Donn Piatt

**Sunday Meditations and Selected Prose Sketches**

Donn Piatt

**Sunday Meditations and Selected Prose Sketches**

ISBN/EAN: 9783337241551

Printed in Europe, USA, Canada, Australia, Japan

Cover: Foto ©Andreas Hilbeck / pixelio.de

More available books at **www.hansebooks.com**

# SUNDAY MEDITATIONS

AND

# SELECTED PROSE SKETCHES.

BY

## DONN PIATT,

*Author of "Memories of the Men who Saved the Union," "The Lone Grave of the Shenandoah, and Other Tales," "The Rev. Melancthon Poundex," "Poems and Plays," etc.*

CINCINNATI:
ROBERT CLARKE & CO., PUBLISHERS.
1893.

# CONTENTS.

# PREFACE.

The Christian mind of to-day, as it has been in the immediate past, is much disturbed by the claim of so-called science. This means that through certain intellectual processes and discoveries Christianity is found to be erroneous and without the foundation of fact that should give dignity and power to its existence.

The church, in its effort to tranquilize the troubled mind, has committed the error found in an attempt to harmonize the two—the so-called science and itself. There is not an intelligent mind on either side that does not recognize the futility of this attempt. They can not be reconciled. If it were left to what we are pleased to call the learning of the world, we would be not only without a recognition of God and life hereafter, but taught to disown both. We may as well face this fact at once. We gain nothing—indeed we lose—by shrinking from or attempting to blind ourselves to the true aim. We are conscious of God as we are conscious of sunlight, and when we attempt to give one born blind a knowledge of light we are precisely in the same condition as when we seek to make God evident through human reason. Through all the ages of recorded and unrecorded past of humanity in all parts of the peopled earth, no human being has ever been, or can be, found who did not or does not feel within himself the existence of a Maker. This is born in us; it can not be obliterated, however much through boasted human reason it may be distorted.

In the same way each mortal is conscious of a part of himself that thinks, wills, and remembers—that is distinct, separate, apart, and superior to the matter upon which and through which it acts. Our poor little processes of thought, dignified with the name of science, give this a name, and call it mind; the servants of our holy church call it soul; but the name throws no additional light on the fact. It begins, continues, and ends in the consciousness of its existence. In the same way, but not with the same strength, we recognize life hereafter. The "I am" of the immediate second is the "I the am" of the next second. I know that I exist. I know that I shall continue to exist, and such knowledge comes from no subtle process of thought. Thought helps us to nothing. One step beyond the inner consciousness and we are in utter darkness.

Philosophy, the vaunted philosophy of the schools, which means a knowledge of the fact and the reason for it, is a delusion. We have the fact, but the reason, or the power to comprehend the reason, has not been given us by our Creator, and therefore has no existence. I ask the learned man what is light, and he answers sadly that he does not know. The blade of grass at his learned feet is as much a mystery as the depths of space into which science drops its little pack-thread of measurement and solemnly makes record. It is not necessary to climb painfully to the outer verge of our little knowledge and gaze into boundless space to have our boasted reason reel back into insanity.

The humblest thing about us brings the same result. Why, I do not know myself; I know only that I exist, I think, I will, I remember, and there it ends. How, then, are we to know God's works? We have the science of astronomy that begins and ends with an enumeration of a few worlds of unending space that are as atoms to the whole. We have the science of geology that digs painfully into the mere skin of our little world, and from it measures epochs. Back of the geologist, with his little hammer, lie the countless ages—the ages that had no beginning—and before him countless ages again; and in this line, as in limitless space, our poor science disappears. Small wonder, then, that the dim-eyed, heart-sick sage of science at the close of life says, mournfully: "I end where I began, and all my years of study have only taught me that I know nothing."

The difference between the extremes, educated and uneducated ignorance, is that the one believes there is knowledge, and the other knows that none exists. The height of all human knowledge is to know that we know nothing.

What an error, then, it is for the ministers of our holy church to accept the pretense and attempt to harmonize religion and science. This is lamentable, but it becomes pitiable when a minister of God accepts the challenge of a scientist as to the existence of God or the truths of religion. He passes from the altar to the rostrum, from the presence of Christ to the man-created idol of wisdom, and accepting the promises offered by infidelity suffers necessarily defeat amid the ribald jeers and laughter of fiends in human shape.

The first offense was eating the fruit of the forbidden tree of knowledge as it grows on earth. Our latest crime is canning that fruit, under a supposed sanction of the church, for common use.

Our blessed Savior appeared on earth, not to teach us scientific truths we can not comprehend, but to appeal to the better nature of humanity as

God made it, and so render us fit for the life eternal
that lies beyond the grave. All He taught was so
simple and so clear that a child can comprehend. It
appeals to what is in us and lifts our instincts themselves into an intellectual guidance. To love one
another, to be charitable to the poor and afflicted, to
be just in our dealings and to love God, calls for no
study by the midnight lamp or feeble groping amid
the works of the Creator. The little space given life
on earth can well be spent in preparing ourselves for
the promised life beyond the grave.

The worst result of all this learned craze is that
found in what we are pleased to call popular education. Education, of course, means that development
of the mind which gives the largest and most satisfactory results of thinking. In the popular course it
means a mere cultivation of the memory, through
which great stores of facts may be accumulated.
Education, in its true significance, is applicable to a
few minds only, and those few differ so radically
that no two are alike as to either quality or character.

The popular belief is that all are alike, and
through one system the common run of minds may
be lifted to the same level. Memory is common to
all, and therefore memory is appealed to and used in
a vast accumulation of facts.

The process is not only unintellectual but fatal to the little mind left us upon which to accumulate the so-called information. The training of the intellectual faculties is not unlike that of the body. A man is given a tool, or a set of tools, and trained to their use. What, then, is the good of a shop full of tools to a man who can not use one, and what is the good of a congressional library to the man who can not utilize a single fact therein recorded? A mere cultivation of the natural or instinctive memory fails to give the necessary use; on the contrary, it destroys the power to use.

To understand this, it is necessary to know what the natural or instinctive memory is. It is based on association. The mind is to its surroundings what the plate of the photographer is to the objects brought before it, save that instead of a separate picture there is a succession of pictures connected one with the other by what is called association. Through every healthy, natural mind there floats continuously a succession of images, and one seems to suggest that which succeeds. Thus it is rain, the rain suggests a flood, the flood the ocean, the ocean the English navy, the English navy the bombardment of Alexandria.

When this flow of images held together by association is arrested and the mind dwells on one, or when it is confined to a few and the flow seems to be an eddy from which the mind can not escape, it is called insane.

This is disease, and our so-called common education brings it on.

The first lesson taught through educational training is that there is no logical sequence between the image presented and that suggested. Take the example given. There is no logical connection of the rain and the ocean. The thoughtful mind realizes this when asked what relation there is between the rain and the bombardment of Alexandria. In fact, there is no logical sequence in any of the steps that led from rain to the bombardment.

As we strengthen the mind, then, we weaken and eventually destroy the instinct. A mere memory is a mark of a weak mind. It is on this account that children, women, and negroes learn—as it is called—more readily than the more thoughtful. As the natural memory is broken up, the logical memory has to take its place. Those things only are retained that have a logical connection. As there are but one in a hundred thousand capable of this, we can readily appreciate where our popular education is left.

The public instructors having a glimmering sense of this difficult task are continually striving to destroy the natural memory, and, believing that all are capable of a like elevation through training, fetch about the same result that comes from disease. The nearer level of mind in the unfortunate pupils may afford enough to break in on the natural memory, but have not sufficient to replace with the logical or acquired memory—hence insanity.

The ordinary result, however, is a cultivation to an abnormal condition of the natural memory and a consequent weakening of the intellect. If this were the only evil we might submit to it, but a worse remains. This unnatural training of the memory through all sorts of stimulants of competition, rewards and punishments destroys the nervous system. It not only fills the land with educated idiots, but with invalids as well. That child that should be on a farm or in a work-shop getting health from reasonable labor, is not only shut in a hot school-room, deprived of natural exercise and pure air for hours every day, that would kill an adult, but carries home a load of books to continue far into the night the death dealing process.

All the tender joys of home, so dear to the memory in after life, are disturbed; all the moral influences that grow from the hearth-stone are destroyed to satisfy this Moloch of education. From the home comes all the good upon which not the state alone, but social life exists and prospers, and the home is wrecked. The state takes the child from its parents and of consequence the citizen from the church, that a popular superstition may be cherished, and the result is, after a century's experience, that insanity doubles upon us every ten years, while crime is such that the question is no longer what are we to do with our criminals, but what will the criminals do with us.

What else could we expect? Admitting for a moment that education elevates and culture refines, have we found the education, are we getting the culture? The fountain never rises above its head, and the crude, coarse machinery we look to as an educational process grinds out only what it is capable of grinding. The mind is recognized as the most subtle, delicate and important part of us, easily disarranged and difficult to care for, and yet we turn this over to the stupid pedagogue who is capable of teaching precisely in proportion as he is incapable of other pursuit. Does sane mind carry his watch to a blacksmith for repair? And yet a machine, as we have said, the most delicate that comes from the Creator, is given to a worse than blacksmith to hammer upon.

The common schools are worse than Godless; they are idolatrous, for the false god worshiped is memory. The tender, youthful victims offered yearly upon the altar of this mumbo-jumbo make life in the interior of Africa or on the Cannibal Islands Christian and respectable.

The Christian faith was not born of human knowledge, and is not dependent on that wisdom which comes of the intellectual processes. It was made part of us when we were first created, is therefore an element in our nature, and while it may be disturbed can not be destroyed, any more than the action of our lungs, the circulation of our blood, or any other function necessary to our physical existence. None know this better than the truly taught. All knowledge, when truly analyzed and sifted down, means merely giving a name to something that we can not comprehend.

An event, when first recognized, is called a phenomenon; when repeated, it is styled a coincidence; when it occurs a third time it is entitled a law, and as such is duly labeled and put to record. Its cause, nature and effect are all alike unknown and unknowable. When, for example, Sir Isaac Newton called attention to the fact that all bodies fell to the earth, and entitled the continued occurrence the law of gravitation, the learned apes in spectacles gravely nodded their hairless skulls and cried, " Great mind, learned man: wonderful progress of science!" And yet what has become of this fact, so simplified as supposed by Newton, among the savants themselves?

Newton himself, in his well known letter to Berkely, recognized the absurdity of the supposed explanation found in the name by admitting the impossibility of such a law acting through a vacuum, and attempted an explanation by supposing all space to be filled with ether, as if that helped to understand what remains to-day an impenetrable mystery. The latest heard upon this subject came from a discussion before the Berlin Physical Society, when two eminent scientists, known to the learned world as Professor Paul Du Bois-Reymond and Professor Von Helmholtz, agreed that gravity was simply incomprehensible, but that it is an "inherent property" of matter.

"Why is it, Professor," asked a student of the late astronomer Vaughn, who starved to death at Cincinnati, "that the sun is said to be the source of light, yet as we leave the earth and approach that great source we pass into outer darkness and cold?"

"My son," was the sad reply, "If you can tell me what light and heat are, I will solve your difficulty."

The latest fad, to use an expressive cant word, among these dealers in scientific mysteries, is evolution. Invented by the imaginative mind of Darwin, it was so improved on by the more logical intellect of Herbert Spencer, as to mean quite another thing from that intended by its inventor, and is to-day so shadowy and uncertain that no two of the learned pundits can be found agreeing upon the precise definition. It differs from gravitation in one remarkable feature, and that is, that while gravitation is a name given to a continuously occurring event, which, whether we comprehend it or not, seems a fact; evolution, on the contrary, is the creature of pure speculation. It serves its purpose, however, and solves all doubt in the mind of its believer by the mere use of the word. When one of these aged phrase-eaters, of recognized scientific attainments, utters that magic word, an awful silence of submissive humility follows, as a grove of little singers becomes mute when a fog obscures the sun.

How little learning has done for humanity a slight investigation will demonstrate. The sum total progress is to be found in material existence. Through the control and manipulation of matter some of us—a small minority—are better sheltered, fed, and cared for than were our ancestors. Are we happier, more moral, or in better health than were our barbarous progenitors? Alas! no. Nicely adjusted machinery, driven by harnessed steam, may pick up and carry us at the rate of sixty or a hundred miles an hour. Has it carried us from our sorrows, sickness, and evil impulses? No, again. These are with us more positively secure than our epito-

mized worldly goods checked in the baggage cars.
Antiquarians tell us of cave-dwellers among our remote
ancestors, who were cannibals, and sucked the marrow from the stone-broken bones of their fellow-men.
The cannibals of to-day have their caves gilded with
gold and graced with silken drapery. They live on
champagne and canvasbacks, *pâte de foie gras* and ter-
rapin, within walls so thick that they can not hear
the moans of dying and cries of starving men, the
marrow of whose bones they have sucked out, each
cannibal absorbing the living of thousands.

Man is to-day what man was thousands of years
ago. Alongside the palace stands the penitentiary,
the poor-house, and the asylum for the insane.
Hovels multiply and crime grows bolder and more
aggressive. "I knew I had struck a civilized land,"
said a ship-wrecked mariner, "for I encountered a
gallows on the coast." That ghastly remnant of bar-
barism is the one great distinguishing feature of civilized life.

From this dark and depressing view of how little
learning has done for humanity, we turn with glad
hearts to that which, if it has not lessened our sorrows or lifted us above sickness, has enabled us to
bear both with a hopeful recognition of a relief hereafter—a relief that is to come from our own recognition of our better selves. "That is all a delusion,"

2

cries the agnostic, who, professing to know nothing, claims to know all. " Your miracles on which you base your belief in the divinity of Christ will not bear the test of evidence. These so-called gospels are fictions, and all your Christ taught was known to the world long before He was born."

Woe waits the poor believer who turns to dispute such questions as these. This learned agnostic, who measures God's creation with his little packthread, and gives nature's mysteries which he can not comprehend learned names, and so disposes of them, will make short work with the evidences of Christianity based on the so-called laws of human evidence. If the agnostic were called on to prove, through such process, the existence of his cherished gravitation, he would be as much at a loss as the poor Christian challenged to demonstrate the divinity of our Savior. If our faith is not in us, there is no intellectual efforts that will put it there; if it is in us, no such process will rob us of its blessed possession.

Putting aside all claim of proof as to miracles, accept frankly and freely Hume's axiom, acknowledge that the gospels are not authentic, and what have we left? The Christ of to-day, that no subtle intellect of a Renan can displace.

" Lo, I am with you until the end of time. I was

with you in the beginning, and will be with you to
the last of earth." It is the Christ of to-day we recognize, as he has been recognized through the ages.

The truth that is as clear as sunlight to the seeing is strangely disregarded in this blind chase after
the vagaries of scientists. Our Savior made no such
contention. He appeared on earth as a humble Nazarene, the son of a carpenter, and gathered about him
as his apostles ignorant tent-makers and fishermen.
He appeared to no school of philosophers, and made
no attempt to teach that learning which we now
hold to be so precious. His few years on earth were
given to appeals to the better part of human nature,
and to teaching us the divine truth, that in kindness
that held charity and forgiveness to each other we
could prepare ourselves for that happiness hereafter
that can be found in the love of Our Father in
Heaven.

His mission, lasting but a brief period, ended in his
cruel death; and, search through the recorded gabble
of the world, and we find stories of brutal conquests—
the rise of empires and the fall of kings, sages, and
poets are told of, and their wise teachings and beautiful words come down to us; but of Christ, of his
life, sufferings, and crucifixion, there is a dead silence; not a word was said, not a sentence went to
record. The great, noisy world rolled on without

Him. This mission of a carpenter's son was too insignificant to command the slightest mention. And yet the divine work went on. A ray of God's sunlight had pierced the gloom, and strengthened and broadened until it embraced all the earth. There are no miracles, they tell us; and yet the low, solemn teachings of this Nazarene, left to the keeping of ignorant laborers, sneered at by scientists, fought by conquerors of all-else, the poor followers thrown into loathsome prisons to rot, given to wild beasts to devour, branded as criminals, and outlawed as convicts hold the earth now and forever. This may not be a miracle, but it can be explained only by a true reading of our Savior's word, which taught us that he appeared to the Christ that was born in us when we came fresh from the hands of our Creator; that it is the better, stronger, and more vital part of our nature, and when awakened gives us a joy no words can describe. Such awakening calls for no learning, no culture, no burning of the midnight oil in vain study of what we can not comprehend. He is with us now; He will be with us until the end of time.

These thoughts, so long known to the church that they have come to be commonplace, are treated with lofty contempt by the learned men, who find more in a little geological specimen than in all the hopes, sorrows, and afflictions of humanity.

# SUNDAY MEDITATIONS.

---

## Searching for the Truth.

It seems to me, while reading the touching life and beautiful teachings of Christ, that the English speaking people are nearer to God than those of any other tongue. This because of the simplicity and power of the pure old English into which these chronicles were translated. Other languages may have a wider scope and a more perfect construction. They may excel in that accuracy so necessary to science, be more musical in sound, more available for eloquent utterance, but they never approach our mother tongue in those qualities of simplicity that make it so easy of comprehension to the unlearned and so touchingly beautiful to all.

And when we bear in mind the object of Christ's mission on earth, the blessing grows in worth upon us. His mission was to the poor, and his teachings intended to give consolation to the humble. Before his advent religion was confined to the rich and well-born. Philosophers had reasoned out the immortality of the soul, and priests had built to them gorgeous temples, where the wealthy alone found food for thought and a foundation for faith. With the mass of suffering humanity religion was a superstition and a fear.

To these last alone came Christ. He asked no learning, no subtle reasoning ; he proclaimed his truths and attested his authority by miracles—miracles that leave one in doubt whether they were the result of charitable impulse or evidences of his authority. But all were addressed to the poor and oppressed. Born in a stable, his brief, sad life was passed among the toiling millions and the wicked, to whom he gave words of comfort, the first that ever fell upon their ears.

He was the first democrat in the history of humanity. His race was a despised race of laborers, hewers of wood and drawers of water. His associates were erring women and wicked men. To these he came, these he taught, and to such as these he left his divine doctrines of love and forgiveness. Born in a manger, he died crucified between two thieves.

Like the prophet of old, he smote the rock for the suffering multitude, and from its flinty heart leaped into light and life the waters—not for the gold and silver pitchers of the rich and well-born, but to flow into lowly places, where down-trodden and oppressed humanity might stoop and drink, and go their weary way refreshed.

To read this simple narrative through tears, one must divest himself of the error modern theology has thrown over the story. As it is narrated, Christ, the sufferer, is man. He has all the ills that flesh is heir to. He has the doubts, fears, anguish, and troubles of poor humanity. If he were while on earth a God, possessed of powers as such, the narrative loses all its significance in its loss of sympathy. Hector is the hero of Homer's great epic, for Achilles was invulnerable. To get at the true meaning of the sacrifice, we must go back to the belief of his simple followers. They regarded him as the Son of God, but a man all the same. Judas Iscariot alone looked on him as the Christian world now regards him, as one who, through his divine power, could protect himself and his followers from all harm. He took the thirty pieces of silver, believing a great miracle would be wrought in their behalf, to lift his master and themselves from the harm of their enemies. When he found what a cruel error he had committed, he returned the money, and went out in anguish to death by his own hands. Peter, in fear, denied his master. Christ himself passed the night in prayer, petitioning for what evidently Judas believed would happen, and that was that a supernatural power would interpose and save him from his enemies. Here is the narrative:

"Then Jesus came with them into a country place which is called Gethsemane; and he said to his disciples: Sit you here until I go yonder and pray. And, taking with him Peter and the two sons of Zebedee, he began to grow sorrowful and to be sad. Then he said to them: My soul is sorrowful even unto death. Stay you here and watch with me. And, going a little further, he fell upon his face, praying and saying: My Father, if it be possible, let this chalice pass from me; nevertheless, not as I will, but as thou wilt. And he cometh to his disciples and findeth them asleep, and he saith to Peter: What! could you not watch one hour with me? Watch ye and pray, that ye enter not into temptation. The spirit is indeed willing, but the flesh is weak. Again the second time he went and prayed, saying: My Father, if this chalice may not pass away, but I must drink it, Thy will be done. And he cometh again and findeth them sleeping; for their eyes were heavy; and, leaving them, he went again, and he prayed the third time, saying the self-same words."

He prayed for what? That he might be saved

the cruel tortures and horrible death in store for him at the hands of his brutal enemies.

Any other version of this sad story robs it of all meaning. Without the intervention of the man, religion is not only without comfort and consolation, but is impossible. To share with creation, the worship of God is to reduce our earth to an atom and the human soul to a nonentity. Astronomy, lifting the heavens into the immensity of space that we can not comprehend, carried with it the old Hebrew theology that made God human that we might know him, and inhuman that he might be feared. We look over the edge of our little horizon, into that never-ending space, and shrink back in horror at a dreary immensity, to think of which threatens insanity—is insanity. We can not go to God, and so Christ comes to us. He is part of ourselves—shares in our wants, weaknesses, hopes, and sorrows. In this direction lies our religion :

> " The good we love and cherish most
> Lies close about our feet ;
> It is the dim and distant
> That we are sick to greet."

As the home is to the world, the religion of Christ is to modern theology, that, aided by science,

3

seeks to become a fact and not a faith. It is cold
and colorless, and without comfort. The church,

> " Like a dome of many colored glass,
>   Stains the white radiance of eternity."

It enters into all the sweet humanities and relieves the sad troubles of our afflicted life as a parent
ministers to a child. It is this that gives us comfort
in Christ, and from this want came the mother of
Christ, fetching heaven nearer to home and nearer to
the heart. To become as a little child, to accept
without questioning the faith offered us, to keep our
religion where Christ left it, within our own horizon,
is all we can ask. It is certainly all that we can get.

The tragic end of Christ's mission on earth has
been held before mankind through centuries as a
sacrifice in which death alone is made the measure
of the atonement. And yet, being man, and as such
mortal, his enemies only anticipated by a few years
what would have been his inevitable fate. It was a
cruel death, it is true; one in which human ingenuity
was tasked to extort pain; but not more so than
many diseases that to-day afflict humanity. The human system is capable of only a certain amount of
suffering. One would scarcely imagine a more horrible torture than to be nailed to a cross and left to
perish from exhaustion. But the violence of the

means used would defeat the purpose, for what with
the loss of blood and intense agony, insensibility
would soon follow. Nature, true to herself, kindly
administers relief at the last moment, when powers
of resistance are exhausted. In the horrible tortures
invented and practiced in Europe when religious persecution reached its inhuman limit, it was found
necessary to prolong the suffering by restoring the
victim through rest and stimulants. Insensibility
and death baffled the fiends in human shape.

It was death, and in the death relief, that comes
sooner or later to all of us. If that were all we
would find ourselves at a loss to account for the divine interposition in behalf of poor humanity. It is
but true that the thought makes one's heart ache,
that one whose pure life of charitable acts and God-
like teachings of love and forgiveness made his life
a miracle, should be howled down by a mob and tortured to death. But to understand and appreciate
the blessing bestowed, we must look deeper and
more wisely to find that there is something more in
death than the pain of dying. To one who has
watched the weary days and dreary nights by the
couch of some loved one, this is painfully evident:
for while the heart aches over the suffering it stands
still at the thought of the separation. Therein lies
the sting of death, therein exists the victory of the

grave that no reasoning makes familiar, no religion can afford consolation. It was not, therefore, that Christ died, but that on the third day he rose again, that brought blessed consolation to the human family. For thousands of years the children of men had seen the grave close over the lost and loved, and from it come back no whisper, no sign, naught but a dead, eternal silence, that found relief only in forgetfulness, against which the heart struggled with an anguish no words could express. "Why do you weep?" asked the philosopher, "tears are unavailing." "Therefore do I weep," was the truthful and touching reply.

Christ threw the bridge of faith over the dread gulf. The grave gave back its answer. Our brief, wretched existence reached into the future of eternity, and what was doom before became only a trial calling for patient endurance instead of despair. Before then religion was a superstition and a fear with the masses. The nearest approach that reason could fetch the intellect of the more cultivated was that our dread of annihilation and longing for immortality were proofs of a future existence; but how slender, cold and comfortless the belief, if such it could be called, compared with the reality of the narrative, told with such simplicity that it leaves no doubt upon the mind:

"At that time Mary Magdalene and Mary the mother of James and Salome brought sweet spices that, coming, they might annoint Jesus. And very early in the morning the first day of the week they came to the sepulcher, the same being now risen, and they said one to another, who shall roll us back the stone from the door of the sepulcher? And looking they saw the stone rolled back; for it was very great. And entering into the sepulcher they saw a young man sitting on the right side clothed with a white robe—and they were astonished—who saith to them: Be not affrightened; ye seek Jesus of Nazareth who was crucified; he is risen, he is not here; behold the place where they laid him. But go tell his disciples and Peter that he goeth before you into Galilee; there you shall see him as he told you."

There are few events more illustrative of the new life that dawned on the world than those attending the death and resurrection of our Savior. "The last at the cross and first at the tomb" were these women. Of apostles, Judas had betrayed and Peter denied him, while all disappeared, hiding in terror from the storm that had so suddenly broken upon them. They who look on death when a human being is born were the first to learn that death meant life, and all that had wrung their hearts in agony on that dreadful day, as it had wrung the hearts of millions, was but another and a more beautiful birth, carrying us from this earth of sin, sickness and grief to where the wicked cease to trouble and the weary are at rest.

Ah! me, what sweet consolation there is in the very music of those words! How life's struggles dwindle before them; how disappointments lose their annoyances, and slander, abuse, desertion of friends and triumphs of enemies—all that the master mind enumerated:

"The whips and scorns of time,
　The oppressor's wrong, the proud man's contumely,
　The pangs of despised love, the law's delay,
　The insolence of office and the spurns
　That patient merit of the unworthy take."

All sink into nothingness before the thought that in a few brief years we will have passed beyond them, into life where their very memory will cease to trouble us. Through the iron gate of death streams the light of life hereafter, spreading its balm upon even our own earthly unhappiness, giving us a taste in anticipation of the blessings reserved for us in a higher sphere and more perfect life than this.

Life on earth is what we have known as death, and death is life in reality. Even this dull, heavy matter of our present being feels a quickening in the change.  Science teaches us that this hand that traces these lines, that is held in form through life, passes after the change into the elements of which it is composed so swiftly that in a brief period all save the bones disappear.  Death then means life, not only in the release of the soul, but of the body itself.

The tendency to clothe a simple fact in religion with a mysterious faith in something greater than the fact, has nearly robbed us of the true meaning of Christ's mission.  What can be more sublime, beautiful, or more consoling than what he has taught us in the resurrection?

## Natural and Revealed Religion.

We know God as we know unending space; as we know eternity; as we know all things without being able to comprehend any thing. It was never designed that we should. We have just enough intelligence given us to make a living out of this hard earth on which we are destined to exist for a brief space. That such intelligence should be given man that makes him capable of a better life than the brutes beneath him, with qualities that, if developed, will lift him to a higher plane and prepare him for a better and purer existence, is all upon which we can base our religion. By religion I mean that divine Power which can satisfy the want born in us that craves divine protection, without which earth is a hell, and existence a horror.

This condition is common to all humanity. Wherever found in the more dense, or in the remotest and most solitary places—among the barbarous, or more civilized—the man is haunted and oppressed, with the same sense of dependence, and has the same eager longing for help, and utters the same prayer for protection. There is no man walking erect, and possessed of any mind, but feels this want. There is no intellect, however cultivated, but recognizes its existence.

This is the condition to-day, and such it has been throughout the ages. All the world's sand-buried records found in Egypt that tell of a high civilization in the dim, forgotten past, has but one clear story, and that is of religion. The tale of empire, the records of great conquests, the history of dynasties, of king-haunted wars, are all blurred and dim, almost beyond comprehension, but deeply engraved on imperishable stone sculptured and yet bright in paint runs on and on the story of religion. The huge temples were palaces, and the palaces were temples, and the god they worshiped was a god of war and vengeance. Swarming about these sand-covered ruins of these gigantic memories of a mighty past are the naked Arabs, and they have one thing in common with these once illustrious dead, and that is the same natural religion. To the ignorant it is one of fear; to the more cultured, one of despair. The savage hears the awful voice of God in the thunder, sees his vengeance in the violence of the tempest, and tremblingly prays to be protected from the very god to whom he petitions in his prayers. They who are lifted by our little learning above this groveling condition may pronounce such belief superstition without freeing themselves from the very fear that brought such superstition into existence. The god of science, the great first cause is the most terrible of all. Beyond human conception, lost in the realms of space at the mere thought of Him, the heart is stilled in terror as the finite mind reels back upon itself in dazed insanity.

This is natural religion, a great realty, a fact that gives our faith its firm foundation. It was the field prepared for the seed our Savior found, and gives us reason for the quick growth that clad the earth with such abundance in His presence, then, as now, and through all time. When asked, then, to prove that once upon a time far back in the centuries, our God, in the form of man, lived and suffered, we say that it is the Christ of to-day who concerns us. His divine teachings through His church have never ceased, and that which won humanity in the beginning wins us now. How strong this was and is, the awful persecutions, that sought to stamp out the truth of God tell us, and we are not to be moved by the sneers and scoffing of modern unbelief.

Of all the stored information among men, the least available in seeking to gratify the religious want implanted is the logic legalized in what is called the law of evidence. This which comes of human experience, and is so useful in our tribunals when we seek to punish the guilty and protect the innocent, fails to be of any service when applied to religion. It is based on the offspring of evidence we call belief, that is involuntary, and has in it, therefore, no merit. And this evidence runs exclusively on human experience. How utterly futile and impotent is this little machinery when applied to God's works, when our brief experience is lost in eternity, and measures less than a mote in boundless space!

"We can not believe a miracle," says this rule of evidence, "until it would be a miracle to disbelieve it." We present a miracle in evidence of our belief and are calmly told to prove our miracle. Of course this is correct in our earthly court, but what becomes of the wise axiom in a creation where to us all things are miracles? Lifting my right arm in response to a thought is as great a miracle to me as lifting one from the dead. The motion of my arm has come to be a common occurrence, and therefore probable; the return of the dead happened but twice in the centuries, therefore is it so wonderful that it becomes improbable and can not be believed.

Nevertheless the mystery remains. No frequent repetition of the event solves its deep obscurity. The horizon of human knowledge lies close about us. It is almost within reach; beyond is blank darkness. And the mystery is in all things, as much in the blade of grass at our feet as in the endless star-lit realms of space.

And we recognize as divine, the teachings of Christ, as they reach us through His Church, because they come to us with all the warmth and light of the sun. They respond to the want within us for divine guidance and sympathy that is more potent than in the body is the appetite for food, or the demand for breath, or loving impulse, and it can not be set aside, silenced or satisfied by the intellectual processes any more than hunger can be gratified by dreams of food, or the lungs be filled and life made stronger by artificial inflation of the lungs. Ask for proof in accord with the human law of evidence that Christ lives, as well ask a child to prove the existence of its mother. The awakened soul hears the voice of its Savior, and a strange peace follows the call. The belief is not that of our courts, but a longing faith that prays to be made firmer by divine interposition, as the drowning sailor clinging to a spar calls on God for strength. True, one is fed, but not satisfied. We believe while longing to believe, and why not? The teachings are sweet, wholesome and life-giving. To live by such precepts and self-denial is to reach a higher plane, and breathe a purer air and be as near content as our life on earth allows. Why should I put all this aside at the arrogant bidding of a man whose pretense to superior learning is a miserable mockery?

Let one, returning from the grave of buried love,

when the very heart seems torn out and left with the dead, be asked to abandon the consolation found in the faith that tells us this is not the end, there is a life beyond, and the mourner will realize the blessings of Christian belief. It is thus we are made better and we are made blessed. From the dreary thoughts of an awful universe; from the cares and ills of life; from the pains and agonizing grief caused by disease and death, we turn to the Church of our Savior to find refuge, peace and that calm content that surpasses in value all the gifts of the world. In its divine results we find its divine origin. No man can read the touching story of our Savior's life on earth, no one can hear His teachings without responding eagerly to both.

A vine planted in a dim cellar grows blindly, groping its way to the ray that penetrates a crevice, and, finding the outlet, struggles into light and life. And so the poor soul, all ignorant or lost in the learning of the world, turns longing to the light, that it may live. There is no comfort in the cold teachings of science, no consolation in a godless world. Homeless, helpless, hopeless and half insane, the soul seeks the ray dropped through the crevice for light and life, found as the blessings of our beautiful religion.

## Cheerfulness a Duty.

We begin life with the discovery that all good things are dull, and we are apt to end considering all dull things good.

What there is in Christianity as taught by Christ to make one sad or even serious, is more than a reasoning being can answer. We are moved to sorrow by the struggles and suffering of one whose brief life was full of trouble, but his teachings are those that should make the heart glad. He brought good-will to men on earth, taught them forgiveness, love, and sympathy, and, that greatest boon of all, he lifted the dark veil of death and showed us that beyond our close, narrow horizon, was life, immortal life.

Aside from this, however, there is no merit that we can discover in being melancholy. On the contrary, a grave man is simply endured, while a sorrowful man is pitied, a morose character is detested. No one thinks it necessary to look upon such a condition as meritorious. Why then should we believe that we are commending ourselves to our Maker by an exhibit of solemnity? And yet intense solemnity is about the only religion in a majority of mankind. A few, at long intervals, compromise upon a smirk that is only skin deep in feeling, and has in it more conceit than a sense of humor, the last being guarded against as a deadly sin. They treat their God as if he were on the watch to catch one of his saints in a broad grin, indicative of that broad way down to eternal punishment, when the grin is impossible.

And yet nature has made this sense of humor a distinctive mark of humanity. Man is the only animal that laughs. What can be more beautiful, and beautiful in its innocence, than the merry laugh of children, unto whom Christ compared the kingdom of heaven? Or the hearty bursts of early youth, full of hope and health? The man or woman who can not laugh is to be feared. Such a creation is but half made up—a monster seeking to possess what he or she can not enjoy. The sense of humor is to humanity what light is to earth, and light is not the sense of seeing—it is life. We only share in every emotion the beneficial results of some law that extends to all creatures. The man, then, who would divest himself of the healthful influences of humor, would be as wise as he who would destroy his sight lest the enjoyment of light might prove sinful. His sight would be gone, but the light remains.

This dark and dreary view of religion is a remnant of the superstitious fear that haunted poor humanity before the coming of Christ. The God of the Jews, as told in those naked chronicles of a cruel race, is a God of vengeance. His patriarchs and prophets were famous, and should be infamous for crimes their God sanctioned. He was the God of war, pestilence, and famine. The little life of his followers was bounded by misery, with no beautiful hereafter to alleviate their suffering. They were not taught to love their God, but commanded to love God and fear him—the last only being possible. Are we commanded to love Christ—is the child commanded to love its mother—or the mother the helpless little creature that is born of her body, but never from her heart? Does one need any command to love the dear, helpless invalid dependent upon one's care? To claim such feeling as a merit is in itself the tangled end of a confusing superstition.

The heathen mythology, as it is called, wherein poets and priests created deities out of their passions, was of the same sort. The speculations of its philosophers were like rockets shot up into the night, that to the ignorant seemed to reach the stars. They exploded only to leave the night darker than before. But what was poetry to the cultured was superstition to the masses, and only one remove in its touches of humanity from the dark and dreary belief of the Jews.

How gladly we turn from all this murky night

of ignorance and terror to the beautiful dawn of life
that came in with Christ. While His life was brief
and full of sorrow, there is nothing in His teachings
or example to encourage the puritanical sourness so
generally mistaken for religion. Because life hereafter is made to appear beautiful, it does not detract
from the healthy sweetness of this life. There is no
reason for the belief that Christ was of a sorrowful
temperament. They who tell the story of his life are
so filled with memories of his miracles, teachings,
tragic death, and resurrection, that they give no space
to aught disconnected from what they considered of
such vital importance. But a close study of their
testament leaves no impression upon the unprejudiced
mind that he was a stern man. The popular mind
in this respect gets its impression from the sad, weak
face painted by the old Italian masters.

Nor is it likely that He differed from humanity
in His manner or ways beyond what His mission demanded. That His first miracle was wrought at a
wedding festivity, and was done in aid of the enjoyment the poor people sought to further beyond their
means, is in proof of what we assert. Let any one
read the story as told, and divesting one's mind of
the glamor of divinity that for our sake Christ re-
nounced, being man among men, and see how

4

sweetly the character comes out from the dim records
left in this respect so obscure.   Here is the story:

"And the third day there was a marriage in
Cana of Galilee.   And both Jesus and His disciples
were called to the marriage.   And when they wanted
wine the mother of Jesus saith unto him:   They
have no wine.   Jesus saith unto her:  Woman, what
have I to do with thee?   Mine hour is not yet come.
The mother saith unto the servants:  Whatsoever He
saith unto you do it.   And there were set there six
water pots of stone, after the manner of purifying
of the Jews, containing two or three firkins apiece.
Jesus saith unto them:   Fill the water pots with
water.   And they filled them to the brim.   And He
saith unto them:   Draw out now and bear unto the
governor of the feast.   And they bore it.   When
the ruler of the feast had tasted the water that was
made wine and knew not whence it was (but the
servants which drew the water knew), the governor
of the feast called the bridegroom and saith unto
him:  Every man at the beginning doth set forth
good wine, and when men have drank, then that
which is worse; but thou hast kept the good wine
until now.   This beginning of miracles did Jesus in
Cana of Galilee and manifested forth of His glory,
and His disciples believed in Him."

That this miracle of the wine was wrought from

no desire to proclaim His divine power is evident.
At the marriage feast to which He and His humble
followers were invited the poor women, mortified at
the lack of refreshments, moved His pity; and what
meant His divine interference in this light is shown
by his reply to His mother, "Mine hour is not yet
come;" that was the hour in which His divine authority was to be tested by His miracles. And from
the conversation and the confidence in which she regards His effort, it is evident that He had imparted
to His mother the fact of His divine mission before
He gave it to the world.

To have been a welcome guest at this feast He
could not have been the austere, unhappy man, such
as His many misguided followers and imitators are
to-day. What that feast was the ruler of it tells us
when he refers to the practice of giving the good
wine first, that, under its stimulating influence, the
bad may pass unnoticed. It must have been a merry
occasion; and as to that enjoyment Christ has so
materially contributed, it is not likely He dampened
the festivities by a cold, forbidding manner.

The tendency to distort through the uncultured
imagination of the multitude has well nigh deprived
us of a knowledge of Christ. One, in reading the
gospel, has to clear away centuries of exaggeration
and error. The love that is part of adoration is soon

lost in awe and fear. We are not willing to accept Christ as He came to us. We work His manger into a cradle of gold, and we banish from our minds as blasphemy the fact that He was reared a mechanic. It is shocking to think that He was a guest at a wedding festivity and enjoyed the feast as other young men. "Ah!" says the Rev. Chadband with a snuffle, " He sought to give the sanction of His divine presence to the holy sacrament of matrimony." Let the Rev. Chadband study the Hebrew law regulating marriages of that day, and he will see what a holy sacrament our Savior is said to have sanctioned.

No, He went to the feast as He walked the earth, clad in His humanity, and doubtless found in its innocent enjoyment a pleasant rest from the mystery of His mission and the dark forebodings of His own fate. He grew in grace and stature, and He sought to win His brother men to His side by reason and persuasion, and men marveled at His words of wisdom, that were as sweet as they were truthful, and He who brought such great joy to men could not Himself have been cold, austere and forbidding.

## The Courage that Suffers.

With all the humanity, the charity, the loving forgiveness, and good will for man shown in the mission of Christ, one is struck with the store placed on courage. Non-resistance based on courage makes of that high quality its truest and purest test. To patiently submit to wrong, insult, and pain, is to be brave without the aid that comes from resistance, however hopeless. No one knows this better than the officer who has seen actual service. There is no duty more trying than to hold a reserve under fire. Men who will go into a charge with a dash, or receive one with coolness when fighting, falter before the danger that can not be resisted.

Not the least trying part of the ordeal is the sense of degradation that accompanies non-resistance. No one questions in the abstract that to submit calls for a higher courage than resistance; but the sufferer asks of himself: Who and what am I that I should be trampled upon? It is hard to realize that Christ appealed to the divinity of our nature from that brutal part which is based on might, and not on true courage. To get at the true meaning of this, one must occupy a more elevated plane than that of poor

material humanity. Once enabled to look down upon
earth, how monstrous and grotesque are our quarrels!
Our brief existence is one long struggle with pain,
trouble, sorrow, and full of the cruelest disappointments. Why should we seek to add to these afflictions by quarrels, persecutions, and abuse of each
other? Frail specters of a brief existence, why
wantonly shorten that existence? Passions of a
wrathful, aggressive sort are therefore insane and
brutal. To look at them from this Christian light,
and act upon such knowledge, demand the highest intelligence and the purest courage. To these Christ
appealed in his teaching of non-resistance.

We must not delude ourselves from these facts,
that a Christian life is here or hereafter one of peace.
We are promised a re-existence hereafter. How that
life is maintained, at what cost it was gained, and
how held, are questions that come to us; for evil did
not begin with this life, nor does it end here.

Through all the teachings of Christ, through all
the blind experience of humanity, we are taught that
evil is immortal. A vast shadow resting upon the
edge of this life swings out, dark and foreboding,
through all space and all eternity. It is evil, and it
wars forever with good, as good with evil, and it
seems to us as if the one immutable law of our nature is war. The dread chills the heart that the evil

nearly equals the good in power. Of a surety so far as this life goes, the evil is in the ascendant. Will it continue beyond the grave?

One might comfort himself with the thought that our brief experience on earth, between the cradle and the grave, is so unsatisfactory that we can not tell, can form no idea of what our mortal existence is to be hereafter. It is as if one born in the beginning of winter were to mature and die as the winter ends, without knowledge of the spring, summer, and autumn that follow. But revelations give us no such comfort. In them evil is immortal and war eternal. That to the virtuous a heaven is promised, that the children of men who have accepted the faith and fought the good fight shall find a home with Christ, where the wicked cease to trouble and the weary are at rest, is true, but it is the safety afforded helpless women and children of a great army, where the combatants only are exposed.

What is this horrible, ghastly shadow that haunts our life, and is never from our thought? That it is not of this world alone we all know, as earth carries daylight in the heart of night, and that but a little way beyond our little circle sun, moon, stars, all disappear in an eternal blackness, later science teaches us; and how much of God's moral light, that like the physical seems to prevade all space, is really limited, who can say? Without being spoken in words, the fear haunts the holy writing from end to end. When Christ says to Peter, " Upon this rock I build my church, and the gates of hell shall not prevail against it," He speaks exultingly, as if the fortress had at last been found against which the powers of evil could not prevail. What are these gates of hell that seem to defy the son of God?

Whatever they may be, courage is the one great quality most dwelt upon, as most necessary to the Christian. And how calm and brave through all his perils was our Savior! He alone felt and realized the trial in store for him. His simple, ignorant followers, regarding him as possessed of supernatural powers, saw nothing in their future to create alarm. He foresaw, and looking beyond this life into that eternal hereafter, we can not tell what he saw to so cast him down that he prayed to be spared the sacrifice. This depression came upon him, according to St. Matthew :

" At that time Jesus said to his disciples: You know that after two days shall be the pasch, and the son of man shall be delivered up to be crucified. Then were gathered together the chief priests and ancients of the people into the court of the high priest, who was called Caiaphas; and they consulted together, that by subtlety they might apprehend

Jesus and put Him to death. But they said: Not on
·the festival day, lest perhaps there should be a tumult among the people. And when Jesus was in
Bethania, in the house of Simon the leper, there came
to him a woman bearing an alabaster box of precious
ointment, and poured it on His head as He was at the
table. And the disciples, seeing it, had indignation,
saying: To what purpose is this waste; for this might
have been sold for much and given to the poor? And
Jesus knowing it, said to them: Why do you trouble
this woman, for she hath wrought a good work upon
me? For the poor you have always with you; but
me you have not always. For she, in pouring this
ointment upon my body hath done it for my burial."

Of all the tragic utterances ever recorded there
is not one like this: "For she, in pouring this ointment upon my body, hath done it for my burial."

At that feast of unsuspecting friends and followers, the ghastly phantom of death sits unseen by
all save the son of God, whose body is being already
anointed for the burial. A little while longer and
these simple believers, these fisherman and tent-
makers who have left their humble callings to follow
Christ, will have the poor with them, but not their
God and prophet. They will look no more upon that
face whose quiet courage gave them confidence, as
his sweet voice gave them comfort. Scattered, per-

5

secuted, driven like beasts from the haunts of man,
putting the mark of death upon all they baptized in
the new faith, they will each find his sad end wide
apart from the others, and looking from earth to the
sky into which he disappeared, and see the sun rise
and set, and the stars take in eternal silence their
glittering way, but no Savior.   There will be left to
them, as to the children of men for all ages to come,
only the memory of His sweet words, the high future
of His heavenly promise.   He taught them the wisdom of God, He bequeathed them the courage of
martyrs.   They were to learn that as the children of
earth come into life through the throes of death, and
die from insiduous disease or slow decay, so all good
is born of violence, and is lost through fraud.   So
long as religion meant life hereafter, that antago-
nized the comforts and luxuries here, it was met with
a deadly resistance.   Since it has accommodated itself to the enjoyment of the good things of earth,
peace reigns among men.

We never weary of reading and meditating upon
the briefly but beautifully told story of that feast
where the woman annointed the head of our Savior.
His mission was drawing to a close.   Already His
deadly enemies, the high priests and the ancients of
the people, were gathering about Him to compass
His death.   He sat at the feast loved and worshiped,

and all about Him seemed peace and pleasantness. But after the precious ointment was poured upon His sacred head, under our zealous remonstrance, He revealed the dark forebodings He had concealed. He says sadly and with such true force in its simplicity: "For she, in pouring this ointment upon my body, hath done it for my burial."

The days of brutal abuse, the horrible persecution and the horrible death, all were gone, and the poor lifeless remains alone were being anointed. To the son of God came the same strange warning that often visits the children of men. As the great German poet has said:

> "There is no doubt that there exists such voices,
>     Yet I would not call them
>     Voices of warning, that announce to us
>     Only the inevitable. As the sun,
>     Ere it is risen, sometimes paints its image
>     In the atmosphere; so often do the spirits
>     Of great events stride on before the events,
>     And in to-day already walks to-morrow."

And what a morrow broke on humanity! After the ages of chaos and night, what a calm, sweet dawn came to us of earth!

## The Giving of Alms.

"Take heed that you do not your alms before men to be seen of them; otherwise you have no reward of your Father who is in heaven.

"Therefore when thou doest thine alms do not sound a trumpet before thee, as the hypocrites do in the synagogues and in the streets that they may have glory of men. Verily I say unto you they have their reward.

"But when thou doest alms let not the left hand know what thy right hand doeth:

"That thy alms may be in secret and thy Father, who seeth in secret Himself, shall reward thee openly.

"And when thou prayest thou shalt not be as the hypocrites are, for they love to pray standing in the synagogues and on the corners of the streets that they may be seen of men. Verily I say unto you they have their reward.

"But thou, when thou prayest, enter into thy closet and when thou hast shut thy door, pray to thy Father which is in secret; and thy Father, who seeth in secret, shall reward thee openly."

What a sweet, subtle knowledge of our nature and its needs is found in the above passages, where charity and prayer are classed together and so beautifully defined. That which is done for a reward must be satisfied with the reward. The man who, through an exhibit of his piety, strives to win the admiration of his fellow men, must be content with that compensation. The true Christian, who seeks the approbation of Christ through a purification of himself, will find his reward in the harmonizing and improved health of his own nature.

Both charity and prayer are for the benefit of the one who gives and petitions. Prayer is but another name for confession, that follows a recognition of our own sins from which we seek to cleanse ourselves; while charity has little good beyond the development of all that is kind and generous in our own nature.

The centuries have but little changed our nature. The Jews had, as we have, the men who sound trumpets over their giving, and standing in public places, pour out their prayers for the ears of men and not the heart of Christ. Doubtlessly the Hebrews were besotted then, as we are now, with the thought that charity was meant almost exclusively to benefit the recipients and not the giver. They, too, probably, had their organized charities, orphan asylums, homes for aged poor, and hospitals for the penniless sick. And these fat, substantial citizens, who by

close dealings and hard bargains had accumulated
wealth, gave pennies from hoarded thousands to or-
ganized charities, and thought thereby to have purchased a peace with their Creator.

How our Savior must have amazed that people,
of all mankind the most avaricious and hard, by
these strange doctrines! What a struggle he had to
obtain a hearing and secure any consideration. But
that he spoke to the poor, and that his wise, kind
words went to their hearts, where they were treasured, his revelations would have been lost to humanity.

It is well for us that his advent was in advance
of an enlightened press. How the leading journals
of Jerusalem would have sneered at, ridiculed and
reviled the poor carpenter and his ignorant followers! The subsidized organs of a commercial people
would have seen in him only a dangerous communist
or an insane fanatic, making an attack on the very
foundations of social organization. The Moses and
Sons, Aaron and Brother, Rothschilds, and other leading citizens, did not differ in any respect from the
same class of to-day. We, too, have our Christian
statesman, whose charity is accompanied with trumpets, and who gives God good advice in a loud voice
in public places.

Then, as now, the charity was reserved to the

deserving poor. The old delusion exists to-day that the sole purpose of charity is to help the poor, as that prayer is a cunningly devised process through which to conciliate God. We can not help the needy. Were all the accumulated property of the world thrown into a common heap and divided equally, it would not be many days before the strong and cunning would leave the improvident and weak to suffer. "The poor ye have always," said Christ; and so long as we have wicked, selfish men, weak men must suffer. And how utterly hopeless we make the task of relief when we restrict our efforts to the deserving poor, and how little of Christ is there in the restriction. When Christ bade us administer to the sick, He did not say the deserving sick; nor when we are bid to feed the hungry and clothe the naked, does He qualify by saying the deserving hungry and the deserving naked.

We know that the wicked stomach and the sinful back suffered as keenly as the righteous stomach and back, and both sorts were His children. Deserving people indeed! His beautiful life was passed amid the poor and sinful. He was the associate and friend of vicious men and fallen women, and died at last between two thieves who were not deserving in the eyes of men, yet He carried the poor wretches with Him into heaven. The great heart went out to all the children of men, and it teaches us that true charity is a charity to ourselves, an elevating, healthy impulse, and not a calculation.

Does one ever reflect how little we can do for the poor? The difference between wealth and poverty are most imaginary. The beggar in his rags has about as much happiness as the millionaire in his fine linen. Happiness is not in the linen nor the lack of it in the rags. Pain and privation are positive evils, but pain comes to the rich as well as the poor, while hunger and nakedness do not call for much, and are of small account, if their relief were all when placed to our account with God.

Let us build an orphan asylum of the stoutest walls, and beautify it with all that art can give, and we can not replace a mother's love, that makes in its loss the orphan. It is the giving that makes the good; and the poor sister of charity, half mother and half angel, who gives all she has to the poor and sick, little dreams in her self-sacrificing privation that she is getting a reward here that she prays for in the hereafter. Ah! God lift us from the hell of self-torture—this sense of sin, this loss of self-respect— and give us content with ourselves, and the heaven of the hereafter is the heaven of to-day.

The lesson of charity taught by Christ has been

taken up from time to time through the ages, and repeated mostly by women to the human family. Well we remember when a child walking unawares with Christ and being taught that lesson by one whose memory is watered with tears, although she died many years since, after eighty-four years of goodness on earth. It has been indeed since the death that a clearer sight of her sacred life has been given, for the moistened clay that restored sight to the blind man, told of by the chroniclers of Christ, is the clay of the grave moistened with tears, when we see too late all that we have lost.

It was one of the coldest days of midwinter, when on her way along the freezing street, this mother encountered a thinly clad, shivering woman, evidently very poor, and evidently, alas, very degraded. Her thin, ragged gown was in tatters, and her face bore all the brutal marks of intoxicating drink. But she was suffering; how she did shiver in the bitter, freezing wind, and as we stopped she gave such a wistful, hungry look out of her inflamed eyes, as a suffering beast would. The woman appealed to looked anxiously up and down the street; no one was near, and, hurriedly taking the warm shawl from her shoulders, she wrapped it about those of the sufferer, and then hurried on.

Of course, she knew that the shawl would be pawned for liquor, but the impulse had its reward in the charity given to her own heart hungering for good works, and in the lesson that survives to-day as vividly as when it was given.

## The Poor in Spirit.

"And seeing the multitude He went up into a mountain, and when He was set His disciples came unto Him, and He opened his mouth and taught them, saying:

"'Blessed are the poor in spirit, for theirs is the kingdom of heaven.'"

These, according to St. Matthew, are the first recorded words of Christ, and how pregnant of meaning and how beautiful of utterance they are.

The multitude followed him to the mountain. It was a multitude made up of the poor and oppressed. Probably in all that multitude there was not one even well to do in the world's goods. The rich and well-born of that day, as of this, did not seek Christ, nor were they sought for by Him. He had said in the synagogue on the Sabbath day:

"The spirit of the Lord is upon me, because He hath anointed me to preach the gospel to the poor: He hath sent me to heal the broken-hearted, to preach deliverance to the captives and the recovery of sight to the blind, to set at liberty those that are bruised."

Blessed words, that after all the centuries come to us now as fresh as when uttered.

"As dew is to the drooping flower,
  As sunlight to the sea,
To my sad heart, oh! gracious Lord,
  Are thy dear words to me."

He was known to the poor, and they had followed Him to the mountains. The strange magnetism of His beautiful presence, the sweet, wise utterances, had gone to their hearts, and as trustingly as sheep are led by the shepherd these poor creatures went to their Savior and gathering about Him, listened, amazed, to the first kind words given them through all the ages. Their redemption was at hand. The curse of God, put upon Adam and all his race, that by the sweat of the brow should their bread be earned, was turned to a blessing.

Let us realize the condition of humanity at that time. Take from us all that christianized civilization has done for toiling millions; wipe out the intelligence that has spread to the many; make life a struggle for a bare subsistence, scarcely one remove from the condition of a brute—nay, worse, for the brute has its master interested in its health and strength—and our wonder is that His words reached such deadened hearts, and so wakened them to life that they were not only

received but treasured. They were so treasured that
for over three hundred years these hearts were the
only tablets upon which they were written. All that
the divine Master taught on earth were passed from
parent to child, with not a word lost nor a truth
misstated. What greater miracle than this!

Nor does the miracle end here. Sunlit science
has sent the heavens off into the unfathomable immensity of space. It has taken from us the sun,
moon, and stars. It has made a mote of our earth
and atoms of humanity. It has taught us to know
that we know nothing, and that all the boasted
powers of the intellect touch only one little point
of a great circle, whirling beyond our poor comprehension into never-ending space and through all
eternity. But it has not taken from us our Christ,
and to the learned as well as the unlearned there is
comfort and refuge in His love, in His protection, in
His wisdom.

" Blessed are the poor in spirit, for theirs is the
kingdom of heaven."

These poor toilers without hope, who saw only
between the cradle and the grave hard, unrequited
labor, degradation, and abuse. and beyond the grave
nothing—brutes in human form, brutes with unde-
veloped manhood in them. possessed only of a strange
longing for some better life and higher living—they

were spoken to, not by earthly prince or potentate, by no prophet, poet, or philosopher, but by a God whose words awoke life in the dead—the dead through thousands and thousands of years—and so He gave sight to the blind, healing to the sick, and deliverance to the imprisoned. He gave them their manhood; He breathed hope into their deadened hearts; He taught them that that which had been their curse should hereafter be their blessing. The sweat of the brow was no longer to be the badge of slavery, but the rain of heaven, that would develop all our being into health.

Since then servitude is the better process to a higher manhood. The masters pine, and wither, and disappear, the slaves grow strong, and in time become the masters. The brave races now on earth, who have conquered rough nature and made the earth a pleasant abiding place, came up from servitude.

It is but a few centuries since our ancestors wore iron collars about their necks and labored under the whips of their masters.

Christ was loved and worshiped by the poor and crucified by the rich. He is to-day forgotten by the one and loved by the other. So long as human nature remains as it is, as it was, and as it promises ever to be, money-getting will be its curse, its great sin. It deadens the moral nature, destroys the taste, and so hardens the nature that the divine command of "love one another" is impossible. This was the one sin Christ could not forgive, the one sinner whose repentance He made almost impossible. To the frightened cry of the rich man, "What shall I do to be saved?" He responded sternly, "Give all thou hast to the poor and follow me." Fear, not love, dictated the question; justice rendered the answer.

Christ demanded no impossibility. The leopard could as well change his spots as the rich man his nature. Our Savior commiserated other sorts of sinners. He consorted with the wicked, looked affectionately upon Mary Magdalene, forgave the woman caught in adultery, so kindly that His heart seemed to go with the pardon; He even carried the crucified thieves into heaven with Him; but for the man who bartered his soul for earthly gain he had no mercy, no compromise; he must cease, as it were, to be, before he could begin to serve.

A study of human nature confirms the justice of his decree. There is nothing that so deadens the soul and destroys the humanity as the abject pursuit of gold—the greed that accumulates for the sake of the accumulation. The yellow demon of the mine is the enemy of mankind, the one cruel, hungry, despotic devil that feeds on its worshiper and blights all that he touches.

Christ drove the money-changers from the temple, but He could not drive the love of money from our hearts. He left His curse—He who cursed so little and blessed so much—upon the money-getters. He lifted the beggar from the gate to the heaven of the good, while He assigned the rich man to eternal torment. And yet to-day, as of old, His temple is thronged with the money-changers, who drop their coin into the boxes of the poor as toll wherewith to pay their way along a beaten road to heaven. And who among us, after all the centuries through which the admonition comes, seasons his prayer with the comforting reflection that during the day he, in imitation of our Savior, parted with some of his possessions in charity?

The poor are Christ's true friends; the rich, never. The rich man's religion is fear and faith, and his salvation is paid for. "Two men do I honor," said a philosopher, "and no third. One is the hard-handed, honest laborer, and the other the man who, devoting himself to God, serves as Christ's representative on earth in teaching ‘peace and good will! to man on earth and glory to God on high.’" And

when such shall have passed from the earth they
blessed to the heaven they are to enjoy, Christ will
meet and give them welcome. They are of those he
came to comfort, and in the many chambers of his
father's house they will find their home.

## Pity for the Fallen.

Jesus went into the mount of Olives.

"And early in the morning He came again into the temple, and all the people came unto Him; and He sat down, and taught them.

"And the Scribes and Pharisees brought unto Him a woman taken in adultery; and when they had set her in the midst,

"They say unto Him, Master, this woman was taken in adultery, in the very act.

"Now Moses in the law commanded us that such should be stoned; but what sayest thou?

"This they said, tempting Him, that they might have to accuse Him. But Jesus stooped down, and with His finger wrote on the ground, as though He heard them not.

"So, when they continued asking Him, He lifted up Himself, and said unto them, He that is without sin among you, let him first cast a stone at her.

"And again He stooped down, and wrote on the ground.

"And they which heard it, being convicted by their own conscience, went out one by one, beginning at the eldest, even unto the last; and Jesus was left alone, and the woman standing in the midst.

"When Jesus had lifted up Himself, and saw none but the woman, He said unto her, Woman, where are those thine accusers? Hath no man condemned thee?

"She said, No man, Lord. And Jesus said unto her, Neither do I condemn thee; go and sin no more."

Of all offenses, through all ages and all climes, the one that meets with the swiftest and cruelest punishment was that selected by the Scribes and Pharisees to tempt our Savior. This is one connecting link between humanity and the brute. Nay, it is all brutal. It is not where the man ends and the beast begins, for with that wrath once aroused the creature made in God's likeness is all brute. It is fierce as hell and cruel as the grave. The savage man is a tiger, the civilized man a savage. It is as unreasoning as fate, cowardly as mean; so shameful as to be without shame, and all men and all women will approve—nay applaud, as if the wrath were divine and the vengeance heroic.

How grandly Christ accepted the position of judge, suddenly, from wicked motives, thrust upon Him, and clearly He measured the offense, and looking from the victim to the offended, rendered His judgment. How touchingly beautiful His pardon: "And Jesus said unto her, Neither do I condemn thee." It was for man to accuse and for man to condemn. Our God, the Lord Jesus Christ, has no accusation and no condemnation.

There are some stars so remote in the depths of space from our earth, say astronomers, that their light has not yet reached us. In like manner there are some truths taught by Jesus that have not yet got to us. Traveling slowly but surely through the experience of the ages, they will reach humanity after humanity has been prepared for their reception. Nearer, oh! Christ, to Thee, that we may shorten the space that shuts out Thy truths.

As the qualities debased in prostitution are the most beautiful given us, the degradation is the deepest. Upon those qualities rest all the sweet romance of youth, all the ennobling qualities of manhood, all that is tender and sweet in family ties. The home could not exist without them. On them is founded the holiest love the heart may know, in the love of a mother—in the strongest affection of which we are capable, that of the parent for the child. To have these dimmed, tarnished or destroyed is to take the beautiful from life and leave us only sin and shame.

Christ wrote upon the ground as though He heard them not.

He left the passions to still themselves, the tumult to subside, and when He lifted His God-like eyes and gazed upon them the decision went in advance of speech—yea, it had been decreed by the law of Moses that the woman taken in adultery should be stoned to death. That was the fate of the victim, but what of the offenders? Christ spoke through the law to the law-breakers, from the crime to the criminals:

"He that is without sin among you, let him first cast a stone at her."

That was his finding, that his judgment, and as it went to record, there it stands the law to-day. But how little heeded. The God-like presence of our Savior awed the brutal crowd, "And they who heard it, being convicted by their own conscience, went out one by one, beginning with the eldest, even unto the last." But Christ being gone, they returned with stones in their hands—yes, stones in their pockets and stones in baskets—and for nearly nineteen hundred years they have been stoning to death the weak creatures they degraded, whom our God would not accuse nor condemn.

Prostitution is the sale of one's self for the gratification of the purchaser, and Christ held the purchaser alone responsible. They who have made this loathsome subject a study tell us the one great cause

is poverty. There are other causes, of course, but
they are as nothing to one found in destitution. The
pangs of hunger, the lack of shelter, the absence of
enough clothing to shield the frail body, these break
down and destroy the sweet modesty of youth, the
holy instincts of maternity, and all the pure attributes that fitted woman to be the mother of God and
the salvation of humanity. In the fierce competition
for the necessities of life, the hungry generations
tread the weaker down, and then, devils as we are,
we punish them for falling.

Talk of the torture of the crucifixion. Great
God! let one go about our streets at night, or into
those dens of pollution, and note what frail, delicate
humanity can be made to suffer and still live.

The average duration of life is that of the penitentiary and formerly that of the slaves on southern
plantations. Five years of life, condensed into it a
century of suffering. Look upon the poor painted
creature upon the streets, and try to realize that she
is of the same humanity that makes your mother,
your sister, or your child. Once she was as pure and
precious as they. Her wretched finery does not keep
out the cold; intoxication inflames without satisfying
her hunger. She is sick without sympathy; her
heart hungers for a home it can not find. The world
to her is a world of beasts. She is outlawed. You

can not swindle a rogue without being forced to restitution; you can not beat a rogue without being punished; but a fallen woman may be robbed, beaten—yea, murdered—with impunity. She can not appeal for protection and gain even a hearing. "It will not do," cry the Pharisees of to-day, "to recognize their existence by giving them aid, sympathy, or protection. Let us pretend that the evil does not exist." And so we shut our eyes and ears to this horrible sin, although it grows upon us as poverty extends its gaunt presence, and, crowded out of obscure haunts, it invades public places and taints the atmosphere of all our thoroughfares. As the duration of such life is, as we have said, an average of five years, we can see the multitude of helpless creatures this moloch consumes. We can not divest ourselves of the responsibility. We can not turn our backs on those Christ lived and died for.

Stuff the cotton of your comfortable creed in your ears, close your saintly eyes as you sit in velvet-cushioned pews, and hear only the poundings upon the marble pulpit, for outside upon the corners, close upon your daily walks, the Christ whose mercy you ask is being crucified. We shudder at the burning of a hotel where many people are hurried into eternity. The wreck of a railroad train fills us with horror. We send missionaries to distant heathen,

while all about us, night and day, with thousands on
thousands, degradation and death, in horrid torture,
work, unrelieved and unmolested.

We want the gospel of love and loving **forgiveness** for the victim; stern, unrelenting justice for the
wrong-doer. We must cease to be cruel. One virtue
with us makes a man; the loss of one ruins a woman.
Give a man courage, and he is acceptable; suspect
even a woman's chastity, and she is lost forever.
Follow Christ. Avoid the sin, but seek the sinner.
Remember that his beautiful days on earth, brief as
they were, He passed among the poor, oppressed, and
erring. Mary Magdalene walked with Him, and ministered to His wants. Are you purer than Christ,
that you should shrink from the poor, wretched
Magdalenes of to-day?

How common it is for us to count obstacles as
impossibilities, and saying to our mean, cowardly natures, there is a lion in the path, turn from our duty.
While the law punishes the victims, society seeks to
ignore their existence. Even with the church itself,
the refuge for the sufferer is a prison. "You have
fallen, oh, my sister! Henceforth for you God's sunlight shines no more. The money changer, the miser
abhorred of Christ, the thief, nay the murderer, being
repentant, may again enjoy the sweets of life, with a

hope of heaven ; but you, be buried alive, give your body to fasting and toil and your soul to prayer. For you, to whom Christ said kindly, 'neither do I condemn thee,' the world stands outside with stones for thy torture and thy death."

## What we owe to Woman.

" The Pharisees also came unto him, tempting him and saying unto him, Is it lawful for a man to put away his wife for every cause?

"And he answered and said unto them, Have ye not read that he which made them at the beginning made them male and female?

"And said, For this cause shall a man leave father and mother, and shall cleave to his wife; and they twain shall be one flesh?

" Wherefore they are no more twain, but one flesh. What therefore God hath joined together let no man put asunder."

How slow the world is to appreciate what Christ did for humanity in lifting woman from her degradation to her appropriate sphere. To her we owe all that makes life endurable. From the mother comes the home and all that makes home beautiful. To her we are indebted for our manhood, indebted for the pure, sweet romance of youth, the strength of middle age, the dignity of and love for declining years. She rounds out and makes perfect our life, that were so broken and dreary with any part lost or destroyed. Before Christ old age was a burden.

Now the dimmed sight, the bending form and whitening head of the dear parent draw so strong upon the heart that we water the grave of the departed parent with the same bitter anguish we give the little narrow resting place of our first-born when cruel, relentless death takes our heart out of us in the loss.

There were virtues known to humanity before the coming of our Savior. Love of country, honor among men and honest dealing were extolled and practiced. But they had no color, were cold and comfortless, until the woman in us was brought out and the forgiveness of sin, the love of the enemy and a belief in manhood for manhood's self, came to soften and sweeten life.

Reason would have taught us the existence of God as science teaches us astronomy; but only as naked, hard facts, from which, only half understanding, we shrink, appalled at the vastness of the conception. We had to be born again under the guidance of the son of Mary, blessed mother of God, to draw nearer in gladness to his holy presence.

Christ left us but few precepts, but as the acorn holds the oak these few precepts hold all that are necessary to our happiness and our salvation. One wonders so little is said upon the subject of marriage, when seeing how much depends upon the home marriage makes possible. And yet the wife came with the mother of God as daylight follows dawn. He walked from house to house in the land of the Hebrews, and He said nothing in rebuke of the abuse the patriarchal law entailed. He knew that in the fullness of time the abuse, under the holy teachings of His precepts, would disappear. In like manner He said render unto Cæsar the things which are Cæsar's, and unto God the things which are God's. Ah, well He knew that when the world came to recognize its Christ, pure democrat that He was, it would be an open question as to whether there was any thing due to Cæsar, all being owed to God.

He who confided His mission to His mother before He gave it to the world; who walked the earth the associate and friend of women ; who cast the devils from Mary Magdalene and made her His friend and companion ; who pardoned so kindly the woman condemned to death for adultery—knew that man was but half made up without the fairer, kinder and more perfect part found in woman's nature.

And so it comes that while the apostles saw Christ only on Calvary, we see Him at our hearth-stones and take Him, in our wives, children and parents, to our hearts.

The old heathen poet told of two loves that were gods of men's idolatry : One was of the earth— dark, fierce, turbulent and fickle; the other of heaven—pure, steadfast and beautiful. The first is passion, the only love known to humanity before the coming of our Savior; the other is affection, the love of the household. It may be that the earthly love urges on the union of two hearts, but it passes away, and the other enters, never to leave. How little, then, do they know of the true, binding tie of the household, of the home, who talk of free love? There may be, as there doubtless is, a free passion, but there can be no such thing as free love. It is free lust— the wanton impulse of the beast—and can not be tied down to any law or made subject to any control. Nor can it be destroyed. It is a part of our earthly nature and necessary to our existence, but woe awaits the poor creature who accepts it as a guide and builds upon its promise. The fire that is a good slave is no worse master.

It is the unity of hopes, fears, joys, sorrows and of interests that creates the love of married life. And it grows stronger in sickness, sorrow and disappointments, in poverty shared together, than in prosperity and the gladness of success. It can take a deeper root in one little grave, reach nearer heaven from that soil, in its flower-fringed branches, than it can from feasts and merry-makings. One's little wife may not be beautiful—no more than one's mother or one's child—but ah, she is the little wife from whose kind eyes came consolation in the hour of disappointment and perhaps shame. All the world may not believe in you, but she believes in you. The mother of your children teaches them to love and reverence you, and her sad yet patient face, her gentle hands and loving heart, have held through all the years that little home a haven of rest and comfort, while the cruel world roared without.

Free love! Who wants to be freed from the love of his mother or the love of his child? And, God help us, who wishes to be freed from the tie woven by little hands at the hearthstone, although the little hands have long since moldered into the dust of the grave?

How sweet it is to know that the homely ways of life are pleasant ways, and full of tenderness and beauty to us. In at the door comes the son of Mary, and life's cares are soothed and a sunshine from heaven lightens and beautifies all poor places, so that one looks upon them lovingly and remembers them in after life with tenderness and regret. They were hard days, ah, my wife, in that time of youth when we two made our little fight with the world, but love sweetened the toil and softened the disappointments, and out of the sickness, the sorrows. the failures, the death, came the reward that now makes the life pleasant to the memory. In all the lands of Christendom are the homes, many rich and multitudes humble, but in all Christ dwells, bringing happiness. Blessed be the name of Christ, and blessed be the name of Mary, mother of Christ!

### The Casting Out of Devils.

To one who studies the new testament with care, with loving care and tenderness, it is curious to find that while portions of the precious book are literally believed, others again, of equal importance, if any inequality can be found, are ignored and forgotten.

The enforcement of some precepts has caused centuries of wars, and their so-called propagandism has decimated the human race. It is a strange contradiction in poor human nature that made the Prince of Peace grand teacher of good will to men on earth, the author of the cruelest persecutions and abuse the world ever knew. And because Christ said that his coming would cause dissensions we must not conclude, as many do, that he sanctioned them. It was not until after his doctrines became respectable that they changed their character. It was when Christianity passed from the keeping of the poor to the control of the rich that men began to render unto Christ that which pertained to Cæsar. The missionaries went forth with the Bible in one hand and the sword in the other, to enforce glory to God in the highest and good will and peace to men on earth.

There are two phantoms—one fair and tempting,

the other gaunt, ghastly and murderous—that follow close upon true religion, and are mistaken by the
multitude for that which they only shadow and obscure. The one is fanaticism and the other law and
order. They are the dead'y enemies Christ denounced
but did not destroy. Long years after His sacrifice
the one took up, repaired and embroidered His sev-
ered garment ; the other seized His cross, and sword
in hand, sought to enforce, through violence, His precepts of peace and forgiveness.

This is mostly the Christianity of to-day in organized religions. Now the conviction that is so in-
tolerant that it will not bear opposition is a doubt.
No man threatens you with death for disputing as
a fact that the sun shines or does not shine. But
when one has a painful doubt lurking at the base of
his belief he grows furious at your encouragement
of it.

Thus it is that the Christianity which should be
as open and broad and generous as the day is gathered in parcels and hid in churches, as if they were
forts bristling with deadly arms against those who
doubt as the sectarian himself doubts.

Fanaticism is a grave evil, but it is mild because
less insidious than Cæsarism, which flings out the
garb of Christ as the banner of law and order.
Christianized Cæsarism is the attempt to render unto

one person both that which is Christ's and that which is Cæsar's. It attempts to harmonize the gratifications of the one with the self-denial of the other. It gilds the cross and makes it ornamental. It drapes the robe of our Savior over the purple and fine linen. It organizes charity, formalizes faith, and gives the sanction of the highest respectability to the humble Nazarene and His rude apostles. It calls in science and builds belief on geology, and stretches far into the heavens on astronomy. It purposes reaching heaven by easy stages, on a macadamized road that is comfortable and respectable.

Of the two, fanaticism is the lesser evil. Better the violent conflict, the stake, the torture and great fights than thus to live with slow decay that antedates the death. Ah! when Christ so bitterly denounced and doomed the rich man he realized the danger of riches. They eat into and destroy both true religion and its gaunt, cruel specter, fanaticism. An eloquent essayist tells us that the routes to shrines so long as they remain shrines, can be traced by human bones of the pilgrims who perished while seeking the holy places. When these shrines change to marts of trade the roads grow safe, for men care more for their goods than their lives or their religion.

To accomplish this union of Christ and Cæsar,

to make fanaticism possible, it was necessary to ignore certain parts of the new testament while earnestly insisting upon a literal obedience to others.

Among the miracles wrought by Christ, the one most dwelt upon in the testament is the casting out of devils; and yet how few give the strange fact a second thought, and pause over an event such as this to ask, What can it mean?

"And they came over unto the other side of the sea, into the country of the Gaderenes.

"And when He was come out of the ship, immediately there met Him out of the tombs a man with an unclean spirit,

" Who had his dwelling among the tombs; and no man could bind him, no, not with chains;

" Because that he had been often bound with fetters and chains, and the chains had been plucked asunder by him, and the fetters broken in pieces; neither could any man tame him.

"And always, night and day, he was in the mountains and in the tombs, crying and cutting himself with stones.

" But when he saw Jesus afar off, he ran and worshiped Him.

"And cried with a loud voice and said, What have I to do with Thee, Jesus, thou Son of the Most

High God? I adjure thee by God that thou torment me not.

"(For He said unto him, Come out of the man, thou unclean spirit).

"And He asked him, What is thy name? And he answered, saying, My name is Legion; for we are many."

We are aware that wise doctors of divinity, and learned doctors of medicine have after consultation, told the Christian world that this being possessed of devils meant that the afflicted were insane. Clearly as words can express His meaning, Christ does not teach this. He tells us not once, but frequently, that it is demonianism. Now either Christ knew that the poor creatures were insane, and yet was willing to pander to the superstition of the day, or He was ignorant of the wonderful fact the science of medicine has since claimed to develop.

We may close our precious book and shut out revealed religion on either proposition.

No, Christ teaches us all that later experience confirms: that lying outside the little circle of our material life, and sometimes penetrating it, is a world of life other than our own, that more or less influences our earthly existence. And what significance this gives to prayer—that cry for help to the unseen Holy to save us from the control of the unseen evil.

How much have we done in life that, looking back upon, we wonder at—follies that seem to have been without motive. No less of sin. Who upon any other ground can account for the boy murderer of New England, whose horrible butcheries of children fill one with horror and amazement? We are told that there is a flow in the tide of our vitality that reaches its lowest ebb between midnight and dawn, when the dying release their hold of life and pass away. It is between those hours we waken to turn and toss upon a couch that seems to be surrounded by a strange, weird atmosphere, through which we look upon our own follies and sins as they never appear at other times. How close we are upon the border line between this life and the life to come, and from mysterious influences we can only feel what strange promptings are given us.

Are not the dead about us; and if demons may possess the bodies of men, may not the good spirits lend a holy influence to the better promptings of the soul? Christ has so taught. His prayers were addressed to his Heavenly Father as a child's petition is to the loving heart of a tender parent. The world is full to-day of strange manifestations that startle the multitude and confound the learned. We thought to have exhausted in our knowledge the laws of nature and explored to their farthest mystery all there was to comprehend. The result is faith in ourselves, but no faith in Christ or Christ's teachings. We have built to ourselves a religion on science, and sent our astronomical God far from us, into the depths of never-ending space. All less than this is superstition, ignorance, and falsehood. The dead materialism of the day rejects all else than that which touches the senses. To the educated of our time the earth rolls, cold and Godless, through eternal space. Christ is dead and forgotten, and beyond the brief troubles of our little life there is naught. This frightful condition does not yet touch the poor nor the earnest teachers of the church, but when it does, God in his mercy will send the sheeted dead to walk our streets, to waken us from an unbelief that is worse than annihilation.

## Good One Day in Seven.

We formally set aside one seventh of our time for meditation upon holy subjects and prayer to God for divine protection. This is less than fourteen and a half per cent taken from our sins and devoted to our souls. Is it, then, of so little importance to us that we can afford to thus trifle with it? What business man, what merchant is there who would prosper in his undertakings who would thus give to them so small a part of his time and attention? Is this policy of insurance, with its payment of fourteen and a half per cent for a treasure in heaven, what Christ contemplated in his teachings? Here is what he says:

"No man can serve two masters; for either he will hate the one and love the other, or else he will hold to the one and despise the other. Ye can not serve God and mammon."

The Christian of to-day illustrates the truth of what our Savior uttered, for he has compromised theoretically upon giving one-seventh of his time to Christ, and ends practically in devoting all of it to mammon. The fever of the week will not end its inflamed throbbings at our bidding upon Sunday, and the servitor of the world carries to the house of God all the care and anxieties of the week. The prayer becomes a mere formality, the song of praise beats unmeaningly upon the ear, for the mind follows the troubled heart back to the counting-room or work-shop, or field, or office, where the hopes and fears are.

It is so hard to learn that revealed religion has reference almost exclusively to this life. Christ's precepts teaching us how to live are few, simple, direct and easily understood, while all that He said of life hereafter was spoken in parables, and they, too, begin and end with the preparation necessary this side of the grave to fit us for the unknown hereafter.

As well might one hope to have the soul lifted from earth into heaven by the divine music garnered from the centuries by the church, without being taught and trained to comprehend the strains, as to expect to enjoy the heaven promised us without the life-long preparation left us by Christ. To one born blind light is as unknown as the religion of our Savior to the worshiper of mammon. Such blind followers, believing in the goodness of God and the forgiveness of sins, fondly hope that after all mercy will intervene and undo all that justice has decreed. They little dream that they make such mercy impossible. Study the laws of our physical being and note how inexorable they are. They never forgive. The wrong done our body, be it in mutilation of limb or to the injury of our health, is followed with fatal certainty by punishment against which we cry in vain. We were shown at Mt. Vernon a bullet that had been shot into the bark of a tree. It had healed over and the tree continued to grow, and here, after a hundred years, the bullet was found, the remote but positive cause of its fall. All about the wound the stubborn fiber had hardened into knots until slow decay brought death at last. And about the wound of our moral nature goes on the hardening of the heart so often spoken of by Christ. God may forgive the sinner, but never the sin. We may nurse the broken limb and salve over the wound, but the mutilation ever remains. How terrible the thought that every wrong done our moral nature has like consequences, and that we are doomed to enter the great hereafter maimed and sick.

After telling us that we can not serve two masters, how earnestly he warns us against the cares of this life, the hard service of mammon:

"Therefore I say unto you, Take no thought for your life, what ye shall eat, or what ye shall drink; nor yet for your body, what ye shall put on.

8

Is not the life more than meat, and the body than raiment?

"Behold the fowls of the air: for they sow not, neither do they reap, nor gather into barns; yet your heavenly Father feedeth them. Are ye not much better than they?

"Which of you, by taking thought, can add one cubic unto his stature?

"And why take ye thought for raiment? Consider the lilies of the field, how they grow; they toil not, neither do they spin:

"And yet I say unto you that even Solomon, in all his glory, was not arrayed like one of these.

"Wherefore, if God so clothe the grass of the field, which to-day is, and to-morrow is cast into the oven, shall he not much more clothe you, O, ye of little faith.

"Therefore take no thought, saying. What shall we eat? or, What shall we drink? or, Wherewithal shall we be clothed?

"(For after all these things do the Gentiles seek); for your heavenly Father knoweth that ye have need of all these things.

"But seek ye first the kingdom of God, and his righteousness; and all these things shall be added unto you.

"Take therefore no thought for the morrow:

for the morrow shall take thought for the things of itself. Sufficient unto the day is the evil thereof."

How sweet and soothing are these words coming from Christ to the anxious, careworn sons of toil. Look up, be cheerful. God lives; the seasons come and go each in its appointed time, changeless in their change; the earth, hard as it is upon the children of men, has yet flowers that bloom and birds that sing, and the pleasant sunlight is every-where. The struggle, hard as it is on earth, is but brief. A hundred years hence, and where will be these cares and hopes and fears? Be content, be kind to each other, and remember that we are all children of the kind Father who cares for the birds and flowers, said Christ, and therefore cares for us.

How much of the misery of this life comes from those brooding anxieties, from imaginary troubles. Alas!

> " We look before and after, we sigh for what is not;
>   Our sincerest laughter with some pain is fraught.
>   Our sweetest songs are those which tell of saddest thought."

What mother hath left her child for a time, and returning found its eyes widened with fear and its little lips trembling, but takes the infant into her arms, and says: " Don't fear, my babe; I was not far away; I am with you?" And so Christ gathers us to Him, and so He gives us tender assurance of His loving care.

Nor must we be guilty of the common error, the sin, for such it is, of supposing that in this or aught else left us by our Savior, we are to despise this life or turn from this world, believing thereby that we are making ourselves more acceptable to Him. This earth is a beautiful earth, given us not to abuse, but enjoy. It is full of pleasant ways for innocent enjoyments that purify and elevate our nature. Note in the sermon to the toiling, care-worn millions, how lovingly and gently He speaks of the lilies of the fields. He had seen and loved the flowers, as He had seen and heard the birds. He briefly referred to these in illustration of what He sought to teach. But had He not also looked upon the lofty mountains, along whose sides to-day the cloud shadows chase each other, on the solemn woods, or the ever-changing sea, and loved them as He did the flowers and birds? How often, in his houseless wanderings, had He seen the sun go down, then, as now, unchanged, in all these centuries, in its still glory of cloud drapery, and gazing into the depths with His tender, beautiful eyes, through the glowing sea of fading light, to the cold, chilling, never-ending space beyond, felt as feels the Christian to-day, that God is good to give us, even for this brief life, such a lovable home. All, then, that is beautiful in nature, all that is refined and elevating in art, are ours to enjoy.

## The Need of Faith.

"And when He was entered in a ship His disciples followed Him.

"And behold there arose a great tempest in the sea, insomuch that the ship was covered with the waves; but He was asleep.

"And His disciples came to Him and awoke Him, saying, Lord save us; we perish.

"And he saith unto them, Why are ye fearful, O ye of little faith? Then He arose and rebuked the winds and the sea; and there was a great calm.

"But the men marveled, saying, What manner of man is this, that even the winds and the sea obey him?"

The lesson sought to be taught us in this touchingly beautiful narrative of a strange event in the life of Christ is the importance of faith. "O ye of little faith," cried our Savior when awakened by His terror-stricken disciples. They had seen Him performing miracles with the power of God; they had seen the peoples moved by His godlike presence and His words of divine wisdom, and the wild winds of the stormy night and the yeasty waves drove out from their minds that they were with their master, whose ill man alone could compass. He spoke to the winds and the waves; He said, "peace, be still," and the winds, thus rebuked, ceased, and the wild waves subsided.

To how many storms raging in our own hearts, filling our being with fear, despair, the anguish of wicked disorder, dark as the clouded night and wilder than the wildest storm that ever tossed lawlessly along a boundless deep, storms that have changed our being and driven us out to deeds of violence and cruelty—to how many such storms have we awakened our Savior that He might cry "Peace, be still," and so give us rest and hope and happiness.

After all the centuries the faith is as necessary to us as when the wearied Son of Man sank to sleep upon that troubled sea. And what a picture those few simple words present to the thoughtful mind. Through the ages that have followed His advent men have so accustomed themselves to regard their Christ as their God, that His labors, trials and sufferings on earth as a man are obscured. He was one of our own helpless race, and all the ills that beset us were his to encounter. We are prone to say to ourselves, "But he was God—what are our sufferings to the Almighty?" And so Christ passes from us. To retain the truth in all its vividness we must return to the

story as told by his apostles.  Preceding this very
miracle we are told :

"Now, when Jesus saw great multitudes about
Him He gave commandment to depart unto the other
side.

"And a certain scribe came and said unto Him,
Master, I will follow Thee whithersoever Thou
goest.

"And Jesus said unto him, The foxes have holes
and the birds of the air have nests; but the Son of
Man hath not where to lay his head.

"And another of His disciples said unto Him,
Lord, suffer me first to go and bury my father.

" But Jesus said unto him, Follow me, and let
the dead bury their dead."

He was weary.  He sought to end the labors of
the day, and the multitude that gathered about,
poor, hungry hearts, would have more.  They sought
to look upon His kind face, they longed for His
strangely wise utterances, and so He sought refuge
in the vessel that was to carry Him and His disciples
to the other side.  And how sad is his response to
the scribe, " The foxes have holes and the birds of
the air have nests, but the Son of Man hath not
where to lay his head."

He does not say the son of God, but of man.

He was given on other occasions to referring to His Father in heaven; but now, footsore and weary, hungry and sick at heart, He tells the scribe that He has no home in which, among loving hearts, He can find shelter. He hath no place to lay His head. Ah! blessed head, how we long to pillow it upon our tenderest affections! How we long to give the one friend of humanity a home! And yet who among us is more kind, more patient, more charitable, with all the love we express and all the teachings His words and example have left us?

He went aboard the rude vessel to escape the multitude, and like a tired child lay down to sleep. He was so wearied, so worn out, that the great storm, with its fierce winds and waves that washed the decks, did not disturb His deep repose. Christ slept. God never sleeps. How difficult it is for us to recognize the dignity of truth. A fact to be acceptable must not be homely. The Jews would not accept their Messiah for that He was born in a manger. More stupid than the Hebrews, we will not permit Him to remain there. They expected Him to come in glory and power, and we lift Him there, not content with his lowly lot, and so we misuse the truth. The inexperienced hunter looks a mile away for game that springs up at his feet. We can not see that in

9

our anxiety to make Him other than He was we deny
Christ as completely as did the Jews. They could
not see him in the humble carpenter born in a stable;
we can not see him as man at all.

Far darker and more painful is that skepticism
that shuts him out entirely. This is the horrible
teaching of to-day. We are wiser than Christ;
we are more learned than His simple disciples and
the blind followers of all the generations who accepted the faith He taught with the simple confidence of children. We are wiser than they. We
accept only what we can comprehend. We dispense
with faith for the light of learning. Alas! the old-
est sage, the wisest of men, after a lifetime of
thought, closes his book, and looking out upon creation with his study-dimmed eyes, says mournfully:
"After all these years of thought and research I have
been taught to know that I know nothing." He has
counted the age of the earth by the unerring records
of geology, and footing up the millions of years,
finds before and after the incomprehensible eternity.
He has reached the stars, and beyond lies, what?
Never ending, incomprehensible space. He can not
comprehend the very sunlight; no, nor a little flower,
nor a blade of grass, nor, above all, himself.

We accept the sunlight we can not understand:

we enjoy the flower. In like manner must we take to our hearts the divine precepts of the Master, and above all the faith that lifts from our troubled hearts all the dark brooding cares of this life, and all the painful doubts of the life hereafter.

·,·

## Confession of Sin. ˜

"And when He had said this He breathed on and said unto them, Receive ye the Holy Ghost:

"Whosesoever sins ye remit they are remitted unto them; whosesoever sins ye retain they are retained."

How humanity, in all its needs, hopes, fears, in all its weakness and strength, remains the same through recorded centuries, the brief story of Christ's life and teachings tell us. With all our progress in material prosperity we are to-day the same feeble creatures that gathered about our Savior and followed him as the flock follows the shepherd into desert places, that they might get comfort and wisdom from His beautiful words.

And why should it be otherwise? Let us build to ourselves grand houses, give to each a palace of stout walls and double-plated windows and strong doors; let us make to ourselves summer in the dead of winter, and cool retreats from the heat of summer, and wasting disease and ghastly death will enter and abide with us. We may build against the wild elements, shut out the burning sun, the biting winter wind; but we can not build against the ills of life,

that are part of our nature. Where are the walls
that can shield us from ingratitude, chilled affection,
selfishness, avarice, meanness and the thousand ills that
flesh is heir to? Said a friend: "I went to the palace of the rich man with the petition of a poor widow
dying of a cancer, who asked relief for her hungry
and helpless children. I waited in rooms where art
had exhausted its last resource in all that was beautiful. Huge mirrors extending from floor to ceiling
seemed to double the wealth of palatial decorations.
The ceilings were gems of frescoed excellence; the
walls had fortunes in the form of pictures on every
panel; all that has been done in bronze and marble
to revive the almost lost science of Greek beauty appeared in every recess; the carpet beneath my feet,
woven by hand, had probably a poor laborer's life in
every square foot. And while I waited for the servant to carry in my card I heard a moan from the
sick room within so sad, deep and agonizing that it
seemed to come from the very grave. I thought I
had left with the poor dying widow all the misery of
which life is capable. That moan taught me my error. Death, the great democrat, knows no distinction."

This is so well recognized that its utterance is
a platitude. It is common-place, worn so threadbare that while the preacher speaks it from his pul-

pit his congregation sleeps. We all continue struggling fiercely for these things, as if their possession lifted us above all suffering and made disease and death our friends, in the way we want them. And if it is not worldly possessions that own us it is some fevered ambition worse than bodily sickness.

And yet all the real estate a king may possess, with forests of brown Rembrandts' depths of lighted gloom, and sunny fields and lofty mountains, does not hold as much of the human heart as one little grave. The cemeteries of the earth are after all the kingdoms of earth, and hold in their narrow limits all that we possess.

And how do we feed our little vanity over our material progress, and claim that humanity is wiser, better, happier from what we have gained? The iron rails with which we so laboriously network our land fetch wide points closer together, while the telegraph seems to annihilate space. And how are we better? The telegraph sets shores world-wide apart to whispering to each other. Has that telegraph reached that other life, and can it fetch to us a loving word from the dead in whose graves we buried our earthly happiness?

Poor creatures are we after all. The coral reefs of the South seas come up from unknown depths to present great sea-walls against the ever stormy, restless ocean, and so solid and enduring that man can not imitate them. And the builder is a worm.

The Church of Christ is founded on the wants of humanity, and in its relief no greater is given than that found in confession. A sin once committed seems to burn into our being until we find relief in telling of it to another. This is a trait in human nature even when uninfluenced by religious feeling. "To make a clean breast of it" is a popular saying that every one recognizes. To tell of the dark transaction even when confided in confidence to another seems to give that other a share of the burden. What parent is there who has not remarked the sense of relief the little one seems to experience after telling through tears and with trembling lips of some transgression that has lain like lead upon the little heart? Who of those learned in the law, with practice among criminals, has not noted in his client the same result?

This is not remorse—it is the reverse of that. Remorse means simply the fear of detection. The murderer, for example, lives in the constant dread that his horrible secret, that he has sought to bury with his victim, may be brought to light; and in his effort to hide he oftentimes betrays his crime. No, the fact remains that we feel instinctively that there is a process through which the sin-laden soul can be relieved, to gain which the self-convicted is willing to brave discovery and accept punishment.

What a power, then, this gives to confession as a part of our religion! Who among us, when troubled with some vexatious worldly affair has not found comfort in transferring the case to the keeping of a lawyer? Who, when watching by the bedside of some loved sufferer, has not felt relieved when the long-expected physician comes to share the responsibility? In the same way, but far more effectual, we go humbly to the good minister of God, our advocate before the bar of the Almighty, our physician of the soul, to relieve our inner being of its heavy burden. It is prayer reduced to practice; it is making a reality of an emotional desire to be cured. Trouble not your soul, oh! Christian, as to what may be between your minister and his Master. Judge not lest ye be judged, when God alone is the arbiter. Remember that of the twelve ordained by the sacred hands of Christ himself, none were perfect, from Peter who denied to Judas who betrayed Him. Let us look in deep humility to our own transgressions, leaving the ordained to answer for themselves at that awful tribunal where in the end we must all appear.

## The Love of the Beautiful.

"And they send unto him certain of the Pharisees and of the Herodians, to catch him in His words.

" And when they were come they say unto Him, Master, we know that Thou art true, and carest for no man ; for Thou regardest not the person of men, but teachest the way of God in truth.  Is it lawful to give tribute to Cæsar or not?

" Shall we give, or shall we not give?  But He, knowing their hypocrisy, said unto them, Why tempt ye Me?  Bring Me a penny that I may see it.

"And they brought it.  And He said unto them, Whose is this image and superscription?  And they said unto Him, Cæsar's.

"And Jesus answering, said unto them, Render to Cæsar the things that are Cæsar's, and to God the things that are God's.  And they marveled at Him."

The heathenish tendency so marked among modern sects, to seek the favor of the Creator by a contempt for His works, has really no foundation in the teachings of our Savior.  Of all this beautiful earth, with its flowers, birds, sunny fields, and solemn wood, its shadow-haunted mountains, and restless seas, its ever-changing seasons, and glories of light, that are of the earth, man alone is vile. And yet he seeks to win favor by affecting to despise all that is better than himself.

It is not possible that He who had such an un-bounded love for his fellow men should not have as kindly looked upon the humbler but more perfect work of the Creator. "In the many mansions of my Father's house there is room for all his creatures." And the house was not larger than His heart, that gathered in and held lovingly and tenderly all living things. The very sparrows that sold in the market two for a penny were known and cared for by our Savior, who gave His heart's blood in testimony of the truth, that not only opened heaven to us here-after, but tendered peace and good will to the human family on earth.

The humility He continually teaches has in it no degradation, no slavish, superstitious bending of hu-manity before a vindictive God, but the humility that takes from us the false pride that arrogates to an ant-hill all of creation. For how many thousands of years did the human family see the sun rise in the east and set in the west, and say this light was made for us, and for us only! How science took the sun from us and gave it to such depths of space the mind of man can not comprehend them! How science removes God Himself, making Him the center of that which has no center, for it has no limits! But science no more than Christ can take the false pride out of our nature. As heaven was made for us earth is to be despised. We mangle, and abuse, and feed on the inferior animals, and yet the poor creature we mutilate and torture through our work is no more ours than the sun that we now gaze upon in awe; and that is after all only the one light in millions on millions that illumine the portals of God's creation.

All that we win from unfeeling matter, all that we make our own from the elements, are ours, so far as we may control and use them. But these dumb animals, with their pitiful, pleading eyes, are not ours to torture, abuse, and kill. This is the pride, the vain conceit, Christ would have taken from us, and not the love of the beautiful of earth, for the keen enjoyment of which He has given us such a great capacity.

A great philosopher has told us that we may repeat a truth until it loses all meaning. We may add that a falsehood can be dwelt upon through generations, until it becomes in the minds of men a truth. Of this sort is that fanatical self-denial that finds no good on this earth and reserves its conceited self for the heaven of the hereafter. God is to be insulted, if that were possible, by a loud condemnation of His works on earth, and with puritanical hypocrisy we are to turn our backs on Him and His in a vain effort to make ourselves other than what we are. It is well to go to our closets and confess our sins in secret to our Creator, but to fit ourselves for that holy communion it is good to show some kindness to the poor creatures dependent upon our care, to extend Christian charity and forgiveness to our fellow-men, and, above all, to be prepared to thank our heavenly Father for this beautiful earth, and to ask His aid to fit us better for its inheritance.

Would we pass our Sundays in meditation, let us go to the fields and woods, or down by the ever-changing sea, and drink in God's goodness in His beautiful works. Nor is it to be found in nature only. Art is as much His as aught else. Who has stood before the grand old cathedrals of Europe, where the humble faith of generations is worked in columns and arches and towers until the marble mocks the clouds, or knelt within where one's prayers seem carried to heaven on great waves of melody, and not felt the soul lifted above the cares and pains and disappointments of this life?

And with what beautiful simplicity He makes answer to these cunning inquisitors: " Render unto Cæsar the things that are Cæsar's, and unto God the things that are God's." He had asked for a coin, and uttered those grand words over the money. The Jews had a government that was a theocracy, their politics were their religion, and their legal enactments came direct, they claimed, from God himself. But Cæsar had intervened, and separating religion, such as it was, from government, brutal as that was, built a foundation for a double duty. It was little that Christ gave to Cæsar, and all that was left he gave to God. Our duties as a citizen harmonize with our religious obligations. We may pay tribute to the power that gives us law and order, but nothing beyond.

Municipal government is for the benefit of the governed, and the tribunal to try such is in the governed. The brutal conquest of the weak by the strong, the lust of power, and the greed of gain, that pervert governments from their just ends, create no just demand for the tribute Christ authorized to Cæsar.

We, however, have improved upon the Cæsarism of the day in which Christ spoke. A deadlier enemy to Christianity appears in that Cæsarism that seeks to make religion fashionable. Christ was denied by the Jews because he was born in a stable and was by trade a carpenter. The humble mechanic is ignored and a god substituted. Were our Savior to reappear on earth, with the lowly following of fishermen and tent-makers, our church members would be horrified and gravely disheartened.

Our religious Cæsarism elbows poverty out into the cold, for that it is not respectable. It would go hard with it to make an exception in behalf of the Divine Founder of Christianity and his chosen twelve. Yet He has said to us that a slight to or abuse of the humblest is an offense to Him that will rob us of the heaven hereafter. And well it may. If we can not receive the poor in our churches because of their poverty, how can we find happiness in their association when they are to meet their Divine Master and friend?

We have so arranged our Cæsarism that we can be religious without being moral. The good will to man on earth is lost in the glory to God in the highest, and the glory resolves itself in mere forms that are as dry and hollow as husks. The husks may be gilded, but they are husks all the same. Christ gave little to Cæsar and much to God, and we give little to God and much to Cæsar—for are they not one? Ah! let us return, and, filling our empty pitchers at the divine fountain, prepare for heaven by developing heaven as Christ taught us on earth.

## Blind by the Wayside.

"And it came to pass that as He was come nigh unto Jericho a certain blind man sat by the wayside begging;

"And hearing the multitude pass by he asked what it meant;

"And they told him that Jesus of Nazareth passeth by.

"And he cried, saying, Jesus, thou Son of David, have mercy on me.

"And they which went before rebuked him, that he should hold his peace; but he cried so much the more, Thou Son of David, have mercy on me.

"And Jesus stood, and commanded him to be brought unto Him, and when he was come near He asked him,

"Saying, What wilt thou that I shall do unto thee? And he said, Lord, that I may receive my sight.

"And Jesus said unto him, Receive thy sight, thy faith hath saved thee.

"And immediately he received his sight, and followed Him, glorifying God; and all the people, when they saw it, gave praise unto God."

Of all the afflictions to which poor humanity is liable among the saddest is the loss of sight. To those possessed of wealth and surrounded by friends it is to be a helpless object of compassion; but when to this is added poverty how horrible is the affliction. Those we love, who may demand our care through our affection, and own the means to save them from want, the sense of dependence, the loss of so much that makes life even endurable, are troubles hard to endure; but when the patient gropes helplessly along the highways of life, thrust aside in the cruel competition of hungry, heartless multitudes, trampled upon and abused, suffering from hunger, thirst, shivering in the pitiless winds of winter or fainting in the heats of summer, how horrible is his or her fate! Nothing but that great blank night forever about one; nothing but one's thoughts, dreary as the moonless, starless night for all time, until death adds the tomb and brings relief!

With what touching truth Milton tells of this in his Samson Agonistes. When we remember that the immortal poet is speaking of himself the beautiful words have a touching significance:

> " O, loss of sight, of thee I must complain!
> Blind among enemies, O, worse than chains,
> Dungeon of beggary, or decrepid age!
> Light, the prime work of God, to me's extinct,

And all her various objects of delight
Annull'd which night in part my grief have eased—
Inferior to the vilest now become
Of man or worm, the vilest here excel me ;
They creep, yet see—I dark in light, exposed
To daily fraud, contempt, abuse and wrong ;
Within doors or without, still as a fool
In power of others, never in my own ;
Scarce half I seem to live, dead more than half—
O, dark, dark, dark amid the blaze of noon,
Irrevocably dark, total eclipse
Without all hope of day.
O, first created beam, and thou great word,
Let there be light,' and light was over all,
Why am I thus bereaved thy prime degree ?
The sun to me is dark
And silent as the moon
When she deserts the night,
Hid in her vacant interluner cave.
Since light so necessary is to life;
And almost life itself, if it be true
That life is in the soul,
She all in every part—why was the sight
To such a tender ball as th' eye confined,
So obvious and so easy to be quenched,
And not as feeling through all parts diffused,
That she might look at will through every pore ?
Then had I not been thus exiled from light,
As in the land of darkness yet in light
*To live a life half dead, a living death,*
*And buried ; but O, yet more miserable,*
*Myself, my sepulcher, a moving grave—*

10

*Buried, yet not exempt,*
*By privilege of death and burial,*
*From worst of other evils, pains and wrongs,*
But made hereby obnoxious more
To all the miseries of life."

What a cry of agony is there! What must be
the suffering that comes up and reaches the heart
through beautiful words. The expressions of pain,
whether of body or mind, are generally wails without words. The next to reach our inner feeling and
make us sympathize with the sufferer are homely expressions. They are the truest eloquence. To know
this one has only to compare the sad utterances of
Christ when, wearied and depressed, He turned from
the multitude, whose sick He had healed, and to
whose mental and moral wants He had ministered, to
a certain scribe who had proposed to follow Him to
His home, and said, " The foxes have holes and the
birds of the air have nests, but the Son of Man hath
not where to lay His head." To compare this to the
stately poetic utterances of the blind poet: The one,
with his great heart longing for love and sympathy,
stands alone. In all the world there is no home for
Him—not one friend upon whom He can lean—no
home in which He can find rest. And He tells this in
homely words, that come nearer to the inarticulate
cry of suffering. The other, in a burst of agony, re-

lates his terrible doom, but in such stately, measured poetry that the beauty of the utterance robs it of half our sympathy.

We once waited on an eminent physician of Paris who made diseases of the eye a specialty. He gave two hours every day to the poor, who thronged his rooms for medical treatment, for he was famous as a learned man of quiet judgment and rare wisdom. Waiting for our turn, we saw him approach a poor girl:

" You are quite blind, my child ?"

" Quite blind, Monsieur."

He examined the clouded balls, turning up the lids gently, and said:

" You should have come to me a year ago; you have been sadly neglected, and yet I believe I can help you."

A blind smile, pitiful to look on, came to the face of the poor girl. The joy that cometh with the morn already shone in upon her darkened being.

To another woman he said, after a careful diagnosis:

" I can not help you—your case is past medical skill."

Ah, God! what a look of wild despair paled into that poor face as, with trembling lips, that could utter no sound, she turned away!

And a strong man tottered to a chair; on hearing his doom he uttered a cry that went straighter to the heart than all the solemn, measured sentences of the blind Milton.

They, these poor people, could not see much; but they saw probably the poor, dependent little ones ahungered and cold, turned out upon the world without their bread-winner, to starve.

We thought were this physician Christ, could he by a single word restore the sight, how readily would the crowd fall down and worship him.

And so He went about the earth healing the sick and giving comfort to the afflicted, when it came to pass, as He drew near unto Jericho, a blind beggar sitting by the wayside heard the multitude go by. The ear, quickened by the loss of sight, caught the name of the strange being who went among the children of men curing the lame so that they walked, and the dying so that they lived, and the blind so that they saw. What a thrill of hope shot through his darkened being! Ah! if he would only heal him and he cried out. Christ heard the cry. What appeal from afflicted humanity does He not hear? And while His followers rebuked the agonized sufferer, He turned and bade them fetch the blind man to Him, and Jesus said to him, "Receive thy sight— thy faith hath saved thee."

And yet to us, after the centuries, it is but a parable. How many of us sitting blind by the highway of life hear Christ going by and do not cry out, "Jesus, Son of David, have mercy upon me?"

True, it has been told us that if we ask it will be given us; if we knock it will be opened to us, for His love is as boundless as His forgiveness. But it is the law of our being that some one time in our life the good we seek passes within reach, and Christ, without our seeking, comes to us. Ah, me! how seldom it is that the quickened hearing of the blind catch the meaning of the sound, as salvation sweeps by, and cry out for help from the Son of God. Alas! it is our fate to be born blind; the aching, the troubled soul can not know the blessing, the joy of that light that, through the door of heaven opened by our blessed Savior, flows down, filling our world, making all things beautiful; that light which gives health to the soul, peace to the heart, and happiness to our troubled existence.

What a comfort it is to remember that He who went about wearily and in sorrow doing good when one of us, now our Lord, can give sight to all humanity and sweet content to all of us who in the suicide of crime have already a foretaste of the hell hereafter. Cry out, oh! sinner. as Christ passes, " Son of David, have mercy on me."

## The Love of Children.

"And they brought young children to Him, that He should touch them, and His disciples rebuked those that brought them.

" But when Jesus saw it He was much displeased and said unto them, Suffer the little children to come unto Me and forbid them not, for of such is the kingdom of God.

" Verily I say unto you, Whosoever shall not receive the kingdom of God as a little child, he shall not enter therein.

"And He took them up in His arms, put his hands upon them and blessed them."

There is probably no passage from the life of Christ more quoted and lovingly dwelt upon than this. Nor is this to be wondered at, for the event fetches our poor humanity so directly in contact with heaven. Our love of children is not only one of the strongest affections, but it is the purest.

They who teach us the harmony and uniform beauty of what they are pleased to call the laws of nature find it difficult to fetch death in accord with their teaching. Sleep, life itself, with all its mysteries, may be law, but death is violence. We strive in vain to make it harmonize with any part of our being. Death and its attendant pain are in antagonism to us, and mean war on nature. No teaching nor training, no attempt to look the inevitable in the face will make the dread thing familiar and less terrible. When one dies the world ends, and from that ending we shrink and cower, let our hearts be ever so brave, our faith ever so firm. We say they who are tortured by disease find relief in death. The heart-broken and sorely troubled find repose. Brave men and heroic women have calmly met his approach, delicate girls have meekly folded their thin hands above their terror-stricken breasts, and babes have been folded in his arms with trembling little lips and wide-staring, terror-stricken eyes—but none, unless insane, have sought that refuge willingly. The inevitable in all else can be made familiar and met half way with endurance, but death never.

"Why weepest thou?" asked the philosopher of a sufferer, "thy tears are unavailing."

"Therefore do I weep," was the touching response.

But of all visits of this dread enemy the most terrible is when he comes to the household, as he comes to every household, to claim the little one whose cooing voice is the music of the heart, whose little footsteps make the long hidden, silent affections of our inner being awaken to exquisite life.

Where is the parent who has fought off his dread approaches through the long, anxious days and dreary watches of the sleepless nights, who has hung in breathless agony above the cradled bed and saw the loved form waste away and the poor life weaken, and thought of all the winning little ways—who has not been prostrated in prayer and begged hard and long of God to spare the breaking heart, this unendurable affliction, this great agony that seemed impossible for the mourner to survive? They tell us of the efficacy of prayer, that God hears and grants our petition when it is carried to Him on the wings of faith. Alas! poor mother, the words go up in sobs from a broken heart like bubbles from a drowning man, and the little one dies all the same.

Blind leaders of the blind. This misdirected doctrine has done more to rob the afflicted of religion than all the teachings of science or the sneers of unbelief. The heart-broken stares in blind amazement at the dead and cries in agony against the cruel, iron-heeled fate that in spite of prayer has crushed out a heart. No; prayer may cleanse the heart and purify the being, and like cries and groans, give relief after a time, but it turns not death away. Christ in the garden prayed in agony to be saved, and prayed in vain. Who since then may have what was denied Him?

And when, in those fateful hours between midnight and morn, when life's tide ebbs and the little breath becomes more feeble, and the tiny pulse slips away from all feeling, and at last the loved one is still, and the long preserved quiet of the house is broken with agonizing cries—a sorrow is burned into one that no time, no religious consolation can soften or erase. Years and years after the keen heartache will return as one looks through tears at a lock of sunny hair or an old, half-worn little shoe. One's earthly possession, one's real estate that is priceless, can never be sold or mortgaged or given away, is a little narrow grave. The dear form molders into dust and disappears, but it never leaves the heart; the babe is one's precious babe through life. Perhaps forever.

Ah! me, what comfort there is, what sweet consolation to read these loving words " Suffer the little children to come unto Me and forbid them not, for of such is the kingdom of God."

" And He took them up in His arms, put His hands upon them and blessed them."

The afflicted says " He who has no children has taken my poor little one into His arms and put His

11

tender, loving hands upon its head and blessed it. Peace, oh! my heart. Christ lives."

We might lose all of the blessed Testament but that one passage, and yet true Christianity could win and control the world.

There is no love like unto that love. Said a profound jurist to us:

" A mother's love survives the deepest degradation of which the female nature is capable, and it is capable of a lower state than man's nature. When a woman comes into my court claiming the custody of her child I always grant it. She may be a bad woman and yet a good mother, at least the best if not the only mother the child can have. In this way I have at times saved both mother and child. For the sake of the child the mother will at least strive to appear virtuous. It is a rare event for a father and son to be engaged knowingly to each other in crime. It is never the case with mother and child."

Given by God, they lure us to heaven. Fresh from the hands of their Creator, pure and sweet in their innocence, not contaminated by sinful life, they fall about us like flowers from Paradise. Such as they are is the kingdom of heaven. A wise man has told us that in our old age, when the frame weakens and the faculties decay, the mind returns to, first its early youth and then its childhood. We pass from life as we entered, and the mother's teaching goes with us to that other life.

Deep and strong as the lesson of love is in the passage we quote, there is yet a more important one taught in the way of faith. When Christ says that such is the kingdom of heaven He means that confidence, that faith, that are such traits of childhood before contact with earth brings suspicion, disappointment and all the ills that sad experience entails. This lesson is taught in nearly all the life of our Savior. What is learning but doubt; what can science give us but disbelief? To reap the full benefit of all so beautifully given us by the Son of David we must approach Him with the faith of children, and confidingly take from His divine teaching the beautiful lessons of love in life, for such is the kingdom of God and the heaven promised us hereafter.

## Respectable Christians.

The attempt made to worship two masters, so strongly prohibited by our Savior, ends in our giving nearly all to Cæsar and very little to God. How strange it is, after the centuries of teaching, that in our striving to harmonize the worshiping of the two we should separate morality from religion. In Christ of course they mean one and the same thing. With us the line is drawn between the two, and both roads lead to heaven. The morality of modern Christianity means to be respectable. The world has come to be commercial, and if one meets promptly his moneyed obligations he is considered eminently fitted for heaven. He may fail in all else, and his failures will be considered eccentricities and indiscretions, not intefering in the least with his respectability or claim to Christian fellowship. The marble pulpit preaches to velvet-cushioned pews. It is not considered in good taste for the modern apostle to awaken respectability by unpleasant reference to the sins of to-day. Truths lose their meaning through frequent repetition, and so the sins denounced over eighteen centuries since in Jerusalem have been repeated until they cease to irritate, and rather add to than awaken from the slumber of indifference. The respectable Christian of to-day may be a Jew in his dealings—so that he be a Hebrew in his devotions, it is well with him.

We complimented a young divine on the devoted conduct of his congregation.

" Yes," he responded, sadly, " the way in which my little congregation in the Lord sing, pray, exhort, and cheat each other is very refreshing."

A delegation of pious colored men waited on their pastor one day, who had been making himself extremely disagreeable by denouncing theft, indolence, uncleanliness, adultery, and other sins.

" Brudder Campbell," they petitioned, "can't you stop talking so much about stealin' and sich, and give us one day ob good ole-fashioned praise-de-Lord religion ?"

The poor, benumbed intellect of a helpless race struck in a rough way the Cæsarism of modern religion. It is allowable for us to gain heaven through the praise-the-Lord devotion while nursing our sins, provided we pay our debts and so are respectable. The belief is general that there is a diplomatic gallery in heaven, where the rich and well-born, clad in purple and fine linen, sing operatic music in front of a huge organ. Beautiful music must be acceptable to the Lord, for it is the one form of prayer that more surely lifts the soul from the business and degradation of sinful life; but the hands that hold the harps must be clean, and the voices those of the pure and innocent to please God.

We have often thought, in this religious Cæsarism that exists to-day, of the consternation that would fall upon a congregation were Christ and His chosen twelve to walk into a fashionable church. Travel-stained, foot-weary, badly appareled as they were, how religious Cæsarism would gather away its skirts and gaze in trouble at the very founders of their faith!

Ah! how hard it is to realize that Christ was disowned, denounced, and crucified for that He was not respectable. The Jews were looking anxiously for their Messiah, who was to come in clouds of glory to slaughter and subdue their enemies, and lo! He appeared an humble mechanic, born in a manger, teaching love and loving forgiveness. Poor human nature is the same to-day as it was in Jerusalem, and has been through the centuries. We persecute the Jews for doing only that which we practice to-day. What would be thought of the rich man to-day who would give all he possessed to the poor? His heirs, under the solemn sanction of a court, would consign him to an asylum for the insane; and yet the terrible condemnation of the rich man, written in unfading words above the portal of every palace on earth, remains to be read of all men.

And so it has come to pass under our religious Cæsarism, that our worst men are our best Christians. The cold, calculating, selfish creature who carefully observes religious forms, who pays his debts, and is therefore respectable, walks in the ways of righteousness, although he may oppress the poor, crowd his debtor to the wall, torture his enemy, and live through life without one generous impulse. His charity is of an organized sort—a huge machine that grinds out alms to the worthy poor. He does not belong to the class of hypocrites denounced by Christ. The religion of the Jews was a terrible religion of vengeance, with a God made up of the worst qualities of humanity, that he might be feared and understood. But their religion was the ten commandments, and the sinner who prayed in public places was forced to a pretense that made him a hypocrite. But we have harmonized all that. Our sinner is not a hypocrite—he is one who deceives himself. Modern theology teaches him that Satan is the servant of God, and he has compromised with the enemy. The husks he lives on are the husks of corn husked out over eighteen hundred years since, and are therefore very dry and without nutrition. The walls of his temple are massive—too thick to admit the groans of the oppressed, the cries of the poor, the wailings of despair.

There is no more deadly enemy to true religion—the religion of Christ—than selfishness, and the essence of selfishness is the model Christian, who gathers in the good things of this world in one hand while he holds the beguiled cross in the other.

"I have been looking in the trap that holds our little rogues, the weak fellows," said the late Chief Justice Chase, when governor of Ohio, after a visit to the penitentiary, "and now I will dine with the big rogues, and next Sunday we will all go to church and thank God that we are not as they are—in the penitentiary."

How beautifully Christ tells us this in His parable of the prodigal son:

"And He said, a certain man had two sons:

"And the younger of them said to his father, Father, give me the portion of goods that falleth to me. And he divided unto them his living.

"And not many days after the younger son gathered all together, and took his journey into a far country, and there wasted his substance with riotous living.

"And when he had spent all there arose a mighty famine in that land, and he began to be in want.

"And he went and joined himself to a citizen of that country, and he sent him into his fields to feed swine.

"And he would fain have filled his belly with the husks that the swine did eat; and no man gave unto him.

"And when he came to himself he said, How many hired servants of my father's have bread enough and to spare, and I perish with hunger!

"I will arise and go to my father, and will say unto him, Father, I have sinned against heaven and before thee,

"And am no more worthy to be called thy son; make me as one of thy hired servants.

"And he arose and came to his father. But when he was yet a great way off his father saw him and had compassion, and ran and fell on his neck and kissed him.

"And the son said unto him, Father, I have sinned against heaven and in thy sight, and am no more worthy to be called thy son.

"But the father said to his servants, Bring forth the best robe and put it on him, and put a ring on his hand and shoes on his feet.

"And bring hither the fatted calf and kill it, and let us eat and be merry.

"For this my son was dead, and is alive again;

he was lost and is found. And they began to be merry.

"Now his elder son was in the field, and as he came and drew nigh to the house he heard music and dancing.

"And he called one of the servants, and asked what these things meant.

"And he said unto him, Thy brother is come, and thy father hath killed the fatted calf, because he hath received him safe and sound.

"And he was angry, and would not go in. Therefore came his father out and entreated him.

"And he answering said to his father, Lo, these many years do I serve thee, neither transgressed I at any time thy commandment, and yet thou never gavest me a kid that I might make merry with my friends.

"But as soon as this thy son was come, which hath devoured thy living with harlots, thou hast killed for him the fatted calf.

"And he said unto him, son, thou art ever with me, and all that I have is thine.

"It was meet that we should make merry and be glad; for this the brother was dead, and is alive again, and was lost and is found."

One of the lessons taught in the above parable is the subject of our meditations. The careful, prudent, selfish son, who saw his more repulsive brother depart without a sigh and noted his return with jealous envy, is rebuked, as our excellent, respectable Christian will be when, standing naked before the gates of heaven, he asks to be rewarded for having cared for himself.

## The First of Democrats.

There is one trait in the character of our Lord and Savior upon which it is great comfort to dwell, and that is his democracy. He was the first and last true democrat of all the ages. Others claiming to be such are only demagogues—shallow pretenders or charlatans, using their brain to perfect their acting. Or worse yet, they are men soured by failure and envious of others' success. But His nature was sweet, and while He denounced the sin He had room in His mighty heart for the repentant sinner. But looking through the rags He saw the man, and penetrating the robes He recognized the hypocrite. His brief, beautiful life was passed among the poor, the humble and the sinful. He was born in a manger and died between two thieves. He was the friend of the convict, the poor, weak creature crowded to the wall and trampled to the earth, and He was the consoler and companion of the poor laborer whose bent back, bowed head and hard hands told of a life-long struggle for life. He had but little time to be with us, and that little was given to those who had only their humanity to plead. He did not seek the learned nor the great of earth, nor the rich and well born, in the few years alotted to Him on earth. And has no one thought how significant is the fact that He, whose mission·was of such vital importance to the human race, was with us as man so brief a period? One would think that He should have been immortal, living through the centuries, to repeat the teachings from His own eloquent lips unto all humanity. But that divine presence would have conquered for us. What would have been left for the endeavor, the grand struggle that purifies the heart and elevates our being until we are worthy, and being worthy are prepared for that heaven His divine goodness has prepared for us? He led us through suffering; He taught through example and He sealed His truths with His blood. Were He with us, a God in His immortality, He would do our work; or if not, we would be filled with despair at the thought of His perfection that we are ordered to attain. It was necessary that He should be man to convince us what man could accomplish.

We can not say that Christ lived only after His crucifixion, but we say that His doctrines took life from that dreadful event, and revelation was given only when the heaven opened in terror to receive the God rejected by humanity He sought so earnestly and lovingly to aid. There was a resurrection in that death few of us pause to consider. How that which

poor humanity supposes for the moment to end their
annoyance sometimes dates its power.  The cruel
crowd that howled about our Savior in His last tor-
ments, went to their homes believing the presump-
tious Nazarene was ended.  It was not that the veil
of the temple was rent, and that the skies were darkened and the earth shook as in an agony that their
crime became manifest, but that the beautiful truths
He had uttered to the down-trodden and oppressed
took new life, and of that dim and dreadful past
come down to us clad in the mantel of immortality.
Cæsar dies in the opening of the tragedy by the master mind of men, but Cæsar's ghostly shadow holds
the stage until all go down in a common ruin.  The
horror that comes upon us when we think of God
being rejected in scorn and torture well nigh drowns
out the sorrow His sad life and death should give us.
He came among us as a man, to suffer the lot of such
and die; but how hard it is to reconcile ourselves to
the insult that made His death so horrible, now that
we know and knowing love and worship Him.

It is necessary for us to keep this in mind.  He
was one of us.  All that He did we can accomplish,
or striving to accomplish, can make ourselves worthy
of His love, help, and protection.  Let us, then, contemplate His character as it was in its humanity, and
so contemplating, weigh well His utterances.  In His

earnest simplicity, in His true, sweet, loving endeavor to take humanity to His heart, what a democrat He was! There is no man who ever died for man, no patriot with swelling heart and eager protest of eloquence, ever uttered more that was possessed of higher scorn for the oppressor than these few simple utterances :

"Then spake Jesus to the multitude, and to His disciples,

"Saying, The scribes and the Pharisees sit in Moses' seat.

"All therefore whatsoever they bid you observe, that observe and do: but do not ye after their works; for they say and do not.

"For they bind heavy burdens, and grievous to be borne, and lay them on men's shoulders; but they themselves will not move them with one of their fingers.

"But all their works they do for to be seen of men; they make broad their phylacteries, and enlarge the borders of their garments,

"And love the uppermost rooms at feasts, and the chief seats in the synagogues,

"And greetings in the markets, and to be called of men, Rabbi, Rabbi.

"But be not ye called Rabbi: for one is your Master, even Christ; and all ye are brethren.

"And call no man your father upon the earth:
for one is your Father, which is in heaven.

" Neither be ye called masters: for one is your
Master, even Christ.

" But he that is greatest among you shall be
your servant.

"And whosoever shall exalt himself shall be
abased; and he that shall humble himself shall be
exalted."

"Call no *man* your father upon earth," and call
no man your master. The grand equality before
God of all on earth here taught sweeps away two-
thirds of earth's idolatry. Where are your princes
and potentates; where the rulers who make broad
their phylacteries, and enlarge the borders of their
garments, and love the uppermost rooms at feasts,
and the chief seats? Miserable actors are they,
who would be subjects of laughter as they are of
scorn, but that they can torture and abuse in their
" insolence of office."

And we have immortalized the man who said to
us that all men are born free; but Christ gives the
words significance by adding, "and before God are
born equal." On the broad platform of common suffering, coming helpless and naked into life, and going
to one common bourne, the grave, we are all the

children of God, and any distinction that creates an inequality is a sham and a mockery.

Who that has stood in the low hovel that was once the home of Scotland's greatest poet and patriot, and looked over the fields where he toiled as a serf, does not hasten to pardon his sins that they may acknowledge his nobility? He had the sanction of our Savior in his heartfelt, earnest protest against oppression; in his lofty scorn of rank, that held itself above toiling, suffering humanity.

And how strange it is that God's great work, claimed to be in His own image, should be held the least valuable of all our worldly possessions. Houses, lands, bonds, gold, satin-lined carriages and gayly caparisoned horses, all that pampers the body and deadens the soul, are rated above that for which all these things were made. And yet the little helpless being that came to us through a mother's agony adds nothing to that affection in such surroundings, which makes its life so precious. Nor when the life, through tender nursing and loving care, gives to manhood all that moves the heart to joy or tears, and makes a being so near and dear that it can not be measured by money, it lives in itself, and has no gain from what the world rates so far above it. Genius that gave birth to great thought, patriotic impulse that lives through great deeds, come from

lowly homes and cradles as obscure as the manger
that held our Savior. And yet the world dwarfs
God's work in deep mines, mows it down by thousands in great battles, and tramples it in scorn along
the highways of life. The world crucified Christ,
and it crowds down His humble followers. And yet,
O Christian friends, in the purple and fine linen,
there is a horrible disease silently at work under your
gay apparel, and ere another Sunday's meditation
meets the light your friends will hurry your well-
clad yet loathsome body out of sight, and your naked
soul will stand shivering before the bar of God, no
better than the poor laborer you so despised in life.

> " For so the world goes,
> And so the stream flows,
> But there's an old fellow nobody knows,
> Who setteth all free,
> On land and on sea,
> And maketh the rich like the poor to flee."

And how grand the church is that through all
the ages has taught and plead and obeyed, regarding
God only as master, and opening her doors as her
heart to all alike! In that sanctuary that is God's
temple all vain differences disappear, and the poor
laborer, beside the proudest potentate, receives the
same recognition, the same relief, the same salvation.

## Love for Our Fellow-men.

" Give to every man that asketh of thee; and of him that taketh away thy goods, ask them not again.

"And as ye would that men should do to you, do ye also to them likewise.

" For if ye love them which love you, what thank have ye? for sinners also love those that love them.

"And if ye do good to them which do good to you, what thank have ye? for sinners also do even the same.

"And if ye lend to them of whom ye hope to receive, what thank have ye? for sinners also lend to sinners, to receive as much again.

" But love ye your enemies, and do good, and lend, hoping for nothing again; and your reward shall be great, and ye shall be the children of the Highest; for He is kind unto the unthankful and to the evil.

" Be ye therefore merciful, as your Father also is merciful.

" Judge not, and ye shall not be judged; condemn not, and ye shall not be condemned; forgive, and ye shall be forgiven.

" Give, and it shall be given unto you; good

measure, pressed down and shaken together, and running over, shall men give into your bosom. For with the same measure that ye mete withal, it shall be measured to you again.

"And He spake a parable unto them, Can the blind lead the blind? shall they not both fall into the ditch?"

The selfishness of accepted religion is a strange fact, when contrasted with the sacrifice of self, taught by our divine master. Without the pronoun "I" religion were not possible to the great mass of civilized humanity. With such to save one's soul makes up the sum of all effort. Such Christian egotists do not reflect, that to have salvation acceptable we must live in the hereafter with our identity the same as on earth. There is as little comfort as philosophy in the popular translation to passionless bodies, cold, white robes, and everlasting harpings before the throne of God. Who contemplates death with courage from whose heavy heart has been taken the hope of looking again on the dear face of one's mother or father, with all the homely lines of the careworn but loving face? Or, who hopes for a heaven where one could not clasp the lost little one or the loving wife? Where is the mother who would not die to save her child, or be damned to insure its eternal felicity?

This is religion—the religion that made our Christ suffer torture and indignity that we might live.

What were heaven to the selfish, or the mean and avaricious?

"Oh! my wife!" cried an enthusiast, "a million of years will pass in looking upon my loved Savior's face before I shall want to see yours, so much greater is my love of my Redeemer than my love of earthly things."

And we have heard the above repeated, by ministers of the gospel, in illustration of what should be our devotion to God. Blind leaders of the blind. The earthly love thus discarded as a feverish, unhealthy desire for the not only unattainable but the undesirable, is the very foundation of heaven itself. We turn insanely from all that Christ taught, lived, suffered and died for.

There are earthly ties that stretch from life into eternity, and hold us to a hope of a heaven that would not be a heaven without them. Who would leave even this green, sunny earth for the cold, golden streets that Christ, speaking in parable to a money-getting people, sought to picture as attractive that which eye had not seen, nor ear heard, nor the mind of man conceived. We long for that which God has made so precious and Christ has promised us.

Said a home missionary in the city of **New York,**
" I ministered to a poor widow woman who was dying
in a tenement house, of a disease that had long been
regarded as incurable. She had become known to
the police through her devotion to her evil children.
Scarcely a term of court passed that one or the other
was not arraigned for some grave offense. She was a
hard-working, honest woman, and her clinging so
faithfully to the miserable family won for her the
respect, if not the admiration of the police. Therefore, when she begged to see her children before she
died, I had one son brought from the penitentiary—a
hardened villain; he was sentenced to ten years for
burglary. The other son we brought in from the gutter, and the daughter from a worse locality. That dying scene was so pitiful that it made the heart ache.
There was the poverty-stricken appearance of the
apartment, that is always the more obtrusive when
an effort is made at cleanliness and order. The poor
woman looked from her pale, thin face and hollow
eyes upon these children who had given her so much
pain, but love survived all. She stretched out her
skeleton arms and moaned piteously, like a dying animal. I have known a cow to moan that way after
her young. She placed her thin hands upon their
heads—on the close-shaven head of the convict—as
if she were blessing them. I prayed long and earn-

estly for them all, and then I strove to administer to her the consolations of religion. I told her that her weary strife would soon be at an end, and her dear Savior would say, 'Well done thou good and faithful servant; enter into the Kingdom prepared for you.' Her dying eyes were on her children; every gasp of breath was a pain and a moan. At last she gasped, 'Don't ask my salvation—I don't want it—I don't want to be parted from my children—let me go with them. God never heard my prayer before to save them—let him hear this.'

"And so she died. I shall never forget that night if I live a thousand years. It was bitter cold and storming, and the frost seemed to hurry to claim its own, the corpse, in through the crevices, and holes, and rattling windows; but it was not so cold as the stony hearts of those sons and daughter. The convict asked with an oath if we were done with him; the inebriate begged for money to procure whisky, while the daughter's lamentations were worse than their indifference; but the mother's love lived through their degradation, and went with her to where that love and devotion made the wings of an angel."

It is a lamentable error we have taught ourselves that Christ's words, and, above all, Christ's unselfish example, are addressed to the individual, and that we can separate from the human family, and each one steal selfishly into heaven. For such there is no heaven—for heaven means happiness, and there is no happiness here or hereafter for the mean and sordid. So long as the memory of Mount Calvary and its cross remains to the human race, with their sublime example of Christ dying for humanity, the beauty, purity, and virtue of self-sacrifice will beam in eternal light of God before us.

We may well differ as to the sanity of Old Ossawattomie Brown, and shudder at the thought of the servile insurrection he planned, and yet no one can contemplate that old man, who wrote the emancipation proclamation upon the mountains of Virginia long before Abraham Lincoln dreamed of it, as he stood, a hero, manacled and hurt, amid his fierce enemies, and not feel a thrill of admiration as he said so simply, and yet with such moving eloquence, " Had I done this thing for my own race, you would have praised it as right, but being done for the negro, it is a crime." At least he was brave, sincere, and self-sacrificing. Are there other qualities necessary to lift a motive, however mistaken the intent, into admiration? These few simple words, after all, struck the manacles from the limbs of four millions of slaves, and all that followed is vulgar ambition, of the earth, earthy, in comparison.

To love God, we must love our fellow-men. To

follow Christ into that heaven His death prepared for us, we must be ready and willing to die for others. Good will to man on earth precedes and makes possible the glory to God in the highest, and may the example of our Savior soften our hearts towards each other as His great heart forgives us our transgressions.

## Unjust Stewards.

"And He said also unto His disciples, There was a certain rich man which had a steward; and the same was accused unto him that he had wasted his goods.

"And he called him, and said unto him, How is it that I hear this of thee? Give an account of thy stewardship; for thou mayest be no longer steward.

"Then the steward said within himself, What shall I do? for my Lord taketh away from me the stewardship; I can not dig; to beg I am ashamed.

"I am resolved what to do, that, when I am put out of the stewardship, they may receive me into their houses.

"So he called every one of his Lord's debtors unto him, and said unto the first, How much owest thou unto my Lord?

"And he said, A hundred measures of oil. And he said unto him, Take thy bill, and sit down quickly, and write fifty.

"Then said he to another, And how much owest thou? And he said a hundred measures of wheat. And he said unto him, Take thy bill, and write four score.

" And the Lord commended the unjust steward, because he had done wisely; for the children of this world are in their generation wiser than the children of light.

" And I say unto you, Make to yourselves friends of the mammon of righteousness; that, when ye fail they may receive you into everlasting habitations.

" He that is faithful in that which is least, is faithful also in much, and he that is unjust in the least, is unjust also in much.

" If therefore ye have not been faithful in the unrighteous mammon, who will commit to your trust the true riches?

" And if ye have not been faithful in that which is another man's, who shall give you that which is your own?

" No servant can serve two masters; for either he will hate the one and love the other, or else he will hold to the one and despise the other. Ye can not serve God and mammon."

The teachings of our Savior are mainly devoted to the duty one owes himself and the duty we owe to others. The principal object of His mission seemed to be the purification and harmonizing of our life hereafter, of which he says but little. And while that little is vague in outline and wanting altogether in detail, the rules of conduct on earth are clear, positive, and incisive.

Since His appearance on earth, instead of attempting to accommodate our lives to His teachings, we have striven with much ingenuity to make His teachings in accord with our worldly life.

To accomplish this the more easily, we slur over, as of secondary importance, the Christian law of life on earth, to build a religion on life hereafter. As we can not be as perfect as our blessed Savior, we will reserve our efforts until such time hereafter when, divested of the passions, sickness, and weakness of the flesh, we can strive better in the spirit. In this way, as we have tried to show, religion has come to be something apart and different from our real life here, and pertains to the hereafter. Therefore we can readily render unto Cæsar things which are Cæsar's, occupying all of six days of the week, and unto God the things which are God's on the seventh.

Therefore is it that we can be hard on Christ's friends and associates, the poor—crowd them down with insult to starvation, abuse them for daring to complain, and then go to church on Sunday and listen to Hebrew sins nearly nineteen hundred years of age, preached from a marble pulpit, while we dream, in a velvet cushioned pew, of a heaven where the rich and well-born, the educated and refined, meet in ever-

lasting praise before the throne of God. " Give us
this day our daily bread," beats unmeaningly on the
ears of those who have robbed thousands of their
food. Through the thick solid walls of the temple
no whisper of the world's misery reaches in to disturb the harmony of a religion Christ came to destroy, or to waken the self-satisfied from dreams of
a heaven that is impossible. We reason to ourselves
the imitations of Christ until that solemn time when
corruption shall put on incorruption, and the ethere-
alized being in robes of light shall be lifted above the
temptations of the flesh. In the meantime we are
clad in corruption and to corruption we give the best
of our time. We have accomplished what Christ did
not even attempt, but told us was impossible. We
have harmonized Cæsar and God. We serve with
philosophical indifference the two masters.

How little in all the centuries has humanity
changed! We are suffering to-day from the unjust
stewards. With a land teeming in plenty, we have
from every part cries of want. For years past it has
been a demand for work. Now it deepens into an
agonizing cry for bread. " Give us this day our daily
bread," cry the half starved from the naked hillsides.
" Give us this day our daily bread," repeat the unjust, full-stomached stewards in their cushioned pews
and fine linen, while the deep-toned organ and mel-

low voices send up praise to God in the highest, without good will to men on earth.

It is rendering unto Cæsar things which are Cæsar's for the unjust steward who has stolen from the poor to defend his stealings by force. We rob and then we murder, if the victim complains. This is law and order. Christ has said to the faithful, if a demand is made for the cloak one must give the coat also. But Cæsar says that if the laborer, who is worthy of his wages, makes complaint that he gets no wages, and is noisy and disagreeable, give him the bayonet instead of the bread, for society, that rises above Christ, and is based on law and order, must be preserved.

To-day the land is filled to overflowing with abundance. Granaries are full of the golden corn, the nutritious wheat; the fatted cattle cover the plains and hills, and yet millions are starving, out of employ, while the millions at work are weak from lack of sufficient food. And why is this? Because the unjust stewards come between the labor and its just reward. The unjust stewards, worse than locusts, have consumed all of the substance of the land in their riotous living.

There is but one thing left that is sacred in the eyes of Cæsar, and that is debt. And our country is the debtor, and it is the law that it shall be held by the throat until the last cent is secured. Pay what thou owest and pay it quickly, interest and capital, in gold. What matters it that labor starves, the Shylocks must have the coin or the flesh, and possibly both.

This is hard when the debt is justly owing, but it is something beyond the endurance of flesh and blood when the unjust stewards have forced on us unjust debts. We may submit in silence to the presence of men who, in just dealings, have accumulated riches through economy and shrewdness, however hard and tyrannical they may be; but armed resistance to the wicked oppressor is the law of God. We submit to the processes of law in the punishment of crime, that the innocent may not be made to suffer; but law or no law, crime is to be punished. It is well that society be protected and preserved, but the man and the family antedates the social organization, and when the law fails to accomplish evenly what the law was created to do, society is resolved into its original element, where each man is a law unto himself.

It was never ordained, and can not be endured, that one man should hold another in slavery, white or black, and when through any combination of circumstances this happens, the social structure has lost its significance, and is no longer, in the eyes of God or man, worth the preservation.

"Resistance to tyranny is a service to God," said the patriot of old, who marched proudly to the scaffold to die for men. Seen through the softening haze of a hundred years, the grand truth rises in grandeur as distant mountains, in assuming the hue of heaven, become a part of heaven. It is in the vexed present that we are confused. The poor laborer, ridden over and crushed by the Juggernaut of a heartless corporation, lacks something of the heroic in his hollow cheeks and ragged clothes. He, too shot down in the streets, serves his God and dies for his fellow-men. Will time soften into beauty the sad event, or only cover it in the darkness of oblivion? Christ, who died at the hands of a mob, had no bayonets at His back to enforce law and order. Would He have used them had they been available? Fool, Christ was crucified in the name of law and order. He was the rioter, with His twelve tent-makers and fishermen, and that great commercial center, Jerusalem, solemnly adjudged Him death lest He endanger the social and political structure of their day.

Violence is of no avail save in self-defense. It is the law of the sword that he who lives by it shall die by it. It carries death in its scabbard and death in its hilt. The government that can not sustain itself save on the bayonet ceases to be for the common good. It is only the instrument of the unjust steward.

Every man is an unjust steward who wrongs in any way his fellow-men. In this God made stewards of us all, and He is the master to whom we must render our accounts. And who among us, when we look into ourself before asking the help of God, can say, "this day I have wronged no man?" And what a mockery is the prayer if one has been the unjust steward, and seeks to deceive God as he deceives himself and his fellow-men. It is not that we have been charitable, patient, kind, and forgiving, but have we been just? and not being just, what is there left upon which to base divine mercy?

Ah! fools, what are the few years of troubled wealth, with their anxieties and hearts filled with anguish of hidden wrong, to the peaceful content Christ's teachings and example give to the lost opportunity that made earth a foretaste of heaven, and heaven a continuation of all that was good and happy on earth?

## "Son, Give Me Thy Heart."

One can not dwell long upon the memory of our Savior's life on earth without finding that it is our feeling, more than our judgment, through which we are contemplating His acts and character. And after all, this is our better guide through life. We owe so little to reason and so much to affection. On this last is based the household. On this we build up the home; and to test its importance, let any one ask himself how much there is outside worth contending for. The walls of one's home are the boundary of one's happiness. All else is cold and comfortless, vain hopes and cruel disappointments. The dove returned to the ark, but the raven did not return. All that is gentle and of Christ in us finds its better development in the household.

This is not only the teaching of Christ, but the law of our being. We share it in common with the beasts. Among the animals the fiercest become gentle, the stupid intelligent, the most timid grow brave in the care and defense of the young. Who has not seen the poor little bird pretending to be hurt and helpless, that it may turn one from its nest, by an appeal to all that is cruel in our nature? God help us, that is the way in which we are adjudged by all animated nature with which we are brought in contact. And we must not deceive ourselves with the belief that this instinct is dull and indiscriminate. There is a subtle intelligence therein that is unerring. Beware of the man shunned by children and dogs; also the human being who can not laugh and has no sense of music. Such are human only in form ; the beast of prey lurks within. We know a cemetery beautifully adorned with woods and ponds. The superintendent, a man of rare qualities, enforces with care the law that prohibits killing within its limits, and its woods and ponds are frequented by wild animals that cease to be wild, by strange birds, shy water-fowls that elsewhere find refuge from their great enemy, man, in barren wastes and wide, unfrequented marshes of distant seas; yet here they regard the throng of humanity with tame indifference. What subtle intelligence, as mysterious as the telegraph, has spread over the continent, telling these innocent, inoffensive creatures that there is one spot devoted to the dead, where the spirit of Christ lives, where His law of kindness prevails? The sparrow may fall to the ground, but the pair is not sold in the market for a price.

Christ, looking through the cruel evil of our nature, saw the divine possibility beneath, and sought in the feelings to develop all that is divine and beautiful of our being. As life is so brief, this labor would be without motive almost, but for the fact that it fits us for the heaven hereafter. It is the error of the day, as it has been the error of all time, that the development of the intellect alone elevates our nature and brings us closer to the divinity; and yet the end of our knowledge is that we know nothing. We climb with pain and labor to the outer edge of our existence, and gaze over into the blank, deadly, unanswering space of eternity. Christ came as a parent to his children, to teach us kindness, charity, forgiveness one unto the other, and not as a philosopher, giving us facts and the reason for them; for while there is divinity in our hearts there is nothing godlike in our intellect. He could not have made us comprehend the blade of grass plucked from the field; and could He have done so, we would have been no nearer heaven than we are in our ignorance.

It is in this error that we wrong ourselves and our children. We no longer train the young in the ways of moral conduct. We teach them science, instruct them in art and are amazed to find that they are not virtuous. The most civilized in this process is the most wicked. One of our profoundest thinkers has said that he could not comprehend why a knowledge of arithmetic should be followed by a love of

truth, justice, and honest dealing. It was a shrewd
parent that asked of a leading university what the
extra charge would be, aside from the academic course
of boating and boxing, to have his son taught to write
and speak grammatically. It would be a wiser parent
who would offer to pay large sums of money to have
his child instructed in the ways of Christ, which mean
the self-sacrifice found in self-restraint and a development of our kindlier nature. The day is not distant when our much-vaunted common-school system,
wherein labor is whimsically taxed—for labor pays
all—to secure free schooling to the rich—will be regarded as an evil. The fathers based our government
wisely upon the virtue and intelligence of the citizen.
We believe in the intelligence only. We educate to
keep our children out of the penitentiary, through
their superior shrewdness, and we can not see that our
civil-service is bad, because all service is rotten. We
laugh at the fabled story of the boy Washington saying to his father that he could not tell a lie, because
the precocious wisdom that dictated such a heroic
speech would have impelled the embryo patriot to
have uttered a volume of lies.

"All healthy children," said a cynic—which means
one who not only sees evil as it is, but is fond of seeing
it—"are born cowards, liars, and thieves." Of course,
for they are born weak and helpless. With developed

strength comes the courage that resents a wrong, and
then again the higher courage that can forgive it.
And because of this weak, helpless condition, that
developes, if left to itself, all that is selfish in our nature, we are said to be conceived in sin and brought
forth in iniquity, and the doctrine of total depravity
is taught. It is said of little children that Christ
opened His arms to and bade them come to Him.
The germ of all goodness is there, much nearer purity
than at any time subsequent in life, for weak helpless-
ness has its sweet, confiding nature where it finds protection, and that, too, through the feelings rather than
the intellect. Each parent realizes this, although so
few are found capable of profiting by it.

The religion of the intellect is sunlight on **ice.**
It blinds one, while it chills the heart.

We knew an able and learned man who took delight in listening to the Rev. M. D. Conway. This
reverend gentleman is a brilliant man. He takes
Christ from the cross every Sunday to dissect the
body and demonstrate the absurdity of superstition.
His sermons are intellectual gymnastics, and yet as
near true Christianity and the wants of our spiritual
nature as sky-rockets get near the stars. We admire
such sky-rockets, not because they go so high, but for
that we are so low. Conway's learned parishioner had
a child sicken and die. He saw his poor little boy nestle

in the arms of death, and his heart ached with unutterable agony.  Groping blindly for relief, he sent for an earnest, humble clergyman, a good man, only to pray with him over the body of his child.  He learned through this sad experience that one drew nearer to God through the heart than through the intellect. Death taught him to fear God, love Christ and be content in knowing nothing.  What was it to him that he could weigh the sun, measure vast space, count accurately the age of the world, and know that lightning carried our messages and steam did our work? He would have given all he knew and all he possessed to have one little throb from the heart stilled in death, or for one breath to the dear lips that never, never again would utter that music of love that is the life of the parent.

Christ's precepts were few and precious, but His examples were many and His love boundless.  One can not open upon any page of His record without finding the appeal to our better feelings, to our nobler nature.  We have read the story of the poor woman who was miraculously restored to health by touching with faith the garments of our Divine Master. With what simplicity the story is told:

"And a certain woman, which had an issue of blood twelve years,

"And had suffered many things of many physicians, and had spent all that she had, and was nothing bettered, but rather grew worse,

" When she had heard of Jesus, came in the press behind and touched His garment,

" For she said if I may touch but His clothes I shall be whole.

" And straightway the fountain of her blood was dried up, and she felt in her body that she was healed of that plague.

" And Jesus, immediately knowing in Himself that virtue had gone out of him, turned Him about in the press and said, Who touched My clothes?

" And His disciples said unto Him, Thou seest the multitude thronging Thee, and sayest Thou, Who touched me?

" And He looked round about to see her that had done this thing.

" But the woman, fearing and trembling, knowing what was done in her, came and fell down before Him, and told Him all the truth.

" And He said unto her, Daughter, thy faith has made the whole; go in peace, and be whole of thy plague."

In every instance of a miracle wrought there is not only the story told illustrating the power of God, but there is a subtle and almost hidden meaning to be drawn from it by the thoughtful believer. In the

above we are called to note Him surrounded by the
multitude. Many touched Him in the crowd, but it
was only the poor, suffering woman who stole up to
Him in a pitiful way and touched His garment with
that faith that makes and marks the Christian, and
she alone of the multitude, who had a reward. How
many of earth's children crowd about our Savior,
and how few touch His garment with that faith which
gives us health. And the bloody issue that now fills
our land with starvation and violence, finds so few
willing to seek the remedy that comes through a belief in Him or His teachings of even-handed justice,
kindness, charity, mercy and forgiveness. With our
hands at each other's throats, we seem to have forgotten our duty to each other and our hope of heaven
hereafter.

14

## The Wonders of Nature.

We have been communing with nature—nature that leads us up to nature's God. We have been for days and nights a denizen of the wide, sunny fields, the willow-fringed brooks, the deep, solemn woods. We have looked upon those stars of earth, the wild flowers that grow in beauty and sweet perfume and boundless profusion, with no other hand to plant, guard and train but God's. We have listened to the song of wild birds, that in their melody defy human imitation And we have said: "These are for us." And yet, in all the years of absence, since early youth, the trees have whispered, the brook has babbled, the flowers have bloomed, and the birds sang. When we shall have passed away, to be forgotten by men, these delicate, beautiful things will live on as if we had never existed.

This is an old, old thought, and yet, in our selfish egotism, never to be realized. For us the sun rises in its dewy freshness of morn and sets in its golden garniture of clouds. To us the moon and stars make the night beautiful in its calm sublimity. The flowers bloom and the birds sing for us, wonderful, precious creatures that we are.

And who returns, as we returned, to the scenes of childhood, to find how life has continued without change in our absence, but is forced to repeat with the poet—

> " I will not say my eyes are dim,
> I will not sing the change
> That 's wrought upon my soul within ;
> Its sadness, still and strange,
> Nor here, by flower and tree and stream,
> Repeat the well-worn lay,
> How we the fleeting shadows seem,
> Immortal substance they."

Who goes from the desolated home, where death has left a black midnight of despair brooding by the hearthstone, bereft of all that makes life endurable, to find the sun shining upon that outer world of life, and not feel, after all our self-laudation, that we are but part, a sad, insignificant part, of this creation, that goes on and on, through all the ages, without us, and utterly indifferent to our existence?

Who under the dark shadow but remembers the sad plaint of the Scottish poet, when, from death in the hovel of all that was fair and dear to him, he sang :

> " Ye banks and braes o' bonnie Doon,
> How can ye bloom so fresh and fair;
> How can ye chant, ye little birds,
> And I sae weary, fu' o' care ?"

Little reck they, in their joyous existence, of the broken heart that makes its despairing plaint in their sunny presence.

It is in time only that the balm sweet nature holds works its cure and aids to heal our wounds. How pleasant it is to have one's life wedded, as it were, to these sweet, innocent things; to have one's memory mingled with all that is beautiful of earth; to go back in recollection to the long, wintry nights, when the mysterious winds moaned about one's dwelling, or when the silent snow whitened up the window-sill like the dead face of a forgotten friend; or when one, in the deep, somber woods of June, saw the sunlight sifted through the wind-shifted leaves, when the whisperings seem those of forms long since moldered to dust in neglected graves.

And how sweet it is to return, after years of absence, and find the stately trees one planted offering a friendly shade to welcome the tired denizen of a peopled earth, to greet and be greeted by the humble animals we may have forgotten, but have not forgotten us. Those shrubs and trees we planted and trained, these animals we cared for, have no ingratitude. They do not repay our love with the unkindness of our fellow-men; and the very ills of the rough life seem small by the side of those that have, making our hearts ache, turned us to bitterness and wrath.

> " Freeze, freeze, thou bitter sky;
> Thou dost not bite so nigh
>   As benefits forgot;
> Though thou the waters warp
> Thy sting is not so sharp
>   As friends remembering not."

Alas! this is not the only lesson taught us by the country. We enter upon the scene, and how sweetly harmonious and peaceful it all appears. From the deep green meadows, the fields of waving grain and rustling corn, through the purple noon's transparent light to the distant, softly rounded, wooded hills, that seem to melt into heaven's blue, all seem one grand harmonious whole. But we look closer. In this quiet stream is the murderous pike, living upon the more helpless fish. Above sits the keen-eyed, lightning-like king fisher. And yet above the wild hawk, like a censor, swung circles in heaven's blue, with cruel beak, watching for its prey. And in the still watches of the moonless nights the owl, on the downy wings of death, unseen, all seeing, floats noiselessly by, the assassin of the gloomy woods. The wild beasts have fled before the approach of man, but sin, cruelty and sorrow remain, feeding on all things fair.

Ah! God, what are these mighty ills, pain and sin and death, that hold their own in the presence of their Creator, marring all his works? Christ, building his church, said the gates of hell should not prevail against it. What are these gates of hell that they should contend with their Creator?

Give us the science that will solve this dread question. Find us the student, the learned man, who can lift from our souls this terrible doubt, and we will carry our gods to the temple of human learning and abandon all other hope of salvation.

All about us is mystery. The blade of grass, the little insect with its golden coat and gauzy wings, whose delicate mechanism fills us with admiration, that seems to be tossed out upon boundless creation without care; the delicate flower; the tiny weeds about our feet—all cease to be wonders only in being common. But the mysteries of all mystery are pain and death. These hideous phantoms loom up, black and dense, between our terror stricken sight and God. From them we turn to our loved Savior, who, passing through both, returns to say: I am the resurrection and the life. In charity I came to you; in love I return. Poor, helpless children of men, wandering and groping in blind despair, listen to the Son of David, for He speaks from beyond the grave, where death is not; where pain is not.

## Avarice and Hypocrisy.

" Woe unto you, scribes and Pharisees, hypocrites! for ye pay tithe of mint and anise and cum-
min, and have omitted the weightier matters of the
law, judgment, mercy and faith : these ought ye to
have done, and not to leave the other undone.

" Ye blind guides, which strain at a gnat and
swallow a camel.

" Woe unto you, scribes and Pharisees, hypocrites! for ye make clean the outside of the cup and
of the platter, but within they are full of extortion
and excess.

" Thou blind Pharisee, cleanse first that which is
within the cup and platter, that the outside of them
may be clean also.

" Woe unto you, scribes and Pharisees, hypocrites! for ye are like unto whited sepulchers, which
indeed appear beautiful outward, but are within full
of dead men's bones, and of all uncleanness.

" Even so ye also outwardly appear righteous
unto men, but within ye are full of hypocrisy and
iniquity.

" Woe unto you, scribes and Pharisees, hypocrites! because ye build the tombs of the prophets, and garnish the sepulchers of the righteous."

To one who studies with loving care the life and teachings of our Savior, there is surprise at first that, while the more atrocious crimes are merely referred to, the heaviest denunciations are bestowed upon money-getting and hypocrisy. A better knowledge of human nature teaches us, however, that our Lord knows us better than we know ourselves. The atrocious crimes of murder, cruelty, arson, robbery, and all that are born of violence, are unnatural and exceptional. They are more in the way of disease, and humanity, from a sense of self-preservation, guards against them without divine admonition. From all ages, in all climes and conditions, we find the criminal code reading nearly the same. How much soever we may differ on other subjects, this receives the same treatment. The man of violence is treated the same as the wild beast possessed of appetites dangerous to life and destructive of peaceful security.

And how much of this is disease no one can tell. Scientists of late years profess an ability to distinguish the skull of a murderer from that of ordinary heads. A learned superintendent of an asylum for the insane called our attention to the fact that disease or malformation lies probably at the base of much that we call crime. He had a lad of twelve years of age brought to him for treatment. The boy, up to a certain late period, was affectionate and obedient. From this he changed to a condition of great irritability, that increased until he became dangerous, having attempted the life of his mother. It became necessary to confine him in an asylum. The doctor made a study of his little patient. He found on shaving his head a place where the heat indicated inflammation, and on further investigation discovered a fracture, with the bone pressing upon the brain. A surgical operation lifted this indentation, and the poor lad returned to his normal, quiet, affectionate disposition and conduct.

How terrible the thought that in our cruel pursuit and punishment of criminals we are hunting down sick and insane people.

To say a word in their behalf is to incur the charge of mawkish sentimentalism. How the money-getting hypocrites of to-day would sneer at our Savior, who promised the heaven to the thief writhing in agony upon the cross that He denied to those respectable matter-of-fact people who pride themselves upon being free of sentiment! Ah, friends of Mammon, there is little in this world worth struggling for that can not be stigmatized in this way. What is the love of parent and child, all that makes the

15

household dear and holy; what is patriotism itself, that lofty virtue praised through all ages by orators and sung of by poets, but sentiment? Who has seen a people rise in their wrath to lay waste and kill for the honor of our flag, and not wondered? for the flag is a painted rag and their emotion nothing but sentiment.

When we have passed from this brief existence of morality to the life hereafter, we shall find Heaven's foundations based on the feeling we have been taught to despise, and Howard, who went through loathsome prisons striving to mitigate the sufferings of criminals, sitting on the right hand of the God who on earth made the poor and wicked His friends and associates.

Christ warned us against that which is a part of our normal condition—our poor human nature—that, if left unrestrained, will inevitably degrade us to a condition where the more horrible offenses are possible. From the selfishness of money-getting comes the desire to do wrong; from the necessity of a process through which wrong may be done with impunity, comes hypocrisy.

Slavery was said to be the sum total of all villainy, and the slavery of sin is its worst form; and this horrible condition can be traced back in nearly all cases to selfishness, that has its most common phase in money-getting, and to hypocrisy, in which a man, striving to deceive his fellow man and his God, ends in deceiving himself. The great curse, the curse of all curses that afflict humanity to-day, is intemperance in the use of intoxicating drinks. War, pestilence and famine are as nothing to this foul, insinuating disease, that degrades the body and destroys the soul. The tears it has wrung from broken hearts would make a sea; the crime it has created would fill hell; the disease it is the author of would make the earth a loathsome pest-house of foul disorders. And yet Christ did not denounce intemperance, because he struck at its root in the selfishness of the money-getter who traffics for gain on the miseries of humanity, and the selfishness of the man who walks over broken hearts to the gratification of a vile passion.

Small wonder that women grow frantic and good men wild in the face of this terrible curse; for the drunkard's grave is found in the utter ruin of the household. Could it be arrested, peace would fall like sun-light on our homes; our prisons would be almost depopulated and poor-houses needless.

God give us wisdom to treat and strength to conquer this horrible curse, that misery may be lifted from the wife, wretchedness from the children and agony from gray hairs!

Hypocrisy, which means we are told, stealing the livery of God to serve the devil in, assumes the worst form when the wearer deceives himself.

It is a law of our nature that we can not assume the unnatural long without making it a part of our nature. The man who says, and repeats for the purpose of impressing others "I hate," ends in hating. The fish of the Mammoth Cave are without eyes, and the hypocrite passes inevitably to moral blindness. The hypocrite, as we have said, begins in an attempt to deceive his fellow-men and his maker, and terminates in making a monster of himself. Who has seen the rich hypocrite, in his velvet-cushioned pew, listening devoutly to that other hypocrite preach from his marble pulpit of sins two thousand years old, and not felt a sense of shame at a mockery that makes the devil laugh and angels weep? The two have eyes that see no duty, ears that are deaf to the cries of distress, that go up in wails of despair about them, while their feelings anticipate death in their foul decay.

And what is the meaning of that terrible warning of Christ to beware of that which kills the soul? Can the soul die? Is there a suicide of crime? Is it possible that through our self-degradation we may wound and at last destroy that which we thought immortal? Let us hope not. Christ, who denounced

the sin, pitied, and promised forgiveness to the sinner.
And yet He has uttered that terrible warning that
comes ringing through the ages like the voice of fate,
to beware of that which kills the soul, and it carries
in it the horrible fear of annihilation. And His words
were not vain. They are our law.

## Man's Intellect.

We, who rank ourselves next Deity in the creation, are troubled to find how little store our Savior places by that upon which we base our claim to consideration—our intellect. We are reasoning creatures, and differ in this from all animated creation. We think, will and remember, and, possessed of these God-like faculties, we arrogate to ourselves an immortality denied the animals. For us was this earth made, and order called from out chaos, and light created and warmth made, that we may have food. For us a heaven exists, where God lives, and but for this one purpose there would be no heaven and no God. We think, will and remember; therefore are we immortal. We have each our individuality; therefore are we immortal. And we cultivate our reason, we seek to penetrate the mysteries of nature; therefore are we like unto God—immortal.

Poor fool, our reason stumbles upon the threshold. It gropes blindly, seeing nothing. It reaches out and touches nothing. And the learned man says, "Listen. I see naught, I feel naught, I touch naught; your belief is foolishness, your faith a superstition." Even so. We know that we are immortal because

Christ was mortal. He died, and the marble-jawed death that through all the ages had been dark, cruel, and silent as the grave, at his bidding revealed its precious secret. Every minute a mortal dies, and every minute, through ages on ages, a cry of agony went up, for that the grave had closed like fate over the life of one lost forever. But the angel of the Lord rolled away the stone, and from the dark, mysterious depths, Christ crucified, Christ who had died, walked forth and gave us what reason failed to teach or learning find.

And Christ, appealing to our affections and not our intellect, selected ignorant, simple-minded men to be His disciples, and confided His mission to His mother before He gave it to the world. There were in that day, as in this—

> "Kings of thought,
> Who wage contention in their time's decay,
> And of the past are all that will not pass away."

He might have appealed to such. He might have gathered learned priests, sages, and philosophers about Him, and making them the depositories of His treasures, left His divine mission in their hands. But He had nothing to leave such as these. In all His life on earth there is not one scientific fact given us. For thousands and thousands of years, the children of men saw the sun rise and set, and they said it was made for us, and moves for our comfort. The stars were studied, that they might foretell the future of men. Comets in their minds were messengers sent to tell us of wars, pestilence, and famine. Did Christ see and hear these errors, and could not He who taught us such precious truths about ourselves have also taught us the truth of these things, and so clear the brain of falsehoods? Doubtless. Yet He did not. For, after all, of what avail is such learning?

When a man dies the world ends. For the brief, troubled years of his life, what gain is there in measuring bits of space, weighing the heavenly bodies, or counting back, by milestones given us in geology, the dim age of our earth? It is of these things one concerns himself when the dread hour of parting approaches? The greatest and most learned of men has closed his eyes in that sleep which knows no wakening, with no thought of the scientific truths his mind may rise to in that other and higher sphere hereafter. Alas! no, his heart, if he have any, longs for the presence of the dear wife, or child, or parent, who faded from his poor arms long, long before! Many a monarch would give his crown and his earthly possessions for one little breath to animate into life again the dead child before him. In the presence of these things the material creation resolves itself into atoms, and is to us a barren, lifeless waste.

It is pathetic, and at times pitiful, to note the childlike faith and simplicity with which these humble tent-makers and fishermen follow their Lord and Master. He came when the work and teachings of the prophets had come to be traditionary. God seemed to have withdrawn Himself from the self-styled, chosen people, and the miracles worked in their behalf had grown dim in the distance of a past the priests alone kept in memory and taught their followers. Nothing tends to make a religious faith bigoted so much as doubt. The fear in the mind of the believer that his belief is not a truth excites the combative; for one does not question a palpable fact, such as sunlight or night; and to deny a faith founded on that which lies outside and beyond our experience, is not only to insult the believer, but to disturb in his own mind that which it is his desire to believe. Christ came in fulfillment of the prophecies, but in deadly antagonism to the teachings of the prophets. The God of Israel was a God of vengeance; Christ taught a God of love, pity and forgiveness. The church rose in arms against this. The Messiah it looked for was to come in the glory of mailed hosts, to kill or enslave the enemies of Israel. The Son of David, the carpenter born in a stable, was first an object of contempt, and then, when His power was shown and His teachings took hold upon the heart of the people, He was regarded with hate and terror.

He did not come down from the mount, about whose summit the clouds gathered and the deafening thunder rolled, with the law, to lead the tribes in bloody wars to great victories; He consoled the afflicted, healed the sick and raised the dead. And yet He exacted as high courage from His followers as the mailed prophets of old. He demanded the courage of endurance, that harmonized with the love He taught, and He gave them an example of both qualities. Hence it was that He recognized the public baptism of John the Baptist, and organized a church wherein His followers could be seen. He had scorn and contempt for the mere forms of the Hebrew church. He questioned their meaning and violated their commands; but He would accept no one who feared to assume His dress, that meant persecution and death. He bids Peter put up his sword, but at the last supper he regards Him in pity, akin to contempt, as one who will deny Him when the hour of trial comes.

This is the meaning of baptism. It was the public initiation of members who could brave the sneers of the world and die in meek submission un-

der the stoning of a mob or in the arena of wild
beasts. This is all changed now. We do not realize
to-day that it requires the same courage to deny the
divinity of Christ that distinguished the early Christian when he avowed his belief. The true Christian
now must pass from that to what baptism implies,
which opens to love, charity, forgiveness of our enemies, and the self-denial that consults the good of
others. Without these the mere form comes to be
the dry husk that Christ trampled in scorn beneath
His feet. Baptism means a continual submersion in
the healing waters of God's love. Are we honest in
our dealings, are we kind and patient in our ways,
do we control our selfish passions and confess our
sins with heartfelt resolve to sin no more? Then
are we baptized in the water that was made holy by
the blood of our Savior. If we are, He will smile
upon and forgive us. He will not give us riches, nor
honors, nor health, nor the love of children, nor the
praise of men ; but He will give us that which is
dearer than all—peace of mind, power to endure,
purity of soul, that, beginning heaven on earth,
passes that heaven into the promised hereafter.

# SELECTED PROSE SKETCHES.

## A Tribute to an Humble Friend.

I have but now returned in melancholy mood, from a funeral. Now, do'nt laugh. It was the burial of a dog, and the dog was solemnly interred in the family vault, with more real mourners than the average lot of deceased humanity is honored with.

Poor little Frank departed this life without any resignation whatever, for he objected to the latest moment to his taking off. He was old, with all the infirmities of age, half blind, nearly deaf, and quite toothless; yet to the last he looked up to me with a pathetic protest in his dim eyes. Frank would not "say die" even when all was dead but his brain, for he went off from paralysis.

This member of our family was given us fourteen years ago by Frank Gassaway, at Washington. I exhibited my usual eccentricity by being a friend of Gassaway. I recognized in him a man of genius, and take comfort in the fact that the Prince of Wales and Labouchere, of London *Truth*, confirm my opinion by pronouncing Gassaway's poetry some of the best, most beautiful, and original in the English language. Frank Gassaway is naturally a good fellow, but he made the not uncommon mistake of thinking it clever to seem bad. The really clever bad man strives to appear virtuous, and gets in the way after a while of being to some extent what he pretends. The reverse is the history of the good fellow who takes on the character of smartness as a wrong-doer. He ends by being what he has striven, with much persuasion, to make others believe.

However, it is about Frank the dog, and not Frank the poet and humorist, I took pen in hand to memorize. Frank the dog came to us from Frank the poet not long after he got his eyes open (I mean the pet, not the poet), and was a black-and-tan so diminutive I could stow him away in my pocket. He grew apace, and at an early age developed the intellectual traits that made him a noted member of our domestic circle. All the peculiarities and tricks that subsequently made him noted were evolved out of his own inner consciousness. His education was badly neglected by us. He was self-taught, and had all the conceit that comes of such teachings.

He discovered, for instance, at an early day that the meals were the most important events in our household, and his keen interest developed itself into noting the hours and recognizing the bells, especially the first and second bell of a morning, and his activity in getting us all into the dining-room was to the last extent comical. He would run from room to room, barking up each member of the family, and never resting until he had all present and accounted for.

As I have been remarked through life as a man never known to keep an engagement unless I was to be married on it, and of consequence generally late to my meals, I worried Frank beyond endurance. The pleasantest sleep with me is that which comes, regular as the day, between the two bells of the morning meal. There is an ebb in the tide of life that seems to reach its lowest level about three or four A. M. of every day. At this time patients dying from exhaustion lose their frail hold on life, and pass to that silent unknown where the wicked cease to trouble and the weary are at rest.

I know this has been contradicted by physicians, who assert their bills of mortality do not sustain the assured fact. My very clever physician and friend, John A. Murphy, explained this by saying that people who die from some wasting disease are apt to slip their cable at that time, but it did not hold good in cases of violent dissolution, as one could die from an accident at any hour.

This then with the living is the hour for wakefulness, and the so-called unrest which our wicked Lord Byron calls attention to when he says, " It is not the night but the next morning that fetches unpleasant memories," or words to that effect, for I have not had a Byron about me for twenty years.

Well, about four A. M. his Satanic Majesty awakens me for a little intercourse when seated on the footboard of my bed; he runs over not my sins, but my follies, for the enemy of man has discovered long since that we suffer from the last-named and not the former. It may be that in that other world we shall be punished for our wickedness in this; but here below—or above, if you will—we suffer from our folly. In the sin committed we get some recompense, very inadequate I admit, but it is something. In our folly we give ourselves away, and get nothing but humiliation and shame in return. Having ended, somewhat exhausted, my matinee with Satan, he would leave and I turn over to sleep. The bells for breakfast denied this slumber, and then Frank would come to my door and continue his noisy demonstration until I responded by rising.

Often when writing in my den, and far more deeply interested in my work than any reader I ever secured, Frank would dash in with his wild barking to let me know that a hungry family waited below.

If I paid no attention to his summons, he would race out and shortly return with Tiny, a diminutive female black-and-tan, and Nibbs, his royal Nibbs, a Scotch terrier, and the three would bark at me until I followed them to the dining-room.

I have often marveled at Frank's power to communicate to his dog associates my delinquencies, and tell them how to help him, but he did. This is not stranger, however, than the fact observed by naturalists that animals have among each other a language of their own. There is Spring Grove Cemetery, for example, near Cincinnati, of six hundred acres. Shooting, trapping, and other brutal assaults on the poor, harmless creatures below us are forbidden. The result is that the place is thronged with game, as we call it, and the wildest and most shy elsewhere sing, fly, and swim unconcerned amid the grinding rattle of carriages, and even guns fired over the graves of dead soldiers fail to disturb them.

It is well known that wild fowl, strangers to Ohio, are frequently seen on these cemetery ponds. How they come to be there is the mystery. I suppose some wood-duck or wild-goose of our region meets a stranger away off on the coast of the Carolinas amid the rice-fields, and tells him that if he have occasion to cross Ohio, there is a nice place near Cincinnati where he can rest secure and get a good square meal.

Frank's knowledge of English was limited, but perfect as far as it went. A servant could put his head in at the door, and say any thing but breakfast, lunch, or dinner, and Frank would pay no attention to the communication. But let any of those magic words be uttered, and the little fellow would be up, all excitement, and chase in every member of the family.

He had a high contempt for the cat and parrot. He did not consider them ornamental, and as for any useful duties about the house they were not worth a Confederate bond. The parrot had, as parrots are wont to do, picked up a few choice phrases, and among the rest calls for the dogs. Now, although Poll imitated the voices of various members of the family in a skillful and superior manner, she never deceived Frank. Lazily asleep on the rug, the little fellow would open his eyes and look contempt at the parrot, and it needed no words to say, " You miserable green-coated humbug, you can't fool any body."

Our diminutive friend developed his sagacity in early youth. One night Dick Troin was writing in the library of our house at Washington, and was disturbed by the fuss Frank was guilty of on the sofa behind the pen-driver. He would whine, growl, bark,

16

and jump until Dick looked around and saw the little fellow trying to cover himself with the afghan. Seeing that he was noticed at last, Frank dropped the afghan he was tugging at, looked wistfully at the writer, and then barked. Dick, understanding the appeal, kindly covered the little fellow, that, curling up with a satisfied air, was after as quiet as a mouse.

Ever after, when nine o'clock came of an evening, Frank's mistress would say, "Come, my little man, it is bedtime," and he would solemnly proceed upstairs to his bed. This was at the head of the stairs in the hall above, and one night he was sent to it, and in a few minutes he came down rapidly, barking with much animation. His mistress, rebuking him for such unseemly conduct, ordered him back again. He went reluctantly, with head and tail down. In a few seconds, however, down he came again as before. Knowing that something unusual was the matter, I returned with him, and my dear wife, believing the long-expected man had arrived and been discovered by Frank, accompanied us. We found that Maltese Tom, Frank's enemy, a huge cat, had curled up in the poor fellow's bed. Frank looked at the intruder, then at us, as much as to say, "Did you ever see such impudence?" Tom was rattled out and Frank duly installed with the comfort well over him. As I retired that night I saw that Tom had returned, and was lying sound asleep on the dog. Frank evidently thought that kind hands had added a cover to his couch, and, as the night was bitter cold, he had accepted the addition.

Writing of winter; one very cold and stormy season found poor old Frank suffering from the rheumatism. He was so crippled in his old age as to be scarcely able to move. He slept in his mistress' room near the fire, and during the day kept up a mixture of whine and growl that would have been comical had it not been so pathetic, for his grumbling complaint came of extreme pain. Of a morning he would crawl out of bed, limp and stagger over to the window, pausing every few steps as if about to give it up. On reaching the sill he would rear up and look out. If the sun was shining, he would remain out of bed all day; if not, and the morning was stormy, he would turn his old gray-haired, wrinkled face away with a disgusted expression and crawl back to bed, where he would growl and whine like a little old man, complaining of his wretched condition and the neglect he suffered.

Frank was strangely devoid of the affection that marks the dog generally. He was animated by a high sense of duty. He felt that he was born to a mission, and, while he abstained from crowding his

convictions down the throats of others, he was careful not to be influenced by any past favor or affection.
When any suspicious character came about, Frank,
feeling that he could not try conclusions of brute
strength, had a way of attacking the culprit in the
rear by swiftly and noiselessly approaching and biting
at the calf of the intruder.

A lightning-rod man once jumped from his wagon
and came toward our door. Frank saw my expression of disgust and made for the intruder. He was
a tall, broad-shouldered piece of animated nuisance.
Frank passed him, unobserved by the victim, and
turning, gave the bore one nip with his needle-like
teeth. The fellow roared and seemed to jump a rod,
"Gewillikins!" he cried, seeing Frank, "I thought
I was snake-bit!"

The only instance I ever saw in him of affection
Miss Austine Snead, the clever correspondent, put
to record. She was a great friend of Frank's, and
met him after four years' absence. Frank singled
her out from the group of late arrivals at our home,
and went wild in his expressions of delight.

Women are sneered at on account of their fond-
ness for canine pets. The sneer is the shallow expression of a shallow brain. Our sublime egotism
belittles all of God's works but ourselves. We alone
are worthy His creation, and this in face of the fac

that in His divine wisdom he gave the dog qualities superior to any we possess. The dog ranks us in courage, devotion, duty, and gratitude. Had we one-tenth of the attributes that mark the dog, it would not have been possible for us to crucify our Savior.

Dogs are my companions and friends, and good company they are. I never met but one friend who could talk ten minutes on any other subject than themselves. It is a very tiresome subject. Dear old Jerry Black was the only exception; he encouraged a fellow in the fellow's egotism, and it was delirious. Dogs are the best listeners on legs.

### Little Christy's Christmas.

It was Christmas eve, and Christmas eve always fetches snow in Christmas stories. In the locality I treat of snow made the rule, clear weather the exception. It had been falling at intervals all day and as night came on, the storm, if I may use such a word when there was no wind, gave us heavy flakes, that fell as silently as the ballad sung of, that is said to execute the freeman's will. It contributed its silence to the busy city, and padding the thoroughfares, stilled the noisy horror of the stony streets. Heavily laden cars, so crowded that passengers hung to them like a swarm of bees to the limb of a tree, and each pulled by four smoking and weary horses, moved noiselessly, save after each stop, when driver and conductor joined in yells and whip-cracking at the worn out and much-tortured beasts. Drays, carts and heavy wagons hurrying home from work passed without the rattle that usually warns people on foot of their approach. From the black sky above came the white snow, like blessings that turn to evil as they touch the earth.

The streets were thronged, and the toy shops and fancy stores, lit with electric lights, were crowded by people purchasing presents for the Christ day, that of all others tells of good will to little folk on earth.

Ladies, from silken-lined and silver-plated carriages, now fringed with winter's white, and patient coachmen that resembled so many Santa Claus, filled their warm vehicles with all sorts of bundles, while men, from fur-clad brokers and merchants to poor mechanics, were sturdily tramping through the storm, with their hands and arms full of gifts for the dear ones at home. The patter of little feet and the sound of sweet voices, now echoed in the heart, claiming their day, the crowning glory of all the days in the year.

One of the crowd who trudged along had the heavy tread and coarse dress of a day laborer. In his hand he held the tin bucket that so unmistakably indicates the calling. This poor fellow was also in search of gifts, but seemed hard to please. Standing in the glare of the electric lights, the clerks—especially the female clerks—gave him scant attention. His dull, rugged, pock-marked face had little attraction in it, and his coarse wear indicated small purchase and less profit. Paying no attention to the neglect and snubs he experienced from the attendants, he passed from shop to shop, and after an expenditure of twenty-five cents, found himself possessed of a few toys. They were of the rudest sort.

I pledge my word of honor that an ingenious Yankee could have whittled them out of a few shingles in twenty minutes. Cheap paint in the hands of a ready artist had given to the supposed likeness of the animals produced a wild, insane expression that rendered the resemblance quite improbable. Wrapping them in brown paper he placed them under his **rough coat** and started homeward.

Martin Calkins, for by that name was my man known, a common day laborer, never indulged in the luxury of a car ride, from economical considerations. By walking from his work to his den he could save five cents, which, added to another five, enabled him to pay for a drink at a free lunch and so secure a better supper than he would find at home.

This was Martin's theoretical economy. The practice differed somewhat, as with all of us, for having indulged in one glass he took two or three others, so that when this economist reached his wretched lodging he was full, while his pocket was empty.

This sort of club life Mrs. Calkins resented, and being a woman and ill-tempered generally, let loose her indignation in certain expressions far more forcible than polite. Liquor did not develop good nature in Martin, and regarding Mrs. Calkins as his property, he usually enforced a proper respect for his marital rights by beating her into silence if not submission.

On the night in question he stumbled up two flights of dark, dirty stairs to the room of the tenement house he called home, and opening the thin door with a kick, rolled in.

The interior presented a scene of squalid poverty, in the midst of which, cowering over a handful of coal, sat Mrs. Calkins in a faded calico, pathetically hid under an old shawl pulled close about her shoulders.

The room, brought to view by an ill-trimmed kerosene lamp, would have made a house dog drop his head and tail in abject depression. The low ceilings and walls were almost black from smoke and dirt, while from the corners were festooned cobwebs that seemed moist and hoary with accumulated filth. The furniture consisted of an old bedstead, suggestive of vermin, the bed-clothes thereon made up of dirty blankets edged with a sheet of denser hue, and presenting an uneven topography that evidenced an underlying strata of packed straw. At the side of the bed was a cheap cradle with a child therein that had outgrown its resting place, and slept with its little knees drawn up and head touching the head-board. A pine table and two rickety chairs made the rest of the furniture. The floor was bare, save where stains

17

of tobacco varied the general dirt. The two cur-
tainless windows resembled the eye sockets of a skull
—a haunted skull—for as the fire-light flashed and
fell the empty sockets were filled with sudden glares
that resembled ghostly glances at the exterior.

Martin, shaking the snow from his clothes, as
would a Newfoundland dog, fell into a chair with a
force that made the old split-bottom scream as if its
rheumatic joints were being dislocated in great
agony.

The woman, with a sullen expression, looked at
him from the corner of her eyes without turning,
and said: " Well, have you brought me what you
promised ?"

" Brought myself," he answered, "and that's
about all."

"So I expected," she replied, more to herself
than her husband. Then, after a long pause, added:
" Want supper?"

" No, I do n't," he responded.

" Oh! of course not. Do n't want none. Got
yourself full of oysters and whisky, while we starve."

" What's the matter of you, Meg? Now, out
with it, old woman. What is it, I say?"

" Oh! you do n't know, of course you do n't.
You are so innocent, you are. You did n't promise
me money to-night to take kid and me to see my

folks, and you hav n't put all the money down your mean throat. Oh, no; and you ask me what's the matter!"

Martin Calkins was that most hideous of all beasts known as the husband at common law—the creature that absorbs the wife and the wife's right No slave of the south, or anywhere else, was so oppressed as the wife of such a husband. Blackstone tells us that it is his right to chastise her. Practice has taught that it is in his power to kill, provided he does so by slow torture, of blows and abuse, and fails to put her out of her misery with a knife or an ax.

The discussion on this occasion ended, as such generally did, in Mrs. Calkins getting her ears boxed and her wretched anatomy well shaken. She took her punishment in silence, as a matter of course, only shielding her pale, thin face with her arms, as she was averse to appearing before her neighbors with blackened eyes and a scarred countenance.

The brute Calkins had several times been arrested for this violence to his wife. In every instance, however, she refused to prosecute. This is generally the case, and is attributed by our sentimental world to a slavish love and submission on the part of the wife. The fact is, as the punishment consists of fine and imprisonment, the wife and chil-

dren are the main sufferers, for, while the brutal
bread-winner is maintained in jail, the family remain
at home to starve. If the law were so amended as
to put the wife beater at work, and give the wages
to the family, the wifely love and submission would
not be so apparent. Even then the poor woman
would be in terror of immediate death when the
beast had worked out his term of imprisonment. I
believe with Bergh that the better punishment would
be the whipping-post in the public square, or say
hanging.

Soon after the beating, the wife went to bed,
leaving her husband by the dying fire, smoking his
pipe. He sat for hours gazing at the few coals that
gave out little light and less heat. All about him,
throughout the dismal tenement house, were heard
noises that indicated that the huge honeycomb of
filth and poverty was enjoying its Christmas eve.
There were shoutings and poundings, coarse and
shrill voices singing, and through it all came the
strain of a fiddle that sounded like the wail of an old
female opera chorus singing in hades.

We have, it is claimed, sixty-five millions of souls
on this continent of ours, called the people of the
United States. Of these about five millions read
newspapers, and about three of the five read books.

Now, we of the book-making and book-reading

few, have certain superstitions by which we are influenced. One of these is that we number very nearly that of the entire nation, and the other, that through our intellectual efforts we are doing a tremendous business of a missionary sort, toward elevating the masses.

The white caps of a local storm have about as much control of the measureless depths and boundless limits of the ocean as this little class has of the sixty-two millions. Immediately beneath lies the unmoved and unmovable weight of dead ignorance, and beneath that again the monsters of the deep, in all the forms of vice flesh is heir to. The educated few are in influence about as the fly upon the wheel. And how they labor and look wise in their efforts at reformation of humanity! And what a quantity of beautiful little Christmas stories we have, telling all about a class of laborers they know as little of as that class knows of them.

We do not know, and can never learn, it seems, that the deep yet delicate affection we have for one another comes of culture and training in the precepts of our Savior, and as we pass down the scale of humanity we lose all of that and approach the brute creation.

Martin's love for his child, if I may use that sacred word in this connection, was of the sort, but of less intensity, that a cow feels for her calf or a lion for its cub. And as such animal he sat brooding over the dying fire, thinking of what a fool he was to have burdened himself with a family.

Awaking at last from a sleep that nearly tumbled him from the old chair, he proceeded to pull off his heavy spiked shoes that he softly placed upon the floor; rising noiselessly as he could from his creaking chair, he stole toward the bed.

Every plank he pressed, however, had a voice of warning, and, pause as he might, feel his way as cautiously as he could, his approach was accompanied by sharp cracks, unheard during the day.

He paused by the side of the bed; his miserable wife lay in a heavy sleep; the storm had passed, and at that moment the full moon from the clear, cold sky, sent through the dirty windows a flood of light. How he longed to put his brawny hand upon that slender throat, and by one muscular grasp, end her life and his struggles together. Resisting the temptation, more through fear than affection, he continued his stealthy way until he reached the foot of the bed, and there found a poor, little, almost footless stocking suspended from a nail. He took the cheap toys from his breast and carefully thrust them into the stocking. Having accomplished this he rolled into bed.

Christmas morning broke with dazzling bright-
ness upon the city, and the cold, sunlit air was tremu-
lous with the cries of children, explosion of Chinese
crackers and the merry jingle of sleigh-bells. Mrs.
Calkins was the first of her little family to rise, and
she began at once her household cares. The day was
the same to her as all other days. She rekindled her
fire, using with caution a small quantity of kerosene,
and then seizing a bucket went out to the common
hydrant below. Detained there awaiting her turn,
and by some gossip with neighbors made more than
usually interesting by the quarrels, fights and killing
of the night before, she found, on her return, that
Martin had gone out.

This absence did not disturb the wife. She was
accustomed to the morning drink, which, on this sacred day, would probably take until noon to end. It
is a little singular that when a man, owing to his
poverty, can not buy any thing else, he can procure
bottled insanity. I wish some economist could find a
reason for this, and, if possible, a remedy. I suppose
the profit in liquor dealing is so great that a wide
margin of credit exists, and is limited only by the
gutter. When an inebriate gets so low that he is a
dirty nuisance the credit ceases, and he can only get
drunk for cash.

Mrs. Calkins, having put her poor breakfast to

cook, wakened her boy, the only living child out of four born to her wretchedness, and proceeded to dress the little four-year-old in his best clothes. These best were rude enough, and with a rough ablution in cold water set the little fellow on his feet.

The boy was unusually impatient on this occasion, and got some shaking and blows with the open hand for his hurry. As soon as released he ran around the foot of the bed, and with a cry of delight returned with the toys he had discovered.

"See, Musser!" he cried, his little face brightening, "wot dood Santy Claus fetch me." He held up, grasped in his two little hands, the selection and purchase of the night before.

Now, while the mass of grown people among the uncultivated, have dull, inexperienced, and hard faces, their children, under six years of age, generally possess not only innocent countenances, but strangely sensitive, and thoughtful ones, as if fresh from the hands of the Creator. They are unspoiled by the rough life to which they are born.

Little Christy, although his cheeks were hollow, lips thin, and eyes unnaturally large, actually appeared beautiful as he appealed, in his delight, to his mother.

The delight was not reciprocated. The angry woman saw in the toys some of the money that had been promised her for a trip to the country with her child. The wrath, at this find, was intensified by jealousy engendered by the child's preference for the brute of a husband, who had long since beaten all love out of her heart.

A flash of anger lit up her careworn face very like a gleam of heat lightning over a dark cloud, and, seizing the toys, she thrust them in the fire under the hissing pan.

The look of mingled amazement and grief on the child's face was pitiable. Its thin lips trembled, tears welled into the large eyes, and a choking sob, not of grief, but of an attempt to repress its grief, came convulsively from its throat. The attempted repression was a failure. With a wild cry the poor child started forward to rescue its precious gifts. The mother met the move with a stinging slap on the ear that nearly threw down the little sufferer. At the same instant the wife felt herself seized by the throat.

Martin had entered the room unseen by the wife, and took in the situation at a glance. Without a word he pinned her to the wall. She saw death in his face, and as he swung her around to dash her again at the wall, she uttered a wild shriek that rung through the entire house. It was her last. She fell senseless to the floor, and her husband was about to finish his work with a kick in the head, when the door was burst open and half a dozen stout men seized and held him. The woman was put to bed, the poor-house physician sent for, while at the same time the police were called in and Martin was tumbled into a patrol wagon and carted to prison.

The cause of this disturbance, little Christopher, stood, at first, dazed. Then, recovering from his amazement, he saw his father being dragged away, and, all unnoticed in the confusion, followed the police with their prisoner down the stairs. When the patrol wagon was driven away, he ran after, diving through the heavy snow in a vain effort to keep the vehicle in sight. He failed in this, of course, and when it disappeared he stopped, looked about him, and began crying.

The child was lost, and according to received authorities known as Christmas stories, after wandering for hours, and when half starved and nearly frozen, he should have been picked up by a fur-clad, full-stomached, miserly old broker, at that moment full of remorse at having abandoned his daughter at an early age of this child, and lived through all his years with no other occupation than the sinful one of accumulating money. Of course little Christopher should prove to be the millionaire's grandchild.

Heaven forbid that I should doubt the existence of such fur-clad, full-stomached old brokers. I have known quite a number of them, and from what I saw, consider them men liable to abandon their offspring for the sinful accumulation of filthy lucre. But that such operator in Wall street should have an attack of sudden compunction and a waif at the same time is not probable, but it is possible, or it would not be so frequently rehearsed in novel and play. This, however, was not little Christy's luck, and as I am dealing with the hard realities of life, I can not venture to lug in the conscience-stricken broker aforesaid.

The boy did encounter a burly policeman, who at once recognized a lost child, although Christy was in sight of his home. A society for the better protection of children had not only issued an order to have strays of this sort taken to the nearest police station, but had offered a reward for each rescue. It is astonishing what a number of stray children were found after this regulation.

The station to which Christy was carried, had in it a number of cells, for temporary confinement, and while the officer was making note of the newly found in the dingy, ill-ventilated hall, a rough face was pressed against the bars of a near cell, and a husky voice said:

"Christy."

The child with a cry of "Dad" dashed forward, and thrust his little arms through the bars.

"The kid is mine," said the prisoner, "Can't you let him in?"

"The devil it is," responded the officer, and then added: "Don't know about that. Might kill him, as it is charged you did the mother."

"I guess not," was the quiet reply, "I whacked her on account of the kid."

At this point Christy began crying in a low pitiful way. The policeman, not knowing what better to do, opened the iron door, and Christy, with a cry of delight, sprang into his father's arms. This so moved the hardened conservators of the peace, that one emptied his pocket of candies meant for his own children, while another, remembering it was Christmas day, sallied out and returned with a number of toys for the little fellow.

I know that this seems improbable, but when I add that this benevolent guardian of the peace was shortly after discharged for leaving his beat to take a doctor to the bedside of his sick wife, my skeptical reader will feel satisfied.

Seated upon the floor of the warm cell, the child ate his sweets and played with his toys, looking up at intervals to assure himself that his dad was yet present. The heavy air of the badly-ventilated place told at last upon the little chap, and he dropped into a sound sleep. From this he awakened in his father's arms, and looking up saw the stars twinkling through the bars of the prison windows. And thus little Christy's Christmas came to an end.

### The Worries that Kill.

That part of our animal economy, supposed to be the seat of the affections, is considered so elastic that the above phrase causes laughter. And yet, at rare intervals, something vital gives way, in that part of us, and the man, or woman, renders up the ghost as completely as if some well defined disease, recognized by the medicated world, had struck its fatal blow.

A broken heart is not only laughed at, but the scientific gentlemen, who know all about it, insist that the heart is nothing but a pump, placed within for the better control of the circulation, and has no more feeling in it than the bone of the big toe. And so, in their wisdom, they transfer the affections to the brain.

What positive rot all such speculations are. I knew an officer in the late war, who was shot in the head, and lived some months after. The bullet entered at comparison, and was supposed to have traversed benevolence, firmness and lodged in self-esteem. The man died, of course, but he went on dying, in about as sensible a manner as he had lived. We who nursed him, could not perceive any loss of intellectual power. The test was scarcely fair, for your average army officer is not one of those brilliant specimens whose gain or loss of the thoughtful processes can be easily marked and recorded.

We locate the intellect in the skull, because we feel it is there. The late Jeremiah S. Black was wont to say that a legal argument by William Evarts made his head ache. In the same way we put the emotions in the heart. We feel them there.

The poor fellow watching at the bedside of a stricken wife, or the mother hanging over the cradle of a dying child, gauges the progress of the dread disease by a sinking sensation at the heart, which clouds the brain, dims the eye, and sends the breathing up through sobs.

It is not the thought that kills, or even tires; it is the worry of the heart, and this writes wrinkles on the brow of care, and sickens, if it does not shorten, life.

"A great man to be successful," wrote a French Bohemian, attributing his axiom to Napoleon, " must have a good digestion and a bad heart."

Fretting over the affairs of life is like friction in machinery—it heats, wears and retards. The car-wheel was made a success by an invention that brought a soft, cold material that might melt, but could not heat, in contact with the axle.

That the heart is the seat of emotions is better proven than phrenology, although we have all dropped into that bumptious theory. In phrenology, that is so generally accepted, the mind is broken into bumps or organs. This absurdity prevails, although, when we come to investigate philosophically, we find every organ a head in itself. What, for example, is comparison, ideality, without every other intellectual organ entering into it. I will take any one organ and run quite a great man on it. Now nature is not only logical but economic, as well, and above all, strangely secretive. While the countenance, played upon incessantly, remains something of a mask, it is not likely that bumps would be embossed on the skulls, telling to the fingers of a quack the inner secrets of a man's characteristics—characteristics unknown to the man himself.

Astrology was better, palmology as good, while pedalogy, started by an ingenious friend of mine, is quite as conclusive. Who sees a fat foot, for example, and is not satisfied that the structure above is lazy? A high, well arched instep indicates delicacy of organization, even if seen dangling under a gallows. This is all arrant nonsense, but not more so than the so-called science at the other extremity.

Well, the troubles of the heart have little to do with those of the head, nor are they much better understood. It is through such ignorance that consolation and condolence are so very exasperating.

The sympathy, for instance, that comes in through funeral ceremonies is very trying. At the moment when one longs to be alone with one's dead, all one's friends and neighbors come in and gaze. The beast of an undertaker arranges the remains that are lying upon one's breast, for public inspection, and all the crowd, speaking in bated breath of the weather, the markets, the health of the neighborhood, pull on long faces and pass by the coffin to take a last look at the departed they care nothing for. Poor heart, that wants to drive them all out and clasp, in agony, the cold form of the dead and fairly shriek into the closed ears for a return of one who never, never, more may come back to bless us!

> " Why weepest thou ?   Thy tears are unavailing.
>     Therefore do I weep."

It was this shrinking from the undertaker and the public on the part of a sensitive wife that gave rise to the cruel report that the great war secretary, Stanton, had committed suicide. The afflicted widow had, through accident, seen an undertaker preparing her dead child for burial. The brutal manner in which the poor little corpse was being treated so shocked her that she vowed that thereafter none but

18

loving hands should prepare her dead for the grave. The undertaker, therefore, saw the body of the eminent statesman only in the coffin, and his duty was confined to screwing down the lid. This abrupt departure from common usages, of course, gave rise to strange rumors.

It was my good fortune to know Edwin M. Stanton intimately as a brother from my boyhood until death separated us. My brother-in-law, Judge Nathaniel C. Read, of the Supreme Court of Ohio, gave Stanton his first office, that of reporter, and Stanton was wont to make Mac-o-check his summer resort for years.

Doubtful as it may seem to the secretary's many enemies, and he left behind him an army of such, he was of a deeply religious nature. Possessed of a sensitive temperament, he was subject to great extremes of gayety and gloom, and had withal powerful vitality. His powers of endurance were amazing, and a force of character, stimulated by an indomitable will, made him master of all situations and of himself. All men thus fitted to this life cling to life with an obstinate tenacity.

He was dying of an incurable disease while in the department he controlled with such amazing vigor, but, at the bidding of his will, death postponed his doom until his task was ended.

I saw his remains the morning of the night he
died. With hands crossed upon his breast, his resolute face was softened with an expression resembling
that of sleep, and I know from what I saw that the
renowned story of his suicide was false. The stormy
life of a noble character, marred with more ignoble
passions than ordinarily falls to the lot of man, had
passed into silence and memory, quiet as a child.

This incident has carried me from my theme.
Of the more beautiful emotions of the human heart,
humanity is strangely ignorant. Take for illustration the touching care and love of a mother for her
crippled or deformed child. What pity we extend
to the parent, unaware that in the loving care there
is a source of great comfort. The same result occurs
in the nursing of any loved patient.

James Whitcomb Riley tells me of a humorist,
the wittiest, most delicate and pure of all that toil in
our midst, who lived devoted to his invalid wife, and
in her death suffered as no man ever suffered before
over a like loss. The little wife, through helpless-
ness, was more to the poor fellow than a healthy,
hearty helpmate would have been.

One summer passed at Oaklands, amid a great
crowd of hay-fever patients, I remember vividly, from
the fact of an artist stricken with paralysis coming
to pass the summer months accompanied by his wife.

The painter was on the shady side of life when he married a little girl young enough to be his daughter. Paralysis followed, and the wife became his nurse. Her quiet care, her unpretending devotion, called forth much admiration among the throng of people at that summer resort. She was his hands, feet, voice—his all—and folk looked on wonderingly and pitied the poor woman, and when the old man died, which he did one night, we all felt relieved, and said : " Now the little widow will have some comfort."

Somehow or other she did not seem to realize the great blessing that had come to her. She wept much in a quiet way. Her eyes grew cavernous and her cheeks hollow. The poor thing, avoiding sympathy, passed hours alone. It was so absurdly different from what was expected, and ought to have been the fact, that a feeling of impatience, nearly akin to dislike, sprung up and spread.

One morning the widow failed to appear at breakfast, a meal she seldom honored by eating. As knocking elicited no response, a slender mulatto boy was tossed through the transom to unlock the door. When that door was unlocked, we found the little widow lying on her back, with her thin hands meekly folded on her breast—dead of a broken heart. At least, the fashionable doctor pronounced it heart disease.

That which was thought to be a grievous burden had, in fact, been a blessing. When the old man, numbed in brain and crippled in body, found a refuge in the grave, all that she had of life, all its tenderness, love, and sweet, helpful dependence disappeared with him, and her little horizon darkened down to death.

## Humors of the War.

When General Fremont, then in command of the Middle Department, was suddenly ordered to intercept Stonewall Jackson after that pious old Confederate had chased General Banks and his little command from the Shenandoah Valley, General John Charles, as true a soldier and as capable an officer as the government possessed, placed his surplus baggage, sick and wounded, at Petersburg, under the command of Captain Lee, with one full company, to care for the property and people left behind.

I write it Captain Lee, for to tell the truth I have forgotten the name of the gallant young fellow, the hero of my sketch.

The captain was not well pleased with the duty assigned him. He grumbled not a little at the ignoble service of sitting guard over old tents, blankets, sick and wounded, while the army marched away to glory. And glory it would have been had Fremont been really in command of an army. Aside from Generals Cluserit's, Schenck's and Milroy's brigades, he had worse than nothing, for the force was made up of what was known as Blenker's division, German in name, but in reality the scum and dregs of all nationalities represented in New York, where the scoundrelism of the earth makes yearly its foul deposit. Blenker's division was an armed mob of thieves, with as much fight in them as discipline, and not enough of either to make the men other than a burden to us, that demoralized the entire force. For example, when Fremont first hit Stonewall's heavy forces near Strasbourg, a forced march of an hour would have hemmed them in between Fremont's army and that under General McDowell. Fremont saw the chance and issued his orders accordingly. The response was a deliberate halt in the road, and two-thirds of our force unslung their kettles and deliberately went to cooking breakfast. No remonstrance, no threats nor hard swearing could move the solid mass.

General Schenck, grim as the god of war, sat on his horse, surrounded by his staff, and saw the Confederates sweep by and the golden opportunity to gobble gone forever.

I can see now, as if the event were but an hour old, the gallant young fellows forming that staff—the handsome Cheesebrough, the cool, impassive Este, the witty Crane and impetuous Feilding Lowry, all cultured gentlemen, brave and gentle.

" Well, fellows," I said, " we are being taught that something more is necessary to make an army than the officer. While warlike Europe has spent a thousand years in the creation of a private, our wonderful government spends its vast energies in the creation of an officer. When that wonderful production is completed we stand off and say, 'Behold our army.'"

Again, at Cross Keys, subsequent to the above, when Stonewall was forced to make a stand, these cowardly thieves left Cluseret, Schenck and Milroy to do the fighting, while they wandered over the country, singly and in gangs, robbing farm-houses and murdering unarmed men.

My little story, however, has nothing to do with the march of that army, but seeks to tell what happened to our unhappy captain, left in command at Petersburg. With him the time wore on drearily enough. His camp was infested with copperheads *au naturel*, for he had selected a stony eminence, and from hidden recesses came out the ugly reptiles at all hours, while around were copperheads on end, quite as malignant, if not as poisonous. Of these the females were far the more noisy and disagreeable.

A woman comes into the world and grows up so surrounded and protected that she never learns and appreciates the beauty and efficiency of head-pummeling as a guard against tongue-wagging, and she is therefore free to let loose her opinion on all occasions. Captain Lee had a turn for female society, being young, handsome and gallant, but he soon tired of attempted attentions that were received in scorn and garnished by such pleasant epithets as " Lincoln hireling," " cowardly Yank," and " Lincoln pup."

One sunny afternoon the captain was sitting, or rather reclining, before his tent, looking vacantly at the beautiful scenery stretched out before him. Below, and more immediately near, were the golden fields shimmering in the sunlight. Beyond ran the forests, with their deep green foliage, and far out, framing all in, were the blue summits of the distant mountains, that seemed to melt into the soft summer skies. It was hard to realize that in this beautiful, peace-loving stretch of nature man's evil nature had hidden death in its cruelest forms, and over all spread the dark pinions of brutal war, dropping mourning and desolation on the homes of all the land.

Our captain had not much poetry in his soul, and probably at that moment was thinking of where he could find some fresh bread and butter, instead of side meat and hard-tack, that made his digestion suffer at the mere thought. Whatever his thoughts may have been, they were interrupted by the guard, who, pausing on his weary round, shaded his eyes with one hand for a moment, and then cried:

19

"I say, Cap, what the devil is that coming down the hill yonder?"

The officer sprang to his feet, and, bringing his glass to bear, had the happiness of a new emotion.

"What the devil?" he muttered, "it looks like a flag of truce. By George, it is a flag! Hullo, there! My horse! Hurry up, several of you! Mount quick, I say!"

It was a flag of truce, and as it approached, the captain and his escort had ridden down to meet it. The captain was kept from laughing by the novelty of the fact. The leader of the cavalcade he met was mounted on a switch-tailed hat-rack, with marks of collar and traces on its lean body, that added to its grotesqueness by the infernal pace, so common to Virginia horses, that makes the animal look as if it had on each side a separate organization, and harmonized the two through a general understanding to move one side at a time. The rider was dressed in common butternut homespun, turned into a uniform by having pieces of red flannel sewed to the shoulders, an old-fashioned sword, that had come down through no end of militia musters from the revolution, was slung to his thin form by a common saddle girth. The sallow face was shaded by a broad-brimmed slouched hat, that was made conspicuous by a white and red cockade, fresh from the barnyard, sporting the tails of at least a dozen unfortunate roosters. He carried on a stick a dirty white rag, while his two companions, or squad, as badly rigged and mounted, one on a mare that showed by her uneasiness, that a colt had been left behind, were to be known as soldiers only by their heavy old muskets.

Our captain called a halt, and demanded the reason for this extraordinary appearance.

" I come, sah," was the response in the purest Potomac dialect, " from General Tomkins, to demand the immediate surrender of Petersburg."

" The devil you do," was the captain's brusque response.

" Yes, sah."

" Will you tell General Tomkins for me that if he wants this God-forsaken town, just come and take it."

" Very well, sah ; then General Tomkins ordered me to say to you, sah, to remove the women and children, for he will open on the place immediately."

" Tell General Tomkins," snorted the captain, " for me, that as the women and children are secesh, he can open and be d—— to him and them, too. The more he kills the merrier it will be."

" General Tomkins is a humane man, sah, and despises a war on women and children. To avoid unnecessary bloodshed, he demands your surrender."

"You have my answer—pound away.  I won't surrender!"

"Very well, sah; I shall so report."

And, so saying, he gravely saluted our captain, and, turning, rode away.  As he did so the bereaved mare made a vigorous effort by rearing and kicking to rid herself of her rider.  Failing in this she took the bit in her teeth, and went off at a speed highly complimentary to the brood mares of Virginia.  The bearer of the flag and his remaining squad of one man paced off in a sober, sedate manner, while the rider of the bereaved mother, with his long legs and arms flapping wildly, disappeared over the hill as Captain Lee and his orderlies made the place ring with their peals of laughter.  The flag of truce, however, did not respond to this merriment.  Their mission could not be relegated to the things that amuse.  They carried war and desolation's nakedness back to the mysterious General Tomkins.

Our captain lost no time trotting back to camp.  He had the long roll beaten, the company hastily drawn up in line, supported by such of the sick and wounded as could stand.  This gallant little force was informed that the enemy, under General Tomkins, was about to make a raid on Petersburg, that he would probably open on them with artillery, and as they had none with which to respond, it would be necessary to assume the offensive as soon as the demonstration was made. This was responded to by such hearty cheers as the honest throats of American soldiers—God bless them—are always ready to give, and our hero, sitting in grim silence, on his steed, awaited further developments.

An hour passed, and then to the captain's amazement the flag of truce again appeared; this time without the bereaved mare. Captain Lee rode down.

" General Tomkins, sah," said the flag bearer, " is humane—yes, sah—a gallant soldier, sah, but humane. He has his guns in position, under a superior force, and he again demands a surrender to avoid unnecessary bloodshed, sah."

"See here," said the captain, "you have my answer, and if you come cavorting down this road again I'll open on you. Do you understand that?"

" Yes, sah—a flag of truce, sah."

" Oh, go to ——," well it was a rather warm climate, not then abolished by Colonel Ingersoll, and our hero rode back to his command. At the head of his small forces he awaited the attack. He waited in vain. The woods upon the mountains, into which the flag of truce had disappeared, remained silent as a cemetery. The sun went down, the stars came out, and yet the thunder of the threatened artillery failed to awaken the echoes of the mountains; one by one the sick and wounded dropped off, and the anxious commander, taking all necessary precautions for the night, broke ranks and sent his soldiers to their tents.

The place remained undisturbed through the night, and early in the morning a squad of Connecticut cavalry—a force always bumming around stealing horses, and making themselves generally disagreeable to both sides—galloped into camp with some prisoners, and among the rest the bearer of the flag.

" How d' ye do?" asked our captain of the warrior under the red flannel straps.

" Purty well, sah ; how d' ye find yerself?"

" Why did n't you open on us yesterday?"

" Well, sah, fact is we had no artillery."

" The devil! Why did you not come in and take us anyhow?"

" Why, you see, sah, when you beat the long roll and formed, we thought you were too much for us."

" That so?"

" Yes, sah, only three of us all told."

" Then I have the honor of addressing General Tomkins?"

" You have, sah."

It was a neat little game of bluff, in which our captain won by a call.

## Churchyard Reveries.

For many days past I have been engaged superintending the erection of a vault and monument at the old churchyard of Mac-o-chee.

I call it old, for it was among the first, if not the first, God's acre dedicated to the white dead after the Indians left their graves, to vanish westwardly into tradition. I remember well an Indian burial-place that I often visited when a boy under what is now a garden to the residence of Mr. John Nash, not half a mile from this Catholic cemetery, in which I am preparing a place for my dead. The Indians were not given to monuments, and there was not much to indicate the graves, or the boundary of the lot. I remember well, traces of a trench that old George Martin, a pioneer much given to fishing on Sunday, and whisky at all times, told me contained the bodies of the warriors killed when the Mac-o-chee towns were surprised and burned by the white settlers from Kentucky.

I remember, too, the Indians themselves. A remnant of the Wyandotte tribe lingered about Upper Sandusky in my youthful days, and it was no uncom-

mon event for a number of them to visit our settle-
ment, offering skins and maple sugar for sale. A
mingled feeling of fear and curiosity held me in their
presence, and having heard very wild stories of their
wars, in which Martin figured as a tremendous fellow,
I hung about the copper-colored sons of the forest
quite fascinated.

Cooper, the novelist, has fixed in the American
mind an impossible Indian, and this silent, brave and
intensely solemn creation will go down to future ages
as the Indian our fathers persecuted and destroyed.

I have come, through much observation and a little thought, to regard national traits as superstitions.
Mankind, in the main, is about the same the world
over. It is an article set on end, with a turn for
cooking and the capacity to laugh. Some cook better
than others, and some laugh more readily and louder;
but to deny a people a sense of humor, as Cooper did
the Indian, is as absurd as making a wooden-headed
saint out of Washington and a fiend incarnate out
of Burr.

The Indians from Upper Sandusky, coming
among us, turned the skins they had to sell into
whisky, mainly, and became thereafter vociferously
cheerful. In this condition they kicked the squaws,
and got slashed over their heads with knives by those
gentle beings, which treatment brought forth roars

of laughter, which grew hysterical when a mother-in-law took a hand in the family disturbance.

There was among them one old Indian known as " Capten Johnny," who would have made a fortune as the clown of a circus. He had a way of hoisting his heel and kicking himself when disappointed or disgusted with himself, and saying, with some emphasis and the gravest face, " Me dam."

The rough pioneers of the valley were fond of retailing old " Capten Johnny's " jokes. One, I remember, quite illustrative of his solemn style, for the old fellow never laughed. He was quite struck with the intelligence exhibited by a bob-tailed pointer dog, owned by an officer. And the old " Capten," turning it over in his aboriginal mind, came to the conclusion that the dog's sagacity, so superior to the " Capten's " own hounds, came of the fact that his tail had been amputated. Tails, he thought, weakened the intellect. " Man got no tail—man see good —see afore, see 'hind, all good, when no drunk."

Having arrived at this sage conclusion, the next step was to try his theory on one of his own hounds. By shortening the tail, he thought to strengthen the canine intellect. To this end, he requested a woodman, engaged in hewing a piece of timber, to hold across the log the tail of his hound while he cut off the appendage with a broad ax. As the heavy ax

came over with a sweep, the woodman, either alarmed
or pretending to be, gave the poor dog a jerk, and
Captain Johnny cut the poor animal in two. Dropping the ax, he exclaimed solemnly:

"Hip—by dam—two short a most," and went in
pursuit of another.

To return from the dead and almost forgotten
Indians to the buried whites. St. Elizabeth, of the
Mac-o-chee, is a rude Catholic burying ground, holding the remains of mostly poor folk—so poor that,
were they not Catholics, there would be few remind-
ers in the way of monuments, to keep the dead in
memory. Two or three more pretentious structures
tell of wealthy or well-to-do families, but the majority are of those in the humblest walks of life.

The place is exceedingly beautiful in its surroundings. Situated on one of the low, softly
rounded and richly wooded hills that frame in the
Mad River valley, far off to the west and south the
eye takes in the wide stretch of fertile plains, with
streams willow-fringed, and farm houses half hid in
orchards, until, on the dim horizon, earth seems to
melt into heaven. "A blue country," as Ruskin calls
such, and as beautiful a specimen as I ever had the
happiness to look upon. Off to the right one catches
the gleam of the village spires that rise above the

beautiful maple-shaded place, and I find myself weaving the sounds into the music of words:

> And now, as in that far-off time,
>    The village sounds are dear;
> The cry of children and the chime
>    Of bells break on the ear.
> My playmates, then, are bearded men,
>    The men tread old, and slow,
> Or sleep within God's silent glen
>    Where broods the long ago.

These, with the clip, clip of the workmen building in the warm spring sunlight a house for me and mine when we shall have passed away and left nothing but this vault and monument to hold our name in memory, make the voices of solitude.

How we cling to this hope of a memory. I wander, book in hand, among these graves, and note the humble records in humble lines. Born so and so—died so and so, and then a sentence from the Bible. That is all. Brief story of a busy life—a life full of hopes and fears, triumphs and disappointments. What comedies, what tragedies, with the whole world for a stage, have been enacted, for when a man is born the world begins, and when the man dies the world ends; and how important it all is—for each, in his own estimation, is a center, a hub, as it were. He can not realize that when, upon some very unpleasant proposition, assisted by a doctor, and wept over by three or four, he drops out of this life, his exit will scarcely be noticed, and all his affairs, to which he was so necessary, will go on as if he had never existed.

The last grand struggle for a memory is made in the cemetery. He, though dead, asserts himself above his grave. Here are the immortal stones, with names cut deep into them. Some are leaning over, moss covered and gray, as if in extreme old age—and others are down, as if fairly exhausted with holding up the legend of a name—and all scarcely legible. " Sacred to the memory of"—poor man, in all this wide world there is not one who remembers, or dimly remembering, cares for the departed, whose very bones are dust.

Gray tells us of the mute, inglorious Miltons, lost in his country churchyard. Is the Milton who was not mute, or Shakespeare, or Cæsar, or any of the world's great, any more fortunate in that respect than these humble toilers ? I think not. Let us see.

In counting the past we fix in our minds a period, at which to begin—we start at the creation. Looking forward, we help ourselves to another date known as the day of judgment, when the world shall end. We ignore the awful truth, that before our date of beginning, back through the countless millions of ages, lies eternity, and before us, through the same countless ages going on, and on, and on forever, is the future. Here we are, then, unseen motes in the now, taking to ourselves an immortality of fame. Already, the blind Homer is fading in the dim distance, and the blind Milton diminishes with passing years. Shakespeare will follow, all glittering insects that flash for an instant in the sunlight, and then disappear forever.

What are crumbling monuments in the light of eternity? They seem solid and slow of decay to us, precisely as this atom of a world in the boundless space that stretches on and on without limit, with its countless worlds, seems to us a huge affair. It is not even as a grain of sand upon the shore.

It is well for us that we are not all Bob Ingersolls, and know too much, or rather think we know it all. We ate of the tree of knowledge, but neglected to steal from the tree of life. We lack the strength, then, to entertain our information. When a man crawls up beyond traditionary teachings to the edge of the world, and stares out upon blank, cold, unending space he is stricken with blindness or insanity. One can not think truly of God and retain his reason, as he can not see God and live, as the Bible tells us. Therefore is it that we take refuge in Christ; the sweet, loving, humble Savior, and through His mercy enjoy our homes and accept our graves.

Sitting among these poor graves, with a cross over each, erected by loving hands, and covered by grass and ground ivy, watered by tears from broken hearts, I thought what a cruel ceremony was this burial of the dead, without the consolation Christ's religion gives. And how brutal are the men who go about striving to destroy this comfort.

It is, on this account, I have no patience with our Colonel Ingersoll. Of course, he is powerless among the better educated, the thoughtful minds that hold Christ's religion as not only perfect, but precious. It is with the ignorant, the poor, who have no opportunity for study, no time for thought, that the wrong is being done.

Through all time, the more fortunate class, the rich and well born, have had their religion born of the brain, rather cold and uncomfortable, but nevertheless a faith to lean upon. The great mass of earth's toilers had no such consolation until Christ appeared on earth, and became the friend of the oppressed and downtrodden, the teacher of the great untaught.

Like Moses of old, He smote with His rod of truth the hard, flinty earth, and from its rocky heart sprang into light and life the waters of God's religion, not for the rich and well born, to fill their silver pitchers and relieve their delicate thirst, but to flow along in lowly places over the earth, where the poor and suffering may stoop and drink, and go their way strengthened and happy.

I heard Colonel Ingersoll on one occasion, and I langhed, not so much at his humor, which is great, as at the man. To see a stout gentleman, in a swallow-tailed coat and white choker, prancing up and down a stage on a Sunday night, assailing Moses, struck me as extremely ludicrous. The theater was crowded by, I should say, some two thousand men, and of the two thousand one solitary individual had read Moses, and that was the fleshy gentleman engaged in assailing him. I thought of Sidney Smith's irreverent man who spoke disrespectfully of the equator.

I never saw illustrated before the hold Christianity has taken on the popular mind. Colonel Ingersoll could ridicule Moses, he could even express his doubts as to God, but a slight allusion to our Savior was followed by a dead silence, that indicated that any attempt at ridicule or abuse in that direction would shock even this hardened, shallow, indifferent crowd. The friend of the poor, the afflicted and oppressed, who died teaching us that the road to Heaven was through kindness to each other—" Glory to God on high and peace and good will to men on earth "—holds His own in the hearts of humanity, even in the hell of a theater, with a theological end-man raising a laugh at the expense of Moses.

This gentleman claims to know all about every-thing, and yet, when on this occasion, he asked him-self whether he believed in an existence after death, he said he did not know.  I do not claim to be clever, and never sought to instruct any one, and yet, had Colonel Ingersoll been asked, "Do you believe you exist now?" he would have considered the questioner a fool.  And yet, both beliefs rest on the same foun-dation.  This thing we call " I," " me," " myself," that thinks, wills and remembers, believes, feels, knows that it exists.  It feels, knows and believes that we existed yesterday and will exist to-morrow, and forever.  It is as easy to make us comprehend anni-hilation as it is to convince us that we do not exist.  I have heard divines spend hours, in far-fetched argu-ments and questionable facts to prove the immortality of the soul, when each soul within hearing felt its ex-istence, and could not, by any process of reasoning, be brought to comprehend non-existence—or an-nihilation.

Sitting alone amid these neglected graves of the poor, I read the great truth on every weather-stained, moss-obscured tombstone about me.  The untaught toilers of the earth have put briefly and in quaint words their unshaken faith to record.  In the Indian burying ground, not far off, is the same faith.  And on no part of the earth can a man be found who is not born with that consciousness, that belief, in him. Why then waste time in proving a fact, that only puzzles one when an attempt is made to disprove it?

Again, if this little life of ours here be all and end all of existence, death would be as easy and natural to us as sleep. But, as we are born into this world in a painful strife—we are born into that other existence in a struggle. Pain comes, and pain goes with us. There is no preparation we can make that will familiarize us with the dreaded change. The old man, with two-thirds of his physical being already buried, looks forward to interests in this life as keenly as the young.

All men are mortal save the man himself, says the poet. We never take death into our confidence. I look at the narrow cell in this vault I have selected for myself, and try to realize my mortal remains being shoved in and walled up, when the hand that writes this and the body I have so long regarded as " me " shall be left there, in darkness, to moulder in decay. But I can not bring it home to a palpable, familiar sense. I know that in a brief period—Oh! so brief—I shall be taken down on some unpleasant medicated proposition, and get worse and weaker from day to day, when at last a cry of anguish will go up from the one dear being—the one, the only one in all this world who truly believes in me—and the neigh-

20

bors will gather in with very long faces, and much seemly solemnity and no grief, and then follow the hearse, while talking of the weather and the crops, to this, my final home on earth. But I can not make it familiar—nor pleasant.

This musing, in the still solitude of a neglected graveyard is all well enough, but for myself to afford food for worms and meditation is not so agreeable!

I was once making excellent time from Bull Pasture mountain, in Virginia, during the war, when we had been defeated by the Confederates, with the late Colonel Crane, when that gallant officer turned to me and said:

"I don't want you to suppose, Donn, that I am scared. I am not. But, my dear fellow, you don't know what a singular prejudice I have against dying just at this time."

And what a mockery is the funeral! If the procession were reduced to the actual mourners, one hack would carry it all. Lucky is the man who can fill one hack. I have a seat vacant now in mine.

## The World's Grumblers.

The threatened return of the cholera to our afflicted land reminds me of a man I once knew who improved the occasion of a visit from that awful scourge to develop a trait peculiar to a class given to not only looking upon the dark side of all events, but forcing others to occupy the same standpoint.

This world of ours has been likened to a vale of tears and a valley of tribulation. We come into it with a cry, live through it in sorrow, and go out with a howl of anguish, not only on the part of the poor actor making his exit, but all the sorrowing friends and relatives join in the lamentations.

One would suppose that under this state of melancholy fact, the dictates of duty, and no less philosophy, would teach us to make the best of it, and so train our thoughts and cultivate our conduct as to see and feel the few blessings bestowed upon us.

This is the fact with a majority, and I believe we would get along quite comfortably were it not for a class of grumblers who go about growling at all things, and not content with feeling miserably themselves, insist on everybody else sharing in their stupid wretchedness. The poet Rogers sang:

> " Such joys I find in melancholy,
>  I would not if I could be gay."

Sweet musical words, but a cursedly mean sentiment when it finds expression in vulgar discontent.

Our salutation, when we meet, is " How are you?" The response should be " Jolly, I thank you ; hope you enjoy the same blessing." This is seldom the response. The party of the first part and the party of the second part immediately fall into a detailed account of his or her bodily ills. If talks about our aches and pains were suppressed, two-thirds of the conversation of civilized life would cease. If to this interdicted subject be added the weather, humanity would relapse into brute silence. I forgot that female discourse on dress and servants would yet remain and the chattering continue.

It is amazing to listen and hear humanity, set on end for some wise purpose, devoting so much of the brief time allotted us on earth to a careful detailed diagnosis of head aches, back aches, stomach aches, and that peculiar misery that defies description. Accompanying this are the cases, kind and unkind, that have been found available or suggested by friends once in their time afflicted in the same way.

I think this might be improved on if, instead of seizing each other by the hand, and vibrating the arm, like a pump-handle, a most senseless ceremony, each should seize the pulse of the other, and proceed to count the same with running comments, more or less discouraging. After this, these tailless monkeys should thrust out their tongues, and have the coats of the same investigated and reported on.

The comical part of this business lies in the patience with which each listens to the other. He or she knows, however, that his or her turn comes next, and the luxury of unloading sickening accounts of sickness will be granted.

The thought has often struck me that the great foundation stone of the Catholic religion is to be found in the confessional. This not only relieves one of his sins and makes the poor clergyman better acquainted with the wants and weaknesses of his congregation, but it is such a luxury to be able to talk of oneself without the penalty of having the recipient talk back on the same bore of a subject.

Once upon a time I tried this infliction. I did not assume the garb of a priest, and sit on a hard seat within the reach of a bad breath. I was not capable of that torture, but while passing the summer at Berkeley Springs, Va., I encountered a homeopathic specimen of manhood in the shape of a little poet.

He carried his so-called poems about him and persisted in reading them to every one he could corner for that purpose. I never could bear that jingle of two words at the end of an idea, unless I wrote them myself, and the guests at Berkeley were of the same turn. They fled from the approach of this nuisance on legs, as if he had been the cholera.

I saw the poor fellow wandering about in such a melancholy manner, with his eyes that had all the intensity of a pickled shad, in search of a victim, and I said, " Medicated scientists have risked their lives in experiments made to benefit humanity, why should I not take the same risk ? Why not test my powers of endurance ? I am a journalist. Patient endurance is a great quality for success in that pursuit." I did not make any will, for I had nothing to leave, nor did I fortify myself with old Virginia whisky. I took a sad, lingering look at the purple hued mountains, the bright sunlight, and a receipted board bill, and had Otway Randolph Gnat read me his much renowned poem on Berkeley.

How readily, with what joy, he took the roll of MS. from his bosom, and began reading before we could reach the shade.

It was one of those exasperating doggerels, abounding in rhymes and puns, that makes the impression on one of an uncertain stream trickled down one's back. It was a regular treadmill, where, tramp as lively as you may, you never get on or up. The

moments seemed hours and hours ages of torture.
I felt the over-excited brain gathering the blood
of my body to my head. A dreadful pain set in. I
felt that life was in danger, but I could not stop.
It was like those dreadful scribblings on walls that
one sometimes encounters, and one must read, although reading is disquiet.

Otway Randolph Gnat came to the end at last.
"Now is the time for heroic courage," I thought;
and I said—may the Lord forgive me for lying!—
"Otway, my boy, that is exquisite! I am delighted.
I can not part from it. Would you mind going over
and culling such passages as you may think the
finest?"

He read it all over again.

I seized the awful MS., and cried: "Otway, I
must read this to my friends!" I fled in a dazed
condition to my room. For days I was ill, and at
times delirious. I drove my sorrowing friends from
me by shouting: "Ah ha! isn't this beautiful?" and
pouring out a torrent of doggerel that my fevered
brain had caught up and retained.

The experience was, however, of great benefit
to me. I found after that I could listen to a so-
called debate in the senate without flinching, and to
this day I can listen to a detailed account of all the
ills my every acquaintance seems troubled with, and

not only save him or her from the penalty of a return diagnosis, but retain a look of deep interest that
has won for me the reputation of the most fascinating conversationalist alive.

A friend told me of a stout, ill-tempered Irishwoman in the car who had a poor, forlorn-looking
female seat herself beside her. The unhappy creature began pouring into the ears of newly-found listeners her misfortunes in the way of family sickness.
The Irishwoman bore the infliction for some time in
silence, and then almost annihilated the mournful
talker by asking fiercely:

"Phat in the blank is all yer blankety blank
throubles to me, ye ould idjiot!"

It would not be polite to sit down on every
grumbler in that way, and yet the nauseous details
of one's sickness is about as rude as such a snub
would be.

What I sat down to write, however, was of a
melancholy man who read the cholera reports and
repeated them to all his acquaintances and patients,
for he was a physician. He was the most learned
fool in that line I ever knew. Strange infatuation
people have, that to cultivate the memory betters the
judgment, when the fact is the better the memory
the poorer the intellect.

Dr. Aberuthy Snyder had a most tenacious memory. We called him Old Statistics, from a habit he had of remembering the figures and forgetting the facts. He had a way of saying to one abruptly: "Do you know what happened on this day three hundred years ago?" The response would be, of course, in the negative. "Well, sir, I am astonished; yes, sir, astonished; the ignorance of some people is annoying. This day precisely three hundred years ago General Pillicoddy crossed the Po and changed the face of Europe."

When the cholera broke out among us, Old Statistics was in his element. With a face and a manner that made him a condensed funeral, he went about with a history of every plague that ever destroyed humanity on the tip of his tongue, and he created a panic at every turn. It was on cholera reports, however, that he was most effective. Coming down to breakfast at our boarding-house, he would solemnly announce: "One hundred and ten cases and ninety deaths within the last twenty-four hours— awful! awful! The dread disease is on us. It is the Asiatic cholera in the most malignant form."

"Has medicine no remedy, doctor?" would ask a female boarder, frightened into a subdued condition of ready-to-take-any-thing-that-moment.

"No, madame; pained to say no. Calomel

21

guarded with opium, or opium stimulated with calomel, seems to be the only medicine—but in vain."

" Why, doctor?"

" Well, madame, it takes calomel eight hours to affect the liver; the patient dies in four."

" Why do you call it a remedy, then?" growled an old bald-headed, bottle-nosed boarder.

" Because, in very mild cases, sir, the patient escapes cholera, and dies of inflammation of the bowels—or brain, sir, if he happens to have one, which, I am sorry to say. is seldom the case."

" What can we do, doctor, to avoid this dreadful scourge?"

" Medicine is at fault. We can only warn you to be careful of your diet." This was a signal for general consternation, for he would continue: " We only know that it is a disease of the bowels, and whether caused by the food we eat, or aggravated by such, the fact remains that the stomach is affected. Don't touch cowcumbers, or you perish. If you want to die immediately, eat hash. Preserves and pickles are poison. If any man hankers after the worst and most malignant form of Asiatic cholera, let him eat bread pudding. Fruit is fatal. Hot bread in any shape is death. Pork, sir, pork! Bless my soul, what a question! One sausage is good for four cases."

"What in the devil is a man to eat?" snorted the bald-headed boarder.

"Rice, sir, rice—boiled well in water. Nature planted the food by the disease. It came from the rice swamps of India, and nothing saved the millions that survived but the rice. It is nutritive, and of easy digestion."

"Well, I believe I'd rather have the cholera. Another sausage, madam," said the bald-headed boarder, firmly.

"Go on, sir, go on. That is what the grocer Green did, round the corner, sir. Eat heartily of sausage and tripe at breakfast. Went to his grocery. An hour after boy came in to purchase six cents worth of cheese. Could not see the grocer—store empty of grocer. Boy stole raisins, candy, ginger snaps and things. At last boy climbed on counter and looked over. There, sir, lay the grocer Green—dead, sir, dead in four hours, as you will be if you eat more of that sausage."

The bald-headed man did die that day—of apoplexy. Our doctor said he did it purposely, that he might give the lie to his prophecy.

After breakfast the doctor would stalk down town, paper in hand, and to each acquaintance met on the way he would foretell an increase of the pestilence, until his pathway could be traced by the wild and scared faces he left behind.

The mortality among the doctor's patients, friends, and especially at our boarding house, was frightful. That the animated gloom survived only shows the mysterious ways of divine providence.

## The Shaw in London.

It is the policy of the English government to fetch barbarian princes to London as we cart Indians over a continent to Washington, that they may be awed by the power of the people that has conquered them. While the captured potentates are in the daze consequent on strange sights and strong liquors, treaties are made highly advantageous to the civilized party, of the first part, and damaging to the untutored party, of the second part.

I doubt whether this policy is of much avail to the governments practicing it. As we descend the scale of intelligence, we find a corresponding ascent in cunning. In the end, civilized diplomacy finds itself outwitted in the most humiliating way. The savages wined and dined—escorted to and fro, like "Brer Rabit's tah-baby, say nothin," but they have their own views all the same, and take in all the good things with a pretty clear conclusion as to the purpose, that is not complimentary to the entertainment.

Said a chief once, at Washington, "Great father, big chief, much fighters, big guns, way out—no good then—whip 'em all time."

When General Manypenny, of Ohio, was Indian

commissioner he had the strange belief that Indians were human beings, and sought to civilize them through cooking stoves and kind treatment. He was defeated by border ruffians. The borders are made up of criminals escaping conviction and convicts escaping punishment. They steal from the Indians to sell to the whites, and from the whites to sell to the Indians. When they trade their medium of exchange is bad whisky, that does not make a man drunk, it makes him insane.

I remember Mannypenny brought on a delegation of Indians from the then far West. They were guileless children of the plains. The first tunnel they were plunged in on the Baltimore and Ohio Railroad, they drew their knives and uttered the most fearful yells. On emerging into daylight, the women on the train were observed clasping with both hands their back hair with an expression of mingled fear and resolution comical to contemplate.

At Washington they were quartered in a hotel. The day after the proprietor of that ornate indigestion remonstrated. He told the commissioner that those Indians were beasts, and never left their rooms save for the purpose of running down the chambermaids, and robbing them of their false hair, and otherwise abusing those foolish virgins.

The commissioner repaired to the hotel, and

gave the heads of the nation, through their interpreter, a long, solemn discourse on the usages of civilized society at that hotel.

The next day the wards got drunk and threw the servants, male and female, from the front windows. Fortunately, the awnings below saved the poor creatures from severe harm. Brown called in the police, rallied his boarders, and drove the children of the plains to the street. The commissioner gathered the delegation together, and quartered them in boarding houses.

The Indians were at first delighted with their quarters, but soon learned that a Washington boarding house was a portion of that punishment awarded the wicked hereafter. Mrs. Surratt was hanged by a court martial for keeping a Washington boarding house. At least I never could find on what else the poor woman was convicted.

The day came when these wards were to take leave of their great father, and depart for their home upon the plains. They were all ill, and walked with difficulty into the presence of the president. The usual speeches were made, and the Indians lingered. It was evident they had more to say. The interpreter shook his head at them. He positively declined to say it. At last a chief stepped forward, pointing majestically to the president, and then with scorn at the commission, said:

"Big father, little father, be dam."

Then, with a deep grunt of satisfaction, they all moved off.

I happened at London when that ignorant, brutal, vulgar barbarian, the Shah of Persia, was being ovated by designing English politicians and their snobbish followers. I did not take much interest in the Persian fellow. The polygamous potentate of Persia was to all save England, that had designs on him and his provinces, a very limited production of far less interest to me than Private Dalzell, Eli Perkins, or Ward and Grant. I, however, heard some stories about the clubs that were somewhat amusing.

I learned that all the precious jewels with which his royal person was covered, were false stones bought of the house of bondage, run by Moses & Sons, pawnbrokers.

The most entertaining, however, was a story of how His Royal Scorbutic Majesty fell in love with the ballet of the opera. He loved all the ballet, for the heart of your Persian monarch is a sort of an omnibus, and always has room for a few more. After each performance this son of the sun and brother of the moon, would pace to and fro rubbing his royal hands, and between Persian cries of delight, call all his divinities to witness, that he had never seen such ravishing forms—the art of manufacturing legs for public exhibition had not yet reached Persia —nor such rapturous jumping. He sent his prime minister and barber, with a proposition to the ballet. It was to add the entire corps to his seraglio. The gay young troop treated the proposition with contempt. Why, each one had a little seraglio of her own, and, besides, they all were under contract with their manager, and there would be the mischief to pay if that were broken; for each member believed, in her terpsichorean heart, that she was the bright particular star of the troupe, and anon jealous conspiracies would give way and she beam out as a star.

One little girl, however, and the brightest of all, lent a willing ear to the proposal. Her real name was Susan Powers, but she wrote it Susette Violanti. This little blonde drove a contract with the tonsorial minister to the effect that his master was to deposit £5,000 in the Bank of London to her account, and added several stipulations such as suggest themselves to the common ballet mind. The preliminaries being complete, the ballet dancer was summoned to appear before the Persian monarch, at the palatial residence assigned him by the British government, when it appeared that this honored guest from the land of poetry and dreams wished to be entertained in his hours of retirement by a dance.

"But, your Majesty," cried Susette, "I can not dance without music."

"Music!" responded the royal animated show-case of paste diamond. "Music, of course not, go at once and get some music."

The officious official rushed to the street and captured an astonished hand-organ and monkey.

"That is not music, your Majesty," laughed Susette, merrily, "that is a dreadful noise."

"Noise!" asked the royal brother of the moon and light of all Persia, "what's the difference?"

Susette explained. She wanted certain instruments, an orchestra, in a word, and immediately some of his majesty's suite were detailed as such, and while the instruments were being procured, the possessor of fifty paste Koh-i-noors smoked and mused upon the strange results of western civilization as developed in legs and motion.

When the instruments and improvised musicians were brought together, and the order given to play, the noise was more horrible than the hand organ. Little Susette struck her delicate fingers in her delicate ears and screamed. The beguiled Shah was more puzzled than before, and when told that his subjects could not produce the required music, he

made a few remarks of a personal nature in his native
tongue, that caused even the swarthy faces of his
faithful followers to pale. He adjourned the performance for a prize-fight, gotten up for his entertainment between a noted peer of the realm and a
noted prize-fighter. The alarmed vizier consulted
Susette.

"What can I do?" he cried in despair. "His
Majesty threatens to bow-string us all."

"Send for our director," said Susette, "He'll hammer the noise out of those fellows if you pay him
enough."

The director was sent for. All musical directors
have dirty nails, take snuff, and are ill-tempered.
Between pinches, this potentate of the opera studied
the situation.

"I can furnish His Majesty with a very good orchestra of my own," he said.

"But will they go to Persia?"

"They will go to the devil, if you pay them."

"And be his subjects, liable to the bow-string?"

"Certainly, with a liberal allowance of beer and
tobacco."

"But His Majesty has given his order, He does not
permit his orders to be questioned or changed."

The director took huge pinches of snuff. He
could not solve the difficulty.

"Musicians," he said, "are not made; they are born. Adam, a man, was created in one day; a first violin is the result of many generations. His Majesty's orders are impossible."

"Perhaps so," replied the poor vizier; "that is our system of government. The Shah is born to a right to try the impossible, we are born to suffer from the failure. You can have your own price for the effort, and my head if you fail."

A compromise was agreed on. The director was to furnish musicians of his own while instructing the barbarians.

"Can I wallop them?" he asked.

"Undoubtedly."

"That is something. It won't help on the music, but it will relieve my feelings!"

The music was procured and the sovereign of Persia made happy in a little ballet of his own. The orchestra to be gotten up out of Persians, as the director prophesied, did not prosper. By the time the Shah reached Paris, the first and second violins had disappeared. They were subsequently arrested by the police of London, striving to make a precarious living as musicians, and sentenced to hard labor as nuisances. The trombone committed suicide, while the bass viol and clarionet were in a hopeless state of idiocy. The drum alone remained of a sound mind and sound execution. But one can't have an orchestra out of a drum, and so the attempt was abandoned. The regular orchestra performers, however, were happy, content, and quite willing to go to Persia or the devil, as the director had said, upon reasonable pay and unlimited tobacco and beer.

Susette grew in favor, and, without doubt, Persia would have had an English queen but for the unhappy fact that at Paris the Shah succeeded in adding two French performers to his troupe.

In the first performance thereafter, Susette saw, or thought she saw, her eastern master bestowing too much favor on the newcomers, who really threw their shapely legs—I beg pardon, limbs—much higher than she, and, stung by jealous wrath, the plucky little Susette planted a succession of right and left blows, and sundry kicks on the persons of her rivals that were more vigorous than graceful. The French rallied and a general engagement came off.

For awhile the Shah labored under the delusion that this was part of the ballet, and enjoyed it hugely, but when he saw that two-thirds of his troupe had black eyes and bloody noses, while Susette's lovely countenance resembled a colored railroad map of England, the truth dawned on his eastern intellect that he was being treated to a revolt of the harem, and calling in his eunuchs, he immediately ordered the bow-string for the entire troupe. It called out the full force of European diplomacy to save the politest capital of the civilized world the scandal of such an execution. It put an end, however, to the Shah's private ballet.

What a shame that these writers of comic opera should cudgel their dull brains for plots when such a charming story as this exists in fact.

## Our Inventive Cranks.

Who has not met, at unpleasant frequency in life, a pale, slender, sunken-eyed and seedy man, who invents? Who is there has not wished himself dead, or the inventor in hades, on such occasions?

Conquering a continent with a scarcity of laborers has developed our ingenuity to a point of insanity. Our patent office at Washington is packed with devices of stranded cunning. The law of our being holds good, and for one success we have a thousand failures.

The late war was fought to a successful conclusion, not alone by bayonets and artillery, but by agricultural implements, that enabled the North to produce all upon which we lived at home, while it sustained a million of men at the front and another million swindling the government in the rear.

We look about us and find ourselves hedged in by inventions. The revolving chair I sit in, the table I write at, the portable book-stand, the pen, the ink, the paper, in a word, every article I use comes from the brain of invention, and is stamped as patented by the government.

Yesterday my dentist inserted a buzz saw in my

grinder and, working a treadle with his right foot, made me wish I were dead.

" Where, in the name of Satan, did you get that instrument of torture?" I cried, with my few remaining teeth on edge, and my poor nerves tingling in anguish.

"It was invented by a farmer to shear sheep," he responded, " and failing at that was picked up by a dentist."

The sheep escaped, to have the torture bestowed on less fortunate humanity.

I witnessed once a farce at the Palais Royal, Paris, when the fun turned on an exhibit of inventions, rejected by the Imperial Commission selected to pass upon machines, offered the grand international exhibition. I remember one instrument, designed to open oysters, that filled the entire stage with its complicated cog-wheels and levers. Another was called Chastity's belt, and consisted of concealed daggers about the waist of the unprotected female, that flew out like a *cheval de frise* on touching a spring.

" Very ingenious, indeed," said an old spectator, " but I would like to know who controls the spring. Monsieur, my wife might spring it on me."

This was taken as a most reasonable objection by the audience that broke into a roar of laughter and applause.

It was about that time that an old American crank appeared at Paris, by the name of Thompson, who proposed to make every article of furniture in a ship, life preserving, in case of wreck. His greatest invention was a life preserver in the shape of a stool. The male passenger was to strap this stool to that part of his person where the legs end and the body begins. Each stool was warranted to float one hundred and eighty pounds, so that when the ship went down the voyager would float out to sea in a sitting position. The female was to be supplied with an India-rubber air-tight bustle that would serve the same floating purpose.

Thompson caught the emperor at Charburg going through a view of the French fleets, and with a life-preserving stool strapped to his inventive person—Thompson I mean, not the emperor—jumped overboard in a rough sea.

Little Louis was prejudiced in favor of life-preservers at the time, and he presented the indomitable Thompson with a snuff box adorned with little Louis' intellectual countenance, set in diamonds. Thompson, of the life-stool, went to taking snuff, and, it is to be hoped, shortened his inventive life in that way.

The most amusing instance, however, that came to my knowledge was in the shape of a Yankee pos-

22

sessed of a sewing machine, then just invented. He managed, as a Yankee will, to get an interview with the Emperor, and told that imperial sham that he could teach him in ten minutes to make a pair of pantaloons in twenty minutes.

The cost of a French soldier had been reduced to five sous a day. If each soldier could be taught to make his own breeches, the cost would be yet further reduced. The Emperor tried his hand at breeches-making, and succeeded. The Yankee sold his patent for a good round sum in cash, and was far at sea when the war department of France discovered that the nether garment, made in twenty minutes, lasted about ten. The knot subsequently invented, was then unknown. A break in the thread raveled the seam.

It was after the Emperor had been taught by experience to regard Yankee ingenuity in its true light that an inventor appeared at Paris on his way to St. Petersburg. He had discovered the process of rifling cannon and applying to heavy ordnance the principle of the minnie-ball. Armed with letters from the Russian minister, at Washington, he was on his way to St. Petersburg to offer the Russian government the use of his invention. He was bearer of dispatches from our State Department, and, as secretary of legation, I helped him on.

The Crimean war, however, was in progress, and travel to St. Petersburg was dangerous and troublesome. Our inventor grew discouraged and returned to Paris. With that impartiality peculiar to our people, he concluded that French money was as good as Russian, and wished to offer his invention to France. I told him the Emperor, through sad experience, had come to be rather shy of Yankee inventors. My friend persisted. An idea struck me. I said: "Return to your lodgings, take out your invention and fire it up the chimney, especially at midnight."

The good fellow, without seeing my object, did as I directed, and in twenty-four hours was arrested as a conspirator and thrown into prison. I hastened to the Minister of Foreign Affairs. I told him that an ingenious American, who had discovered the art of applying to artillery the principle of the minnie-projectile, and on his way to St. Petersburg under endorsement from the Russian minister, at Washington, to offer his great invention to the Czar, had been arrested as a conspirator.

The minister was extremely interested. I had not only an order for the immediate release of my countryman, but in twenty-four hours a commission of experts to test the invention. I shall believe to my dying day that the French fellows stole Roosould's invention for the better improvement of artillery.

Be that as it may, Roosould has himself to blame. He could not be induced to stick to his great invention. He had a thousand. His busy brain teemed with a million. The one important commission that never reported, but as I believed used the discovery, was followed by half a dozen others on all sorts of projects.

One of these, and quite entertaining, was a repeater, in the shape of a musket, that was to carry forty loads, one on the top of the other. The soldier in the quiet of his camp, was to load his musket for the next action. The first charge exploded, fired the next, and so down to the last.

The report on this made solemnly by the commission, gave me a laugh of an hour's duration by the clock. It was to the effect that while the invention was extremely ingenious, and at first sight seemed valuable, a little reflection led to the conclusion that the proposed repeater was impracticable. At long range, for instance, it would have short charges. As the distance lessened, the range would grow long. Again were a soldier, armed with this repeater, to be wounded or killed, his musket would continue discharging, and probably with injurious effect to his own comrades. In case of a panic, where arms were thrown away by flying troops, their flight would be hastened or ended by bullets from their own muskets.

It is scarcely necessary to say that the repeater was not adopted by the French government.

The report, made in dead earnest, reminded me of Squibobs, our first humorist, on the effort made to create a flying artillery, by strapping mountain howitzers to the backs of mules. There was no question, the report said, that in the celerity of movement great progress had been obtained. The practical advantage gained, however, in action was not so clear. The natural disposition of the mule to kick rendered loading extremely difficult and accuracy of aim quite impossible.

Again, while it was quite natural for a mule to turn his rump to the enemy, it was impossible to make the animal comprehend on which side the enemy was.

In the only action had, the lieutenant continued, in which the experiment had been tried, the firing was very promiscuous, both as to time and aim, the mountain howitzers being sowed in a disorderly manner, shooting into their own forces as much as at the foe. While the enemy fled, in much disorder, some twenty miles, the lieutenant's force could never be found again. It was his grave conclusion that it had been kicked to pieces by the mule and mounted howitzers.

My mind has been turned in this direction by the experience of a guest—a most ingenious gentleman, of an inventive turn, who came to pass some weeks with with me at Mac-o-chee. He came loaded down with inventions gotten up more for his personal comfort than with an idea of profit.

Among these was "Walcutt's patent bed cooler and mosquito guard," which consisted of a huge fan suspended above the bed, so worked by cunning machinery that the weight of the occupant kept it moving for ten hours. As we are without mosquitos at Mac-o-chee and the nights are so cool that we sleep under blankts, I told him that it was scarcely necessary to set up his invaluable invention.

He persisted, and at the dead hour of midnight the household was startled by a crash, followed by yells such as have not been heard since the Indians left.

These awful noises came from my inventive guest's apartment, and seizing a light and a revolver I hastened thither. I found the door locked, and as the frightful noise continued I threw myself against it, breaking it open, and was met by a volley from a revolver that knocked the candle from my hand and sent bullets whizzing by me. Believing that burglars, bent on murder, were within I emptied my revolver promiscuously in the dark, and that had the effect of redoubling the cries.

Our guests arrived with lights and we found no burglars about, but our friend on the bed under a mass of ruins. It seems that he had been startled from a dream of murder, and rising confused had been hit by his fan, and blindly resisting the blow, had gone into a general engagement with his own machinery. The revolver I had encountered was another ingenious contrivance, fastened to the door to repel burglars.

My friend is altogether in a bad way, with a broken arm, black eyes, and bruised shins, while I and my other guests have an able-bodied and pious clergyman returning thanks for our escape from immediate death.

### Prorogation of Parliament.

We put ourselves under the diplomatic shadow of our minister to witness the process by which Her Gracious Majesty the Queen can rid herself and the country of her Parliament and enjoy her little estate at Osborne, her brown stout and stout Brown in peace. Since, dead is Brown, but to memory dear. We had no idea that this proroguing was such a troublesome, tedious business. It bothers Her Gracious Majesty and old Gladstone, now in feeble political and physical strength, to get clear of their Parliament. The prorogue has to be sent by special messenger from Osborne, Isle of Wight, where the Queen, aided by her constitutional advisers, makes it some days in advance. Whether it is baked, fried or boiled I do not know. From the way it is spoken of by the press I am inclined to think it is hatched. The journals say the council sat upon it. Be that as it may, it is exceedingly slow and tiresome.

We prorogue things in the States with more ease. We all know that when the hour approaches for our representatives to return to their constituents things grow more lively and rapid than ever. The only part our chief executive takes in proroguing is to approve all the steals the last house gives birth to.

When Henry Clay prorogued James K. Polk, he merely shook his long finger at the little speaker and thundered out: " Go home, —— —— you, where you belong." It was not necessary to use in the prorogation of James K. such strong language, but the Kentucky statesman was a very profane man. I am pained to write it, but Henry made use of a great many bad words that had better be forgotten. But he did prorogue James K. in that abrupt manner, and it seemed to serve the purpose. J. K. went home.

We accompanied our envoy extraordinary to the House of Lords, and arrived there about 1 P. M. It was proposed to prorogue at 2 P. M. We could scarcely call it a good day for peers, for not one could be discovered on the benches below, nor when the Commons appeared at the bar to be dismissed for the holidays did over half a dozen respond to the summons. This formal matter is evidently not treated with much respect.

The spectators were mainly made up of General Schenck's little crowd. But spectators are not encouraged, as I have noted before. One American lady, the brilliant pen-driver, Mrs. Barnard, arriving too late for the shadowing protection of the diplomatic wing, was arrested at every entrance. Nothing

23

but her cool perseverance and General Schenck's popularity with the ministry enabled her to win her away to the charmed interior. As it was, her approaches were slow and tiresome, and she met retiring, evidently baffled and disappointed, titled English ladies who were accustomed, in all human probability, to go where they pleased at all other times.

There was evidence of a hitch somewhere. We sat patiently for the prorogue to make its appearance four weary hours. In the meantime all sorts of rumors were afloat. One said the original prorogue had been lost in the channel while crossing over, and Her Gracious Majesty the Queen had to make another. Then it was asserted that a railroad collision had occurred, and that the prorogue was under no end of smashed-up trains, with three hundred volunteers digging it out. Another rumor had it that Her Gracious Majesty, after consultations with John Brown, had positively refused a prorogue, and the ministry were on their official knees begging the old lady to let them rest a while.

In the meantime, at intervals, a gentleman in knee-breeches and a sword would hurry into the vacant hall below, perspire freely, and then hurry out. One of these looked in the corners and under the seats, as if some peer had dropped his prayer-book. Justice Miller corrected this by saying that an Englishman's prayer-book was the book of "The Peerage," and that it could not be dropped. General Schenck suggested that probably he was looking for the prorogue. Two hours went by without any demonstration, and weary hours they were. Waiting for dinner when one is hungry tries the patience and the stomach. Waiting in a dreary station for a late train will make one wish he were dead. But neither of these trials compare to that of a small party of restless Americans deprived of their tobacco and denied the exquisite privilege of putting their republican feet above their republican heads, with short intermissions for refreshments in the way of mixed drinks, while waiting for a worn-out ceremony of an effete despotism. We could not even talk politics. The State Department in Washington has but one instruction to its diplomatic agents in Europe, and that is to keep the eagle caged.

"Oh! look here, General," cried one of our party, "I've only twenty-four hours to do London. Can't you hurry this thing up a little? I haven't seen the Tower yet."

"My Christian friend," responded the minister, "my right to hurry up the British lion might be questioned."

"I wish somebody would twist his royal old tail,"

sighed the impatient citizen. "I want to see the Tower and the waxworks."

"But, General," asked a fair lady, "suppose the prorogue does n't come, what then?"

"A mutton-chop and a glass of ale," responded our minister.

At last a gentleman in robes, accompanied by a gentleman without robes, entered the deserted house, and Robes, taking up a huge card, proceeded to read, with the singsong chant peculiar to "Luds" when engaged in this sort of thing. It took old Robes some time to get through with this. When he ended, the other man, without robes, threw himself in a kneeling position into a chair and continued the chant without a card. His position indicated prayer, but the way he clung to his hat and cast uneasy glances to one side, as if in search of his umbrella, proved that his thoughts did not elevate to any extent. Ending this prayer old Robes cracked a joke, at which both laughed heartily as they passed out.

Then we had nearly two more hours of patient waiting. General Schenck, requesting two of his stoutest friends to awaken him when the prorogue arrived, dropped into a gentle diplomatic slumber that lasted until a slight disturbance below indicated the coming event. Six peers of the realm, clad in robes and ermine, with their aristocratic intellects covered with beehives and surmounted by cocked hats, marched in. Accompanying them came also four clerks in knee-breeches and beehives.

Also at the same time and place appeared divers and sundry articles of bedroom and kitchen furniture, such as a crimson pillow and a gilt poker, and other things said to indicate something that had been buried in Westminster so many hundred years ago that no one is certain to what they all amount. Our minister informed us that the bills that had not yet received the sanction of Her Majestic Majesty were to be approved. And the manner of the approval was for a clerk to bob up and read the title, then four clerks bobbed up and bowed, then one of the six commissioners said, solemnly :

" Qui vi qua vi stouc a lum navi buck."

" What's that, General?" queried one of our party.

"Old Norman French," replied the Minister, promptly.

" Oh !" said the questioner, much relieved.

After this interesting ceremony, that was so touching that some of our more impulsive Americans shed tears and wished a prorogue might be imported to America, we had the Queen's address, that was chanted by a miserable cove who seemed to have a cold in his head. Then we had more old Norman

French and a dismissal, upon which all ran out—the "all" meaning six peers and two commons—like schoolboys. So ended the impressive scene.

I have witnessed several impressive scenes in my time. I was present when Andy Johnson was sworn in as Vice-President. I once saw a hog go over the falls of Niagara; it was a frightful fall of pork. I was by when Snapp delivered his maiden speech in Congress. But all these and many others fade into insignificance before this imposing—imposing is the word—ceremony of prorogation in Parliament.

I do not wish to be impertinent, but I would humbly suggest to Her Most Gracious Majesty that if she could keep about her august person an assortment of first-class prorogues, so as to send one off at an early hour, and not to keep fellows waiting, it would altogether be pleasing, if not profitable.

## The Whig Party on its Travels.

It is generally believed that the Whig party is dead. This is a popular delusion. That it went out of active political life is very true. When the Democratic party went South for its health, the Whig party retired to the shades of private life and lived on its respectability. This is rather poor sort of living, but some people seem to thrive on that diet. The venerable surviving Whig party does. It may be seen in the person of the Hon. John B. Buntywag, at any hour after 12 M., and before 5 P. M., by any respectable individual of good family possessed of a swallow-tail and a card. Should the card have a crest the owner is all the more welcome. It is well to purchase a few of that sort. They can be had at the same price as plain ones, and when you visit the late Whig party they oil the hinges of aristocratic doors and facilitate an interview—if that is desirable. But, considering our brief existence and its uncertainties, such as ferry-boats, railroad collisions, Tammany securities, and Erie stock, one wonders at anybody wishing to know the late Whig party.

It lives in the person of the Hon. John B. Buntywag. The Hon. John B. has been in the Senate of the United States. His father was in the Senate before him. He is educating his son for the Senate, and it is proposed, so long as a male heir is furnished the line, who escapes the lunatic asylum or the refuge for hopeless imbeciles, to have a Buntywag in that honorable position. As the only qualifications necessary are the name and intense dignity, the training does not call for much expenditure of brain.

Last summer the Whig party visited various public resorts. It could be encountered at any fashionable watering place. It was noted for its dignity and reserve. It was always uneasy lest some low fellow, male or female, would speak to it. Were any such to address this family it would immediately fall from its high estate, and be lost forever. The consequences were that the Buntywag family, anticipating such ruin, was continually on the defensive. In the morning, the patriarch would put on, with his clean linen, an additional coat of dignity. He would starch up as it were, and, marching at the head of his little force, descend with great caution to the breakfast room. Every move indicated an apprehension that the enemy might rush out from around a corner and suddenly speak to some one of the family. This was provided for. This was guarded against. If any low wretch dared attempt such an outrage the family was prepared to annihilate the vile creature.

Some envious people insinuate that the progenitors of the Buntywags were soap-boilers. This is not
so. The Buntywags never had sense enough to be
soap-boilers. The great progenitor of the illustrious
Buntywags was a casualty. He was an undertaker—
hence the dignified training of the family. He fell
heir to a man who, dying of the small-pox, cut off his
family and left his means to his undertaker. Old
Buntywag invested in real estate. The real estate
went up, carrying with it the family. This is the
whole story—and not a very entertaining one—but illustrative.

The present family of Buntywags is timid. The
Whig party always was timid. When the slavery
agitation came on, the Whig party deprecated it, and
said the agitators were low fellows, and ought to be
discountenanced. If they were properly discountenanced the agitation would cease. The old Whig
scow resembled the venerable gentleman, who, going
on ship-board, put on his nightcap and retired to his
berth. When the storm came, he sent word to the
captain to stop that hollowing, as he could not sleep,
and for heaven's sake keep the sailors from running
about the deck, as they shook the boat so it made
him sick.

Mr. John B. Buntywag and family were traveling for pleasure. A more unhappy set were never

caught abroad. Fear, we are told, is contagious.
Mr. Buntywag took the disorder and gave it to his
family. They could not sit comfortably in the cars
for fear of collisions. They drank bad brandy and
starved themselves into hideous headaches from fear
of cholera that was three thousand miles away. On
steamboats Mr. Buntywag and his interesting family
slept in their clothes, twisted through their life-preservers, each for fear of explosions. Mr. Buntywag,
once a gentleman of weight, was losing flesh every
two minutes, his good wife had screamed herself into
the bronchitis, and his two admirable daughters were
all the while looking around for something to be
frightened at.

Mr. Buntywag was distinguished in his appearance. Somewhat short in stature, he was, as I intimated, corpulent. He indulged in white waistcoats,
and many-colored handkerchiefs, that tied tight
around his neck, with a very red face above, with
pop-eyes, gave out an idea that he was indulging in
a very genteel mode of suffocation, or every man his
own gallows. Mrs. Buntywag was a delicate lady of
refined sensibilities. The two daughters were promising girls—promising I say, for as yet they presented
the appearance of only two very fine frames—having
shot into womanhood without waiting for the under-
pinning, framing, or plaster.

The party arrived at Niagara one warm July morning, Mr. Buntywag seeing nothing but thieves and pickpockets around him, and death and destruction ahead.

Our hero issued from the Cataract House in state —the neckcloth tied tighter than ever; the two daughters marched before, he had his wife under one arm, a good stick under the other. With the husband-at-common-law, the wife and stick always go together, at least they do in Blackstone. Mr. Buntywag is an old-fashioned husband-at-common-law, had his eyes about him, and saw on the railroad before the hotel, a huge blue box, to which were attached two horses, while a man stood on one side and blew a horn. Between every blast he sang out, "To Suspension Bridge, Maid of the Mist, the famous whirlpool, Brock's monument, and other natural curiosities —all for one dollar!" Our friend did not understand, but he guessed it was to go somewhere. The thing looked safe, and Mr. Buntywag seated his family and himself, and the nuisance—I mean the box—was pulled away.

After a short ride the party were brought in sight of the Suspension Bridge, that like a net scarf was flung over the great gulf below. Mr. B. prepared to cross—the two daughters walked before—he had the wife under one arm, and the stick under the other. At the moment Buntywag and family invaded the bridge, a large number were promenading to and fro, and a hack, with an old lady known by the name of Mrs. Swansdown, was slowly wending its way toward the Canada side.

The sublime view broke on Mr. Buntywag's sight, and he became alarmed. He looked 'way down, down into the depths where the blue waters were boiling and tossing like millions of angry devils. What a narrow passage—what thin threads held them up two hundred and fifty feet above death!

His heart throbbed—his brain became confused. He quickened his steps—he poked his daughters with his stick—then pushed on. The walk turned to a run. With a short shout, now frantic with fear, he pulled his wife along, and poked and beat his daughters, who screamed terribly. The visitors seeing and hearing this awful uproar became alarmed. They thought the bridge was falling, and fled amain. The women screamed, and the men shouted. The hack driver, startled by this uproar in his rear, whipped his horses into a gallop, shaking the bridge and adding to the terror—after he had knocked over a deaf old gent, who was silently drinking in the beauties of nature. Mr. Buntywag and family made good time— they did seven hundred and fifty feet in an incredibly short space of time; but the crowd had the start, and they rushed out upon the Canada side, much confused, and greatly frightened.

The old gent was picked up considerably damaged, and carried into the Elgin House. The crowd was indignant, and would have pitched the respected Mr. Buntywag over the bridge, had not Mrs. Swansdown created—as she was in the habit of doing—a diversion. Attempting to get out of the hack window, she stuck fast, and half in and half out, she screamed dismally. The crowd laughed and Mr. Buntywag escaped.

At Niagara, people are rushed about. There is no place on the face of the earth where so much walking is done. You climb up, and you scramble down—you are dampened at this point, and drenched at that. You cross over and walk, you return and walk; and, by a wise arrangement, by which you are got along, your pockets are lightened at every step. There is a tradition extant to the effect that when the Wandering Jew visited Niagara he was whipped by a hackman, and so cheated and ill-treated that he made sixteen attempts at suicide by leaping over the falls with a copy of Bancroft's United States tied to his neck.

Two days after the stampede on the suspension bridge, Mr. Buntywag and party—for he now had Mrs. Swansdown under the protection of his paternal

stick—might have been seen picking their way under
Goat Island Cliff, on their road to the Cave of the
Winds. Custom had imparted some confidence to
Mr. Buntywag, and he bravely led the van. But
when, turning a corner, he came in full view of the
American Falls—that came down at this place like a
river of brickbats, shivering into a million of frag-
ments on the iron rocks with a roar like fifty thous-
and wheelbarrows on a bowlder pavement—Mr.
Buntywag called a halt, and shook in his boots.

At the extreme termination of the path on which
they stood, a ledge of rocks projected almost into the
Falls, in fact, upon a portion of them the water fell,
and was dashed into silvery spray from their slippery
surface. These rocks have a few feet of even surface,
and upon it, at the moment the Buntywag party
came in sight, a young lady, of slight and delicate
form, stood alone. Her bonnet was thrown back—
her black hair falling in confusion about her neck,
her beautifully chiseled face turned upward, with an
expression of childish delight—and with her hands
clasped, she stood an exquisite figure of life sculptur-
ing; not that she looked too spiritual in the midst of
the awful war of elements. With her face to the
Falls, at her side the Cave of the Winds kept up its
eternal din—for the winds, forced by the flood into
the Cave, gathered power every few minutes, and

broke from their imprisonment with a shout like thunder. In a moment she stepped lightly upon the path, and taking the arm of a gentleman who seemed much amused at this specimen of childish daring, they walked away.

A notion of immense bravery entered the soul of Buntywag. He seized Mrs. Swansdown's arm, and ere the old lady was aware, had pushed her to the ledge of rocks, where our little heroine had so lately stood. His huge stick contained an umbrella in disguise—unscrewing the top, he drew out the shade, and hoisted it above their heads. But the fates that tumbled over the Falls were against Buntywag. A gust of wind seized a fold of the "snowy drapery," and flung it over the devoted couple. The frail umbrella was beaten down—the water came in torrents—and Mrs. Swansdown, thinking the last day had surely arrived per telegraph, threw her arms convulsively around Buntywag, and fell upon him. Buntywag, who had his hat beaten down over his eyes, when the old lady came upon him, gave up, his knees failed, and the unhappy couple fell to the earth. Still grasping the broken umbrella, our hero looked very like a drunken Neptune trying to shield from the rain a corpulent Naiad. It was scandalous.

Two men from the neighboring lodge rushed forward, and, seizing the unfortunates, dragged them over the rocks into the path. Mrs. Swansdown opened her eyes, and exclaimed, with much indignation : "Drat that man, he'll suffocate me yet."

The lady I have described, while standing near the Cave of the Winds, with her companion, had ascended the hundred feet of the Biddle stairs, and now sat resting upon the bench at the top. They were looking upon the little "Maid of the Mist," that rolled upon the boiling cauldron below, when a fearful shriek smote upon their ears. Then another and another, with shouts and groans, and the stairs shook as if they were being wrenched from their foundation. A crowd was surely rushing up the spiral stair. The first that emerged was a fat, old gentleman—he bounded up the stairs like a crazy elephant. The next was an elderly maiden lady, with note-book ; she bid fair to overtake the fat gent, and bets two to one might have been safely offered. The next were five young ladies, with two beaux, who lead the way and shrieked the loudest. These were followed by a dandy, in undress uniform and huge moustache. His pace was tremendous — his leaps beyond parallel. 'T is said he never stopped, but jumping into the cars, when last heard from was on Broadway, New York. Last came Mr. Buntywag, poking his beloved family along, and all in full cry. After they had passed the astonished strangers, no more seemed on the way ;

but far below they heard some dismal groans. The gentleman ventured down in search of the distressed; he made some fifty steps, when he came upon poor Mrs. Swansdown, stretched out and groaning aloud. To all his questions, her only answer was, "Oh! I'm dislocated. Go for a post-mortal examiner!"

It seemed that Mr. Buntywag, on the return from his late adventure, when half way up the winding stairs—sickened with his last trouble—became dizzy with turning round so much—felt the fabric reel under him—and, frightened at the idea of its falling, gave a shout, and began with urging with his stick the party upward. Poor Mrs. Swansdown puffed along a short distance at a lively rate, when she fell exhausted, and was cruelly deserted.

## Berkeley Springs.

Berkeley Springs are three thousand, two hundred and eighty-two feet, three inches above the level of the Washington canal.

The air is so much purer that many people are deceived, thinking Berkeley about twelve thousand feet above the level of the canal; but the above is actual measurement, made on the Baltimore and Ohio railroad by the fare charged. This is high enough—Berkeley I mean, not the fare, that is too high—for all practical purposes.

The Berkeley water is a chalybeate, and tastes, as it comes from the springs, like warm dish-water. When cooled it tastes like iced dish-water, with a slight flavor of old moccasin. Its specific is rheumatism. People come here on crutches. I beg pardon, they come in a stage—over a mountain road, and pay one dollar for a ride of two miles and a half, crutches included. Transportation any where in Virginia since the late civil war is expensive. General Lee, Jubal Early, Jeb Stuart, and others, spoiled the people in this respect. The civil war was a question of transportation. It cost Virginia all her negroes, all her old families, all her Virginia pride, did this question of transportation. But I am speaking of rheumatism—that is not transportation. *Au contraire,* as the Frenchman remarked when asked if he liked the "german." Well, patients come here who are lifted from the stage and go to their rooms on crutches and cusses. In two days they dance the "german" to the music of a stringed band. So many crutches have been thrown away that all the fences about the springs are made of them.

Berkeley Springs, as a place of resort, is very popular with everybody, but the stockholders. The stockholders have come to be very wealthy, and prefer going to Long Branch, where they can contemplate the Administration. Some have gone to Europe and some have gone to—well, never mind where. But very few are seen about Berkeley. One stockholder, however, has a cottage here. It is directly in the rear of the hotel. He is a venerable man of God, of imposing appearance, and does impose on a good many. Whether he will impose on the Lord and get his title clear to a cottage in the skies is further along. I first made his acquaintance when in command as chief of staff at Baltimore, and caught him running the blockade after a wife. He wishes now that he had invested in old red sandstone instead of Berkeley.

The great attractions at Berkeley are the bathing and the band. The walks are delightfully romantic, the mountain views are superb, the mountain mutton ditto, while the table at the hotel is something astonishing for a summer resort. The beds are soft, sweet, and clean, and I don't know of any place where an old couple can get clear of their rheumatic complaints and daughters as readily as at Berkeley. There is some thing in the air—perhaps it is in the water, perhaps the mountain mutton—that inclines one and all to tenderness and proposals. Old fellows get very frisky, and go beauing about the girls in a grotesque manner, while the old ladies actually get dangerous.

The following story was told us by Jones:

"I found myself one day at Lover's Leap (a precipice overlooking the Chesapeake canal and the eastern part of the United States), with a staid, lovely girl of thirty, if a day. The sun was setting in a gorgeous canopy of cloudy upholstery at our backs, while a thousand feet below us was the railway, the canal, and the beautiful swift-flowing Potomac. Beyond these stretched the wide panorama of fields, forest, and mountain, over which the sad shadows of night were stealing and softening all, like the delicate brush of Wyant when putting his imaginative soul into a landscape. I leaned over the rocky parapet, and was about giving myself up to sublime emotions, when I felt a hand upon my shoulder. Looking up, I saw this aged female gazing on me with a certain some thing in her eyes that sent a thrill of terror through my frame.

" We were alone. There was not a soul within reach I could call upon for help. Although the oaths of boatmen on the canal, and even the voices of children came up clear and distinct, I might shout myself hoarse without attracting their attention; and if I did, they could reach us only by a circuit of five or six miles. I shrunk instinctively from that touch, while my youthful and innocent countenance first paled and then flushed with emotion.

" ' We are alone !' she exclaimed.

" ' I know it—and I am unarmed,'—I faltered.

" ' Man,' she said sternly, ' what has that to do with it ? Why talk of arm save the arms of bounteous nature in a scene like this ? Is not your heart softened and your disposition made tender by these surroundings ?'

" ' They are not. Oh, madam—venerable female, spare me ! We are alone. I trusted you. I gave my youthful innocence trustingly to your honor '—

" ' Fool !' she cried, approaching me.

" I sprang in terror to the outer ledge of the dizzy rocks. It would be terrible for me, weighing one hundred and eighty-four, to cast myself from that fearful height, to fall ca-thud upon the geological specimens below, or worse, to disappear in the slimy depths of that old canal, never to be heard of again any more than if one were a mythical dividend of the company. But I was resolved. I took the attitude of the naval commander in Billy Powell's historical painting of the 'Death of Perry,' and exclaimed, 'Thanks to the hand that reared these rocks so high that none may fall from them and live! Advance one step, false maiden, and I die!'

"Alas! there was no pity in her face. I felt my doom—by Jove! I made up my mind on the instant to give Lover's Leap a new name, when I heard a noise that resembled a locomotive on an up grade, or a steam-tug hooked to a seventy-four. It came nearer and nearer. It sounded louder and louder. At last I saw the head and rotund form of Judge Wright come puffing above the summit of the moutain, and screaming, 'Saved! saved!' I rushed at him, seized him in my arms with such violence that he lost his footing and we both went rolling down the declivity, fetching up in a fence-corner on an old sow that was there reposing, and springing up. went off at a canter snorting out 'Woof! woof!' as if crazy."

This was Jones' story, but Jones is not altogether reliable. He has been so spoiled by being followed, flattered, sought, and sued by the women here—being the one solitary beau—that he can not get his heels to the ground, or tell the truth, if he tries.

And this calls my attention to the singular scarcity of this article. We have no end of women and children in Berkeley. Women and children abound. The number of pretty girls, done up regardless of expense, who go tripping about in high-heeled boots, heels directly under the soles, realize the famous description in the Ethiopian melody addressed to Daniel Tucker—

> "She smashed de bugs as she walked around,
> For de sole ob her foot made de hole in de ground.
> Out ob de way Old Dan Tucker."

The venerable Daniel had better cease obstructing the thoroughfare if he knows what is good for him, unless he can by some process come under the head of beau, and then the venerable Tucker is all right.

The report went out one day last week that a beau was on his way to Berkeley. He was said to be young, handsome, rich, and fascinating. The excitement was intense. The New York riots, the dreadful explosion, the last new hat, in a word, every gossipy topic, went down before the expected arrival. We had the youth discussed in groups of two or three, and groups of hundreds. Young ladies talked in their sleep, and those who were reported to know the youth personally became suddenly very popular. At last we learned that the great expected was at the depot, two miles and a half away. We were telegraphed the startling intelligence. Then, like Sheridan's famous ride, he was two miles away; then one and a half, then one, then half, and then we heard the old-fashioned stage lumbering down the mountain side. The great crowd of young ladies and old ladies, fat ladies and thin ladies, well ladies and sick ladies, gathered upon the porch, and eager eyes were fixed upon the leathern vehicle. It stopped with a bang. A gentleman sitting with the driver attempted to descend. He did so with a gay, springy way, that caused him to miss his footing, and he pitched forward into the arms of Miss ——, who weighs two hundred and fifty. The poor girl had a sigh knocked out of her that sounded like sixteen sighs rolled in one. Indeed, old Balsam, who was nodding after his bath on the back porch, thought that sigh was the steam whistle of the tan-yard.

But, alas for our beau! His hat flew off, and with it his wig, leaving the young old man bald as an egg. His teeth bounced out, and his cheeks collapsed, passing him from twenty-five to sixty. One eye followed the teeth, and the girls fled screaming. The poor old beau recaptured the teeth and the eye, inserted both, and then, straightening himself up as well as he could over rheumatism, neuralgia, old age, and gout, looked after the retreating females, and twisting his old mouth into the most querulous expression, he growled out—

" Ugh, Christ ! "

In that expired our last forlorn hope. We have never expected a new beau since.

## Our Fever for Titles.

Every free-born American citizen under the Declaration of Independence, which declares our equality before the law, is born to edit a paper, hold an office, and invent something, generally a religion. In addition to these qualities, he and she, she especially, are permeated with a desire for a title. Whether life on this earth anywhere is worth living, certainly this part under the star-spangled banner and the screaming eagle would be suicidal but for the hope of happiness found in a handle to one's name.

In response to this healthy demand, we have the country filled with majors, colonels, generals, judges, governors, and honorables.

At the end of the late civil war the rush for epaulets was wider-spread than the gallant enlistment of volunteers during the conflict, and the great war secretary, Stanton, with a cynical sense of humor peculiar to him, brevetted all the sutlers, wagon-makers, commissaries, contractors, quartermasters—in a word, every body soliciting the honor. A humorist once said he could not cast a stone in a crowd without hitting a military title. Another wag, wish-

ing to get a seat in a crowded hall, cried out,
"Colonel, you are wanted," and a hundred and fifty
hastened out.

This is our American human nature. We in-
herit the trait from our English ancestors, who with
all their heroic qualities, are born snobs. An Englishman who has braved the dangers of the deep, and
fought unmoved by fear in all the battles of the
world, will bump his head upon the floor in the presence of a lord. He can scarcely breathe in the presence of royalty. He gasps and shuts his eye when
he says, "Your Gracious Majesty." We would bump
our skulls and gasp, had we a chance. When any
scion of a royal family visits our shores, our men
lose their heads, and our women go mad. We have
seen a roomful of the last-named with their sight
glued, as it were, to a prince, and they seemed to be
tasting him in their mouths.

When our laborers combine to look after interests, they call themselves "Knights of Labor." "The
Sons of Toil" would be more appropriate and influential. But the word *knight* has a high, toney sound,
although it was held by the meanest sneaks and cut-
throats of Europe. Knights of Labor indeed!
Much the original pests labored! They sought to
live on the labor of others, and were not nice as to

how they accomplished that comfortable result—generally by violence, and always through fraud.

We once saw some five thousand men parading the avenues of Washington. They went through the most complicated maneuvers. They were dressed most gorgeously, with swords and sashes, and ostrich-feathered cocked hats, and called themselves Knights of something. We thought last Knight, or Knight before last, would be more appropriate. We learned that they were all good, honest, peaceable citizens, mostly tailors, hatters, and shoemakers, who were banded together for benevolent purposes. But why Knights? Why not Good Samaritans or Brothers-in-law? The word *knight*, however, sounded so grand. It was such comfort to be called "Sir Knight." Think of a retail dealer in allspice, pepper, salt, and soap, in a little shop which a stout man could run a stick through, shoulder up, and march off with, being got up in ostrich-plumes, cocked hat, sword and sash, and being addressed as "Sir Knight!" The honest citizen of the grocery would be amazed to know that he had taken on himself the form of a swashbuckler and public nuisance. Knights, indeed! But "men are children of a larger growth."

There is much in a name. One of the most effective and powerful organizations in the United States is the " Brotherhood of Engineers," and it owes much to its title, for it indicates intelligence and a purpose.

Our official titles in the civil service are more indicative of snobbery than aught else. The honorable has come to be the last resort of ambitious imbecility in that direction. A man who serves three days in any official capacity in the legislature is an honorable for the remainder of his life. We read in a Washington journal an obituary notice of the sudden death of the Hon. Cæsar Stokes, who was killed by falling from his cart in a gravel-pit. He was a colored member of the historical feather-duster, spittoon territorial legislature of the District of Columbia.

There was once a joke that ran through the six old hulks that made our late navy, that told of letters being received aboard one of the six, of huge envelopes and heavy seals, directed to Hon. Henry Augustus Singlepit, assistant paymaster of acting paymaster John Hodge, U. S. N.

The most striking illustration of this sort of thing is to be found in our Senate at Washington. A senator carries more dignity to the square inch than any human creature on earth. This is accorded him in his commission. There was a time in the half-forgotten past when the position of senator was merely a pedestal upon which the incumbent was lifted to public notice, and held his own through his abilities.

Now the pedestals hold for us the commonest sort of men; that is all; and the airs these officials take upon themselves are to the more thoughtful simply ridiculous. They are the Sir Knights of the cocked hats, mostly men who have bought their chairs, or had them purchased by corporations seeking to run the government for their selfish ends. It makes a cultured American sink in shame to his shoes to have an intelligent foreigner brought in contact with one of these pretentious solons.

All this hankering after titles, and thefts of pedigree, with the accompanying coats of arms, are unworthy the American people. Our ancestors were good, honest, hard-working laborers, and we are asses befouling their graves when we give way to the snobbery that would deny their existence or ignore their calling. Come, now, let us confess to what we are, and take an honest pride in the brave sons of toil who conquered a continent, and gave us all a nation of which we can be proud.

## The Death Penalty.

We hang a murderer because we are in the habit of doing so. Again, we condemn him to death for that we do not know what else to do with him. Again, we sustain the death penalty from a feeling of vengeance.

These are motives, not reasons. When we appeal to reason, there is a failure in sustaining the practice. Regarding all human endeavor as fallible, it is not wise to do that which can not be undone. True, when we subject a criminal to a loss of freedom we take a part of his life which can not be restored; but if this has been done unjustly we can in a measure recompense the loss. This is not the case when the unfortunate is deprived of life. The law really does what the law condemns. It is claimed that to act otherwise is to traverse the moral sense of the community. This comes not from a sense of justice, but of vengeance. When a murder is committed, the act arouses a feeling of horror and wrath. If time were given and a delay made between the condemnation and the death by the executioner, this feeling would not only subside, but swing over to the other extreme. As it is, the custodians of the condemned find it difficult to keep out sickly sentimentalists with their gifts of flowers and tenders of sympathy.

This moral sense that sustains the death penalty originates in great measure from the clergy. It is strange, but there is no class, and never has been any class, so vindictive and cruel as the followers of the forgiving Savior. We have of record not only the religious wars, the most horrible of all human conflicts, lit up along the past by fires that consumed the helpless, but the story of the Inquisition. Our pious friends of the pulpit abandon the Gospel and fall back upon the theology of the Jews. To be consistent they should preach the full Mosaic doctrine of an eye for an eye, and a tooth for a tooth. Probably they would but that Christian civilization has given us a higher sense of justice and a keener appreciation of our Father in heaven, as taught us by the Savior.

Slowly, but steadily, we have been influenced by our common sense and better feeling to a departure from the old barbaric treatment of the condemned. Time was, and the practice yet remains in some of our newer localities, when it was thought necessary to give full effect to a hanging that it should be public. The judge, in condemning the man to death, solemnly fixed the day and hour, and the public was invited to witness the brutal spectacle. The public was not slow to respond. We learned, after a time, that instead of an awful warning it was regarded very much as a crowd looks on a bull fight, when a wretched animal is slowly tortured to death. The enjoyment of the show was stimulated to some extent by the danger attending the spectacle to the cruel performers. The crowd about the gallows jeered, laughed, sang, and generally got drunk. The criminal, if he went to his death with any composure, was regarded as a hero. Murders have been committed in the very presence of the awful example.

The clergy helped on this sort of perversion of a warning by accompanying the wretch to the scaffold with hymns and prayers and assurances of divine forgiveness. The absurdity of this seemed to strike no one. The victim of the awful crime had been cut off in his or her sins, with every prospect of eternal punishment, while the criminal was swung into heaven. This seems shocking, but is it not fact? To be logical and consistent we must regard the murderer fully forgiven, looking from heaven down upon his victim suffering eternal torture for having passed to judgment without repentance.

We have laughed at the Frenchman condemned

to death for the murder of his parents, who, when asked by the judge if he had any thing to say before sentence, responded that he hoped the court would have mercy on a poor orphan. We do not laugh, however, at the good parson who hurries forward to assist the assassin to a reward denied his victim.

The good people of New York have advanced yet another step. Choking a man to death with a rope has been justly regarded as a clumsy, barbarous practice, and the legislature has substituted death by electricity. It robs the penalty of much that is objectionable, and adds greatly to its terror. The mode prescribed by the law which gives to the judge the power to sentence, but leaves to the sheriff the precise moment when the execution shall take place, throws a dreadful mystery about the killing that will strike the common criminal with horror.

This law is to be approved, not on the ordinary ground used by supersensitive people, that it lessens the punishment, but that in fact it adds to it. We are not disturbed, however, by the pains and penalties attending the death penalty. When a criminal is to be disposed of for having murdered us, we will be quite indifferent as to the measure of his suffering, very much as he was as to ours when killing us.

In this we sympathize with the member of the French Corps-Legislatif, who, when the abolition of the death penalty was being discussed, said: " Messieurs, I am in favor of this measure, but I want the assassins to begin."

## The Dude in Literature.

The tendency to over-refinement that accompanies social life in civilized communities marks the progress of literature. As we have the Rosa Matilda in the one, we have the dude in the other. When people come to think more of the shell than the substance the shell covers, we have a condition that may be very delicate and refined, but is sure to be without strength or originality. We may in this way weaken in our vices, but at the same time we weaken in our virtues. Moralists through all the ages have dwelt upon the effeminacy that follows wealth, and in that the loss of the manly qualities that make real goodness. In this way wars are said to be ennobling, because in spite of their brutality they throw men back on the coarser strength upon which true manhood is based. A coarse soldier, if possessed of the high courage that disregards his own life, has a better chance to be a true gentleman than the civilian of the highest polish without courage; for the true gentleman is one who generously regards the rights of others. If a man has reached that point where life itself is a secondary consideration, he is better prepared to be generous in things that concern life.

All brave men are not necessarily gentlemen, for they may not have the thoughtful culture that recognizes the rights of others ; but all true gentlemen are brave. Without the manhood, this combative quality indicates selfishness intensified. The timid man is weak and selfish, for he can not escape a continuous consideration of his own safety and comfort.

It is not, however, of the effeminacy of excessive refinement in society of which we wish to treat, but that of literature. In our over-training in this direction we are losing both strength of expression and originality of thought. We seek to be excessively nice, forgetting that we may be so nice as to be nasty. The old maid who clad the legs of her furniture in pantalettes unconsciously betrayed the current of her own thoughts. The English people have added quite a number of skin-diseases to the awful list of cutaneous disorders through over-bathing. To persistently wash the natural oil from the pores is to fetch on frightful eruptions.

If one will study the current of literature as accepted by the critics, one will perceive that this excessive refinement is emasculating our works. The word " coarse " has come to be a sentence of condemnation. No poem, essay, novel, or editorial can survive that stigma. Were Dickens alive now, and entering upon his wonderful career as an author, his books would be incontinently condemned as low and coarse. A New York manager of a leading theater said that Shakespeare had ceased to be popular because of his vulgarity. Miss Murfree, in her charming stories of the Tennessee mountains, retains the mountains, but, to suit the taste of all the old maids in and out of petticoats who read the *Atlantic Monthly,* has eliminated the mountaineers. Her characters are so refined that they have ceased to be the hardy dwellers of that region, who make the air blue with their profanity in ordinary conversation. It was Leigh Hunt, we believe, who said that Thomson's " Seasons " were seasons in Thomson's back yard. The day is not distant, as infidelity and refinement progress, when the Bible itself, like Shakespeare, will be pronounced coarse and vulgar—so much so, indeed, that an expurgated edition will be necessary.

Much of this false literature comes of a study of libraries. It is building books on books; weaving second-hand thoughts out of the thoughts of others. The straw itself is thrashed over until it gets to be too fine to be straw even. The great originals gained their greatness through a study of nature and a contact with living men. It was a rough, coarse business, but the result was work we call immortal.

Emerson tells us this, in his clear, ringing sentences, when he says:

"Our age is retrospective. It builds the sepulchers of the fathers. It writes biographies, histories, and criticisms. The foregoing generations beheld God and Nature face to face; we, through their eyes. Why should not we also enjoy an original relation to the universe? Why should not we have a poetry and philosophy of insight and not of tradition, and a religion by revelation to us and not the history of theirs? Embosomed for a season in nature, whose floods of life stream round and through us, and invite us by the powers they supply to action proportioned to nature, why should we grope along among the dry bones of the past, or put the living generation into masquerade out of its faded wardrobe? The sun shines to-day also. There is more wool and flax in the fields. There are new lands, new men, new thoughts. Let us demand our own works and laws and worship."

There is nothing more fatal to the thoughtful progress of a race than to possess a master, in literature or in art. The source of greatness that made the master was in nature, not in books or pictures or statuary. The student, be he author or artist, goes out and studies nature, and renders into work his interpretation. It may be crude, coarse, and faulty, but it is original, and if such student is a genius it will be great. But, the master once possessed by a people, he is studied instead of nature. Thus it is that Italy has had no painters since the master won the admiration of the world, and England no dramatic authors since Skakespeare. Libraries and galleries are good for mediocrity. But the dim-eyed, delicate student or artist, turned out to study for himself, shrinks dismayed from a contact with the real. It soils one's hands and discourages one's efforts. Of course; but we must remember the fabled story of the demigod that in his death struggle gained strength from the earth to which he was cast. He came up dirtier, of course, but he came up stronger, and was conquered at last by being strangled in mid-air. Our authors and artists are dying through the same process, but they die with nice dignity that is very comforting to the critics.

There is a revolt against this dudism going on all the while in the minds of the many. It breaks out at intervals, and when led by genius results in victory. Victor Hugo, for example, fought and conquered the classics of France. Zola to-day, in spite of his filth, holds a great sway the world over—not, as generally supposed, because of his dirt, but that he deals with the real. Walt Whitman in the same way, with no more poetry in him than in a board fence, is held to be popularly a poet. He is not so filthy as Zola, because there is less of him, but he is real. Howells and James, both men of genius, owe their popularity to their realism, which would be yet more potent if they had not such a terror of being coarse. Dickens, we learn from Messrs. Belford, Clarke & Co., has such a popular demand to-day that it keeps them busy to fill orders, while the more refined Thackeray does not pay for the reprint.

We say then to the youthful author, Do not bother yourself about the dignity of your language or the nicety of your style. Study the common tongue; and if you have a thought to express, so word it that the masses may comprehend. You can not fight error with an open hand. Let your polish be the polish that comes from the sharpening of a weapon, and not the glitter of a uniform that means nothing. In ninety-nine instances out of a hundred to be dignified is to be dull, and dullness is death to an author.

26

## Vacant Pews and Worried Pulpits.

The homes, so called, of our larger cities are in a majority of cases without comfort, and in nearly all instances without refinement. The class upon which we once so prided ourselves, made up of families possessed of a competence, and enabled through a reasonable income from steady work to have about their homes some comfort and a few luxuries, is rapidly disappearing. We have left us two classes only, made up of the very rich and the poor. The merchant, the mechanic, and even the common laborer, who once could boast of a humble home of his own, and enough steady employment to make that home comfortable, is rarely met with. We believe, indeed, that he exists only in the imagination of Senator Edmunds. Well authenticated statistics inform us that we have a larger percentage of tenantry to our population than any people on the face of the earth. This not only includes our great commercial, mining, and manufacturing centers, but the rural regions as well. We learn that, throughout the agricultural regions, while the farms lessen in number, the farmers increase.

We know what this means. We recognize at a

glance that the growth of our country in national wealth, which is claimed to be amazing, is not a healthy growth. For that is not healthy which gives prosperity to a few and poverty to the masses.

This has been so long and so generally recognized that it has come to be commonplace, and people weary of its reiteration. We indulge in this weariness for the purpose of calling attention to a consequence that is not so familiar.

It is remarked by observant lookers-on from abroad that our laboring classes are thoroughly ignorant of art, and take no pleasure in contemplating works of art, as do the like classes in the towns of Europe. The reason given for this is that we have no specimens in our highways, and few in galleries. The latter are closed against the laboring classes on the only day a laborer can have to visit them, and that is Sunday.

The wrong done our people by this can scarcely be overestimated. A taste for art can generally be cultivated. It is quite impossible to educate a people in science and literature, for this depends on intellectual faculties that our Heavenly Father, from a wise purpose to us unknown, has been very sparing in distributing. But almost every man is capable of being taught to admire, if not love, the beautiful in art. What an element in the way of social improvement or progress this cultivated taste is we all recognize, and what happens to a race that neglects it we all know.

Now, it is possible for a people to possess the highest appreciation of, and admiration for, art, and yet be semi-barbarous, for the Christian element is necessary to bring about real civilization; but it is quite impossible for a race to be without some cultivation in the way of art, and be civilized at all.

It is not strange to a thoughtful observer, to note that as a nation we are on the down grade. Such an observer from abroad can not cross Broadway, for example, without learning that life and limb are in peril from a community that has more law and less order than any people the world over. He is prepared to learn then that our galleries of art—such as exist—are closed against the poor, and he is ready to receive without wonder the further fact that our churches also are closed against the poor.

It is this last truth that is somewhat new in the way of being recognized, although quite old as a matter of fact.

At a convocation of Protestant ministers held at Chickering Hall last November, on behalf of the Protestant community of New York, the following was officially stated as to the religious condition of the city :

" The population of New York City has for years been steadily and rapidly increasing, while at the same time the number of churches has been relatively decreasing. In 1840 there was one Protestant church to every 2,400 people; in 1880, one to 3,000; and in 1887, one to 4,000."

Now, to this startling admission could have been added another, no less deplorable, and that is that the attendance has decreased more rapidly than the churches, and, in such as now remain open a seventh part of the time, there is an exhibit of empty seats quite depressing to the minister. If we consider the Protestant population only, not one-tenth are church attendants—and not a tenth of these are true believers.

The reason for this deplorable condition was much discussed by the good men making up the clerical convention, and the prevailing opinion seemed to be, as gathered from the utterances, that this disheartening result came from the active interference of the Catholic clergy—or papists, as our friends termed them.

There was much truth in this. These zealous "papists" are certainly making great inroads upon our population; but, admitting that they take large numbers from the Protestant churches, there yet remains a vast population of non-going church people that the so-called papists have not influenced, nor, indeed, as yet approached. What then is the cause of this irreligious condition?

We believe that we can help our clerical friends to a solution of this religious mystery. It comes from a lack of consideration for the masses they seek to instruct. There is a want of sympathy for the poor, that not only shuts the galleries of art from the laboring classes, but closes the Protestant churches also.

These structures, while scarcely to be classed as works of art—for they are carefully divested of all that appeals to good taste—are yet luxurious affairs at which the rich and well-born, in purple and fine linen, are expected to attend. They are more social than religious affairs, and there is no place for the ragged, even if such appeared from a public bath duly cleansed of their offensive dirt. To make this exclusiveness complete, the churches are filled with pews that, like boxes at the opera, are the property of subscribers able to pay for such luxuries. True, certain pews are reserved as free seats for the poor; but the class sought thus to be accommodated are averse to being put in their poverty on exhibition, as it were, even for the luxury of hearing a solemn-toned clergyman whose theological gymnastics are as much beyond the comprehension of the hearer as they are beyond that of the reverend orator himself.

To realize our condition in this respect, let our reader imagine, if he can, our blessed Savior and his apostles entering bodily, to-day, one of these edifices built to His worship. Weary and travel-stained, clad in the coarsest of garments, the procession would scarcely start along the dim-lit aisles before that austere creation of nature in one of her most economical moods, the sexton, would hurry forward to repel further invasion of that most respectable sanctuary of God. Our Savior would be informed that somewhere in the outlying spaces of poverty-stricken regions there was a mission house suitable for such as He.

We must not be understood as intimating, let alone asseverating, aught against this form of Christianity. It is so much better than none that we feel kindly toward it. The religious evolution that develops a respectable sort of religious purity, that builds a marble pulpit and velvet-cushioned pews, is all well enough if it quiets the conscience and soothes with trust the death-bed of even a Dives. We regard a Salvation Army, that makes a burlesque of religion as it goes shouting with its toot-horns and stringed instruments, as to be tolerated, because it is better than the Bob Ingersolls. We only seek to inform the well-meaning teachers of the religion of to-day why it is they preach to empty pews.

Few of us are aware of what we are doing when we close our galleries and churches, and open our saloons to the poor. This last, so far, has proved impossible. But let our hot gospelers, whose creed is based on "*Be it enacted,*" visit any one of the poor abodes of the laborers denied admission to innocent places of amusement on the only holiday they have for such recreation. Such investigator will descend to a sub-terranean excavation dug in the sewer-gas-filtered earth, where the walls sweat disease and death. These are homes for humanity. Or he will ascend rotten stairways to crowded rooms, heated to suffo-cation by pestilent air poisoned by over used breath from men, women and children, packed in regardless of health, comfort, and decency. These are the so-called homes of thousands and thousands; and the wonder is, not that they die, but that they live. We send millions of money with missionaries to foreign shores; to our own flesh and blood we send—the po-lice. Loving care and patient help are bestowed on distant pagans; poor-houses, prisons, and wrath are the fate awarded to our brothers at home.

A little way from these abodes of misery and crime the saloon is open, with its gilded iniquity, warm, cheerful, and stimulated with liquid insanity in bottles and beer-kegs. Do we wonder that the churches are empty and the saloons crowded ?

The advent of our blessed Savior was heralded by the anthem of the heavenly hosts, that sang "Glory to God on high, and peace and good-will to men on earth." The few sad years of our Redeemer's life among men were passed with the poor, the sinful, and the sorrowing. We have to-day much glory to God on high, and no good-will to men on earth.

Your churches decrease in numbers as the population swells, O brethren, because of your lack of Christian sympathy!

27

## Revenue Tariff, a Tax; Protective Tariff, Extortion.

We are prepared, through long observation, to note without surprise the influence self-interest has upon conduct and character, but we are amazed to see how a heated contention obscures the intellect. These were our reflections on reading the Hon. Allen G. Thurman at Chicago assert that a tariff was a tax. This is the fact when considering a theory, but is as wide of the truth as heaven from earth in the face of our present condition. A tariff, when levied for revenue to support the government, is of course, a tax. A tariff levied to benefit certain private interests is an extortion. It is not even plunder under color of law. The tax-collector who enters one's dwelling to secure what the law demands could just as well deprive the householder of his watch and shirt-studs under color of law, as these favored interests use the custom-house to further their business.

A tax means a levy made on property for the support of the government—see Webster or any body else, for this is not only the scientific definition, but that accepted by popular usage. The law courts have long since held it murder to kill by firing in a crowd; and it is no defense to set up that it was done by an officer, and that in so doing he not only took took the lives of six innocent men, but killed a convict.

A tariff for protection means this, if it means any thing. Under pretense of a levy it plunders for private use—nay, worse, for it destroys the levy made for the good of the government. The higher the tariff the lower the income, and this continues until prohibition is reached, and robbery is without limit and the government is without revenue.

We have under the government of the United States some sixty millions of people. The one pursuit of all this multitude is making a living. This can be done in two ways, and no third. These two ways are, one by honest labor, and the other by theft. The great mass, recognizing this fact, labor honestly, or offer an honest labor for their living. Were the entire population to do this few would be rich, but all would be comfortable. A large minority, however, prefer theft to labor. Greed, added to cunning, enables such to steal; and most of them steal with impunity. It is a singular fact that a man thus constituted is not content with robbing another of his living, but is impelled by his brutal nature to rob several men. He will, if he can, sieze on and possess himself of the subsistence that belongs to a thousand men. It is not our purpose to dwell on the peculiarities of this bread-robber. It is a singular fact, however, that this social vampire is deprived by nature of the capacity to enjoy what he steals. The man who accumulates a thousand coats finds that he can not enjoy one. He has costly palaces, in which he is as unhappy as any other animal would be; libraries which he can not read; picture galleries which he can not enjoy; he has carriages that bore him, and wines that he can not appreciate. We call the creature a millionaire and envy him his possessions, thinking what we could do with them, failing to know or remember that his only delight is in the mere accumulation.

However, there is no good in denouncing the class. It is the system that makes such a class possible we are forced to attack. " Ding doon the nests, and the rooks will flee awa'," says an old Scotch proverb.

The instinctive tendency of uncultured human nature is toward this selfish greed, and the history of humanity is a story of fraud through which a few prey upon the many. It has been the dream of the philanthropist to eradicate, and the effort of the just to restrain, this evil. As all men are born free, we jump to the conclusion that all are born equal. The conclusion is incorrect. As no two are alike, no two are equally armed against aggression, and the result is the utter impossibility of securing a right based on a remaking of humanity. Yet the war goes on, and the framers of our National Government thought to strike a deadly blow in favor of even handed justice and equal rights when they destroyed a class in America that had so long dominated the masses in Europe. This was done in wiping out the law of primogeniture and entail. The sons will distribute, they said, all that the parent accumulates, and the government will give no hand to aid in unjust accumulation. As the government was based on the recognized axiom that it was for the benefit of the governed, we had a right at least to have the government on the side of the suppressed. The hope of equalizing and holding humanity to a level in the possession of property through government interference is as hopeless as the attempt to still the waves of ocean by act of congress. But we are neither dreamers nor impracticables in demanding that the government shall not give its aid to what it was created to prevent.

The statement of these truths, which no reasonable intellect can gainsay, fetches us to a consideration of a problem now agitating the popular mind.

A tariff for protection is not a tax. Then what is it? Simply a process through which the fiscal agency of the government is used to insure a profit to certain moneyed interests, altogether of a private sort. With the people of the United States these interests refer mainly to mining and manufacturing. The government with us is merely a trust. It has no property of its own, and no power beyond the mere expression which its form gives of the sovereignty that remains in the people. It can not, therefore, pay bounties to one interest or class of interests without taking precisely the amount wrested from another class. Nor can the government do indirectly that which it is forbidden to do directly. In bringing the crushing weight of the general government into the field of private enterprise, by arresting competition in behalf of a certain favored interest, the government is guilty indirectly of an usurpation that not only destroys its usefulness, but makes it a despotism of the most intolerable sort.

A feeble attempt is made to prove that the authority for this abuse is to be found in the constitution itself, and that the framers themselves acted upon it in the first congress held after the constitution was accepted. Of course, this is a falsehood, easily seen and answered by the impartial student of our history. Through a fear of state jealousy, the first congress sought to support the general government, not by direct taxation, but by customs levied upon our commerce. If in this an incidental protection was given to certain industries then struggling into existence, the fathers found no reason for complaint. This was a tax, and as no tax can be collected that does not injure some one, they sought to minimize the harm. As Henry Clay claimed, it was a tax with incidental protection so slight and so much of a necessity that it could not well be avoided.

This, however, is not the doctrine of to-day. The levy has no other motive, in the mouths of its advocates, but that of so-called protection. What was once a revenue tariff with incidental protection is now a protective tariff with incidental revenue, or, as the Chicago platform phrases it, no revenue at all.

Of course, when this conclusion is reached, we are saved all discussion as to its merits or failings. Born in error, its life of necessity is evil. Let us suppose, to illustrate, that a party were organized whose one principle would be to kill a millionaire on sight, which should be sanctioned by a legal enactment, not only holding the assassin harmless, but paying a bounty on each scalp of a dead millionaire, duly certified to. All discussion as to the merits of such a system would be silenced by the thought of crime involved in the murder. This is precisely the condition of the Republican organization in its advocacy of what it is pleased to call protection—only instead of homicide we have robbery. It is not necessary to prove, for example, that out of sixty millions of people less than one million are enriched. If the entire population were benefited in a material way by such a destruction of our liberties and our constitution, we should pay dearly for our moneyed prosperity.

The public mind is slow to learn that nearly all the misery inflicted on humanity comes, not so much from an inequality of political rights, as from an inequality of property. A man may be poor, and yet content, if he be free, and by freedom we mean master of himself. But, if his poverty is the livery of servitude, he must be wretched; and there is no servitude so cruel as that of unrequited toil. When a man realizes that work is not only uncertain, but when obtained gives him only a bare, beggarly subsistence, with no hope of a betterment hereafter, it is of small difference whether his master is one man or a thousand men. The life given to sustain another, and that other a master, is not worth living. This is precisely the state to which this tariff of extortion has brought us. Our rich are growing very rich, our poor are getting poorer. Every day the gulf widens and deepens between the two, and the middle class of people, neither rich nor poor, but in comfortable circumstances, that formed a bridge between the two, is rapidly disappearing.

We are assured that if the government takes care of the wealthy class, that class will care for the poor. To use the language of the political arena, the capital so nursed by the government will afford work for labor. God help the men dependent on such a delusion as that. "There is nothing more cruel," said Senator Sprague, "than a million of dollars, unless it be a million and a half." A wealthy mill-owner drawing a million and a half from his works will drive his coach and four from castle to castle with his digestion undisturbed and his dreams undistorted, although he knows that his wretched workmen are toiling in rags, hunger, and privation to which the millionaire would not subject his dogs.

We have yet to learn that we suffer more from a power to abuse than from an abuse of power. Legalize a wrong, and the wrongdoer will go to the further limit of his abuse, well knowing he can not be questioned. An abuse of power works ever in the presence of an indictment, which cows the criminal and stimulates resistance. But legalized crime debases the law, while elevating and protecting the criminal. When the time comes that the judge is at the bar, and the convict on the bench, there is nothing left but violence to restore order. But the worst feature of it all is the mantle of respectability it throws over decay. These men who prate about providing for labor, and laboring for the prosperity of the country, can not look each other in the face without laughing. Of this sort is the so-called Republican organization. It is not a political party at all. It is made up of certain moneyed interests, combined for the purpose of using the government to serve their selfish greed. It is altogether a commercial affair, and under it over one hundred and fifty thousand miles of operating railway have passed under the control, and virtually in the ownership, of less than sixty families. Our circulating medium is the property of some two thousand corporations, that contract or expand to suit their own selfish purposes; trusts multiply, until our food, clothing, shelter, in a word all we live upon, are worked to make millionaires; and the foundation of all this stupendous structure to facilitate plunder rests on the extortion allowed by a tariff for extortion, which its supporters style protection, and our friends with strange blindness call a tax.

## The Kingdom of Satan.

How few among the advanced thinkers of our age take into account the social element when discussing reforms! Society is of necessity conservative. All agitation disturbs enjoyment by threatening a change of condition. Better bear the ills we have than suffer in our comfort the ills of progress that implies revolution. When the Arkansaw man asked the settler why he did not repair his roof, he answered that when it did not rain he did not need to, and that when it did rain he could not work at it. This has been laughed at for half a century, and yet it carries a moral that illustrates all attempts at repair. The wrongs that annoy may be borne, for we are accustomed to them and have inured ourselves to their existence. Change, even for the better, breaks up old customs; and human nature is born and bred to a dislike of that which disturbs old habits. The farmer who was given to carrying his grain on horseback to the mill, with the grain in one end of the sack and a stone in the other, felt uneasy at a proposed relieving of his horse; for if the string broke, he argued, the grain would be lost, whereas the stone could be readily replaced.

The great power, however, in society against reform is the respectability it claims for itself. Respectability is conservative. It conserves all wrongs that have been polished to refinement, although the refinement may, in fact, be a shabby sort of veneering and varnish. To illustrate: At Washington, not a century since, it was no uncommon event for an administration to be carted into the executive mansion so far gone in intoxication as to be, if possible, more senseless than when sober. No one ventured to comment on this, let alone denounce the disgraceful conduct. When a member of the cabinet or a senator gives way to this beastly habit, we speak of him in sorrow as a distinguished inebriate. A member of the house of representatives, thus afflicted, is spoken of, without sorrow, as a drunkard. The poor clerk given to intoxication, is a beast, and is treated accordingly.

How poor humanity holds its own in this respect, through all the ages, a few historical facts illustrate. Our blessed Savior, for example, was crucified, not because of His doctrine of peace and good-will to men on earth and glory to God on high, but because He was a Nazarene, born of a carpenter, and not only drove the money-changers from the temple, but made attacks in speeches upon the rich men of Judæa. In thus disturbing business relations and threatening the social order of Jerusalem, He brought upon Himself the active enmity of the respectable classes, and so went down to a cruel death.

No one possessed of an intellect doubts for an instant that, had our Savior allied Himself with the moneyed men and become the advocate of law and order, He would have been gladly accepted by the then prominent Hebrews as the heralded Messiah. The story of Satan carrying Him into a high mountain and showing Him a vast domain that would be His, provided He acknowledged Satan's dominion, is explained from marble pulpits to velvet-cushioned pews as a parable of a political import. It was a sad truth, told in the simple narrative of the situation then as it is the situation to-day. The earth, with all its wealth is yet held by Satan, and is at once a menace and a standing temptation to the reformer. He learns early that he can be Christ in form and Satan in substance. If he holds out, he will be shamed by epithets and pelted with stones as one who disturbs the business relations and threatens the social fabric.

We devote our time to a discussion of dogmas, and waste the precious hours in deciphering obscure passages in Holy Writ, while the great lesson taught by our Savior's life and death lies unheeded before us. In the same crucifixion that terminates his visible presence on earth all reform is crucified.

We take no account of the immense power against goodness that is wielded by society as organized by evil. The gates of hell are golden gates, and the high seats within, and all the crowns, are reserved for the respectable. The virtues then are not offensive, and the vices are gentlemanly. A man may not steal a loaf of bread, however near starvation, but he can defraud others of a million and not only hold his position but win the admiration of all.

We deplore the benighted condition of the Dark Continent, and collect vast sums to convert the heathen, when true Christianity is less known in our midst than in the center of Africa.

It is told of the earlier Christians that they won their way among the pagans by adopting the pagan form of worship. The altars erected to false gods and the unknown god were retained to the glory of the true God. The lesson has not been lost on Satan. When he tempted our Savior, it was not to destroy Christ, but to pervert His mission. What Christ rejected we hasten to accept. With his cross upon our breasts we adore the devil. The thunder on the mountains is the church-music to the accompaniment of which we worship the golden calf.

Not long since a sexton of a fashionable church

in our midst, being called upon to account for having
thrust a poor woman from a velvet-cushioned pew,
said in extenuation that the pew-owners made a
heavy investment in the church, and that the stockholders held their pews precisely as the same class
did boxes at the opera-house, and that paupers had no
more right to the one than the other. What would
happen if the dirty poor were permitted to crowd in
upon the members, and render respectable worship a
nuisance? This church business was like any other
business transaction, and if the non-property holders
did not like it, they were at liberty to let it alone.
They had their appropriate places for worship and
should be content, said the practical sexton.

We do not pretend to give the words of the out-
spoken and sensible sexton. We give his meaning.
And that such was found satisfactory to the congregation is a fact proven by his retention in the place he
so zealously guards.

The social world sets its face against reform and
is potent for mischief. It kills all movements in that
direction by making them disreputable. The history
of all such is curiously illustrative. The most effective weapon of all in this direction is that of epithet.
To call one a crank, if it does not cow the reformer, certainly renders him helpless. This is the
first resort. We remember but yesterday that to

designate a man an abolitionist was to consign him to social infamy. To-day, those who seek to arrest gross extortion under form of law are sneered at as free-traders. The freedom that is honored in speech, press and religion becomes a disgrace when applied to trade. We have a large body of citizens who, looking upon public office as a public trust, revolt against the despotism of party and cast their votes regardless of caucus dictation, and they are laughed at and denounced as "mugwumps." The first Mugwump on record was George Washington, and his Farewell Address has no part so pregnant of meaning as that wherein he warns us against the evil influence of parties, then called "factions." This meant then, as it means now, the Randallism which makes a man lose in the organization that which the party was organized to sustain.

How the reform survives both reformers and its enemies, and becomes an element of life, history tells us. The treason of one generation is the loyal principle of another. The crank of to-day is the hero of the hereafter, and the stones that pelted the martyr to death form an altar at which the same class worships in generations long after.

## Murmurs of the Mac-o-chee.

I met David Donald on the pike the other day. King David was stalking along in his usual contemplative way when we collided.

"I hear'n tell," he said, slowly and solemnly, "that you've been pictering me out in print as the champion cow-boy of Logan county—that I am the bald-headed, shrieking pee-wee of the rollin' prairie."

"Not that, oh! King David," I made response. "I have set you up as the pensive philosopher of the plains, the hermit of Squaw's Rock, the melancholy madman of the Mac-o-chee."

"Well," he said, "it's a free country, specially to fools and fellers in buggies. A man has a right to call another man any thing he pleases, provided he does it at a distance."

"Why, David, I hope you're not offended."

"I'm not partic'lar. They may call me any thing, provided I am called to supper," and so David started on.

There is a deal of quiet humor about this corn-fed Diogones that is meat and drink to me. I remember when the three months' service in the war came to an end at Camp Dennison, and my men were

28

called to enlist for three years or the war, I made an earnest address about "the land we were fighting for," and ended by requesting the men willing to enlist to step forward. Only one responded, and that one was David Donald.

"Well, captain," cried my one recruit, "g'ess if these other fellers all go home me and you'll haf to lick the tarnal rebs ourself."

A year after, I came from my tent one morning on the Gauly to find David on guard. It was a cruel cold day in midwinter. The heavy clouds hung low over the rough mountain country, while a sleet drove fiercely down upon us. Dave brought his musket down with a bang, and, leaning on it, said, in a drawling, melancholy way:

"Well, captain, if this is the land we're fightin' for, I think we'd better let it go."

\*

\*     \*

There is a man who is noted as the meanest man alive by his neighbors. His close-fisted parsimony has passed into a proverb, and, instead of saying "Mean as Garbroth," the old expression, they now say "Mean as Smithers."

Smithers is not his name: but, with the warning before me of the fair author who did up Cape Cod, and the later example of Zola, I am disposed to be cautious.

What a lively time Dickens would have had, poor gentleman, had this rule been applied to him. It is well known that he picked up both names and characters from real life. I believe, however, that, while he exaggerated the characters out of all recognition, he was careful not to fetch character and name together. It is traditionary that Shakspeare was given to the same practice. He deserved punishment more clearly for this than the mythical deer stealing he was said to have indulged in. And he would have had it but for the fact that in his pungent lampoons on the stage the poor author and actor was considered beneath contempt by the rich and well-born whom they pilloried. They little dreamed, those aristocrats, that their names would be not only remembered through his terrible pen, but that it would be an immortality of shame and ridicule.

My neighbor, Smithers, is a thin, stoop-shouldered, cadaverous looking old man, who impresses one with the feeling that the poor-house trustees are neglecting their duty in not furnishing the corpse with a cheap coffin and immediate burial. He is slow of speech, and in his various trades and business transactions wearies his dealers out with his slow-moving, slow-speaking ways.

Life possessor of a barren little farm, with a swamp for bottom land and knobs for highland, from which last the rains of heaven had long since washed the soil down to help bother Eads in his jetties, he lived alone, heaven knows how, until one day, years since, in the midst of the oil fever, it was discovered that from a spring on Smithers's place an oily substance mingled with the water, and the wild cry of surface indications went out.

A company of capitalists was immediately organized, and every effort made to fetch old Smithers to terms.

He proved to be the most aggravating old owner of an oil well ever found. He would take no risks; he could not be tied down to any proposition or purchase. His miserable land was worth absolutely nothing. It might have been sold for twenty-five cents an acre, and then swindled the purchaser. The company began at five dollars an acre, and then worked up to a hundred, and then gained the property only through strategy.

One morning the old miser was alarmed by the information that oil had been discovered on an adjoining farm, and the company had withdrawn all its propositions of purchase. This, as the president of the company said, "fotched him." His signature to a contract was obtained, and with feverish anxiety the old fellow awaited the payment, which was to be in full and in gold.

The affair was consummated in the office of our blind Bismarck, of Bellefontaine, more endearingly known to the popular mind as Bill West. He was the attorney for the company; but the venerable Smithers considered him as legal adviser also, and much time was lost in consultations about nothing, the old miser leading the lawyer out to ask but one question, and that was: "Now, Bill, is it all right?" or give but one caution of, "Watch 'em, Bill; watch 'em; all rascals, every one of 'em rascals; watch 'em."

When at last the affair was ended, and the glittering gold, after several counts, lodged in the old man's pockets, he took Bismarck to one side, and said:

"Now, Bill, you've been my friend; you've stood by me, Bill, and I'll stand by you. I intend to pay you, Bill; yes, indeed; I don't want no man's time for nothing. I thought of that 'fore I left home, and you see I brought you somethin' nice."

And the rural Shylock drew from his bosom three hen eggs, and laid them softly on the table before the astonished attorney. Our Bismarck could see better in those days than he can now, poor fellow, and he was more in need of fees than at this time.

"Maybe, Bill," said the elderly Granger, seeing the lawyer dumfounded, "maybe, Bill, you'd be willin' to take two; now you kin make them oil rascals pay purty lively, you see, and I'm a poor man, Bill; I'm very poor."

"Uncle Jake." said Bismarck, solemnly, "if I were to take two hen eggs for a legal opinion, and it got out, I'd be dishonored. No, I must have three."

"But, Bill, nobody'd know; I'm such a poor man."

"Can't help that, Uncle Jake; plank down the three eggs or I shall have to draw on your gold."

This last settled the controversy, and the old man left the hen product and wended his way home. Bismarck had remarked that the one egg the old man kept his hand on was marked. The other two were not. Bismarck opened the window as soon as his penurious client left, and tossed out the ornithological retainer. He discovered, as his neighbor did, that two of the eggs were spoiled; the only sound one was the marked product that the old scoundrel had hankered after.

Uncle Jake bought a handsome bottom farm with his money, and waxed rich, of course. This business of accumulating lies more in the saving than the making. Old Smithers would have grown

rich where even a Chinaman would starve, or a house
dog grow rebellious. His miserly propensity grows
with his age. The stories told of his grasping avarice —his intense meanness—make the average congressman appear respectable.

It is said, for example, that, the wife of a neighbor having died, Uncle Jake walked over to console
the survivors and learn when there would be a break
up and a vendue, as such sales are called here.
Smithers attended all such with the hope of picking
up bargains, but never got beyond bidding off trash
no one else wanted.

The aggrieved family, assisted by a rural undertaker—the very worst sort of buzzard in human
shape—layed out the corpse, and two pieces of money
were called for to hold the eyelids. Such could not
be found, and Uncle Jake drew slowly two coppers
from his pocket for that purpose.

"I can lend 'em to you, Brother Tompkins, 'till
you find others," he said.

The substitutes were not found, and Uncle Jake
kept his keen, twinkling, hard, little gray eyes on
the corpse. He went out hastily at last, and returned
with two small, flat stones, saying:

"I must be goin' now," and so he removed the
two cents, replacing them with the flat stones, and
then, with a sigh of relief, went home.

Of course such a citizen is very unpopular, and the whole country-side seems to combine to torment, and, if possible, cheat him. This last is not a pleasant operation. When the old man finds some one has the best of him, he turns his entire attention to restitution. As this consists in shadowing the sharper, almost lodging and certainly living at his house, the successful trader has either to quarrel outright or make liberal restitution.

A minister of the gospel traded a likely-looking horse to the old man—a horse better to look at than look for—he was moon-blind; that is, every thirty days the poor animal's eyes turned of a milky color and sight left them. Uncle Jake remonstrated in his mild, whining way, to no purpose. Then came his old practice. Not only did he haunt the minister's house, but he tied the poor animal at the gate; and thus it was from morning till night, without food or water, staring with its moony eyes like a nightmare.

On Sundays, Smithers became a regular attendant on divine service, and at intervals, when the prayer or discourse came anywhere near the trouble on the miser's mind, he would fairly shout out, "Amen!" that at last set the younger portion of the congregation to giggling.

After service, as the minister came slowly from

the meeting-house, Smithers would sidle up to him, and ask, in a querulous whine, "How about that hoss, minister?"

The poor man of God at last paid Uncle Jake ten dollars to take that horse and himself from his ministerial sight.

The old fellow was not always, however, so successful. On one occasion he drove to Taylor & Fisher's warehouse with a load of wheat.

"What yer payin' now, cash down, fur fust-class wheat?" he asked.

"Dollar five," was the response.

"Must have dollar ten fur this wheat; it's fust-class."

"Dollar five, old man."

"Well, say dollar nine?"

"See here, Uncle Jake," said Mr. Fisher, "I am too busy to waste my time bargaining with you. You can take a dollar five or move on."

"Ain't they a payin' a leetle more at the mills?" he queried.

"I believe Armstrong is giving something more."

Away went Smithers, but so slowly that a lad got ahead of him and gave the miller the hint.

"What's wheat?" asked the old man.

"Well, we're payin' dollar five, but they do say that they're payin' more at the lower mill."

29

This was a mile away, but the dealer "gee'd up" and dragged on to the lower mill. There he had the same response, to which was added that it was reported that at the Mac-a-chee mills wheat brought a dollar ten. To the Mac-a-chee mills drove Smithers, only to be sent to Moot's. At this old establishment he found a deaf miller, and the two yelled at each other for half an hour before the poor wheat dealer discovered that at Moot's mill wheat was not being purchased at all.

It was about sundown when he appeared at his first starting place, his poor horses fagged out and the old driver hungry and tired.

"Take my wheat," he cried, "at a dollar five; I'm tired experimenting."

I am led to this screed by an affliction Uncle Jake practiced upon me yesterday, making my letter, I fear, a mail too late. I can comfort myself, however, with the reflection that it is no great loss, and with this humble confession sign myself.

\*

\*　　\*

To my memory the country seems to have been as well filled with quaint odd characters as it was with game. Nearly every man seemed to have been turned out of a peculiar mold and shaped his life by an eccentricity of his own creating. I remember one, a mason, known by the name of "Old Gettysburg" from the fact that he began all his stories, mostly monstrous lies, with "when I was at Gettysburg." We boys fairly doted on old G. He could discount Munchausen and not try.

"Now byes sot yer off eye on me," he would say, for example, filling his stubby clay pipe, "I'm a 'goin' to tell ye about a big gun. It was a gun left over from the Revolution, a prime favorite of Gineral Washington's. It laid along side the road goin' to Gettysburg. Well, one night I was a 'ridin' on hoss back sorter belated, and a storm come up. It was a big storm, I tell ye. The lightning flashed right along bright enough to blind ye, while the thunderbolts jist dropped about promiscous like, knockin' trees right and left, and the rain—well it jist come down in sheets. I suddenly recollected that cannon, and to git out of the storm I jist rode my horse in at the muzzle. I was about comfortin' myself when the stage coach come a thunderin' down the road and the fool driver missed his way and drove heltersplit into that cannon and killed his two leaders dead at the britch."

"And what became of you?" chorused the boys.

"Well, I thought jist quick as a wink what I'd got to do, and I leaped my hoss out at the touch-hole."

Another favorite monstrosity he was fond of telling came up in illustration of his agility. The powder mills of Gettysburg caught fire. There was danger of an explosion that would destroy the town. He was at work topping a chimney a mile off. He immediately, with great presence of mind, dropped his shoes, descended the ladder and run that mile. He got into the mills and tramped out fifty-eight barrels of powder in his stocking feet and so saved the town.

The old fellow's few introductory words came to be proverbial. When one began a fish or bear story or any other boastful narrative, he would be interrupted by a cry from some one " when I was in Gettysburg," and effectually silenced.

*

* *

The man, that to this day holds the affection born in my boyish heart was George Martin. He was what my father called a first-class chicken-coop carpenter, and evidently made by the day and not ' by the job ' he was so slow not only in his work but all things. The time he took to eat was exasperating. He was longer in getting to sleep and certainly in wakening than any man alive. His gait as he moved was as if his limbs were lazily consulting each other as to long premeditated motions, while the sentences that escaped his everlasting masticated tobacco seemed to lounge out of his mouth.

There was enmity between George Martin and one Mike O'Brien. This grew out of a theological difference. I never could discover that either had any religion, but while O'Brien was a stout Catholic to his finger tips, or rather to the tip of his shillalah, Martin had read but one book, and that was Fox's "Book of Martyrs," fearfully illustrated. Hence Martin regarded all Catholics more or less sons of Satan, and O'Brien as especially marked out for damnation. This he helped out by damning O'Brien on all occasions. O'Brien was not slow in reciprocating, and we were frequently favored with controversies that were supposed to be of a religious nature, but so hid under profanity that the theological intent was somewhat obscured, and especially was this the condition when the dispute ended in a fight—no unusual occurrence.

One Saturday evening a number were engaged near the saw-mill shooting at a mark. Martin had put down his loaded rifle to look at the mark and chalk the latest shot. While thus engaged, O'Brien came along quite drunk. It was growing dark, and had it been broad daylight, White's best, of which Mike had been partaking, would have obscured his vision. As it was he quite astonished Martin.

"Gimme a goon," cried Mike, and before he could be arrested he had seized, cocked and leveled the rifle. Poor Martin was bending over scrutinizing the holes lately made in the board, and thus presented a bright patch on the seat of his pantaloons, that Mike mistaking for the mark, aimed at and fired. Had he aimed at any thing else than Martin, he might have hit that great Hunter and theological student of Fox. As it was, Martin heard the crack of the rifle and at the same instant the shrill whiz of the bullet. He left that locality immediataly. He did not wait to pass any whereas or resolutions. He could have given Lady Macbeth's guests a lesson as he retired beyond range.

"Look at the dirthy baste runnin' away wid de mark," cried O'Brien. Nothing could convince Martin that this was not a premeditated attempt on his life instigated by the Pope of Rome.

\*

\*   \*

Fishing is worse than hunting. Well, I don't know. I always thought the last application was the worst. Fishing begins the night before. The amount of preparation necessary is wonderful. What uncomfortable top-boots, what wretchedly fitting corduroy pants, and insane jackets are brought out! Then one is routed at midnight. The poor wife tries to be merry by candle-light over the hot coffee one can not drink, and the hot cakes one forces down to cause indigestion and headache. Any fool can fish. I always felt like a first-class fool on these occasions, and yet I never caught any thing but a first-class cold and a ducking, generally both. Those top-boots always leak, and if they did not you are certain to slip up on a slimy stone and come down in a sitting position.

I did catch something once upon a time. I had selected a pool directly above a rapid, and, throwing out my line, sat by the murmuring stream in a dreamy way waiting for a bite. My companions were off down stream following the current in a lively way, and in a few minutes, being exceedingly fatigued, I dropped asleep. I was suddenly awakened by a jerk, and to my amazement and some confusion I found the line around my neck and the fish pulling at it with terrible force was on land instead of in water. I extricated my neck from the sharp line that cut me like a razor by running up the bank in an undignified manner on all fours, and, to my intense disgust, found I had hooked a good-sized boar, that pulled and squealed and squealed and pulled in wrath and terror. The line was one of the best, light but strong, and, intending to pull the hook from the beast's nose, I took a turn of the line on my hand

and put out my strength. The hog was going at the rate, I should say, of thirty miles an hour, and the sudden jerk bringing his nose to the ground made hoggy turn a beautiful somersault. I must say that it was superb. It was pork over snout of the sweetest sort.

First knock-down for fisherman.

My triumph did not last. The miserable beast regained his hoofs in a twinkling, and instead of continuing his retreat turned and contemplated me. His reasoning faculties were certainly not so bright as Senator Harlan's, for example, but through his hoggish intellect went the notion that I had something to do with his late disaster. As this original thought took possession of his beastly mind his back rounded up, the tail seemed to twist tighter to his animated hams, his jaws snapped, and with a snort, ere I was aware he charged in on me. I felt a thunderbolt go between my legs, and, although I came down on my face, the astronomical observations that I made of shooting stars were amazing.

I regained my feet rather groggy. and before hoggy could renew his unpleasant attention I retreated. He would have followed but for the happy accident of the line getting foul of a willow. And here a bright idea seized me. I ran to the side of my fishing station and got the landing net. I thought I could throw this over my enemy, and holding him down, cut out my unfortunate hook. I tried it on, and had the satisfaction of seeing the hog go through my net easily, if not as gracefully as Harlequin through a paper hoop. Enraged beyond endurance, I selected a handsome geological specimen of boulder of the drift period, and bringing it in violent contact with the hard skull, had the satisfaction of seeing a great geological triumph. Hoggy rolled over, kicked, tumbled and died.

"By Jove, if you haven't killed neighbor Tomkins' white suffolk boar, that cost him three hundred dollars!" cried one of my companions coming up at that minute.

Somehow or other we neglected to tell of this at the time, and left neighbor Tompkins under the impression that his valuable Suffolk had come to his untimely end through a visitation of Providence.

\*

\* \*

I heard a good thing anent one of our solid citizens that I can not help putting to paper. This solid citizen has a taste for liquid insanity, kept by apothecaries sometimes—and of all sorts of liquor he likes that best which somebody else pays for. Davy Gill, compounder of drugs, was called to the back part of his excellent establishment one day—

> "Filled with deleterious med'cines;
> All of whom partook are dead since—"

And left the solid c. sitting by a counter, on which was a jar of old whisky. Davy heard the stopper clink, and returning saw the liquid yet being agitated.

"Bless my soul," cried Davy, "to think of my leaving that jar of poison so exposed!" and seizing the whisky he replaced it on the shelf.

"Vat?" exclaimed the culprit.

"Poison! deadly poison," responded Gill, gravely.

"Mine Got! Dafy, you don't make some mistakes about dot?" roared the solid c.

"No mistake, old fellow—one swallow of that is instant death."

The solid c. turned white in spots. "Dafy, vat vas it?" he gasped.

"*Virginicus nux vomicus*, to kill bedbugs," was the awful response.

"Mine Got. Dafy, I ish det as a log!"

"You didn't?"

"Yes, I did, Got tam! Vat I do right avays to once?"

"Here, quick! swallow this!" cried Davy, pouring out a glass of castor oil. The oil went down at a gulp. "Do you feel a tingling sensation in your toes and fingers?" asked the apothecary.

" Yes, Davy, I tingles."

" Shivers running up and down your back ?"

" I shiffers all over."

" And sweat?"

" I sweats like a leetle pull."

"The oil won't save you," said Gill, solemnly; "you had better hurry to Leonard and let him pump it out."

" The solid c. hurried across the street to Doctor Leonard. Fortunately for him the Doctor was not in his office. He broke like a quarter nag for Doctor Allen ; he, too, was out. The poor man was seen making for Doctor Hale when he suddenly disappeared from public view. An hour after Davy found him in Ed. Jackson's counting-room adjoining the stable. He was stretched upon a lounge, covered with robes and groaning.

" How do you feel, old fellow?" kindly asked the druggist.

" Oh ! I'm det, I'm det !" he groaned.

" No, you're not," said Davy, " I've been looking all over the town for you. I made a mistake; you did not swallow the poison—it was whisky."

" Dafy," said the patient, throwing off the robes and rising, " you is a dam vools. I know all de times, dot vas whisky, an' I von't pay you a tam cent for dot casdor oil."

# CELEBRATED MEN OF THE DAY.

## Washington McLean.

The death and burial of this remarkable man illustrate in a striking manner the singular condition of our community. No man, perhaps, wielded a wider and deeper influence upon the current of human events at a period of a great social and political revolution than Washington McLean, and yet his exit from life was so unmarked by public demonstration that the people scarcely knew of his departure.

We have come in a strange way to measure our eminent men by the political positions they have held. That is, instead of the statue, we regard mainly the pedestal. All that is lofty and ornate in the base is alone considered worthy of our admiration. Having worked all that is of interest to us into party, we take it for granted that each political organization puts into office its ablest leaders, and each party admires its own while living, and all lament unanimously the official dead. The private citizen, on the other hand, whatever his qualities and power,

(348)

passes to the grave mourned only by his personal friends. When Washington McLean departed this life, to have had his merited share of public regard, congress should have adjourned and the departments at Washington been dressed in mourning.

Mr. McLean, however, never held office; although frequently urged to accept positions by his party, he positively declined. He was wont to say, in his terse, incisive style: "It is the theory of our government that the official agent is the servant of the people. He is something more. He is the slave to public opinion, and can not succeed unless he be a base-burner for people to warm their feet at and spit on." He was not of that sort; and while active in shaping the policy of his party, and putting forward as officials men who could aid him in his efforts, he never trammeled himself with official obligations.

In this way no one had a wider and deeper influence not only on the fortunes of his party, but, through that party, on the country at large, It was Washington McLean, for example, who gave "the Ohio idea" to the country, and brought to the front —where he yet remains—" the Ohio man."

My first acquaintance with Washington McLean was memorable. The precise year escapes my memory, but it must have been away back in the thirties. Cincinnati was suffering from what was called negro riots. They were in fact riots of roughs aimed at a handful of abolitionists. The negro was the bone of contention, and the bone took no part in the contest. The poor negro, however, was the sufferer in the end.

To understand this condition we have to remember that Cincinnati, although in a free state, was in feeling a Southern town. All its prosperity came from trade with the South; and locally it had ties of as strong a nature that came of intermarriages, especially among the more wealthy and influential. To be called an abolitionist at Cincinnati, in those years, was to suffer as great an insult as to be styled a thief; and to be caught helping a slave to his stolen freedom was to be outlawed. If I remember rightly, an Englishman, a baker and candy-maker, named Burnett, was charged with, if not caught in the act of, aiding a family of slaves to escape from Kentucky to Canada. He was mobbed, his house and store were gutted, and the poor man narrowly escaped being hanged in the market-house, which then fronted his little establishment. Following this came a notice to the negroes and their friends, the abolitionists, to leave the town. The negroes not only declined the proposed exodus, but it was rumored over the city that they were arming themselves with the openly avowed purpose of resisting the proposed removal to the death. At the intersection of Broadway and

Sixth street, on the evening of the day these reports had been in circulation, an immense crowd assembled. The streets at that time were badly lighted, and in the gloom the masses swayed to and fro with a murmur of many thousands, in that subdued and angry hum which indicates a disturbed bee-hive or an excited mob. Sixth street, east of Broadway, had a sudden dip directly into the negro quarters of Cincinnati. The crowd gathered more than elsewhere on the edge of a black gulf, and at intervals, after uttering wild yells, two or three hundred would start down the declivity; but invariably the run dropped to a walk; this soon came to a halt, and then the mob returned, yelling, with more speed than it had made the charge.

About 9 P. M. several boxes were brought from stores near by, and a temporary platform was erected by the police and some prominent citizens, from which it was proposed that the mayor should read the riot act, and a number of prominent citizens address the mob with soothing words of promise against abolitionists and other disagreeable disturbers of the peace. A few glaring tallow-dips were being lighted, when some flashes of light and a discharge of fire-arms in the valley below, accompanied by a shower of small shot among the crowd, created a wild sensation. The masses surging back along Sixth street upset the badly constructed platform, and in the hurried retreat carried the mayor and his riot act entirely from the scene of disorder.

As no further reports of guns were heard, the crowd returned. It came back slowly and sullenly. In the dim starlight the faint gleam of guns, pistols, and knives could be seen. There was mischief afoot and a deadly menace in the air, when a diversion occurred caused by a number of men coming up Broadway dragging after them a piece of artillery. The crowd opened to the right and left of the gun and squad. Reaching the center of Sixth street, the old smooth-bore was rapidly put in position, aimed in direction of negro-town, and fired.

The effect of the discharge was ludicrous. How much soever the negroes may have been alarmed by that awful roar in the still night, and the rattle of iron clippings from a boiler yard—for such was the ammunition sent among their shanties—the effect upon the mob of whites was amazing. They incontinently fled along the three streets, and frightened crowds could be heard in the distance by a noise that resembled the tramp of flying sheep. I should probably have accompanied the crowded masses but for the Hon. X. C. Read, one of the proposed orators of the occasion, who stood his ground, laughing at the absurd flight. I remained with him. The gun was quickly reloaded and again discharged. When it was directed for the third time, the youth who seemed captain of the squad exclaimed:

"Hold on, boys; we must save our ammunition. The niggers may be on us any minute, now those cursed cowards have run away."

By the red flash of the gun I had this captain photographed on my memory. He was slightly built, red-haired, with a handsome face, and certainly not over eighteen years of age.

Judge Read approached the leader and said: "If those negroes do come out, my boy, you'll be in a bad way now that your friends have run away."

"They're no friends of mine, damn 'em. I'd as soon turn the gun on the cowards as on the niggers. But nig won't come out as long as we stay here."

Nor did they; in which instance they were as prudent as their late assailants. These last only returned after the then guileless police made up its anxious mind to go back and capture that gun. The police moved forward, slowly followed by the crowd; but when the scene of action was reached the artillery had disappeared, and from that on all was quiet on this Potomac. As nobody was hurt, and no great harm done, the affair passed into the limbo of forgotten things, to be dragged out now that I may tell of my first acquaintance with Washington McLean.

30

He was the captain of the gun-squad that had cowed the negroes while it dispersed so strangely the cowardly mob. But all mobs are as cowardly as they are cruel. Had the awful demonstration that darkened the heavens and shook the earth preceded the crucifixion instead of following it, our Savior had never been done to death.

Washington McLean, born at Cincinnati in May, 1819, was of Scottish descent, and of a family noted through several generations for intelligence and great force of character. They were Covenanters in creed, and Democrats from temperament and association. The boy Washington, after a brief period of schooling, was bound apprentice to a boiler-maker. The business suited the youth; he took kindly to it, and was scarcely freed from his service ere he set up for himself. It was a small beginning, but it prospered, and he was ere long sufficiently independent to marry a beautiful and accomplished Kentucky girl, who, from their union until his death, was not only his kind companion, but, with her tact, clear judgment, and winning ways, an element of success to her husband that can not be overestimated.

In the young McLean a singular combination of character developed that grew stronger as life went on. There was not only that force which makes a leader among men in active life, but a turn for thought that caused him to be a great reader of books. He had rare qualities in both directions. His singularly original views were as fascinating as his actions were forcible and effective. He had largely what we call, without comprehending it, magnetism. He seemed to turn men to him without effort. If to this we add one of the kindest hearts that ever beat, we have Washington McLean as he lived and died.

However, words are feeble and almost unmeaning when used to describe the great abiding quality of the dear friend found in his generous impulses. He gave not only his heart to whatever moved that heart, but the active efforts of the strongest nature I ever knew. This was shown not only when he moved the masses throughout the land to make one friend President of the United States, or beset and dominated the Senate at Washington to secure another friend his confirmation as justice of the Supreme Court, but in his every-day life, where the humble and lowly appealed to him for aid. There was nothing weak or sentimental in all this; it was the joyous, healthy expression of a strong nature. When his remains were escorted to the grave by a throng of eminent men, the cortege carried deep anguish to a few and sorrow to the many, but over all the land were men who read the announcement of his death through tears, as memory brought to mind the acts of kindness in the distant past that made his life and theirs one and inseparable.

Washington McLean entered political life at an early age, and never till his latest moments on earth lost an interest in the pursuit. A patriot at heart, he was a Democrat from impulse as well as from conviction. He sympathized with the masses, especially with labor. Originating from that class, he never lost touch with its hopes, feelings, and sufferings. No man ever comprehended more thoroughly the theory of our political structure, no man more earnestly sought to hold it to the design of its immortal founders. He was in this so consistent and courageous that when the civil war broke upon us he was against coercion by the government, not from any sympathy with the South, but from his patriotic love of the Republic. "A government of states, based on fraternal affection, could not be pinned together with bayonets," he said; and when the war was over, he made the remark since attributed to George Pendleton: "We have freed the blacks and enslaved the whites." His high intellectual force and strength of character made him the friend and associate of all the eminent men from Pierce to Chase and Stanton, and he influenced all for good.

An event occurred in his earlier career that, in-

significant in itself, colored and affected his after-life.
In a heated contest in Hamilton county over an election for sheriff in which a number of congenial spirits were thrown together, a quasi-political and altogether social club came into existence, called the
Miami Tribe. Joseph Cooper, a popular leader, had
been elected sheriff of Hamilton county. When he
sought the second term generally accorded that official, he was defeated in convention by the machine,
then in its infancy, that has since grown in its pernicious spirit to dominate politics. This encroach-
ment upon the old Democracy by a subtle and evil
element was resented more from instinct than intellectual intent by the Miami Tribe. This was a secret
association, with nothing to conceal but its existence,
made up of the best men, lately bolters from the
party on a nomination that had no political significance, and it was thought best that for the time being their remaining banded together should not be
known. It was an unfortunate mistake; for when
the fact of its existence became known, the mystery
that enveloped the club gave color to a multitude of
lies put in circulation by the machine.

Poor club! Born in innocence, it died in the violence of a mud-volcano, with a like effect. The press
turned against us and gave long columns of assault
in their brutal vituperation; while from the stump,

in English, such as it was, and in German that
sounded dreadful with its dismal refrain, "Miamis
Thribes," we had a continuous torrent of abuse. The
uproar was deafening. Fortunately the true list of
members did not get to the indignant public. This
fact enabled the more timid to join the enemy.

"Look at our chiefs," cried McLean, "running
into the tall grass to wash off the war-paint. They
will come out good Indians. Never mind, fellows;
keep horns locked and we're bound to win."

But for our gallant leader we should have been
run over and plastered beyond recognition in the
mud. "Despair," he was wont to say, "is the refuge
of fools." There is no assault that can be made on a
man that he can not live down, if he has the courage
to face it. I never knew a man who enjoyed a fight
as did Washington McLean. I doubt whether he
knew what fear meant. I remember his saying, "To
test a man's ability, put a pen in his hand; to try his
courage, seat him in a dentist's chair with an aching
tooth."

Looking over the roll of members, I am surprised to discover what a number of the Miami Tribe
rose to eminence. I find them as members of congress, house and senate; on the bench of the Supreme
Court of various states and of the United States; and
in other high positions. The "Ohio man" was de-

veloped in the Miami Tribe. There are but three left
alive, and the little remainder can well be proud of
the old association. The tomb of each has an honored epitaph in the name alone.

No better illustration of Washington McLean's
character and political ability can be given than in his
putting forward George H. Pendleton for nomination by a National Democratic Convention for the
Presidency. Pendleton was McLean's pupil in politics. An aristocrat by birth and early association,
he was a democrat by tradition that had its origin in
the South, where it was respectable to hold slaves
under a Jeffersonian dispensation. A man of ordinary power, he had a winning way that made him
popular when known; but that knowledge was not
national, and when Mr. McLean willed that George
H. Pendleton should be the candidate for the Presidency, the proposition was at first met with derision.
Mr. McLean soon changed all that. His power of
combination, his control of leaders, and his manipulation of the press were wonderful. And yet the entire Pendleton movement was from first to last under
Mr. McLean's hat. I remember well when one night
he came to my room in Union Square, New York.
and asked me if I could get a strong leader into the
Herald advocating Pendleton's nomination. I told

him I thought I could, but it struck me he wanted
something better than that.

" What is that?" he asked.

"A severe attack on your man in the Tribune."

" The devil! What do I want that for?"

" On the principle that a man is helped more by
his enemies than his friends. Your candidate is being treated with contempt. He is sneered at and
ridiculed. Let the Tribune make a serious assault
on him as a dangerous, bad man, and all that will
cease, and the Herald will take up the cudgel in behalf of Pendleton from a hatred of Greeley."

McLean saw the point, and we immediately proceeded to concoct a savage assault on our candidate.
With much difficulty I got it in on the editorial page
of the Tribune. The day after appeared in the
Herald a defense of the much-abused Ohio politician
and a pernicious assault on the guileless Greeley.

The attempt to nominate Mr. Pendleton proved
a failure, but it gave to McLean's protégé a national
standing which he carried from that out with force
and dignity until his death. The two friends drifted
apart in the later years of public life, and the cause
of the difference has puzzled many. I think I comprehend the reason. When Mr. McLean came to the
support of his candidate, he did so more from shrewd

calculation of chances than from a friendly regard
for his associate, believing, as he did, that, if the
Northwest could be rallied to the support of a Western man, he would stand a fair chance of election.
Mr. Pendleton, feeling the effect of his advocate's
masterly management, not only quietly acquiesced,
but gave himself entirely to the control of his chief.
This bred a condition not favorable to a continuance
of the alliance, for Pendleton sought to use the prominence given him, and make political combinations
naturally looking to his own advancement. With a
politician this invariably means a conciliation of enemies. This, of course, counted out McLean, for, like
all strong, positive natures, his hatreds were as bitter
as his friendships were strong. He not only accepted
his friends, but he selected his enemies with rare
good judgment, and was utterly despotic in his relations to both. The break between the two, McLean
and Pendleton, was sudden, characteristic, and dramatic. McLean heard accidentally of a dinner-party
being under way at Pendleton's house. The guests
were men McLean had been fighting in Pendleton's
behalf. Seizing his hat, he repaired at once to Pendleton's mansion. In response to his card, George H. left
the table and met his chief in the parlors. He approached with his usual amiable look and extended

31

hand.   McLean took no notice of the hand, and said abruptly :

"Since when have you taken to entertaining my enemies ?"

Pendleton flushed from chin to hair, and replied: "Since when have I accepted a master of ceremonies to dictate my guests to me?"

What might have followed is not hard to say; but at that moment Mrs. Pendleton, a lady of rare grace and beauty, swept in and cordially invited Mr. McLean to join the dinner-party.   There never lived a man who had more of the gentleman in him than Washington McLean.   His manner changed magically from wrath to amiability as he said :

"Excuse me, Mrs. Pendleton, for thus intruding on your entertainment.   You see, I got no notice of it.   I had some business with your husband.   But the business will keep ; it will keep, I assure you.   Good-evening."

And so the two parted, never again to meet as friends.

No better illustration can be given of McLean's kind heart and his influence with men of different politics from himself than what occurred during the war, when his old friend Roger A. Pryor was taken prisoner.   This distinguished jurist and soldier had been betrayed into our hands by an act of treachery, and found himself assigned to the same embrasure that held Beall at Fort Lafayette. This man was charged with being a spy and pirate. He was no ordinary man. Colonel Pryor found that Beall had not only good social position, but much culture—was, in fact, a gentleman who, from zeal in the Southern cause, had risked his life in a venture where the odds were a thousand to one against him. Pryor heard Beall's story, and with his judicial knowledge and experience saw that he had a good defense if such were presented by a capable advocate. Beall begged Pryor to appear for him. That the Colonel could not do; but he wrote to Washington McLean a statement of the defense, and asked if a good lawyer could not be procured to appear before the court-martial in the prisoner's behalf. Mr. McLean responded heartily. The lawyer appeared.

All efforts in this line proved unavailing. A court-martial is a body of gentlemen wholly unacquainted with law, who sit without a bar or a jury, and find a verdict in accordance with the wishes of their superior officers. Beall's defense was soon brushed aside, and the finding consigned him to death on the gallows.

From this attempted defense McLean appealed to the clemency of the Executive. President Lincoln listened with that patient attention for which he was

so remarkable. To aid him in this call for mercy
McLean got the President to send for Roger A.
Pryor. Within twenty-four hours that gentlemen appeared under guard at the Executive Mansion. With
the ability of a practiced and successful advocate he
at once entered upon an argument which began by
showing that Beall had been illegally condemned, and
ended with an appeal for clemency. McLean told me
afterwards that Judge Pryor was extremely pathetic
in his plea for mercy. There was not an unmoved
spectator in the room save the man he sought to move.
The President listened, attentive, indeed interested,
but untouched. He made no response in words, but
poor Beall was duly done to death not long after.

It is strange how strongly the belief has taken
hold of the popular mind that Abraham Lincoln was
a man so under control of his kinder emotions that
he could not say no when these were appealed to.
The fact is that, while good-natured in his ways, he
was as firm as a rock in all that his better judgment
dictated. A man of iron will and indomitable perseverance, he had no trouble from his temperament,
which was of the coarsest fiber.

He could not be influenced to intervene in behalf
of the unfortunate Beall, but he did favor Roger A.
Pryor in a quaint and odd manner. Washington Mc-
Lean having begged that Pryor might not be returned

to prison, the President wrote on a scrap of paper an
order directing Pryor to report to John W. Forney until further orders. Of course Judge Pryor hastened
to respond to this pleasant captivity, and was enjoying himself hugely, when a sour old senator from
New England called attention to this extraordinary
treatment of "a red-handed rebel." The President
took the hint and suggested to Pryor that the sacred
soil of Virginia would be healthier for him—and his
absence a relief to the administration.

Mr. McLean's influence in directing the current
of political events was not confined to combinations
that brought to the front influential leaders, but extended, as I have said, to giving force and effect to his
views upon measures that should govern the policy
of parties. He was the author of the "Ohio idea"
before stated, which held that the government credit,
shaped into paper notes, was money, and no more
limited by the supply of gold and silver on hand than
yard-sticks and bushel-measures were. He protested
against giving this money to banks, for such corporations to contract or expand as their private interests
dictated. He asserted that a greenback was a legal
tender long before the Supreme Court of the United
States so decided. I have no wish in a paper of this
sort to enter upon a discussion of the merits or fal-
sity of this proposition. I only refer to it for the

purpose of saying that the storm which shook the financial and political elements from center to circumference was one made potent by Washington McLean. What men it made and unmade, what parties it organized, and what parties it defeated or made notorious are now matters of history.

Of medium height, McLean was strongly built. His trunk was in keeping with his massive head, while his intellectual outlook indicated his thoughtful powers and great force of character. Possessed of a keen sense of humor, it was yet kept subordinate to his earnest nature. He was remarkable for his epigrammatic utterances, many of which passed into general circulation. When asked once, for example, to join a club, he said: "No; don't see the necessity of organizing to drink." Again: "The only club to which a decent man can belong is his own home. If a man can not find comfort in the society of his wife and children, he is no fit associate for gentlemen." Speaking of Stephen A. Douglas, when that gentleman was being brought to the front as a candidate for the Presidency, he said: "He won't do; his coat-tails are too near the ground." Of a prominent politician he remarked: "He is a one-storied fellow, with his eyes in the roof." One could fill a volume with such terse, incisive remarks.

Washington McLean was of a deeply religious

nature, and there is a story afloat illustrative of this, which, if not true in fact, is true to character. It tells of his being seated in the reading-room of the Riggs House, Washington, and, looking out through the large window upon the avenue, made dismal by falling sleet, when he was joined by Robert G. Ingersoll.

McLean knew the great Agnostic—which means a solemn old monkey that goes about protesting earnestly that he can not be expected to measure the universe with its tail : a praiseworthy confession that would be agreeable for so insignificant a fact, were it not uttered with such arrogant conceit, as if a short tail were a crowning merit.

"You should have been here a few minutes ago," said McLean, "to witness a scene upon the street."

"What was it?" asked Ingersoll.

"A poor crippled veteran was hobbling upon one crutch across the street, when a young fellow came along and knocked the crutch from under him."

"What an outrage!" cried Ingersoll. "I hope he was arrested. He ought to be sent to the penitentiary."

"Hold on," cried McLean. "What better are you doing? There are all about us poor old men and women, each hobbling through life on that one crutch of religious faith, and your pursuit in life is to go about knocking that from under the poor wretch. And yet you get indignant over my imaginary scene."

The great characteristic of Washington McLean was his strong American nature. The cold Scotch blood of his ancestors had gathered warmth through many generations from the sun and earth of our continent; and, while he retained the shrewd, brainy faculties of his forefathers, he had, in addition, a warm, generous impulse that was all American. His success in life illustrates strikingly our environments. Born a poor boy, and bred a mechanic, he won his way to great political power and social recognition. The friend and associate of our statesmen, he had a quiet, dignified ease of manner that made him at home in the most refined society. The paper cap of the mechanic that covers sterling qualities helps on instead of hindering success.

Mr. McLean grew old gracefully. In an historic house on Lafayette Square that he remodeled into a beautiful home, he passed his declining years, surrounded by his loving friends and family. He retained to the last not only his well-stored mental faculties, but the strong religious nature that seemed

born in him. If his native city of Cincinnati had
enough repose from money-getting for memory, a
bronze statue in the principal public space would
commemorate Washington McLean as one of her
most eminent citizens.

## Robert Cumming Schenck.

The death of this distinguished man can scarcely be called a loss to the public, for full of age and honors, he has quietly waited in the privacy of his beautiful home for that summons which ends the world to each of us sooner or later. General Schenck grew old with grace and dignity, and when at last he folded his soldier's cloak about him and lay down to pleasant dreams, the mantle covered the form of one who had known not fear nor reproach. His name alone is his honored epitaph. His courage on the field was as high as the courage of his convictions in the political arena, and while feared he was never offensive. He was at all times the true gentleman, and, while loving and lovable as a woman, he was a man among men, and to a high order of intellect added a force of character that made him under all circumstances a leader.

General Robert C. Schenck had no luck. All that he gained in life came from the hardest efforts of his own against adverse circumstances. Brilliant as his career was, it yet fell far beneath his deserving. The writer of this, who was honored by an intimacy that made the confidence of brothers, looks back

from this cold March day, in which his remains are
being solemnly laid at rest, to the far 1840, when the
acquaintance began that soon ripened into a loving
confidence which continued until death came between, and can note each opening opportunity that,
through a malign chance, was not taken at the tide
which leads to fortune.

Such, for example, occurred when President
Lincoln was first called to the presidency. The then
Hon. Robert C. Schenck and I were assigned to
Southern Illinois to do missionary labor in behalf of
the new-born Republican party. The region belonged to the Hon. John A. Logan, and was called
Egypt because of its dense ignorance. This was not
all; the ignorance had a spice of malice in it that
found expression not only in epithets, but in handy
articles of a rather malodorous sort. We learned
that the American eagle sometimes lays rotten eggs.
It was by the merest chance that the eloquent stump-
ers in the cause of freedom escaped personal violence.
Our meetings were large and disorderly. The enemy
came in from a sense of fun and curiosity, and we
had at each appointment a sturdy band of settlers
from New England who acted as police and generally
took the eggs.

One of the amusing incidents of our tour through
Egypt came in the shape of a curious combination

made up of freaks, sick beasts, and second-rate saw-
dust tumblers.  The showman took advantage of our
advertising, and was proving the greater attraction
of the two.  We found it necessary to get at an arrangement mutually beneficial.  We agreed to alter-
nate hours of exhibition.  When the great moral
combination of fat women, anacondas, invalid beasts,
and spangled riders exhibited in the morning, our
attraction in the way of oratory came off in the afternoon.   On several occasions we occupied the one
canvas, and when General Schenck or I stamped
down our emphatic utterances from the roof of the
cages, the sleepy lion or sick tiger would respond
with growls that gave great emphasis to our oratory
and delighted our hearers.  My eminent leader
charged that on one occasion he caught me and our
hook-nosed showman dividing profits between us.
This conclusion was erroneous; I was only negotiat-
ing with the showman for the use of the fat woman
and the anacondas till the end of the campaign.  I
observed that our audiences so mixed the political
efforts with the show combination that dead things
and decayed eggs were less to be apprehended.

Our canvass terminated at Springfield, where, a
short time before the election, we spoke one night at
the wigwam, as the impromptu hall was designated.
Abraham Lincoln made one of our audience, and the

next day, before we left, Mr. Lincoln urged us to return to the jubilee at Springfield should the fierce
contest end in our success. Such proved to be history, and we not only had the verbal invitation, but
were telegraphed for. At the end of the wild jubilee
the President-elect insisted not only upon our remaining, but in accompanying him to Chicago, where
he went to meet the Hon. Hannibal Hamlin, Senator
Trumbull, and others, to consult about the cabinet
then being selected.

There was no mistaking the significance of this.
While President Lincoln was a cautious man, he was
yet fair, and certainly would not have placed so distinguished a man as Mr. Schenck in such an embar-
rassing position without a motive. Mr. Schenck
believed, not from any thing the President-elect said,
but from his significant actions, that he intended ten-
dering him a seat in the cabinet. When, however,
we reached Chicago, Schenck and I making part
of the President's family, influences were brought
to bear that made such selection impossible. The
fact is that it was at Chicago that President Lincoln
struck that vast underlying mass of corruption that
seized on and held the Republican party so long, to
its embarrassment, and now, it is to be feared, its
utter ruin. Robert C. Schenck was one of the purest
men ever called to public life. A wrong-doing was

not only a shock to his moral sense, but when it appeared before him, a personal insult. He was never tempted, for he had that in his presence which cowed dishonesty. This sort of man was not acceptable to the element that was fighting to get Simon Cameron and Caleb B. Smith into the cabinet. Fraud was licking its hungry chops before the rich spoils which a new and untried party and a simple, inexperienced backwoodsman would have in keeping.

Robert C. Schenck was crowded out. He felt hurt and indignant at the way he had been treated, and for some time after had an ugly-feeling for the man he had done so much to elevate. Indeed, this feeling lasted until the threatened war broke upon us, when all personal feeling was lost in the patriotic impulse of which Robert C. Schenck had so much that he saw nothing but the peril of his country.

One can well be pardoned for speculating—idle as such is—as to what would have happened for the good of our country had Robert C. Schenck been called to the war department at that time. His clear, brilliant mind, vast stores of information, executive capacity, and, above all, his high integrity, would not only have been of great service to the government, but have changed the whole current of events which, through four years of war, made a continuous succession of shameful disasters and defeats,

and the tracks of our armies highways of Union
bones. We should now have something to pride
ourselves on other than the heroic efforts of a great
people, and the no less heroic fighting of the men
under muskets, God bless them! When the cold,
calm, impartial hand of true history comes to record
our public shame, as well as our people's glory, it will
point to the humble grave of the soldier and statesman at Dayton, Ohio, as holding a divine possibility
strangely neglected when God gave us the golden opportunity.

Immediately at the sound of the first hostile
gun, Robert C. Schenck tendered his services as a
soldier to the government. The same strange fate of
unfortunate circumstances met him at the armed entrance. The president, accepting the offer, com-
missioned him brigadier-general. Immediately from
the Northern press went up an indignant protest
against the appointment of what it pleased to call "a
political general." It was our idiotic ignorance of
the work to be done that made us regard a little
school on the Hudson, that taught every thing on
earth but patriotism and the art of war, as the only
source of military ability. It was held that no man
was capable of a military command who had not
been perfected in the drill of a private, very much as
if it were insisted that no one could ride a horse until

he had learned to shoe the animal. All the lessons of all the wars, from the day of Cain to the death of Napoleon, failed to teach us that, while the private can be made through discipline and drill, God alone creates the capable commander. We can as well make a successful physician or an eminent lawyer out of a fool as we can organize a school that will monopolize military ability where the net purport and upshot of its course is to graduate abnormal memories.

Be this as it may, it was General Schenck's misfortune to execute a written order, word for word, as it was given him, by which a railroad train was wrecked by two pieces of chance artillery under command of a stray Confederate officer. Ten of our men were killed; and the wrath poured out in ridicule and grossest vituperation, upon the head of General Schenck was without parallel. It would have driven almost any other man from the service. General Schenck was a sensitive man, and I, who slept in his tent, saw the silent agony that made his days gloomy and his nights sleepless torture. But the brave man clamped those iron jaws together and went grimly on. No one unacquainted with the facts can realize the exquisite punishment so cruelly awarded him. Every day the newsboys, threading the camp of his command, distributed these poisoned sheets, in which the awful butchery of the poor fellows, ten in number, was dwelt on as a fearful crime done by a political general. And General Schenck saw the unconcealed doubts in the faces of his men as he rode down their lines in discharge of his duty. How could he hope to win the confidence and control the actions of raw soldiers thus influenced?

Another fact in this connection illustrates my hero's character. That order, which he was compelled to execute, was signed by General McDowell. At any time, by giving that order to the public, he could have shifted his responsibility to the shoulders of its author. He scorned any effort of the sort. The order was a correct order. What he was called on to do was the thing to be done, and he stood by it. He was not the man to use a baby's plea, and wail out a defense of that sort.

As for General McDowell, who saw this storm of abuse hurtling over the land in condemnation of a gallant subordinate, when four little words from him, " It was my deed," would have stilled the tempest, and yet said nothing, we can only point to the fact that a few weeks afterward he was called upon to abide the pitiless peltings of a like blast. In his defeat at the first Bull Run, a battle planned and fought by him with infinitely more capacity and courage than was any engagement later in the war,

32

he met with the most savage criticism and personal abuse from this same press. However, the enlightened press began to see the fact, as the French philosopher expressed it, that " one can not have an omelette without breaking eggs." The lament over the poor dead of McDowell's railroad express died out before the stunning reports of defeats where the dead and wounded counted thousands. We can take up that refrain, now that the blare and glare of war have passed, and we can with a shudder count up the loss of life—God help us!—the lives of the bravest and best men, the men under the muskets, who marched to murder under epauletted imbeciles. I will not pause to enumerate these heroes of defeat, but I will say, as my old heart throbs with pride in the mention, that Robert C. Schenck was not one of them, nor old " Rosey," nor " Pap " Thomas, the one great hero of the war.

General Schenck never recovered from the blight put upon him by an inconsiderate press. The Government at Washington in every field fought two battles, one the military, the other on the political field. There was an army at the North as deadly and dangerous as Lee's army at the South. At almost any moment when confidence should be destroyed, the grim and almost silent force in the rear was ready to move to the front and end hostilities through a compromise that meant destruction to the Great Republic. On this account the press had to be treated with profound respect. It is a great comfort to remember that this same press was like the people, loyal to the great cause. The press had condemned General Schenck very unjustly, but the verdict had been rendered, and from it there was no appeal. Talk about the infallibility of the Holy Father at Rome! It is as nothing to the infallibility of our blessed autocrats of type, the imperial " we " of the press.

General Schenck was never trusted with an independent command until after he was shot out of his saddle at the second Bull Run, when he was rendered temporarily unfit for active service. Promoted to Major-General for gallant service in the field, he was given command of the Middle Department, with head-quarters at Baltimore.

My General was eminently fitted for success as a military man. He had not only the physical courage so much admired and believed in by the common mind, but a moral courage as well, that made his brain available in every emergency. After all, there is very little in this wholesale killing that calls for much intellectual ability. The self-confidence and force of character which distinguish successful military men are in antagonism to the thoughtful processes which tend to make a man doubtful as to his conclusions. However, let that be as it may, he had a taste for military life, and the natural qualities that gave him command on sight.

In his diplomatic career General Schenck met with the same sort of adverse combination that seemed ever ready to leap up and face him when a way opened to fresh honors. Returning from a trip to Europe he saw at Paris a woman's hat, so beautiful that, under a sudden impulse, he purchased and brought it home a present to Mrs. Grant. President Grant returned the favor by making General Schenck minister to the English court. Now, there is nothing of an official nature for an American diplomate abroad to do, and he has generally two secretaries to assist him in doing it. All our diplomatic business is accomplished at Washington, for the simple reason that there is no authority in our constitution by which the power lodged in the President and senate can be delegated to an agent. As a real diplomate is such agent, possessed of power of more or less significance, to commit his government to any negotiation he may be authorized to open, the door is shut to our ever having a diplomatic corps. Our agents abroad are therefore only clerks of the State Department, sent out on high salaries to play at being ministers, *chargés d'affaires*, etc. It is well for these gentlemen that in their assumed role there is no business to transact, for

it is very doubtful if they could make much of a figure if there were.

However, there is a social side in which our clerk
sent to England can figure, and, if he have the talent
and tact, can do so gracefully, and to the credit, not
precisely of our country, but the gig society, as Car-
lyle called the upper classes. In this way James
Russell Lowell won renown, as did his successor, Mr.
Phelps. General Schenck was eminently fitted for
such a part. Easy, graceful, and self-possessed, he
had a scintillating wit and a sense of humor that made
him at all times acceptable to the cultured classes.

Unfortunately my General carried with his commission a quantity of stock in what was known as
the Emma Mine of Utah. He had not only purchased this stock in good faith, but put about all he
owned in that venture. That the Emma was a most
remarkable deposit, and bade fair to turn the thousands of the stock held by the few into millions, all believed, but especially General Schenck. He put his
own money in the mine, and in the generosity of his
character he advised all his friends to do the same.
Now, among these were some titled people, and
therein General Schenck committed an error, for in
time the rumor rose and spread that the Emma was a
failure, and General Schenck was advised to unload
ere it was too late. It was intimated to him that this

deposit was only a pocket, and would soon be exhausted. "I can not do it," said Schenck, "although its failure will ruin me; I have advised too many of my friends to invest, for me take the course you advise." He did hold on, and in the end proved a winner, for it appears that a few shrewd owners had set about freezing the majority of stockholders out, and having accomplished that, the Emma resumed business. But, as I have said, General Schenck had been guilty of advising certain noblemen of high degree to invest, and Squire Smalley, who stands at the palace gate armed with a syringe to protect the gentry and nobility of England from scurvy American citizens, opened upon General Schenck, and, assisted by Moncure D. Conway, evangelical teacher of evolution, supplied the American press with the vilest abuse of our minister for having been guilty of leading my Lord Tomnoddy and my Lady Teacaddy into a loss in the Emma. This vituperation was taken up and continued by the press until a man, the soul of honor, and of an integrity that kept him poor in places where he could have winked himself into millions, was regarded as a common sharper, and a discredit to our name.

On one place, however, Robert C. Schenck could stand and ask no odds of any man, and that was the floor of the House of Representatives. He was probably the readiest debater ever seen in Congress. As Chairman of the Committee of Ways and Means, and, therefore, leader of the house, he would hold the floor and galleries interested for days at a stretch. His short, epigrammatic sentences, often enlivened by wit, and always forcible, irritated his opponents, delighted his partisans, and amused the spectators. He had the rare art of making dry details entertaining.

General Schenck was not a handsome man. Nearly all his life of a slender build, he had a short neck, prominently square jaw, and small eyes; and yet, with all these disadvantages, no man lived who could so readily win the love of women and the confidence of men. The smile on that grim face was in itself conquest, it seemed so sweet and devoted to the one on whom it beamed. He could turn a compliment in a way to rob it of any shade of insincerity, let the flattery be what it might.

General Schenck's life was too busy—too closely pressed by live events—for him to be much of a book student. Quick to learn, he gathered all he cared to know from everyday life and the talk of men. A serious work that he might pick up, he seemed to master from the preface and index; and all the time he had to spare to books he devoted to fiction. His political speeches, therefore, can not be taken as masterful essays on great economic subjects. He was the originator of many important measures, more prominently the bill he introduced and passed to a law, shortly after the close of the war, pledging the government to a liquidation of the bonds in coin. The Hon. John Sherman gets the credit of this measure, and claims it. The humor of this lies in the fact, that Schenck devised this act, and hurried it through, in order to frustrate the Hon. John Sherman, who had then given in his adhesion to the greenback doctrine of payment.

Robert Cumming Schenck belonged to a class of men once prominent, especially in the Northwest, that has almost disappeared from public life. I refer to men who came up from cabins and workshops, sons of farmers and mechanics, whose force of character carried them from poverty to power. Knotty-headed, hard-handed sons of toil, they worked as laborers in the summer for means to gain a schooling in the winter, and then taught school for a living until they gained professions. From this class came our successful business men, eminent physicians, lawyers of potent ability, profound judges, and popular politicians. In the last-named capacity they made the stump the tribune of the people, and were ready teachers of the masses.

This process of honest toil did not train thieves, and this class led in political life when not only marked ability threw luster upon our government, but to be a Swartwout was to be driven from place and from social recognition. For a man to be convicted of bribery was as fatal to him as if he were caught picking a pocket. Henry Clay might fail to pay any debts save those of honor, and Daniel Webster in that direction might decline preference of any sort. But such wrong-doing did not touch their public lives. The people, dazzled by the ability of their leaders, were no less proud of their purity. Now, we have reversed this. So long as a public man meets his financial obligations promptly, he is not only allowed to practice crime as a politician, but applauded if successful. Even this line of demarcation is not preserved. As we make a detective out of a thief, because of his knowledge of thieves' ways, we set up rogues in each party to outwit rogues of the other organization. A Quay, for example, whose career, as told by the New York World, makes Dick Turpin respectable, is not only tolerated by a majority of the people of Pennsylvania, but sustained as the Republican thief that is more than a match for the Democratic thieves.

"Had I a son," said General Schenck, not long

33

before his death, " I would rather see him a day laborer than a politician."

The distinguishing trait of General Schenck, in
which he is most pleasantly remembered, was in his
keen wit, that was stimulated and rendered delight-
ful by his sense of humor. This was rendered the
more fascinating by its unobtrusive use. He had the
rare art of listening, in conversation, and rendering
frank appreciation to the efforts of others. But that
which made him more generally known was his being so very American. He was the most marked example of our national character I ever knew. Born
in many generations on our continent, he took up in
each birth some peculiarity of our soil, climate, and
other environments. This was shown in his intense
love of his native land, which, in his eyes, had neither
fault nor blemish. And this American character was
shown in his happy versatility. He had in perfection
the American hand that can be turned to any use in
life or in emergency. As a lawyer he would have
moved to the front of his profession. As a debater
he had, as we have said, no equal. No man living
had a keener, clearer knowledge of details, and his
happy facility in their manipulation made him an executive official of rare excellence. As a soldier, I
know of no man better qualified for the field.

After a long life of honorable effort, much of it in the most stirring time of our country's peril, in which he took a conspicuous part, he has passed to rest, leaving to his loved and loving children a memory as precious as it is honored by his country.

## Henry Ward Beecher.

The comment caused by the death of Henry Ward Beecher affords means by which to gauge the impress made by that eminent man upon the community. Our people are much given to the measure of a man's greatness after death by the official pedestal upon which he stood in life. There is a popular superstition to the effect that all eminence finds expression in official agency. In this way a member of the house has his elevation second to that of a senator, while a president towers over all. Now, as our government, on paper, consists of a few rules easily understood, and not difficult of application, one would be puzzled at the infatuation that makes great men of its agents. This wonder, however, is solved when we remember that, while much of the wealth of the country depends on the administration of the government, all of it is more or less interested. The brain, therefore, not only is not called in politically, but is actually excluded. The parties at interest want as their agent either a slave or a cipher, and, while there is no open organization against intellect and character, there is an instinctive inclination that is more effective.

" Why should I contribute money to carry the state election," asked a prominent politician, " when I can buy the legislature for half the money?"

Henry Ward Beecher held no office, and yet his death is as widely lamented as if he were an ex-president. Nor can this marked attention be attributed to religious feeling. This eminent man had no hold of that sort. He was a reverend in name, and the broadest so-called liberal known to the country. Born through several generations in Calvinism, the immediate son and trained disciple of the venerated Lyman Beecher, he seemed, at an early age, to have treated the dark, despairing doctrines of that sect as the average preacher does a text which we are told was like a boy who lays down a stick to see how far he can jump from it. Henry went on jumping until the old stick was entirely lost sight of. He continued until he got to be, in his perfect manhood, an eloquent stump orator of the Lord instead of a closely-constructed advocate of what Burns called, profanely, " tyding o' damnation." He was a preacher of politics in the lecture-room, and a lecturer in the house of the Lord, and no man lived who wielded a wider and a deeper influence over his fellow-men than this strange compound of kind impulses, clear brain, and clever expression. He founded no sect; he started no school; he had, indeed, no philosophy;

but could put in choice phrase the kindlier thoughts and better feelings of humanity. Taking the little gold dust of the popular mind, he coined it into a circulating medium.

To sum up, we are called on to consider one who, beginning a Presbyterian, ended an Evolutionist, and carried with him a huge congregation that went through the forms of Calvin's sect while listening to the teachings of Darwin's infidelity. The condition of this congregation of the Lord seems contradictory, but Henry Ward Beecher was consistent with himself. Charity not only covers a multitude of sins, but it tolerates a large amount of absurdity, provided the absurdity is kindly expressed and in learned phrase. That the human race has been evolved from monkeys is as shocking to the common understanding as Calvin's darkest teaching of predestined damnation, but both monkey and devil disappear in the avowal of the loving mercy of the Almighty, and the subtle dissertations of philosophy. Henry Ward Beecher found no difficulty in harmonizing the two.

This eloquent, kind-hearted, and impulsive man wielded a wider and deeper influence over our people and age than any other human being. Beecher was the architect and builder of his own fortune, and he came into the world singularly well equipped for the work. He possessed, to a wonderful extent, that

quality generally recognized and so little understood,
called **magnetism**. To this he added the kind impulses I have spoken of, which impelled him to find
in his associates opinions and feelings in which they
could harmonize. This is a common quality, for men
are gregarious, but he possessed the rare gift of making it practical. Of a sanguine, phlegmatic temperament, he never offended by appearing better than
others, or in anywise different from frail humanity.
Nor did he ever cry, *Allez mes enfants*, but *Venez mes
enfants.* He sent no forlorn hopes to attack the forti-
fications of sin, but led in person, and took all the
perils and privations of the expedition without pretense of any sort. His stout person, carrying a full
stomach and a kind face, suggested good-fellowship,
while his words were the utterances of genius used .
to persuade rather than threaten.

The first half of his life he gave to the advocacy
of reform ; the other and later half, to preaching the
philosophy of content. Reform is not popular; it is
not respectable. All wrong shields itself behind social respectability, and makes the reformer a low dis-
turber of the peace. As an advocate of Abolition-
ism, Beecher suffered. He was in a minority, and
would have gone down with the odorous few, had
not violence intervened on a different issue, and carried the cranks into a great party that, for the mo-

ment, made the North one political organization. This success seemed to satisfy Beecher, and from that out he accepted the more pleasing *rôle* of Christian resignation to the ills of life. Wendell Phillips, on the contrary, having fought to free the negro slaves, sought to free white labor. Beecher seemed to think that white labor could care for itself, under the recognized law of supply and demand. The only duty he saw in capital was a charitable use of accumulated means, and the duty of labor was to be content "on a dollar a day," feeling assured that the dollar, in some shape, would be paid. He gave all he had to the poor and the gratification of his own cultivated tastes, and labored under the impression that such sort of life opened the road to heaven, closed by our Savior to the rich. "Sell all that thou hast, give to the poor, and come and follow me," had an implied condition that the believer was free of hay-fever and had no taste for bric-a-brac.

As a reformer of evils and a reformer of men, preaching Christian content to one, and anti-negro-slavery to the other, he made a broad mark among men. The poor, much-abused Abolitionists rallied to his cry in the first instance, and broadcloth and fine linen gave him their ears and purses in the last. The forms of religion were retained in both. He preached political sermons between prayers all the time. When advocating the freedom of the slave, he invoked the vengeance of God upon the slave-holders. When teaching the philosophy of content, he gathered about him the money-changers, and taught the Divine mercy of evolution between the same hymns and the same prayerful appeals, with a passage of Scripture that came in like a lump of old cheese to promote digestion. Undaunted by the memory of his stern father, Lyman Beecher, he could introduce Robert Ingersoll to an audience, and stand unmoved upon the same platform with Father Mc-Glynn. This was being liberal, but it must have turned the venerable Lyman in his grave.

It is claimed by a few, and thought true by many, that his usefulness in life was injured by the Tilton scandal. This is said and thought in ignorance of poor human nature. There is a point in a man's life when he reaches his zenith and descends on the same curve that marks his course heaven-ward. This lessening of power, and, of course, use-fulness, is attributed in Beecher's case to the ex-plosion of that mud volcano. It is a startling as-sertion to make, but I believe the truth, that Beecher gained instead of lost by that assault. In this I do not claim that his innocence was proven, or that the white soul came out of the fiery furnace untarnished and unmarked by the flames. The contrary was the fact. The only question debated, in mind among his friends, and openly by the public, was his degree of. guilt. His followers stood by him bravely as too good and dear a man to be put down, even by his own act, while the people sympathized with him in wrong-doing, which is only an unforgiveable sin when committed by a woman. Joseph is sneered at, while the wanton Mrs. Potiphar is consigned to several thousand years of infamy.

This is not a delicate subject; it is simply indelicate, and the dudes of literature are shocked into silence by its mere mention. As morbid anatomy we may show sickening specimens, or leave them to science for treatment. But this is not morbid anatomy; it is poor human nature in its normal condition, and a shame to our civilization. The difference of treatment awarded the man and the woman for the same transgression reflects upon men and women. The sister of the one when even charged with the sin is consigned to infamy by the sex that is without forgiveness cruel as fate, while both join in admiration, either secretly felt or openly expressed, for the sinful man. Had the woman told of in Holy Writ been surrounded by women, our blessed Savior would have found his hearers with aprons, yes great baskets, filled with stones, and e'er the Divine injunction could have been uttered, the Son of Man would have been forced to flee for his life, for not only is the woman doomed, but all who dare to pity and forgive her. In this case of protected trial, grotesque and comic in many aspects, and tragic in one only, Beecher escaped unharmed, while poor Mrs. Tilton lies buried fathoms deep beneath the slime of the eruption.

Again we are so strangely obtuse to the fact that while our admiration may be excited by intellectual qualities, or the power that comes of force of character, our sympathies are based wholly upon the human weakness of the hero. In the silly anxiety to construct of George Washington, for example, a demigod, undimmed by faults or failings, that great man is robbed of the loving memory that should be his. These pious eulogists are worried to find that people weary of their wooden god. The sculptor who left him of heroic size, in marble, at the capitol, sitting in stern majesty, half naked, "looking," as the witty Ben Lesley Loose said, "as if he had risen from a cold bath, and was pointing indignantly at the patent office, where his small clothes were," was not further from the truth than the pious exhorters who have eliminated all humanity from our hero.

I have said that there was no question in the minds of the mass as to the guilt of Beecher. The verdict was a Scotch verdict of "Not proven." But there were degrees of mental conviction. To the vulgar he was a common debauchee, and was loved the more on that account. To the discriminating there was a familiarity with vice and the vicious in that direction that was not commendable, to say the least; but they attributed this to his good-natured, easy indifference that permitted questionable characters to sleep in his priestly robes. This was a weakness, but not a sin.

The fact is Beecher was a born Bohemian. The shallow pretenses, the hypocrisy of social life when respectable, made him tired. He longed to throw off the unnatural restraint and feel at liberty. In this way he opened a back door to a class of emancipated mortals, whose very freedom afforded him relief and amusement. These people were learned, witty, and by no means common people, and they flattered the man whom their mere association first endangered and then damaged. But the man thus abused was not permanently injured. He had a strong hold on the people through love for him, and he won their admiration through his courage.

The fact is, no man in this world of ours lives by the consent of others, unless he is charged with murder, and then twelve men may hang him. Men suffer death politically, socially, or otherwise from their own acts. It is the breaking down of the inner man in the presence of abuse that is fatal to him.

The great Lincoln taught me a lesson in this. During the war I met the Hon. Reverdy Johnson of Baltimore, near the executive mansion, and he informed me that he was on his way to see "Old Abe," as he called the President, on some business. Invited to accompany him, I turned, and we found the President alone, seated at a table, studying a number of maps. Inviting us to sit, he said:

"We 're trying, gentlemen, to get McClellan off the James, and do you know the difficulty reminds me of two bulls fighting. So long as the animals keep their heads down, tails up, and their horns locked, there is a good deal of unseemly noise, but no harm done; but the moment one turns to run, the other rips his behind open."

The Hon. Reverdy, a man of a rare sense of humor, laughed immoderately at this homely, yet apt, illustration, and some distance from the White House said soberly:

"Do you know that bull story is equal to anything in Æsop? It illustrates more than the armies. I have often observed that when a man is assailed by his enemies, so long as he keeps his head down and his horns to the front, he is not hurt, and if he has the staying power, as well as pluck, he can not be injured. The people worship courage, while a sense of fair play, common to us all, comes in after a time to the aid of the poor fellow."

Returning from Europe, some years after, I encountered the late Hon. Matt. Carpenter, the mastfed Webster of the West, in the smoker of a train bound for Washington. I found this able, noblehearted senator in a state of deep despondency. He had offended two journalistic reporters by being instrumental in having them imprisoned for stealing a copy of a treaty held in executive session of the senate, and he had not butted one locomotive alone, but all the locomotives in the country. The abuse poured on his poor head was intolerable, and he told me he was on his way to Washington to prepare for his resignation as senator. "There is but one office I want," he said, " and that is a law office."

I told him that would not do, and recalled Lincoln's bull story, with Reverdy Johnson's moral, and added: "Try and fight it out. This storm can not last much longer; it is getting weaker now. After it is over, make one of your brilliant speeches in the senate, on the popular side, and you can go out in a blaze of glory." Carpenter practiced as I preached, and the trouble about his retiring was that neither his own state, nor the party the country over, would permit him to retire.

Henry Ward Beecher fought it out. If his courage at any time failed him, he kept the failure to himself. With a calm, quiet and almost indifferent front he faced the enemy, until, amid the cheers of the crowd and congratulations of his friends, the enemy disappeared.

Henry Ward Beecher did much writing, but never appeared at his best either as author or journalist. He had the divine faculty of thinking aloud on his legs, and moving masses to laughter or tears at his will. While blessed with a charming utterance, and winning his way through words that for the moment seemed inspired, he lacked the imagination necessary to successful authorship, and his books will make but a feeble record of his power. He was a successful actor, and as such will live through generations on tradition, while the flowers so profusely cast by his friends upon his coffin will fade into nothingness, and the inscription on his tomb will require ere long a memory to tell of who he was and what he accomplished.

## Roscoe Conkling.

How few are the orators capable of burying Cæsar, as compared to the number prepared to praise. the late Mark Antony and the living Ingersoll illustrate.

Death not only challenges effort. but in its dread mystery evokes sorrow and sympathy. It is a great misfortune to die, and the surviving friends and relatives seek consolation in tears and praise that are equally vain and senseless. The poor unfortunates have condensed eulogies engraved on their tombs, while the more conspicuous are treated to orations, and,

"When all is done, upon the tomb is seen.
Not what they were, but what they should have been."

In the burial of our latest Cæsar, it was well that the pagan Ingersoll should be selected to eulogize the dead. To bury Cæsar is to put body and character alike out of sight. To praise is not to bury the past, with his bones, but to call the spirit from its forgetfulness, and keep alive its character and career among the living. Our pagan orator has little logic and less imagination; but a delicate fancy plays upon the surface, like sunlight on water, leaving all the depths untouched and undisturbed. Out of the dead Conkling he constructed a great shade that has about as much resemblance to the original as the fantastic folds of a fog-bank have to the marsh from which it originated.

Through all the glittering sentences of the oration we look in vain for some proof that the dead politician was a statesman—or an orator. No measure is told of that he originated or sustained for the betterment of the masses he represented; no one sentence is recalled, of all the speeches, that humanity cares to remember.

He was an honest man, cries our pagan orator; and it is a sad commentary on our civil service that the highest praise awarded a dead official is that he died poor. Have we come to such a pass that a man holding high honors, who failed to take advantage of his trust and so rob the public to fill his private purse, leaves this as his only claim to memory? Such is the fact; and no man did more to fetch upon us this deplorable condition than the dead Cæsar the orator Ingersoll would not bury.

We were content to have had the wreaths fade and the moss grow upon a tomb, to dumb forgetfulness a prey, wherein were hid the evil deeds of a noted character; for Roscoe Conkling had been for

34

many years out of public life. But to have this picturesque but exceedingly unpleasant person held before the people as a model of excellence is more than
our sense of propriety will allow. To speak ill of
the dead means a wanton assault on a memory; and
after all, the late New York politician did not orig-
inate the wrong he made crime, but only practiced
upon a system he found ready to his unscrupulous
hand. We could well leave the grave to hide the
evil he had done, in the memory of what he might
have been with other environments, but we can not
consent to this mischievous attack on the integrity
of a memory that yet lies within the memory of the
living.

Roscoe Conkling was an honest man, if by hon-
esty we mean the clean hands with which he left
public life. And yet no man ever lived who covered
with his eloquence and concealed behind his high
character so much impurity. Too proud to steal
himself, he was not too pure to wink at theft in others. He was not only willing his henchmen and
allies should steal, but he hastened to shut off all investigation and protect criminals from being made
convicts, and convicts from being punished. Of
course this eminent man would have scorned to defend a common fence for vulgar stealings: but when
the administration itself, in the hands of the highest

officials of the best government under the sun, went into the business, the elevation of the criminals lifted crime into respect, and the senatorial robes could be spread unsoiled to cover and conceal the swag of an administration.

All this was not without compensation. The able advocate who, returning to practice at the bar, made a fortune every year in retainers alone, by pleading cases before judges of his own creation, was not the man to make a present of his powers as an advocate to a combination that was as heartless as it was unpatriotic and corrupt.

God knows Grant's administration needed not only such a defender, but precisely such a bold, unscrupulous leader. It was his task to marshal and hold to the front the Republican party in Congress. There were a few conscientious men there who sickened at the corruption; and there were many timid men there who were startled at the half-hidden mines of dynamite over which they were called to march. Conkling inspired the one with courage and the other with confidence.

This was a huge contract, an undertaking that might well appall a less resolute and more conscientious man. We came out of the late civil war with three armies left over for the government to care for. One was an army of thieves, the other of prostitutes, and the third of cripples. All three of these armies moved on the capitol. They found in command there the man who, being considered the greatest captain of his century, from the fact of his being on horseback when the confederacy fell from sheer exhaustion, had been made a political platform of, and ruled the country as he had the army, on a principle that made the justices of the Supreme Court members of his staff, and members of Congress his subordinate officers.

Under this system of administration, so ignorant that it almost defies belief, fraud ran riot, and the foulest corruption sapped the very foundations of the solid political fabric erected by the fathers. The corridors of the capitol were crowded with a lobby made up of fast men and loose women, upon whose adamantine cheeks iniquity was fairly enameled. The departments were given over to cunning schemers, who depleted a treasury filled to overflowing by a war tax that had kept a million of men in the field. At the executive mansion the very air was heavy with a sewer-gas of moral corruption, and the cabinet itself was embarassed by penitentiary liens upon its members.

From all this foul environment Roscoe Conkling walked apart. No lobbyist, nor dishonest contractor, nor fraudulent official dared approach him. He held a position where he could have winked himself into millions. He had that strange personality and pride of character that made the slightest intimation of personal wrong-doing an insult. And yet this did not prevent his defending wrong in others. He, however, illustrated the truth of ·Walpole's misquoted saying, which tells us that every man has his price. Conkling's price was political power, and it was freely given him.

No prominent man ever lived so poorly equipped to be a popular leader as Roscoe Conkling. To the vanity of a woman he added a manner at once so offensive and aggressive, that it was said of him that he made an enemy whenever he shook a hand. And yet these very qualities gave strength to the control awarded him in a corrupted civil service by the President. In return for his support of the administration he was given full, unrestrained, and complete control of the patronage of New York. His constituency was shifted from New York to the executive mansion. His adroit colleague from New York was so amazed to find the atmosphere about the President so chilly, and his recommendations treated with such contempt, that he was forced from office. Official patronage is the breath of life to a senator, and Conkling's associate had to be a slave or a cipher in order to hold his empty honors in the chamber.

Such was Conkling's hold on Grant that his brother-republican senators feared to offend him; for they saw but too clearly that when a senator refused to acknowledge his imperious leadership, political death was that senator's immediate fate. Thus it was that Sumner found himself deprived of his senatorial prominence, and Carl Schurz was relegated to private life. Detested by the Democrats, distrusted by the Republicans, and feared by all, yet such was the power of the patronage given to his especial use, that he stalked the chamber with the pride and insolence of a dictator, and marshaled his forces as if they were slaves dreading the crack of a whip. And he won his spurs. No scandal drifted near the White House, no attack by reformers or Democrats threatened the Executive, that Roscoe Conkling did not start up, gun in hand, to repel the threatened danger.

When, for example, the San Domingo infamy reached the public, and it became known how a combine had bought for a mere song a rotten debt of a negro government, and sought through annexation to fetch their bonds to par, Sumner assailed it; and while Conkling's resonant voice was echoing along the fretted ceiling of the senate chamber, the President of the United States occupied the lobby, hat in hand, using his personal influence to force the infamy through.

In like manner the French arms outrage, sanctioned by Grant and sustained by Conkling, was fought over in the senate. But five hundred pages would not serve to tell of the iniquities conceived at one end of the avenue and concealed under thunders of eloquence at the other. Roscoe Conkling could be awakened at midnight not only without offense, but eager for the fray. He paid well for the corrupted use of official patronage given without reserve into his hands.

We have said he was distrusted by his Republican associates and detested by all. That the distrust was not without foundation, his conduct in the Tilden-Hayes contest abundantly justifies. Conkling saw Grant's term of office drawing to a close, and well knew that Grant's successor could not be depended upon for a constituency. If he had any doubt of this, the nomination of Hayes at Cincinnati solved it beyond question. The cold, quiet, self-possessed, politically unknown man of Ohio was the equal of Conkling in intelligence, and his superior in force of character. Modest of manner, he was yet self-possessed and positive in his personality. He was not the man to be the tool of the moneyed combinations about Washington, nor dependent on any man in the senate for a vindication of character or career. Conkling could not afford to have such a Republican succeed the rough, ignorant soldier who had so long served him as a constituency. Roscoe could afford to have a Democrat President, as in that case he could put the Executive between himself and his humble office-holders and office-seekers.

Now, had Roscoe Conkling risen in his place in the senate and denounced the purposed inauguration of Hayes as an infamous outrage, he would have won for himself all that Ingersoll has uttered in his eulogy. He did nothing of the sort, but, continuing in caucus with his Republican associates, he intrigued with the Democracy to the ruin of his friends. He was the author of the electoral bill that meant the Hon. David Davis to hold the casting vote; and so clear were his tracks and ill-concealed his motives, that a Republican senate treated him to the discourtesy of refusing him a position on the very commission he had conceived of and carried through to a law.

During Hayes' administration, the shadow of the picturesque senator never darkened the doors of the executive mansion. Under the rule of the Ohio lawyer the moral atmosphere cleared, and the moneyed combinations disappeared from about the departments. They lingered about the lobbies of congress in a shame-faced sort of way. lacking the sanction of the Executive and the support of senatorial eloquence.

St. Edmunds came to the front, and, sustained by the ample cloak of philanthropy that covered the class legislation of a paternal government and in the name of God robbed somebody, Conkling's occupation seemed a dream of the past.

Roscoe Conkling's exit from public life was in keeping with his startling career. Restless under the loss of power, he conceived the violation of our unwritten constitution in a third term of Grant. History tells how this was defeated by Blaine and enjoyed by Garfield. We all know how the Achilles sulking in his tent was brought to the field by a solemn compact that was to restore the able politician to his breath of life—his source of power found in the official patronage of the great State of New York. This compact was violated in the selection of James G. Blaine as Secretary of State. That selection sealed the doom of both the President and Conkling, for the resignation of one was followed by the assassination of the other. The senator of a sovereign state threw up his high office because he could no longer control the patronage found in a rotten civil service; and the crack of an assassin's pistol told the world that our civil service, steeped to the chin in corruption, had culminated in murder.

Of course no sane mind connects Conkling, directly, with the crime of Guiteau; and yet the re-

35

volver fired at Washington was loaded at Utica. Fraud breeds violence, and the men who plot treason against good government are sure to find some one, more zealous or insane than the rest, to put their scheming to the proof of expression in act.

This is the story of Conkling's public career, and it finds significance in being the story of our civil service. Are the good citizens of the great Republic, who seek to send down to their children's children the blessings of self-government, prepared to condone the fearful wrong, because of a sickly sentimentality that would bury in one narrow grave all memory of a crime that covers a continent in its evil consequences?

## Charles Stewart Parnell.

When the startling news of Parnell's sudden death
went abroad, it was accompanied by the rumor that he
had committed suicide. This, in the shape given by
report, proved untrue, and yet in a certain sense it was
the truth. He had committed the suicide of crime,
and what followed, in the loss of moral life, and later,
in the end of his physical existence, were but inevitable results. So long as Charles Stewart Parnell
stood in the sunlight, before the world, with clean
hands and a clear conscience, he was not only the
uncrowned king of Ireland, but one of the most conspicuous figures in all Europe. He was second only
to Bismarck, and it is doubtful, if the Iron Duke had
faced such obstacles as those with which Parnell had
to contend, he could have left the German Empire
as an immortal monument of his fame.

The task given Parnell was to harmonize Ireland
before attacking the most powerful government on
earth. The history of Ireland, up to within ten
years, was an awful record of internal dissension.
Irish impulse was Irish insanity. A state of nature
seemed a state of war. It was said of them that
they fought every nation's battles but their own.

How they were taught to know themselves, and in that knowledge learn their strength, is the record of Parnell's great work. All after came easy.

To comprehend this, one has to know an Irishman. For good or ill he is irrepressible. The only disposition that can be made of a turbulent Irishman is to kill him, said the English oppressor, and there was much truth in the observation. The attempt to get rid of him through migration proved a failure. He was as dangerous and troublesome in the United States as at home. Indeed, the immigrant was more of a menace here than at home, for with us he made, through the value of his vote, our government hostile to Great Britain, while at home, broken into factions, he fought other Irishmen.

Parnell stilled this sea of strife, and, for the first time, brought a great people into position to demand what heretofore they had pitifully sued for. The little island is so close to England, that to hold it as an alien enemy is to cultivate a cancer in the stomach. When, therefore, the entire people of Ireland came to the front, it chilled "jingoism" to the bone, and made a quality that entered into the negotiations of every treaty the world over. Russia's road to India, for example, laid through Ireland. The ministry of Her Gracious Majesty brought Parnell from jail to the house of commons, and begged to know his terms. Any other leader would have compromised with wrong, taking one-half, but Parnell demanded a home rule that had a parliament at its head and the constabulary as its foundation. It was secession in all but name. To escape such impossible results, the English government abandoned nearly all the oppression that had made revolt in Ireland a necessity. In ten short years, under Parnell's lead, the Irish people made a progress, politically, socially, and in material, that had been accomplished in no century preceding.

The secret of Parnell's power is strangely hidden. His character had the charm of profound mystery, his career the fascination of the picturesque. Without the qualities of an orator, he won through his oratory. Cold as an icicle, and almost repellant in his solitary ways and silent reserve, he had the most enthusiastic following and warmest friends that ever blessed and sustained a popular leader. St. Patrick was not more reverenced nor the Holy Father more implicitly obeyed.

Was ever greater power given one man? In his place among his peers on the floor of the commons, he was regarded with admiration or hate, but ever with a tinge of awe and fear. It was felt that the same hand that guided all Ireland, so strangely, held in control the darker and more desperate elements of that turbulent people. Ever along the ragged edges of the slate-tinted cloud played the silent lightning of assassination. While patriotic and poetic under the Roman robes of a Brutus, or the graceful drapery of a Charlotte Corday, to strike for freedom, it was atrocious in a dirty peasant driven to desperation, by his houseless family famishing for bread, to strike down his immediate oppressor. Recognizing his proud pre-eminence, his fame and name went out over all the civilized earth. The millions of exiled Irish, scattered over our fair land, looked proudly up at thought of him, and all united in prayer in his behalf, and all from their hard-earned wages sent him great sums to sustain his poor followers and strengthen their patriotic efforts.

In the very hour of his greatest triumph for his people, at the loftiest height of his brilliant career, he suddenly turned aside to commit the suicide of crime. Fame, fortune, power, all went out as suddenly as darkness swallows night after vivid gleam of lightning. What remained was but the specter of Parnell. The pitiful struggle that followed was but the fierce anguish of despair. The world sickened at the wild, impotent efforts of the strange form that so resembled Parnell, and yet was bereft of all the grand qualities that but a brief time before awakened love and admiration. The immortal past of the great man was gone, and soon this thing would drop exhausted and be buried out of sight.

The church in Ireland, in the painful emergency, acted promptly. How painful the act of condemnation was to the church no words have told, or will ever tell. The poor priests of that suffering land, robbed, abused, sneered at, and despised, found in Parnell their friend and champion. They loved their brilliant advocate and brave leader. From every alter in all the island went up each morn heart-felt prayers in his behalf. To not only tear him from their hearts, but from those same altars anathematize the criminal they had so nearly canonized as a saint; to rebuke the thronging thousands of his insane followers; above all, to part with all that had been gained in the cause of Ireland, called for a fortitude and courage far greater than had been demanded in the darkest conflicts of the past, for all the while there rang in their ears the jeering laughter that told the delight of their enemies. To condone the crime, to forgive the criminal, and bid him go on as the multitude demanded, made a course that was not possible. The Parnell they sought to pardon no longer existed. The laurel that crowned the living hero, in his suicide of crime, but decorated decay.

The closing hours given his mortal remains and the somber surroundings that shadowed in the last shock of agony were strangely in keeping with the solitary, mysterious career of this remarkable man. From that house, so close by the sea that the storm in the hoarse roar of the surf requiemed his dying moments, while the rain and spray spit upon the windows and the wind shook the walls, no cry for aid or sympathy went out to a world that had abandoned him. Of all " who followed, flattered, sought, and sued," no one was found to hold his dying hand or do him reverence. Abundant are the tears and piercing the cries of anguish now from the multitude mourning a dead chief, but the sad event they memorize dates back over a year, when the grand leader committed the suicide of crime.

After all, the fact comes home to us that Parnell's death was necessary to Ireland's progress. All the good he did, and it can not be over-estimated, remains and will remain, and the only man who could have endangered the good accomplished was Parnell himself. What he designed and what undoubtedly he would have attempted, the fulfillment of Ireland's dream of national independence, was and is a dream, which to realize would plunge Ireland into deeper woes than the unfortunate people ever experienced before. It is well for them that the holding fast to the good they possess, the effort at advancement should be conservative, and. therefore, practical. In this way the cruel tragedy that robbed Ireland of one great leader may make room for many leaders, all re-solved to take up what Parnell threw down, and so lift old Ireland to the plane her piety and patriotism make worthy of her.

## James A. Garfield.

This eminent man, looked at from a social point of view, was the most charming of men. His fine, healthy physique overflowed with animal spirits, and, added to this, was a keen sense of humor and a companionable turn. The fascination of his presence, however, came in on a defect. He was extremely sensitive and modest. He lacked entirely what phrenologists call self-esteem. With large love of approbation, that made him ambitious, he was without the quality that creates egotism, hence he had the subtle flattery found in the tireless practice of listening.

In using these terms, because they make a common language, the reader must not suppose that I am giving in adhesion to the so-called science of phrenology. It is a snare and a delusion. Denying that the mind is a unit, and that using gives it diversity, I also deny that it presents a variety of organs, each one of which, carefully analyzed, constitutes a complete head, or, in other words, has perfect independent power of expression. What is ideality, for example, without all the other intellectual organs; or, indeed, what is any one of the organs, or all combined, without the animal powers and impulses necessary to life and use? The great Napoleon disposed of the so-called science when he said: "Nature is secretive, and never gave bumps on a man's head that a blind idiot could read by the mere feeling of them?"

Garfield recognized this. His explanation of the facility possessed by the phrenologist of hitting on the prominent traits of a subject was characteristic of the man, and told of one of his beliefs not generally known.

We were discussing the subject in my library at Washington. Garfield was telling George Douglas and myself how, when a young man, on his way to college, he stopped over at New York and expended five dollars in getting a chart of his head from the Fowlers. The ready bump-reader gave him the head of a Webster and Marshall united, and then said:

"Young man, all these rare qualities are nullified and rendered utterly useless by the absence of self-esteem; where that organ ought to be there is externally a hollow. You will make friends, but never a following."

George Douglas laid his head on Garfield's knee and cried:

"General, where is that bump?"

Garfield kindly put his hand on the head of the gifted young journalist, and said:

" Young man, I would give a thousand dollars an hour for that development of your skull."

The late President ascribed the phrenologists' facility of discovery to a spiritual faculty, since called mind-reading. He explained that when the operator puts his hand on the head of the subject, he fetches himself in contact with the mind itself, and utters what he receives. Garfield was a confirmed spiritualist, and extremely superstitious. " This life on earth," he was wont to say, " is but a shadow of the life we can not see. The immortality we believe in did not begin at birth, any more than it ends in death. We have been born many times, but we never did begin. To admit a beginning is to recognize an end. With this mystery about us, how vain and foolish to make our life on earth the one sole object of our existence."

He gave me many instances of the interference of a mysterious power in his own life; interferences that he modestly claimed did not differ from those experienced by others, save in the fact that he recognized them. Of many of these strange events he told me, and I restrained from repeating them because, being confidential utterances, they are, therefore, sacred. On one occasion, noticing Frank, a little black-and-tan terrier, turning himself round and round before curling up for a sleep, he said:

"Do you know why that little fellow goes through that ceremony before lying down?"

I professed utter ignorance.

"Because he came of a wild ancestry that trampled down the grass in that way to make a bed. We call that instinct, but the practice continues after the reason for it has ceased. How much of that there is in humanity which keeps up abuse long after any—I won't say reason, but—excuse for it exists."

"To ignore a fact," he said, on another occasion, "because it is not dignified is stupid. All science is based on vulgar facts. We know that the earth is round because the ignorant sailor sees first the top of the mast of the coming vessel, and, after a time, the hull. Newton saw significance in a falling apple. Emerson calls Spiritualism rat-hole revelation. The Jews saw about the same of Christianity. It was born in a manger. If Emerson dared, he would class the manger with the rat-holes."

Garfield had a seance with Slade. Before doing so he procured a double slate, hinged and locked, with a bit of pencil inside. He was a stranger to that stupid curiosity, Slade, who is a bad man, and scarce one remove from an idiot. Putting his slate on Slade's mantlepiece, he soon became deeply interested in the strange manifestations that went on in the broad daylight. He quite forgot the precaution he had taken, and was about leaving when Slade said:

"You have forgotten your slate."

Garfield took it, and, going to his hotel—the Metropolitan—opened it, and found written in the center two words. They were: "Credit Mobilier."

Garfield had all the affectionate nature of a child, with the sensitiveness of a woman. He was given to putting his arms about the necks of his friends, and calling them odd names. Jeremiah S. Black once said to him:

"Garfield, you go into a fight with the horns of a bull and the skin of a rabbit."

The able judge did not mean that his friend had the cowardice of the one or the brutality of the other, but that, with his power to hurt, he had a sensitiveness that made his punishment out of all proportion.

One looks back at the Credit Mobilier affair now with no little amazement. Of all the congressmen implicated in the charges, blindly made by the press, Garfield suffered the most. It was, at the time, impossible to be heard in his defense, or, indeed, to be heard in defense of any of the congressmen indicted by public opinion.

Trial by newspaper is the most cruel and unjust

known to humanity. A man is found guilty in the indictment. If, after his condemnation, he comes forward with his proof of innocence, he is pronounced a tiresome bore, for the subject has lost its interest in the loss of excitement. The only road to escape is to quietly live down the accusation. This Garfield did. When nominated, through accident, by a popular party, his record, of course, became the record of the party, and to question it is to get abused, or, perhaps, beaten. In the canvass no one attempted to defend the candidate. The whole thing was simply ignored. Yet Garfield was innocent of any wrong-doing, as was every other congressman implicated.

Let us see: Oakes Ames, a wealthy member of congress, who stood high in public and private, said, for example, to another member: " I have some stock I am carrying for you. It is of the Credit Mobilier Company, which is a great success."

The member said: " Thank you."

It turned out that said company was a wicked contrivance designed to swindle the government. How was the member to know that ? There are not, probably, five men in the United States to-day who know what the member was supposed to know by intuition. Had the offer been made by a lobbyist it would have been different. But here was a gentle-

man of recognized standing, a Massachusetts millionaire, and a reputable member of the House. The
only victim who asked to see the charter and learn
something of its nature was Garfield. The odd
name of the company excited his curiosity. Credit
Mobilier—what was that? The Hon. Ames was too
cunning to comply with the request. Well he may
have been.

The name of Credit Mobilier was borrowed by
George Francis Train from a French company insti-
tuted by the Count de Morny. Train's corporation
came from a Pennsylvania legislature, and was secured to cover a construction company for the Pacific
railroad, that was being built on government bounty.
The members of the Credit Mobilier were the directors of the railroad, so that the contract for construction was made by men acting in one capacity, with
themselves acting in another, and so covered a tremendous swindle.

The stock under this state of fact was of immense value. Messrs. Durand and Harry M'Comb
discovered that Oakes Ames had taken to himself
more shares than he had a right to, and undertook
to blackmail him out of them. Ames knew, as well
as they knew, that a suit would be fatal to all con-
cerned, and so resisted. He told the complainants
that he had placed the stock " where it would do the

most good," and gave them the names of certain members of the House and Senate as the recipients. The object of this is plain enough now. If the suit was actually pressed to an issue, and Ames lost, he could account for the stock. If, on the contrary, he won, the stock would remain his, for he had not gone so far with his honorable friends as to lose their values, and they were important to him, for at that very moment he was on the verge of bankruptcy.

Ames was right in his reasoning. The suit only went so far as to be put on paper, and the papers were carefully locked in a lawyer's safe in New York.

Probably the affair would have ended there had not the New York Sun got an inkling of the transaction, and, through some unknown means, possessed itself of and published the papers.

The public mind was in a morbid condition. Corruption in high places had become so bold and shameless that an excited people demanded exposure and punishment. The wildest cry went up, not against the real wrong-doers, but the unhappy congressmen Oakes Ames had sought to make stalking-horses of. It seems strange to look back now and see the man who openly avowed his intent to corrupt, who said he "placed the stock where it would do the most good," petted and sympathized with, while the unfortunate victims were hounded to the echo. The Hon. Hooper, a solid man of Boston, and member of that House, although a leading director of the Credit Mobilier, not only escaped censure, but lived beloved and died lamented.

Of all the men accused, James A. Garfield suffered the most. How near he came to suicide the world will never know. Night after night the writer of this walked the streets of Washington with him till far past midnight, and I believe that, had it not been for Dr. Garnett and James G. Blaine, he would have sunk under the torture he suffered from the press. The high courage of the one and the skill of the other were potent to save at that perilous time. The way Garfield leaned on Blaine at that period left little wonder, on my part, that he called the Maine statesman to his side when he became President.

The torrent of newspaper abuse that seemed to select him from all his companions, guilty as himself if any were guilty, as the one on whom to center its sarcasm and vituperation, seems singular now that this same press holds him aloft as a martyred saint.

The lesson taught in this noted transaction is that the public likes to be bullied. The men, such as Bingham and Kelley, who came boldly forward and said, in the language of Statesman Tweed,

" What are you going to do about it ? " suffered little or nothing, while sensitive men, such as Garfield and Colfax, were fairly hounded down.

Of like sort were the attacks on Garfield in the De Golyer affair. Messrs. Chittenden and Parsons appeared at Washington as agents of a wood-paving company at the time when Alec. Shepherd was expending twenty millions on the streets of the capital. It was the interest of Chittenden and Parsons to magnify their services in the eyes of their employers, and so Parsons, having employed Garfield to make a legal argument before the Board of Public Works upon a contingent fee, the amount of which was not stated, Chittenden wrote the company that they had captured the chairman of the House committee on appropriations. Garfield was subsequently paid five thousand dollars as his fee.

On this letter and fee Garfield was condemned, and yet it was not shown that he knew of the letter, or that any congressional action was obtained through him. On the contrary, the fact was patent that at the time of his employment as counsel all the appropriations for the District of Columbia had been secured. It is true that the compensation seemed in excess of his services, but in these days of heavy fees to lawyers and doctors that ground of attack is not tenable.

If the sensitive American people want to save themselves from such shocks they should lift their representatives above temptation by allowing a liberal compensation for official services. In a carefully prepared system of temptation through mean pay, they make themselves *particeps criminis* to the wrong-doing when it occurs.

James A. Garfield had his faults, but they did not lie in the direction of money-getting. He occupied positions where he could have winked himself into millions. Instead of belonging to the noted many who grew mysteriously rich on five thousand a year, all he possessed when he was elected President was a modest little home, shingled in with mortgages.

A man of scholarly turn, his social habits were strangely temperate. He drank wine sparingly, and could only be lured from his library by a dinner party where men of intellect were found to make a feast of reason. He was a most charming guest at table, for his wit and keen sense of humor lived above the stimulants so necessary to the ordinary diner-out. A record of the nights when I have heard him talk with such men as Jeremiah S. Black, William M. Evarts, Henry Watterson, Governor Warmouth, and others of like ilk, would make volumes of *Noctes Ambrosia* equal to old Christopher North. On such occasions, and in his library, he presented a strange contrast to Garfield the partisan. As the last he was bitter, and author of the famous advice given to the Union soldiers, to vote as they shot. Personally, among friends, he was, to the last extent, independent and liberal.

There is no difficulty in harmonizing this apparent contradiction, and that without detracting from the excellence of his character. Had the Democratic party presented upon the floors of Congress the political doctrines advocated by Jeremiah S. Black, Michael C. Kerr, and others, at table, Garfield could not have well explained his opposition. But the Democracy, as a party, offered nothing but assaults on the Republicans, and Garfield defended his organization.

Once, when I charged him with blind partisanship, he said:

"Yes, yes; I know. But a man's party is like his own mother. One knows the dear old lady is not perfect, has a temper, perhaps, and is willfully unreasonable at times, but she is one's mother all the same."

James A. Garfield was personally the most lovable of men. His kind-hearted impulses made him promise, at times, more than he could perform; but his efforts satisfied his friends, and left the friendship strengthened. There is but one act of his life that appears in strange contradiction to his character, and that is his letter to Secretary Chase in regard to Rosecrans' campaign, while he, Garfield, was Rosecrans' chief of staff. In common with his other true friends, I shrink from it, and can only hope that some circumstance, to the world unknown, existed then to justify the writing.

Garfield's cruel death silenced all enmity, personal or political. The calm, dignified patience with which he awaited the pale messenger, after he was wounded, won the love, as the horrible event awakened the sorrow, of the world. Without claiming for him the title of martyr—for I can not see what he died to maintain—I can see that he was a victim to a monstrous system of civil service, which our government had developed. High as he stood in the estimation of the nation, he is yet higher in the love and admiration of those who were so fortunate as to know him best. In their hearts is his truest monument, and it is to their loving appreciation that the bronze and marble owe their grace and beauty.

## Richard Realf.

It was on a strangely mild day in midwinter of '59 that I stood smoking a cigar under the porch of my father's house at Mac-o-cheek. This home was half cottage and all cabin, for it had been built of logs, while the Indians yet lived in the land, and the additions and improvements since had softened without entirely concealing its origin. I was looking, in a lazy, dreamy way, over the level, willow-fringed plain of the valley, when a strange figure seemed to lounge in on my field of vision. It moved slowly into nearer sight from behind a clump of lilacs and elders, and I saw that a wayfarer and a stranger was approaching. He had the worn, slovenly look of former circumstances. His broad-brimmed felt hat hung limp about his pale face and over his long hair, while his coat, dark, loose, and threadbare, had a touch of poverty's adornment in the fringe along the lower edges. His shoes, city made, had proved too light for the service required, and were in pitiful seams and holes.

As he approached and ascended the few steps of the porch, I saw a slender man, of medium height, with a pale face marked at the time by a neglected scanty beard and a scared hunted look.

Without removing his hat or dropping the evident lot of soiled linen done up in a dirty handkerchief, he came closely to me, as I rose from my chair, and said:

"I am Richard Realf."

This announcement carried no light to my questioning brain, but I started when he added, in a yet lower tone:

"Secretary of State to Ossawattomie Brown's republic."

John Brown—Ossawattomie Brown—who wrote the emancipation proclamation on the mountains of Virginia, long before President Lincoln's bayonets tore the compact with hell from the Constitution of the United States, had just been hanged, and the country covering a continent yet thrilled with intense excitement over the bold attempt of the fierce fanatic.

Small wonder Richard Realf announced himself in a low, almost-whispered confidence, for all about us were men who would have hanged the secretary of state to the nearest tree with as little compunction as they would a mad dog.

My response to this startling information was not dignified, nor very friendly, for I said:

"The devil you are!"

Noting the gleam of fear that flitted over his pitiful face like a flash of heat lightning, as he half turned as if to fly, I more kindly gave him my hand, and asked him to be seated. He sank into a chair with a sigh of relief, and I noticed that his hand I held for an instant was not only shapely, small, and soft as a woman's, but that it was thin and feverish.

"You need rest and food," I said to the poor fellow.

"Yes," he replied, calling up a wan smile, "I believe I am starving."

I seized the poor, little bundle, and, bidding him follow me, showed the honorable secretary of state to the guest chamber of the old house. Telling him to lie down, I made an effort to remove his wrap, and found the unhappy man had compromised by making his somewhat voluminous mantle do duty as a coat. He said, with a feeble smile, that he had been forced to leave his luggage in the keeping of a hotel man.

Leaving him to rest while a meal was being prepared, I first took council with my brave little wife; and after, at her suggestion, called in the family. It is said that a council of war never fights. This because it is made up of men. Women advise fighting. They are the more combative in council, and

37

the women of our house were unanimous in their
resolve to harbor, conceal, and protect the fugitive.
My dear mother, an earnest Abolitionist, because of
her Virginia birth and life, wherein her sensitive
nature was pained by the cruel practices of slavery,
warmly espoused the cause of Realf, and proposed
locking him in a huge storeroom we called purga-
tory, for that it was without either light or ventila-
tion.

My honored father said little. When called on
for advice, he merely remarked that, " as this gentleman claimed to be secretary of state to a government
that has evidently been hung, I think the better way
would be to give him some money, and tell him to
move on."

My father had all the dislike to slavery held by
the more humane Southerners, but, like them, he
had a profound respect for the guarantees of the
constitution. When the South threw over the sacred compact, as my father held it, and appealed to
arms, he sent eight of his name—sons, grandsons,
and nephews—to the field, and to the day of his
death remained an ardent and active enemy of the
Confederacy.

After the eminent fugitive had strengthened
himself with broiled chicken, hot corn cakes, golden
butter, fresh eggs, and coffee, the very odor of which

would revive the dead—and he ate and drank with
the relish of a hungry man in good health—he seemed
to pull himself together, and entered with zeal, and
some cheerfulness, into the various schemes proposed by the sympathizing family for his better protection. The last one devised was to disguise the
ex-secretary of state in the wearing apparel of an
elderly maiden then doing service in the household.
Realf laughingly assented to this, and added that,
with a little dark pigment, he could use the color
of the race he had striven so dangerously to benefit.

The success of this, however, depended not only
on the confidence and discretion of the servants, but
as to whether our neighbors had observed Realf's arrival.

This was before the appearance of that mysterious pest known as the tramp, and wayfarers were
few, and the country people, keenly observant not
only as to strangers, but their own movements, permitted no one to pass without challenge and gossipy comment. We soon learned that our poor
friend had not escaped observation, and before night
set in more than one neighbor had questioned us as
to the late arrival. An eminent politician at Washington said of another, sadly entangled in the Credit
Mobilier scandal, that, " when a man takes to lying,
he should remember that he has choice of lies, and

select the one having the most truth in it as likely to give him the least trouble." We acted on the spirit of this wise axiom before we had heard it reduced to words, and, putting our fugitive in a spare suit of my clothes, that required but little alteration, and cropping his somewhat luxuriant locks, we changed his name from Richard Realf to Ralph Richards, and introduced him as a distant relative from the East.

We soon recognized that the man we harbored was a gentleman, a very courteous, kind-hearted, graceful creature, full of poetry, and loving romance as he hated real life. As to the ways of this hard, fierce money getting world, he was as innocent as a babe. Ere the end of his exile among us he became quite an exasperating burden on account of an utter indifference to the value of money. He expended our means with an ease and liberality so peculiar to the poets and long-haired patriots from downtrodden places in Europe. I doubt which, the fear of detection or the loss of his hair, gave him the deeper concern. This love of the locks he shared with the brother patriots referred to, but, fortunately, he differed in being cleanly. The European connection between soiled linen and a sacred cause I never could comprehend, unless upon a suggestion once made by the witty Governor Tom Corwin, of Ohio.

We were sitting together one night, listening to an eloquent, animated piece of real estate dwelling upon the woes of Italy. "The people may be cast down, but they rise from the touch of mother earth like the fabled god of old, stronger, and more terribly fierce than before," he cried.

"I see, I see," whispered the governor to me; "that accounts for it. They come up stronger and dirtier every time."

At the period I write of, I had acquired some notoriety as a reformer, being the editor of an eccentric journal called the Mac-o-check Press, friend of man, that devoted its pungent columns to making itself disagreeable to despots in general, and the slave-holders of the South in particular. Dr. Gamaliel Bailey, one of the most suggestive minds of the day, had created the free soil party out of the old abolition cause. He saw the absurdity of a political organization, not only outside of the constitution, but in deadly antagonism to that foundation of our government. So he got up the platform which acknowledged the right of slavery in the states, and fought its further spread to the territories. Seward, Salmon P. Chase, the elder Birney, John P. Hale, Ben Wade, Charles Sumner, and the more practical men of the anti-slavery class, saw the wisdom of this, and so the little party was organized. It was a beautiful party as far as it went, or, to express oneself better, what there was of it. It had an unhappy lack of votes, and, being opposed to the selfish interests of the masses, had small prospect of an increase, until the Barn-burners of New York and the death of the Whig party threw out of employment thousands of voters, who, to use the words of Daniel Webster, "did not know where to go," and so gravitated into the party that eventually elected President Lincoln.

I refer to this, not only because it is a part of my story of Realf, but because I note a tendency to-day among orators, editors, and historians to claim for the efforts of the then anti-slavery advocates the eventual triumph of their cause.

Looking back now to the earnest and gifted men, a group of rare excellence in mental gifts and moral character, it is sad to realize how little they accomplished. Had not the fanaticism of the Southern people blazed into civil war, we would to-day be hunting slaves at the North and hanging abolitionists at the South. The youthful enthusiast in the cause of reform feels at last, whether he lives to learn or not, that the intellectual processes in the advocacy of right seldom, if ever, reach the masses they are used to influence.

A few statistics give us the fact and the reason

for this disheartening result. We have a population of fifty millions. Of this it is a liberal estimate to say that five millions are readers. Of the five about three read books, and all read newspapers. Of the book readers two-thirds are devoted to fictions that have no moral purpose or influence. The journals, or more properly newspapers, are what the name indicates, printed records of current events, mostly of a shocking, bad sort, and depending, as they do, not upon circulation alone, but advertising, for their success, are, of course, cautious not to offend by the expression of views in favor of reform. Reform is ever unpopular. All wrongs lie in the consent of the wronged, and what with the fierce support of those who thrive on the abuse, and the dull, heavy, ignorant conservatism of the masses, martyrs are readily made, so that we need not wonder that, horrible as slavery was, it had the press and the pulpit, the business interests and the selfish greed of the many to sustain and maintain it. So effective was this that the term Abolitionist became one of keenest reproach, from which men shrank, and even to this day it retains a part of its taint.

The real obstacle to reform, however, was in the impossibility found in reaching the popular mind. At the time of meeting Richard Realf, I belonged to the class that believed when the argument was made the cause was won. I did not see that the argument was unheard, nor did I then know that for one influence of an intellectual sort, even when heard, there were impulses born of passions and self-interests, that made moral progress impossible.

Editing a newspaper favorable to freedom, that gained quite a circulation and no little notoriety, I found that its success was based entirely on its power to amuse. While stumping the state with Salmon P. Chase, I saw that where we had hundreds our opponents of the Whig and Democratic parties gathered thousands, and those two political organizations agreed on one point only, and that was in denouncing us as Abolitionists, negro worshipers, and altogether very vile, low fellows, to be shunned generally, and in extreme cases worthy of being hanged.

I said to my gifted associate, Salmon P. Chase, one day: " The trouble with this people is their dense ignorance. Do you know, passing, as we do, from county to county throughout the state, that, leaving out the larger towns, we will not find a house with a book in it, other than the Bible and a medicated almanac? What is the use of striving to move such a mass of ignorance by eloquent appeals?"

He responded, in his way, by calling my attention to the progress made by humanity before printing was known, and that God, in creating man, had made him self-sustaining, inasmuch as evil was temporary only, while good formed the solid foundation of all things; that outside of book-making and mere intellectual efforts, elements were at work that would eventually triumph in the confounding of the wicked and the establishment of justice.

His words proved prophetic, although the means were then unknown to this great and good man. Our enemies in plunging us into that terrible war did for our cause, what we could not have accomplished ourselves. Indeed, our part in the work was so small that it might have been omitted.

Realf had struck the outer edge of the notoriety accorded me as a reformer, and walking nearly three hundred miles, mostly by night, found refuge in our house.

I made a pilgrimage to Columbus, for the purpose of consulting Governor Chase about the poor refugee. I knew before he could be taken from Ohio to Virginia, a requisition would have to be made. The governor listened much interested to my story, and after some consideration, said he thought our alarm uncalled for. Beyond a bare mention of the name, and the fact of such an office as Mr. Realf claimed to hold, the governor had seen nothing. He thought as Virginia had hanged John Brown, and dispersed his followers, with the consent, if not approbation, of all men, Virginia felt satisfied, and that no effort would be made to hunt down so obscure a man as my friend Realf.

We soon found that the governor was right in his view of the case. No detectives nor United States marshals appeared to haunt our happy valley, and the name of Realf disappeared from the press after such brief mention, that the public soon forgot that it had ever appeared. This seemed to annoy Realf, more than his danger had moved him. He not only assumed again his name, but had it inserted at the head of the Mac-o-cheek Press, as associate editor.

The fact was, as I subsequently learned, that Realf had not then been identified in the public mind with Ossawattomie Brown's attempt in Virginia. The poetic tramp was, at the time of Brown's insane attempt, in Texas, and having imprudently revealed his knowledge of, and association with the feared fanatic, he barely escaped a mob by being arrested and taken to Washington City, in irons. The poor fellow suffered from both sides, of those who did know of him. The pro-slavery advocates thirsted for his blood, and the abolitionists, thinking that he had turned informer, were equally wrathful. Mr. Redpath, in his life of Old Ossawattomie, prefaced it with some pungent remarks, bearing on Richard Realf, which he afterward corrected.

Realf fled like a frightened hare from the authorities at Washington, and while fleeing, read in a newspaper a further use of his name in connection with Brown, and fearing a new development connecting him with the affair he plunged into yet deeper obscurity.

It is difficult, at this day, to appreciate the excitement that followed Brown's arrest and execution. The North was shocked and startled at the daring attempt, while at the South there was a general belief that only a surface indication had been developed, and that lying back of it was a huge plot of a servile insurrection ready at any moment to explode. The women went tearfully, trembling, and in prayer to bed, while fathers, husbands, and brothers slept on knives and revolvers. One can not blame, nor wonder, for of all horrible things known to humanity, a servile insurrection is the most horrible. The women could well pray to God for protection to avert the awful calamity, for when it came there was nothing but a prayer for immediate death to escape its horrors.

In making my poetic refugee an assistant pen-driver, I soon discovered that he had not the remotest knowledge of what was needed in an editor, and equally remote information as to his value as co-worker on that sprightly emanation of journalistic wisdom. His bills and editorials were alike long and heavy, and while the one were shadowy and indistinct, the others were painfully near and palpable.

It became necessary to discharge my associate editor. It was a painful duty, and to escape that I resorted to stratagem. He had a lecture written on Shakespeare, that he had delivered at Brighton, England, under the patronage of Lady Byron and other distinguished male and female people. I suggested, that next to the cause we advocated, I thought the people were most ignorant of Shakespeare, and I believed he could do well (the Lord forgive me) in throwing light upon the Bard of Avon, in the face of the public.

To this end we had a trial at the flourishing post-town of West Liberty. Richard Realf's lecture on Shakespeare had a successful run of one night at our nearest post-town. That Fourth of July designation of a village means, generally, a whisky saloon and a hundred inhabitants, but in this instance it is a lovely little maple-shaded burg, nestled under a wood-crowned hill, overlooking the lovely valley of Mad River.

It had, at the time I write of, but one hall, and that in the top story of the Ordway block, and the

roof for a ceiling, and this slanting to the end where
the platform was erected was so low that the lecturer
had to be cautious in his gesticulations, lest he skin
his knuckles, or bump his head on the plaster above.
Lit with a few malodorous coal-oil lamps, on the
winter night in question, and heated by a roaring
stove, he had the beauty and intelligence of West
Liberty to perspire and applaud an eloquent disquisi-
tion on an immortal of whose work no one of that
brilliant assembly had ever read a line. A select few
of us supplied the lights, fire, audience and applause.
To insure the last, armed with sticks and umbrellas,
we not only led but thundered to such an extent that
Ordway's hall was in danger, and the startled loafers
about Cook's saloon and Brownell's grocery hurried
in, filling the little hall and stairway with an anxious
crowd, eager to know all about Shakespeare, and the
cause of this (to use a popular expression) unexpected
"boom."

The lecturer was delighted with his success. It
had been gotten up on subscription, and the entire
amount realized came in all to ten dollars and fifty
cents, the ten coming from the pocket of the senior
editor, and the fifty cents from the amiable post-
master. The sum was handed the ex-secretary of
state. Armed with this, and supplied with a well-
stuffed valise, Richard Realf, ex-secretary of the John

Brown republic, passed from our vision into the busy world never to return.

While at our home Realf gave me, from time to time, fragments of his autobiography, through which were hints of a mysterious origin. His mother must have been a remarkable woman, for Realf was a man of genius. He told me of her taste for poetry, and how she had educated him in a poetic way, until he astonished her with verses of his own when scarcely able to lisp them himself. A knowledge of his precocious turn coming to the ears of a lady—Lady Stafford, if I remember rightly—she took upon herself his education.

I learned subsequently, and not from Realf, that a sister of his, a servant in Lady Stafford's family, interested that literary woman in her brother's behalf.

Elevated to this novel position, the wonderful boy became a pet of a Brighton coterie that included Lady Byron. Richard, having quarreled with his first patron, found in the unhappy, and somewhat hysterical relict of the noble poet another who took up the task where Lady Stafford dropped it, of spoiling the boy. He had persisted in publishing a volume of sickly verses, in opposition to the advice of his earlier friend, and casting her off, swung to the skirts of the more congenial widow.

The warm interest evinced by Lady Byron for this strange boy gave rise to an absurd scandal to the effect that Realf was an illegitimate son of the noble creator of poetic despair. Lady Byron may have thought this to be true, for we well know, since Mrs. Stowe's remarkable revelation, that the poor woman was quite capable of the wildest beliefs.

Be that as it may, the noble patroness of a spoiled boy soon tired of her work, and gave the youth such treatment that he suddenly disappeared. He was not seen, nor heard of, by his friends, for nearly a year after, when ragged, half-starved, and quite ill, he appeared at his mother's house.

He told me he had tried his fortune at London, like Chatterton, and like Chatterton, would have starved, but for a benevolent old baker, who donated bread to him every day, until his return home.

The literary circle at Brighton, having won their elephant, soon wearied of their burden, and finding the poetic pet was inspired by Mrs. Stowe's " Uncle Tom's Cabin," and sought, as the friend of man, to free the colored race of America, they made up a purse, and shipped him to these shores. At that time Ossawattomie Brown was the hero of Kansas, and Realf, seeking him, offered his services. The rough old fanatic had no use for a poet, and so made

Richard a piece of fringe-work to his imaginary republic.

We never met after his departure from Mac-o-chee. I heard of him from time to time, once in the army, but the hearing was not of much encouragement. A man of genius, with his delicate nerves outside his clothes, he seemed to have worried through a life, in a blind sort of way, leaving behind only a few poems to tell that he had ever been.

THE END.

www.ingramcontent.com/pod-product-compliance
Lightning Source LLC
Chambersburg PA
CBHW031058110726
47900CB00003B/981